The

SECRET OF THE AGES

ROBERT COLLIER

ROBERT COLLIER PUBLICATIONS, Inc.

Robert Collier Publications, Inc.
Thirtieth printing 1999. First published in 1926 by Robert Collier, New York; revised edition 1983.
ISBN 0-912576-11-1
Printed in the United States of America on acid-free paper.

Robert Collier Publications, Inc.
1248 N. Lamont Dr.
Oak Harbor, WA 98277
360-679-8981 Phone or Fax

Contents

PART VIII. GO YOU AND PROFIT BY THEIR EXAMPLE

INTRODUCTION

The World Is Yours When You Master The Secret of The Ages!

You can have anything you want—money; a better job; honors; time for travel; for study; for good times; recreations; the love of those dear to you; anything that is good; when you learn the Secrets of the Ages and find your powerful Inner Mind deep within you.

You and only you are the true Master of your Destiny! The POWER to be whatever you want to be, to get what you want in life, to accomplish whatever you are striving for, lies dormant, sleeping within you until you call upon it. You need only to bring it forth and put it to work. HOW to do that is what you will learn in this book. Psychologists the world over agree on this: that the MIND is all that matters. *You can be whatever you make up your mind to be.* You need not be sick. You need not be unhappy. You need not be unsuccessful. You are not a mere clod on this earth. You are not a beast of burden, doomed to spend your life on a job of drudgery in order to meet the monthly bills.

William James, the world-famous Harvard psychologist, estimated that the average man uses only about 10% of his actual potential mental power. Think of it! Only 10%. He has unlimited power—yet ignores 90% of it. Unlimited wealth all about him—and he doesn't know how to take hold of it. With powerful forces slumbering within him, he is content to continue in his daily grind—eating, sleeping, working—plodding through a dull, routine existence. Yet all of Nature, all of life, calls upon him to awake and bestir himself!

You are one of the lords of the Earth, with *unlimited potentialities.* Within you is a power which, properly grasped and directed, can lift you out of the rut of mediocrity and place you among the Elect of the Earth—THE DOERS, THE THINKERS, THE LEADERS among men. It rests with you and you only to use this power which is your neglected heritage—this MIND which can do all things!

Whatever your goal in Life is; this book can help you achieve it. What is your ambition? A better home for your loved ones? A new car? More Success in your chosen life work? Greater happiness? Have you become discouraged with your progress—or lack of progress toward your goal? Do factors beyond your control seem to hold you back? Do you wonder and worry about the security of your future? Are fears and worries marring your full enjoyment in life?

If so, the simple methods outlined in this book by Robert Collier can change your whole outlook on life. It can start you out on each new day entirely free of fear and give you fresh courage and a blessed peace of mind that lets you concentrate on getting things done.

Here is a wonderful method to get what you want easily. Sometimes this dream is so strong and deep in us that surely a power mightier than ourselves must have put it there to remind us that we need not be poor, humble creatures; that security and happiness are our birthright. Is there some method that can help us find ourselves and make ourselves the men and women we want to be?

A wonderful method definitely exists and has existed for thousands of years! It was used by the Masters of the East for many centuries. Ages ago the Ancients probed into Nature's Laws and made amazing discoveries of the hidden processes of men's minds and the mastery of life's problems. These Masters searched into Nature's deepest mysteries and most closely guarded secrets; secrets of life and death and strange forces that rule men's lives. The secrets that these Masters discovered enabled them to perform almost incredible feats and to attain heaven on earth. And now those who follow their teachings can gain for themselves all the good things a man can hope for, drive sickness from the body, prolong youth for many years, freedom from fear and worry, obtain great wealth, and lead supremely happy lives.

Now you too can learn the Hidden Secrets that control life. For thousands of years the Secrets of the Ages were hidden in hieroglyphics, symbolism, and sacred writings by the Chaldeans, Indian mystics, Egyptians, Rosicrucians, Atlanteans. These learned men wished to screen their precious knowledge from the vulgar and the wicked. It was not until modern times that archeologists, scientists, psychologists, and writers were able to translate and delve into these Secrets of Life and Nature and catalog them and present them to the general public in language that can be understood by the average man. One of the outstanding writers, who has devoted thirty long years of study and research into how the Masters control the Infinite Energy of the Universe, is Robert Collier. He has learned the simple easy-to-take steps that you must follow to get the things you want most in life—be it money, a new and better job, a trip to Europe, a new and more beautiful home, health, and happiness, and love of family.

In this most-inspiring book Robert Collier tells you clearly and simply what the Secrets of the Ages are, and how to learn and use them. With the help of this book, you will hold in your hands the key to powers so amazing that in ages past they were regarded as nothing short of magical. For this book offers you the Secrets with instructions for applying them to practical, everyday matters.

In easy steps, by applying the wisdom of the ages as expounded by Robert Collier in this book, you have within your grasp the means to make all your dreams come true. You can learn to invoke the Law of Supply so that your pockets will never be empty. You can learn to tap immeasurable resources of genius that lie hidden in your subconscious mind—resources that will enable you to forge ahead in your job and increase your earnings tenfold, or found a new business that will bring you success beyond your fondest hopes. You can gain wealth and health and social success; all you want and more.

And don't think there is anything magical involved in acquiring these powers for yourself. It is simply a matter of learning the hidden Principles that the Masters have discovered thousands of years ago and applying them for yourself. Results will come quickly as you grow in your powers. You will have immediate, incontrovertible evidence that you can make yourself the happy, effective person you want to be.

You won't believe this, but surveys show that only 10% of the people really want and seek and study for Success. The other 90% only have excuses for their lack of ambition and pure laziness. Any kind of study is too much effort for them. They would rather spend all night watching TV. But when you get into this book, you will find it exciting and thrilling. It is like learning feats of magic, and you are like a magician bringing the lady out of the empty closet in front of the audience. Through study and application of the Secrets of the Ages, you can rub your Aladdin's lamp and wave your magic wand, and bring yourself new cards, new friends, new wealth, new homes, and whatever else you desire. Once the Secrets are in your possession, you will not have to depend on luck anymore. You'll know that wealth, happiness and health, are within reach of those who hold the golden secrets to the storehouse of power and gold contained within all of us.

Each of the following chapters contains a Secret that is essential to your progress towards your goals of Wealth and Prosperity. By applying some of the Secrets, you may gain some benefits; but it is only by applying ALL of the Secrets that you will gain the fulfillment of all your golden dreams. Now don't go halfway and then quit—keep on going and you will win the race.

The latter part of this book contains many shining examples of men and women who have made millions from the use of all these secrets and then we explore the gold mines of opportunity waiting for you in this present, fast-moving world.

May all that you have ever wished for come true for you!

God bless you.

Gordon Collier

PREFACE

What Are the Odds Against Your Retiring Wealthy

Can you, in all honesty, say that you are your own master—and not the slave of your circumstances? Are you getting everything you want out of life—the enjoyment, comfort, health, power, and happiness you feel you are entitled to? Or must you worry about meeting monthly bills?

If you are like most of humanity, in order to feed yourself and your family, you keep your nose to the grindstone, daily doing work that is often dull and uninteresting. Once, perhaps, you hoped for millions. If you resemble the majority, you will be pleased enough to plod along in a rut, hoping that it does not get any deeper and swallow you up.

THE ODDS ARE AGAINST YOU - SO FAR

According to George Barber, in his book *Making Good:*

"Out of every hundred men of the age of twenty-five, sixty-six will live to be sixty-five years of age.

"Of these sixty-six, only one will be wealthy.

"Four will be fairly well-to-do.

"Five will still be working for a living at the age of sixty-five.

"The remaining fifty-six will be dependent upon their family, or pensions, or the community, or on social security for the very bread and butter they eat."

Shocking? But true! These figures come from the records of one of our largest insurance companies. Such statistics must be reliable; the companies stake millions of dollars on their accuracy every year.

Which of the hundred will you be, ten, twenty, or thirty years from now? One of the handful of fortunate ones? Not likely—the odds, you see, are against you, unless you make them come your way.

You Can Get What You Want Out of Life

You can, at age sixty-five and later, be enjoying excellent health. You can, up till then and beyond, be enjoying a comfortable financial situation. You can make yourself one of the lucky few that the insurance statistics tell us about.

You need not be a slave to hard luck or circumstances all your life. There is a way to get the things you want—a way completely in harmony with the highest aspirations of the human race.

By means of this method, in short order, you can improve your opportunities or get a better job, a new car, a new home, or travel abroad in comfort. You will be able to gain enough money to satisfy all these normal wants, and more. (How one woman, through this method acquired twenty thousand dollars she needed is just one of the many true success stories you will read about in the following chapters.) You can win health and happiness just as easily.

The Power Within

The power to master your circumstances lies within you. Inside you there sleeps a giant just waiting for your call. He is your subconscious mind, and for him nothing is impossible. All you have to do is wake him, and he will strike off your invisible chains and show you how to make your dreams come true. Your ambitions for advancement, prosperity, and well-being can all become realities once you know the secrets.

"I am the Master of my fate"

Until you have learned that, you will never attain life's full success. Your fate is in your own hands. *You* have the making of it. What you are going to be six months or a year from now depends upon what you think today.

So make your choice now:

Are you going to bow down to matter as the only power? Are you going to look upon your environment as something that has been wished upon you and for which you are in no way responsible?

Or are you going to try to realize in your daily life that matter is merely an aggregation of protons and electrons subject entirely to the control of Mind; that your environment, your success, your happiness, are all of your own making, and that if you are not satisfied with conditions as they are, you have but to visualize them as you would have them be and put your creative power to work in order to change them?

The former is the easier way right now. The easy way that leads to the hell of poverty and fear and old age.

But the latter is the way that brings you to your Heart's Desire.

Merely because this Power of Universal Mind is invisible, is that any reason to doubt it? The greatest powers of Nature are invisible. Love is invisible, but what greater power is there in life? Joy is invisible, happiness, peace, contentment. Radio waves are invisible—yet you hear them. They are a product of the law governing sound waves. Law is invisible, yet you see the manifestation of different laws every day. To run a locomotive, you study the law of applying power, and you apply that law when you make the locomotive go.

These things are not the result of invention. The law has existed from the beginning. It merely waited for man to learn how to apply it. If man had known how to call upon Universal Mind to the right extent, he could have applied the law of sound waves, the law of steam, ages ago. Invention is merely a revelation and an unfoldment of Universal Wisdom.

That same Universal Wisdom knows millions of other laws of which man has not even a glimmering. You can call upon It. You can use that Wisdom as your own. By thinking of things as they might be instead of as they are, you will eventually find some great Need. And to find a need is the first step towards finding the supply to satisfy that need. You have to know what you are after, before you can send the Genie-of-your-Mind seeking it in Universal Mind.

The Acre of Diamonds

You remember the story of the poor Boer farmer who struggled for years to glean a livelihood out of his rocky soil, only to give it up in despair and go off to seek his fortune elsewhere. Years later, coming back to his old farm, he found it swarming with machinery and life—more wealth being dug out of it every day than he had ever dreamed existed. It was the great Kimberley Diamond Mine!

Most of us are like that poor Boer farmer. We struggle along under our surface power, never dreaming of the giant power that could be ours if we would but dig a little deeper—rouse that great Inner Self who can give us more even than any acre of diamonds.

As Orison Swett Marden put it:

"The majority of failures in life are simply the victims of their mental defeats. Their conviction that they cannot succeed as others do robs them of that vigor and determination which self-confidence imparts, and they don't even half try to succeed.

"There is no philosophy by which a man does a thing when he thinks he can't. The reason why millions of men are plodding along in mediocrity today, many of them barely making a living, when they have the ability to do something infinitely bigger, is because they lack confidence in themselves. They don't believe they can do the bigger thing that would lift them out of their rut of mediocrity and poverty; they are not winners mentally.

"The way always opens for the determined soul, the man of faith and courage.

"It is the victorious mental attitude, the consciousness of power, the sense of mastership, that does the big things in this world. If you haven't this attitude, if you lack self-confidence, begin now to cultivate it.

"A highly magnetized piece of steel will attract and lift a piece of unmagnetized steel ten times its own weight. Demagnetize that same piece of steel and it will be powerless to attract or lift even a feather's weight.

"Now, my friends, there is the same difference between the man who is highly magnetized by a sublime faith in himself, and the man who is de-magnetized by his lack of faith, his doubts, his fears, than there is between the magnetized and the de-magnetized pieces of steel. If two men of equal ability, one magnetized by a divine self-confidence, the other de-magnetized by fear and doubt, are given similar tasks, one will succeed and the other will fail. The self-confidence of the one *multiplies his powers a hundredfold;* the lack of it subtracts a hundredfold from the power of the other."

Have you ever thought how much of your time is spent in choosing what you shall do, which task you will try, which way you shall go? Every day is a day of decision. We are constantly at crossroads, in our business dealings, our social relations, in our homes; there is always the necessity of a choice. How important then that we have faith in ourselves and in that Infinite intelligence within. "Commit thy works unto the Lord, and thy thoughts shall be established." "In all thy ways acknowledge him, and he shall direct thy paths."

In this ever-changing material age, with seemingly complex forces all about us, we sometimes cry out that we are driven by force of circumstances. Yet the fact remains that we do those things which we choose to do. For even though we may not wish to go a certain way, we allow ourselves to pursue it because it offers the least resistance.

"To every man there openeth
A way, and ways, and a way.

And the high soul climbs the high way,
And the low soul gropes the low;
And in between, on the misty flats,
The rest drift to and fro.
But to every man there openeth
A high way and a low,
And every man decideth
The way his soul shall go."

—John Oxenham.

Now, how about you? Are you taking active control of your own thought? Are you imaging upon your subconscious mind only such things as you want to see realized? Are you thinking healthy thoughts, happy thoughts, successful thoughts? "That to which I give my attention reveals itself." To what are you giving your attention?

The difference between the successful man and the unsuccessful one is not so much a matter of training or equipment. It is not a question of opportunity or luck. It is just in the way that each of them look at things.

The successful man sees an opportunity, seizes upon it, and moves upward another rung on the ladder of success. It never occurs to him that he may fail. He sees only the opportunity, he visions what he can do with it, and all the forces within and without him combine to help him win.

The unsuccessful man sees the same opportunity, he wishes that he could take advantage of it, but he is fearful that his ability or his money or his credit may not be equal to the task. He is like a timid bather, putting in one foot and then drawing it swiftly back again—and while he hesitates some bolder spirit dashes in and beats him to the goal.

Nearly every man can look back—and not so far back either with most of us—and say, "If I had taken that chance, I would be much better off now."

You will never need to say it again, once you realize that the future is entirely within your own control. It is not subject to the whims of fortune or the capriciousness of luck. There is but one Universal Mind and that mind contains naught but good. In it are no images of Evil. From it comes no lack of supply. Its ideas are as numberless as the grains of sand on the seashore. And those ideas comprise all wealth, all power, all happiness.

You have only to image vividly enough on your subconscious mind the thing you wish, to draw from Universal Mind the necessary ideas to bring it into being. You have only to keep in mind the experiences you wish to meet, in order to control your own future.

When Frank A. Vanderlip, former President of the National City Bank, was a struggling youngster, he asked a successful friend what one thing he would urge a young man to do who was anxious to make his way in the world. "Look as though you have already succeeded," his friend told him. Shakespeare expresses the same thought in another way—"Assume a virtue if you have it not." Look the part. Dress the part. Act the part. Be successful in your own thought first. It won't be long before you will be successful before the world as well.

Speaking of Henry Ford's phenomenal success, his friend Thomas A. Edison said of him—"He draws upon his subconscious mind."

The secret of being what you have it in you to be is simply this: Decide now what it is you want in life, exactly what you wish your future to be. Plan it out in detail. Vision it from start to finish. See yourself as you are now, doing those things you have always wanted to do. Make them REAL in your mind's eye—feel them, live them, believe them, especially at the moment of going to sleep, when it is easiest to reach your subconscious mind—and you will soon be seeing them in real life.

It matters not whether you are young or old, rich or poor. The time to begin is NOW. It is never too late.

PART I

SECRET NUMBER ONE YOUR SUBCONSCIOUS

CHAPTER 1

The Genie-of-Your-Mind

It matters not how strait the gate,
How charged with punishment the scroll,
I am the Master of my Fate;
I am the Captain of my Soul."
—Henley

First came the Stone Age, when life was for the strong of arm or the fleet of foot. Then there was the Iron Age—and while life was more precious, still the strong lorded it over the weak. Later came the Golden Age, and riches took the place of strength—but the poor found little choice between the slave drivers' whips of olden days and the grim weapons of poverty and starvation.

Now we are entering a new age—the Atomic Age, which is really the Age of Mind—when every man can be his own master, when poverty and circumstance no longer hold power and the lowliest creature in the land can win a place side by side with the highest.

To those who do not know the resources of mind, these will sound like rash statements; but science proves beyond question that in the well springs of every man's mind are unplumbed depths—undiscovered deposits of energy, wisdom and ability. Sound these depths—bring these treasures to the surface—and you gain an astounding wealth of new power.

From the rude catamaran of the savages to the giant liners of today, carrying their thousands from continent to continent, is but a step in the development of Mind. From the lowly caveman, cowering in his burrow in fear of lightning or fire or water, to the engineer of today, making servants of all the forces of Nature, is but a measure of difference in mental development.

Man, without reasoning mind, would be as the monkeys are—prey of any creature fast enough and strong enough to pull him to pieces. At the mercy of wind and weather. A poor, timid creature, living for the moment only, fearful of every shadow.

Through his superior mind, he learned to make fire to keep himself warm; weapons with which to defend himself from the savage creatures round about; habitations to protect himself from the elements. Through mind he conquered the forces of Nature. Through mind he has made machinery do the work of millions of horses and billions of hands. What he will do next, no man knows, for man is just beginning to awaken to his own powers. He has split the atom—now he is harnessing its power. He is beginning to get an inkling of the unfathomed riches that are buried deep in his own mind. Like the gold seekers of '49, he has panned the surface gravel for the gold swept down by the streams. Now he is starting to dig deeper to the pure vein beneath.

We bemoan the loss of our forests. We worry over our dwindling resources of coal and oil. We decry the waste in our factories. But the greatest waste of all, we pay no attention to—the waste of our own potential mind power. Professor Wm. James, the world-famous Harvard psychologist, estimated that the average man uses only 10% of his mental power. He has unlimited power—yet he uses but a tithe of it. Unlimited wealth all about him—and he doesn't know how to take hold of it. With God-like powers slumbering within him, he is content to continue in his daily grind—eating, sleeping, working—plodding through an existence little more eventful than the animals', while all of Nature, all of life, calls upon him to awaken, to bestir himself.

The power to be what you want to be, to get what you desire, to accomplish whatever you are striving for, abides within you. It rests with you only to bring it forth and put it to work. You must learn *how* to do that, of course, but the first essential is to *realize* that you *possess* this power, your first objective is to get acquainted with it.

Psychologists and Metaphysicians the world over are agreed on this-that the mind is all that counts. You can be whatever you make up your mind to be. You need not be sick. You need not be unhappy. You need not be poor. You need not be unsuccessful. You are not a mere clod. You are not a beast of burden, doomed to spend your days in unremitting labor in return for food and housing. You are one of the Lords of the Earth, with unlimited potentialities. Within you is a power which, properly grasped and directed, can lift you out of the rut of mediocrity and place you among the Elect of the Earth—the lawgivers, the writers, the engineers, the great industrialists—the DOERS and the THINKERS. It rests with you only to learn to use this power which is yours—this Mind which can do all things.

Your body is for all practical purposes merely a machine which the mind uses. This mind is usually thought of as consciousness; but the *conscious part* of your mind is in fact the *very smallest part of it.* Ninety per cent of your mental life is subconscious, so when you make active use of only the conscious part of your mind you are using but a fraction of your real ability; you are running on low gear. And the reason why more people do not achieve success in life is because so many of them are content to run on low gear all their lives—on SURFACE ENERGY. If these same people would only throw into the fight the resistless force of their subconscious and superconscious minds, they would be amazed at their undreamed of capacity for winning success.

Religion has always taught us to look upon God as a triplicity—as Three in One—but seems to have forgotten that man is likewise three in one, made in the image and likeness of God. For man's mind is a triplicity, the conscious mind, the subconscious, and the subliminal or superconscious mind.

The Conscious Mind

When you say "I see—I hear—I smell—I touch," it is your conscious mind that is saying this, for it is the force governing the five physical senses. It is the phase of mind with which you feel and reason-the phase of mind with which everyone is familiar. It is the mind with which you do business. It controls, to a great extent, all your voluntary muscles. It discriminates between right and wrong, wise and foolish. It is the generalissimo, in charge of all your mental forces. It can plan ahead and get things done as it plans. Or it can drift along haphazardly, a creature of impulse, at the mercy of events—a mere bit of flotsam in the current of life.

For it is only through your conscious mind that you can reach the subconscious and the superconscious mind. Your conscious mind is the porter at the door, the watchman at the gate. It is to the conscious mind that the subconscious looks for all its impressions. It is on it that the subconscious mind must depend for the teamwork necessary to get successful results. You wouldn't expect much from an army, no matter how fine its soldiers, whose general never planned ahead, who distrusted his own ability and that of his men, and who spent all his time worrying about the enemy instead of planning how he might conquer them. You wouldn't look for good scores from a ball team whose pitcher was at odds with the catcher. In the same way, you can't expect results from the subconscious when your conscious mind is full of fear or worry, or when it does not know what it wants.

The most important province ot your conscious mind is to center your thoughts on the thing you want, "Believe that you receive," and then shut the door on every suggestion of fear or worry or failure.

If you once gain the ability to do that, nothing else is impossible to you.

For the subconscious mind does not reason inductively. It takes the thoughts you send in to it and works them out to their logical conclusion. Send to it thoughts of health and strength, and it will work out health and strength in your body. Let suggestions of disease, fear of sickness or accident, penetrate to it, either through your own beliefs or the talk of those around you, and you are very likely to see the manifestation of disease working out in yourself.

Your mind is master of your body. Your body is in effect a little universe in itself, and mind is its radiating center—the sun which gives light and life to all your system, and around which the whole revolves. And your *conscious thought* is master of this sun center.

The Subconscious Mind

Can you tell me how much water, how much salt, how much of each different element there should be in your blood to maintain its proper specific gravity if you are leading an ordinary sedentary life? How much and how quickly these proportions must be changed if you play a fast game of tennis, or run for your car, or chop wood, or indulge in any other violent exercise?

Do you know how much water you should drink to neutralize the excess salt in salt fish? How much you lose through perspiration? Do you know how much water, how much salt, how much of each different element in your food should be absorbed into your blood each day to maintain perfect health?

No? Well, it need not worry you. Neither does any one else. Not even the greatest physicists and chemists and mathematicians. But your subconscious mind knows.

And it doesn't have to stop to figure it out. It does it almost automatically. It is one of those "Lightning Calculators." And this is but one of thousands of such jobs it performs every hour of the day. The greatest mathematicians in the land, the most renowned chemists, could never do in a year's time the abstruse problems which your subconscious mind solves every minute.

And it doesn't matter whether you have ever studied mathematics or chemistry or any other of the sciences. From the moment of your birth your subconscious mind solves all these problems for you. While you are struggling with the three R's, it is doing problems that would leave your teachers aghast. It supervises all the intricate processes of digestion, of assimilation, of elimination, and all the glandular secretions that would tax the knowledge of all the chemists and all the laboratories in the land. It planned and built your body from infancy on up. It repairs it. It operates it. It has practically unlimited power, not merely for putting you and keeping you in perfect health, but for acquiring all the good things of life. Ignorance of this power is the sole reason for all the failures in this world. If you would intelligently turn over to this wonderful power all your business and personal problems, no goal would be too great for you to strive for.

Dr. Geo. C. Pitzer sums up the power of the subconscious mind very well in the following:

"The subconscious mind is a distinct entity. It occupies the whole human body, and, when not opposed in any way, it has absolute control over all the functions, conditions, and sensations of the body; while the objective (conscious) mind has control over all of our voluntary functions. Nutrition, waste, all secretions and excretions, the action of the heart in the circulation of the blood, the lungs in respiration or breathing, and all cell life, cell changes and development, are positively under the complete control of the subconscious mind. This was the only mind animals had before the evolution of the brain; and it could not, nor can it yet, reason inductively, but its power of deductive reasoning is perfect. And more, it can see without the use of physical eyes. It perceives by intuition. It has the power to communicate with others without the aid of ordinary physical means. It can read the thoughts of others. It receives intelligence and transmits it to people at a distance. Distance offers no resistance against the successful missions of the subconscious mind."

In "Practical Psychology and Sex Life," by David Bush, Dr. Winbigler is quoted as going even further. To quote him:

"It is this mind that carries on the work of assimilation and upbuilding whilst we sleep...

"It reveals to us things that the conscious mind has no conception of until the consummations have occured.

"It can communicate with other minds without the ordinary physical means.

"It gets glimpses of things that ordinary sight does not behold.

"It makes God's presence an actual, realizable fact, and keeps the personality in peace and quietness.

"It warns of approaching danger.

"It approves or disapproves of a course of conduct and conversation.

"It carries out all the best things which are given to it, providing the conscious mind does not intercept and change the course of its manifestation.

"It heals the body and keeps it in health, if it is at all encouraged."

It is, in short, a powerful and beneficent force, but like a live electric wire, its destructive force is equally great. It can be either your servant or your master. It can bring to you evil or good.

The Rev. William T. Walsh, in a book published some years ago, explained the idea clearly:

"The subconscious part in us is called the subjective mind, because it does not decide and command. It is a subject rather than a ruler. Its nature is to do what it is told, *or what really in your heart of hearts you desire.*

"The subconscious mind directs all the vital processes of your body. You do not think consciously about breathing. Every time you take a breath you do not have to reason, decide, command. The subconscious mind sees to that. You have not been at all conscious that you have been breathing while you have been reading this page. So it is with the mind and the circulation of blood. The heart is a muscle like the muscle of your arm. It has no power to move itself or to direct its action. Only mind, only something that can think, can direct our muscles, including the heart. You are not conscious that you are commanding your heart to beat. The subconscious mind attends to that. And so it is with the assimilation of food, the building and repairing of the body. In fact, all the vital processes are looked after by the subconscious mind."

"Man lives and moves and has his being" in this great subconscious mind. It supplies the "intuition" that so often carries a woman straight to a point that may require hours of cumbersome reasoning for a man to reach. Even in ordinary, everyday affairs, you often draw upon its wonderful wisdom.

But you do it in an accidental sort of way without realizing what you are doing.

Consider the case of "Blind Tom." Probably you have heard or read of him. You know that he could listen to a piece of music for the first time and go immediately to a piano and reproduce it. People call that abnormal, but as a matter of fact he was in this respect more normal than any of us. We are abnormal in that we cannot do it, because our subconscious minds retain a perfect record of everything we have ever heard or seen, and if appealed to in the proper way, they will recall these images to consciousness.

Consider the case of these "lightning calculators" of whom one reads now and then. It may be a boy seven or eight years old; but you can ask him to divide 7,649.437 by 326.2568 and he will give you the result in less time than it would take you to put the numbers down on a piece of paper. You call him phenomenal. Yet you ought to be able to do the same yourself. Your subconscious mind can.

Dr. Hudson, in his book "The Law of Psychic Phenomena" tells of numerous such prodigies. Here are just a few instances:

"Of mathematical prodigies there have been upwards of a score whose calculations have surpassed, in rapidity and accuracy, those of the greatest educated mathematicians. These prodigies have done their greatest feats while but children from three to ten years old. In no case had these boys any idea how they performed their calculations, and some of them would converse upon other subjects while doing the sum. Two of these boys became men of eminence, while some of them showed but a low degree of objective intelligence.

"Whateley spoke of his own gift in the following terms:

"There was certainly something peculiar in my calculating faculty. It began to show itself at between five and six, and lasted about three years. I soon got to do the most difficult sums, always in my head, for I knew nothing of figures beyond numeration. I did these sums much quicker than anyone could upon paper, and I never remember committing the smallest error. When I went to school, at which time the passion wore off, I was a perfect dunce at cyphering, and have continued so ever since.

"Professor Safford became an astronomer. At the age of ten he worked correctly a multiplication sum whose answer consisted of thirty-six figures. Later in life he could perform no such feats.

"Benjamin Hall Blyth, at the age of six, asked his father at what hour he was born. He was told he was born at four o'clock. Looking at the clock to see the present time, he informed his father of the number of seconds he had lived. His father made the calculation and said to Benjamin, "You are wrong 172,000 seconds." The boy answered, "Oh, papa, you have left out two days for the leap years 1820 and 1824," which was the case.

"Then there is the celebrated case of Zerah Colburn, of whom Dr. Schofield writes:

"Zerah Colburn could instantaneously tell the square root of 106,929 as 327, and the cube root of 268,336,125 as 645. Before the question of the number of minutes in forty-eight years could be written he said 25,228,810. He immediately gave the factors of 247,483 as 941 and 263, which are the only two; and being asked then for those of 36,083, answered none, it is a prime number. He could not tell how the answer came into his mind. He could not, on paper, do simple multiplication or division."

The time will come when, as H.G. Wells visioned in his *"Men Like Gods,"* schools and teachers will no longer be necessary except to show us how to get in touch with the infinite knowledge our subconscious minds possess from infancy.

"The smartest man in the world," wrote Dr. Frank Crane in an article in *Liberty*, "is the Man Inside. By the Man Inside I mean that Other Man within each one of us that does most of the things we give ourselves credit for doing. You may refer to him as Nature or the Subconscious Self or think of him merely as Force or a Natural Law, or, if you are religiously inclined, you may use the term God.

"I say he is the smartest man in the world. I know he is infinitely more clever and resourceful than I am or than any other man that I ever heard of. When I cut my finger it is he that calls up the little phagocytes to come and kill the septic germs that might get into the wound and cause blood poisoning. It is he that coagulates the blood, stops the gash, and weaves the new skin.

"I could not do that. I do not even know how he does it. He even does it for babies that know nothing at all; in fact, does it better for them than for me.

"No living man knows enough to make toenails grow, but the Man Inside thinks nothing of growing nails and teeth and thousands of hairs all over my body; long hairs on my head and little fuzzy ones over the rest of the surface of the skin.

"When I practice on the piano I am simply getting the business of piano playing over from my conscious mind to my subconscious mind; in other words, I am handing the business over to the Man Inside.

"Most of our happiness, as well as our struggles and misery, comes from this Man Inside. If we train him in ways of contentment, adjustment, and decision he will go ahead of us like a well-trained servant and do for us easily most of the difficult tasks we have to perform."

Dr. Jung, celebrated Viennese specialist, claimed that the subconscious mind contains not only all the knowledge that it has gathered during the life of the individual, but that in addition it contains all the wisdom of past ages. That by drawing upon its wisdom and power the individual may possess any good thing of life, from health and happiness to riches and success.

You see, the subconscious mind is the connecting link between the Creator and ourselves, between Vital Force all about us and our own bodies and affairs. It is the means by which we can appropriate to ourselves all the good gifts, all the riches and abundance which Universal Mind has created in such profusion.

Berthelot, the great French founder of modern synthetic chemistry, once stated in a letter to a close friend that the final experiments which led to his most wonderful discoveries had never been the result of carefully followed and reasoned trains of thought, but that, on the contrary, "they came of themselves, so to speak, from the clear sky."

Charles M. Barrows, in "Suggestion Instead of Medicine," tell us that:

> "If man requires another than his ordinary consciousness to take care of him while asleep, not less useful is this same psychical provision when is awake. Many persons are able to obtain knowledge which does not come to them through their senses, in the usual way, but arrives in the mind by direct communications from another conscious intelligence, which apparantly knows more of what concerns their welfare than their ordinary reason does. I have known a number of persons who, like myself, could tell the contents of letters in their mail before opening them. Several years ago a friend of mine came to Boston for the first time, arriving at what was then the Providence railroad station in Park Square. He wished to walk to the Lowell station on the opposite side of the city. Being utterly ignorant of the streets as well as the general direction to take he confidently set forth without asking the way, and reached his destination by the most direct path. In doing this he trusted solely to 'instinctive guidance,' as he called it, and not to any hints or clues obtained through the senses."

The geniuses of literature, of art, commerce, government, politics and invention are, according to the scientists, but ordinary men like you and me who have learned how to draw upon their subconscious minds.

Sir Isaac Newton is reported to have acquired his marvelous knowledge of mathematics and physics with no conscious effort. Mozart said of his beautiful symphonies that "they just came to him." Descartes had no ordinary regular education. To quote Dr. Hudson:

> "There is a power which transcends reason, and is independent of induction. Instances of its development might be multiplied indefinitely. Enough is known to warrant the conclusion that when the soul is released from its objective environment it will be enabled to perceive all the laws of its being, to 'see God as He is,' by the perception of the laws which He has instituted. It is the knowledge of this power which demonstrates our true relationship to God, which confers the warranty of our right to the title of 'son of God,' and confirms our inheritance of our rightful share of his attributes and powers—our heirship of God, our joint heirship with Jesus Christ."

The subconscious mind is the seat of memory. Every thought or impression we have ever had is registered there. The conscious mind remembers nothing beyond what is held in its thought. It must draw upon the files of the subconscious for everything it wishes to recall.

"Considered from the standpoint of its activities," says Warren Hilton in *"Applied Psychology,"* the subconscious is that department of mind, which on the one hand directs the vital operations of the body, and on the other conserves, subject to the call of interest and attention, all ideas and complexes not at the moment active in consciousness.

"Observe, then, the possibility that lies before you. On the one hand, if you can control your mind in its subconscious activities, you can regulate the operation of your bodily functions, and can thus assure yourself of bodily efficiency and free yourself of functional disease. On the other hand, if you can determine just what ideas shall be brought forth from the subconsciousness into consciousness, you can thus select the materials out of which will be woven your conscious judgments, your decisions and your emotional attitudes.

"To achieve control of your mind is, then, to attain (a) health, (b) success, and (c) happiness."

Few understand or appreciate, however, that the vast storehouse of knowledge and power of the subconscious mind can be drawn upon at will. Now and then through intense concentration or very active desire we do accidentally penetrate to the realm of the subconscious and register our thought upon it. Such thoughts are almost invariably realized. The trouble is that as often as not it is our negative thoughts—or fears—that penetrate. And these are realized just as surely as the positive thoughts. What you must manage to do is learn to communicate only such thoughts as you wish to see realized to your subconscious mind, for it is exceedingly amenable to suggestion. You have heard of the man who was always bragging of his fine health and upon whom some of his friends decided to play a trick. The first one he met one morning commented upon how badly he looked and asked if he weren't feeling well. Then all the others as they saw him made similar remarks. By noon time the man had come to believe them, and before the end of the day he was really ill.

That was a glaring example, but similar things are going on every day with all of us. We eat something that someone tells us is bad for us and in a little while we think we feel a pain. Before we know it we have indigestion, when the chances are that if we knew nothing about the supposed indigestible properties of the food, we could eat it the rest of our days and never feel any ill effects.

Let some new disease be discovered and the symptoms described in the daily paper. Hundreds will come down with it at once. They are like the man who read a medical encyclopedia and ended by concluding he had everything but "housemaid's knee." Patent medicine advertisers realize this power of suggestion and cash in on it. Read one of their ads. If you don't think you have everything the matter with you that their nostrums are supposed to cure, you are the exception and not the rule.

You see, the subconscious takes those things that are handed to it as facts and works them out to a logical conclusion. You read or hear that doing such and such will bring on a cold or fever or some other ailment. The subconscious accepts this as fact unless you actively combat the belief, and if you do the things proscribed, it will proceed to give you a cold or fever, even though you had never given the matter a second thought.

This is the negative side of it. Emile Coue' based his system on the positive side—that you suggest to your subconscious mind that whatever ills it thinks you have are getting better. And it is good psychology at that. Properly carried out, it works wonders. But this method has its weaknesses. Suggestion will cure many ills, but not all. When you try to suggest something to the subconscious that is contrary to a long-held or deep-seated belief, you will fail. The subconscious will not accept it. You have to DO something to change its beliefs. You have to CONVINCE it, and in later chapters, we shall show you how.

Suffice it now to say that your subconscious mind is exceedingly wise and powerful. That it knows many things that are not in books. That when properly used it has infallible judgment, unfailing power. That it never sleeps, never tires.

Your conscious mind may slumber. It may be rendered impotent by anaesthetics or a sudden blow. But your subconscious mind works on, keeping your heart and lungs, your arteries and glands ever on the job.

Under ordinary conditions, it attends faithfully to its duties, and leaves your conscious mind to direct the outer life of the body. But let the conscious mind meet some situation with which it is unable to cope, and, if it will only call upon the subconscious, that powerful Genie will respond immediately to its need.

You have heard of people who had been through great danger tell how, when death stared them in the face and there seemed nothing they could do, things went black before them and, when they came to, the danger was past. In the moment of need, their subconscious mind pushed the conscious out of the way, while it met and overcame the danger. Impelled by the subconscious mind, their bodies could do things absolutely impossible to their ordinary conscious selves.

For the power of the subconscious mind is unlimited. Whatever is necessary for you to do in any right cause, it can give you the strength and ability to do.

Whatever good you may desire, it can bring to you. "The Kingdom of Heaven is within you."

But remember this: The subconscious works beneath the surface, and it reasons logically, deductively, from the facts that are given it. It will not go contrary to those facts. If you want to change it, you must give it new and stronger facts to work upon. Not only that, but you must nullify the original facts.

The Universal Mind

Have you ever dug up a potato vine and seen the potatoes clustering underneath? How much intelligence do you suppose one of these potatoes has? Do you think it knows anything about chemistry and geology? Can it figure out how to gather carbon gas from the atmosphere, water and all the necessary kinds of nutriment from the earth round about to manufacture into sugar and starch and alcohol? No chemist can do it. How do you suppose the potato knows? Of course it doesn't. It has no sense. Yet it does all these things. It builds the starch into cells, the cells into roots and vines and leaves—and more potatoes.

"Just old Mother Nature," you will say. But old Mother Nature must have a remarkable intelligence if she can figure out all these things that no human scientist has ever been able to solve. There must be an all-prevailing Intelligence behind Mother Nature— the Intelligence that first brought life to this planet— the Intelligence that evolved every form of plant and animal— that holds the winds in its grasp— that is all-wise, all-powerful. The potato is but one small manifestation of this Intelligence. The various forms of plant life, of animals, of man— all are mere cogs in the great scheme of things.

But with this difference— that man is an active part of this Universal Mind. That he partakes of its creative wisdom and power and that by consciously drawing to him its vital power, and then working in harmony with Universal Mind, he can *do* anything, *have* anything, *be* anything.

There is within you—within everyone—this mighty resistless force with which you can perform undertakings that will dazzle your reason, stagger your imagination. There constantly resides within you a Mind that is all-wise, all-powerful, a Mind that is entirely apart from the mind which you consciously use in your everyday affairs—the superconscious mind or Higher Self.

Your subconscious mind partakes of this wisdom and power, and it is through your subconscious mind that you can reach the superconscious and draw upon it in the attainment of anything you may desire. When you can intelligently use your subconscious mind in this way, you can be in communication with that Higher Self in you which is a part of the Universal Mind.

Remember this: the Universal Mind is omnipotent. And when the subconscious mind is in tune with the Higher Self, there is no limit to the things that it can do. Given any desire that is in harmony with the Universal Mind, you have but to hold that desire in your thought with confident and serene faith to attract from the invisible domain the things you need to satisfy it.

You see, there is just as much of the Creative Force around you today as there was when the world was made. And the Universal Mind, of which your superconscious is a part, is just as capable of making from it anything it desires.

"In the beginning was the Word," says the Gospel of St. John. What is a "Word"? A mental image, is it not? So all that God had in the beginning was a mental image. That was His mold, and into it He poured the Creative Force all about Him and formed the world and everything upon it.

If you are like most of us, you are not too well satisfied with your world as it is. What shall you do to improve it? RE-CREATE it! All you need is the mental image, and the faith to put the Creative Force all about you into it.

An understanding of this explains the power of prayer. The results of prayer are not brought about by some special dispensation of Providence. God is not a finite being to be cajoled or flattered into doing as you desire.

When you pray earnestly, you form a mental image of the thing you desire and you hold it strongly in your thought. Then, if you have the necessary faith that you ARE RECEIVING the things asked for, your superconsious mind (which is part of the Universal or God Mind) draws to you enough of the Creative Force to fill out the image you are holding in thought and to bring it into being.

Throughout the Old and the New Testament, you find the assurance that we are Sons of God, partaking of all his power—that nothing is impossible to us. And from earliest recorded times, a few have proved this to be so.

Jesus cured the sick, He raised the dead, He brought gold from the fish's mouth, He fed thousands with a handful of loaves and fishes. He showed His followers how to perform similar wonders, and everything that He did, He assured us that we could do also—"And greater things than these shall ye do!"

Whence comes such power? Where but from our part of Divinity —from the superconscious mind which is part of the Universal or God Mind.

Most of us think of mind as being merely the conscious part of us, but from the earliest Greek religious writings we have been taught that man is a triune being: 1st, the physical or conscious self; 2nd, the subconscious, sometimes called the "Inner Mind" because it is latent within you; 3rd, the superconscious or "Higher Self".

Go back 2,000 years before Christ to the Upanishads or earliest religious books of India and you find the same belief. The great pyramids were triangular on each side, exemplifying the idea you find on many of their monuments. The Egyptians believed that the "Ka" or "Higher Self" could separate itself from the body at will and perform any service that was required of it, regardless of distance.

You can send your Higher Self to do your will, as Jesus sent His to cure the Centurion's servant. Through it, you can protect your loved ones, you can heal, you can help in all ways.

To do so, however, you must charge it with your own Vital Force. You can never help another without giving something of yourself. You must consciously GIVE of your Vital Force. You must have the faith to SEE your Higher Self doing the things you direct it to do. You must BELIEVE it IS doing them. Given such faith, all things are possible to you.

All around you is the Vital Force of the Universe—the material of which everything is made. And YOU are a Creator, with the God-given power to use that Vital Force as you please, to make of it what you will.

But to create anything of good requires four things:

1—The mental image of what you want. This is the mold.
2—Knowledge of your power, so you can consciously draw to you all the Vital Force you need—breathe it in—and then pour it into your mental mold.
3—Faith in your creative power, faith to crystalize the Vital Force in your mold, until it manifests for all to see.
4—Doing something to convince your subconscious mind—and through it, the superconscious—that you do believe you HAVE received. For instance, a woman who prayed for a house got a board and nail and kept them before her, affirming that they were the beginning of the house.

As I see it, the Universal Mind is the Supreme Intelligence and Creator of the Universe and we are partakers of the Divine Attributes. You are part of it, I am part of it, and anything we do that is for the good of all has the support of this Universal Mind—*provided we call upon it.*

To bring you to a realization of the power latent in you, to teach you simple, direct methods of drawing upon it, is the beginning and the end of this book.

It is not enough to *know* that you have this power. You must put it into *practice*—not once, or twice, but *every hour and every day.* Don't be discouraged if it seems at times not to work. When you first studied arithmetic, your problems did not always work out correctly, did they? Yet you did not on that account doubt the principle of mathematics. You knew that the fault was with your methods, not with the principle. It is the same in this. The power is there. Correctly used, it can do anything.

All will agree that the Mind which first brought the Life Principle to this earth—which imaged the earth itself and the trees and the plants and the animals—is all-powerful. All will agree that to solve any problem, to meet any need, Mind has but to *realize* the need and it will be met. What most of us do not understand or realize is that we, ourselves, being part of Universal Mind, have this same power. Just as the drop of water from the ocean has all the properties of the great bulk of the water in the ocean. Just as the spark of electricity has all the properties of the thunderbolt. And having that power, we have only to realize it and use it to get from life any good we may desire.

In the beginning all was void—space—nothingness. How did Universal Mind construct the planets, the firmaments, the earth and all things on and in it from this formless void? *By first making a mental image on which to build.*

That is what you, too, must do. You control your destiny, your fortune, your happiness to the exact extent to which you can think them out, VISUALIZE them, SEE them, BELIEVE in them, and allow no vagrant thought of fear or worry to mar their completion and beauty. The quality of your thought is the measure of your power. Clear, forceful thought has the power of attracting to itself everything it may need for the fruition of those thoughts. As W.D. Wattles put it in his "Science of Getting Rich":

"There is a thinking stuff from which all things are made and which, in its original state, permeates, penetrates, and fills the interspaces of the universe. A thought in this substance produces the thing that is imagined by the thought. Man can form things in his thought, and, by impressing his thought upon formless substance, can cause the thing he thinks about to be created."

The connecting link between your conscious mind and the Universal is thought, and every thought that is in harmony with progress and good, every thought that is freighted with the right idea, can penetrate to Universal Mind. And penetrating to it, it comes back with the power of Universal Mind to accomplish it. You don't need to originate the ways and means. The Universal Mind knows how to bring about any necessary results. There is but one right way to solve any given problem. When your human judgment is unable to decide what the one right way is, turn to Universal Mind for guidance. You need never fear the outcome, for if you heed its advice you cannot go wrong.

Always remember—your mind is but a conductor—good or poor as you make it—for the power of Universal Mind. And thought is the connecting energy. Use that conductor, and you will improve its conductivity. Demand much, and you will receive the more. The Universal is not a niggard in any of its gifts. "Ask and ye shall receive, seek and ye shall find, knock and it shall be opened unto you."

That is the law of life. And the destiny of man lies not in poverty and hardship, but in living up to his high estate in unity with Universal Mind, with the power that governs the universe.

When you become conscious, even to a limited degree, of your oneness with the Universal Mind, your ability to call upon It at will for anything you may need, makes a different man of you. Gone are the fears, gone are the worries. You know that your success, your health, your happiness will be measured only by the degree to which you can impress the fruition of your desires upon the mind.

The toil and worry, the wearisome grind and the backbreaking work, will go in the future, as in the past, to those who will not use their minds. The less they use them, the more they will sweat. And the more they work only from the neck down, the less they will be paid and the more hopeless their lot will become. *It is Mind that rules the world.*

But to use your mind to the best advantage does not mean to toil along with the mere conscious part of it. It means hitching up your conscious mind with the Man Inside You, with the little "Mental Brownies," as Robert Louis Stevenson called them, and then working together for a definite end.

"My Brownies! God bless them!" said Stevenson, "Who do one-half of my work for me when I am fast asleep, and in all human likelihood do the rest for me as well when I am wide awake and foolishly suppose that I do it myself. I had long been wanting to write a book on man's double being. For two days I went about racking my brains for a plot of any sort, and on the second night I dreamt the scene in Dr. Jekyll and Mr. Hyde at the window; a scene afterward split in two, in which Hyde, pursued, took the powder and underwent the change in the presence of his pursuer."

Many another famous writer has spoken in similar strain, and every man who has problems to solve has had like experiences. You know how, after you have studied a problem from all angles, it sometimes seems more jumbled than when you started on it. Leave it then for a while—forget it—and when you go back to it, you find your thoughts clarified, the line of reasoning worked out, your problem solved for you. It is your little "Mental Brownies" who have done the work for you!

The flash of genius does not originate in your own brain. Through intense concentration you establish a circuit through your subconscious mind with the Universal, and it is from It that the inspiration comes. All genius, all progress, is from the same source. It lies within you merely to learn how to establish this at will so that you can call upon It at need. It can be done.

"In the Inner Consciousness of each of us," quotes Dumont in *The Master Mind,* "there are forces which act much the same as would countless tiny mental brownies or helpers who are anxious and willing to assist us in our mental work, if we will but have confidence and trust in them. This is a psychological truth expressed in the terms of old fairy tales. The process of calling into service these Inner Consciousness helpers is similar to that which we constantly employ to recall some forgotten fact or name. We find that we cannot recollect some desired fact, date, or name, and instead of racking our brains with an increased effort, we (if we have learned the secret) pass on the matter to the Inner Consciousness with a silent command, 'Recollect this name for me,' and then go on with our ordinary work. After a few minutes—or it may be hours—all of a sudden, pop! up will come the missing name or fact before us—flashed from the planes of Inner Consciousness, by the help of the kindly workers or brownies of these planes. The experience is so common that we have ceased to wonder at it, and yet it is a wonderful manifestation of the Inner Consciousness' workings of the mind. Stop and think a moment, and you will see that the missing word does not present itself accidentally, or 'just because.' There are mental processes at work for your benefit, and when they have worked out the problem for you they gleefully push it up from their plane on to the plane of the outer consciousness where you may use it.

"We know of no better way of illustrating the matter than by this fanciful figure of the 'mental brownies,' in connection with the illustration of the 'subconscious storehouse.' If you would learn to take advantage of the work of these Subconscious Brownies, we advise you to form a mental picture of the Subconscious Storehouse in which is stored all sorts of knowledge that you have placed there during your lifetime, as well as the impressions that you have acquired by race inheritance—racial memory, in fact. The information stored away has often been placed in the storage rooms without any regard for systematic storing, or arrangement, and when you wish to find something that has been stored away there a long time ago, the exact place being forgotten, you are compelled to call to your assistance the little brownies of the mind, which perform faithfully your mental command, 'Recollect this for me!" These brownies are the same little chaps that you charge with the task of waking you at four o'clock tomorrow morning when you wish to catch an early train—and they obey you well in this work of the mental alarm-clock. These same little chaps will also flash into our consciousness the report, 'I have an engagement at two o'clock with Jones'—when looking at your watch you will see that it is just a quarter before the hour of two, the time of your engagement.

"Well then, if you will examine carefully into a subject which you wish to master, and will pass along the results of your observations to these Subconscious Brownies, you will find that they will work the raw materials of thought into shape for you in a comparatively short time. They will analyze, systematize, collate, and arrange in consecutive order the various details of information which you have passed on to them, and will add thereto the articles of similar information that they will find stored away in the recesses of your memory. In this way they will group together various scattered bits of knowledge that you have forgotten. And, right here, let us say to you that you never absolutely forget anything that you have placed in your mind. You may be unable to recollect certain things, but they are not lost—sometime later some associative connection will be made with some other fact, and lo! the missing idea will be found fitted nicely into its place in the larger idea—the work of our little brownies. Remember Thompson's statement: 'In view of having to wait for the results of these unconscious processes, I have proved the habit of getting together material in advance, and then leaving the mass to digest itself until I am ready to write about it. 'This subconscious 'digestion' is really the work of our little mental brownies.

"There are many ways of setting the brownies to work. Nearly everyone has had some experience, more or less, in the matter—although often it is produced almost unconsciously, and without purpose or intent. Perhaps the best way for the average person—or rather the majority of persons—to get the desired results is for one to get as clear an idea of what one really wants to know—as clear an idea or mental image of the question you wish answered. Then after rolling it around in your mind — mentally chewing it, as it were—giving it a high degree of voluntary attention, you can pass it on to your Subconscious Mentality with the mental command: *'Attend to this for me—work out the answer!'* or some similar order. This command may be given silently, or else spoken aloud—either will do. Speak to the Subconscious Mentality—or its little workers —just as you would speak to persons in your employ, kindly but firmly. Talk to the little workers, and firmly command them to do your work. And then forget all about the matter—throw it off your conscious mind, and attend to your other tasks. Then in due time will come your answer-flashed into your consciousness

—perhaps not until the very minute that you must decide upon the matter, or need the information. You may give your brownies orders to report at such and such a time—just as you do when you tell them to awaken you at a certain time in the morning so as to catch the early train, or just as they remind you of the hour of your appointment, if you have them all well trained."

Have your ever read the story by Richard Harding Davis of *"The Man Who Could Not Lose?"* In it the hero is intensely interested in racing. He has studied records and "dope" sheets until he knows the history of every horse backward and forward.

The day before the big race he is reclining in an easy chair, thinking of the morrow's race, and he drops off to sleep with that thought on his mind. Naturally, his subconscious mind takes it up, with the result that he dreams the exact outcome of the race.

That was mere fiction, of course, but if races were run solely on the speed and stamina of the horses, it would be possible to work out the results in just that way. Unfortunately, other factors frequently enter into every betting game.

But the idea behind Davis' story is entirely right. The way to contact your subconscious mind, the way to get the help of the "Man Inside You" in working out any problem is:

First, fill your mind with every bit of information regarding that problem that you can lay your hands on.

Second, pick out a chair or lounge or bed where you can recline in perfect comfort, where you can forget your body entirely.

Third, let your mind dwell upon the problem for a moment, not worrying, not fretting, but placidly, and then turn it over to the "Man Inside You." Say to him—"This is your problem. You can do anything. You know the answer to everything. Work this out for me!" And utterly relax. Drop off to sleep, if you can. At least, drop into one of those half-sleepy, half-wakeful reveries that keep other thoughts from obtruding upon your consciousness. Do as Aladdin did—summon your Genie, give him your orders, then forget the matter, secure in the knowledge that he will attend to it for you. When you waken, *you will have the answer!*

For whatever thought, whatever problem you can get across to your subconscious mind at the moment of dropping off to sleep, that "Man Inside You," that Genie-of-your-Mind will work it out for you. In *"The Workshop of the Unconscious,"* published in *"The American Mercury"* some time ago, Professor Brand Blanshard of Yale University gave the five steps necessary to set the subconscious to work on a definite problem:

"1. Specify your problem consciously. Coin it at the beginning into a perfectly definite question. Remember that thinking is not musing, or wool-gathering, or dreaming, or day-dreaming, or 'inviting one's soul'; it is the attempt to find a suggestion that will settle a particular point, and if there is no point to settle, thought is left without guidance.

"2. Mobilize at the outset the resources you already have. Carry the making of conscious suggestions as far as you can; that will start the unconscious ball rolling with a vigorous push.

"3. Take time. The unconscious dislikes being hurried; it will not be bullied. If you attempt to bully it, it will probably go on strike ....Sleep on a decision for a single night—and it will be a better decision. And the more time the unconscious can get, the better it likes it.

"4. Seize the intimations of the unconscious when they come. They may come at any time and in any volume....Stop what you are doing abruptly. Listen quietly but intently to such voices as you can hear; if the time is ripe, you will find that they come in increasing volume and perhaps that in one pregnant half-hour everything essential in your speech or article is there before you.

"5. Don't confuse unconscious thinking with worry. Both, to be sure, are forms of brooding. But in fact they are mortal enemies. Worry is half-conscious fear, and fear freezes the very springs of thought and action....Creative work is impossible to minds preoccupied and distraught. It is pleasant to think that genius blows where it must and will make its way through any circumstances, but there is little truth in the notion....No mind can create while it is divided against itself. For that reason it is well, at times, to give up conscious effort and let the unconscious have its way with us."

Of course, not everyone can succeed in getting his thoughts across to the subconscious at the first or the second attempt. It requires understanding and faith, just as the working out of problems in mathematics requires an understanding of and faith in the principles of mathematics. But keep on trying, and you WILL do it. And when you do, *the results are sure.*

If it is something that you want, VISUALIZE it first in your mind's eye, see it in every possible detail, see yourself going through every move it will be necessary for you to go through when your wish comes into being. Build up a complete story, step by step, just as though you were acting it all out. Get from it every ounce of pleasure and satisfaction that you can. Be *thankful* for this gift that has come to you. It helps if you make a "Treasure Map" of the thing you want. Cut out pictures from magazines showing objects as nearly like those you desire as you can find. Paste these pictures on a sheet of paper and all around them write affirmations to the effect that you HAVE the things you want, verses from the Bible promising us everything of good, etc. Then relax; go to sleep if you can; give the "Man Inside You" a chance to work out the consummation of your wish without interference.

When you waken, hold it all pleasurably in thought again for a few moments. Don't let doubts and fears creep in, but go ahead, confidently, knowing that your wish is working itself out. Know this, believe it—and if there is nothing harmful in it, IT WILL WORK OUT!

But remember that your subconscious must be convinced of the reality of your belief that you HAVE the thing you ask for, so it is important that you DO something to convince it. If you have prayed for a home, go out and buy some furnishing for it, even if it be only some kitchenware from the 5 and 10 cent store. Or get some boards and start making shelves for your closets. If you have asked for money, start GIVING some to charity, as you would if you had plenty. ACT THE PART! As Emerson put it—"Do the thing, and you shall have the reward."

Somewhere in Universal Mind there exists the correct solution of every problem. It matters not how stupendous and complicated, or how simple a problem may appear to be. There always exists the right solution in Universal Mind. And because this solution does exist, there also exists the ability to ascertain and to prove what that solution is. You can know, and you can do, every right thing. Whatever it is necessary for you to know, whatever it is necessary for you to do, you can know and you can do, if you will but seek the help of Universal Mind and be governed by its suggestions.

Try this method every night for a little while, and the problem does not exist that you cannot solve.

Your Silent Partner Within

While the mental planes lying outside of and beyond the field of ordinary consciousness have been until recent years comparatively unexplored by psychologists, and in fact have been almost entirely ignored by western psychology until modern times, the best thought of the present time is in practical agreement upon the fact that on those hidden planes of mentality are performed the major portion of our mental work, and that in their field, are in operation some of the most important of our mental processes.

The exploration of these obscure regions of the mind has been one of the most fascinating tasks of modern psychology; and the mines have yielded rich material in abundance. Many mental phenomena formerly either denied as impossible by the orthodox psychologists, or else regarded by the average person as evidence of supernatural agencies and forces, are now seen to fit perfectly into the natural order of things, and to operate according to natural law and order. Not only have such investigations resulted in a greater increase of the scientific knowledge concerning the inner workings of the mind, but they have also served to place in the hands of the more advanced psychologists the material which they have turned to practical and efficient use by means of scientific methods of application.

The effect of these discoveries has been the presentation of an important truth to the thinking individual—the truth that his mental realm is a far greater and grander land than he has heretofore considered it to be. No longer is the Self held to be limited in its mental activities to the narrow field of ordinary consciousness. Your mental kingdom has suddenly expanded until it now constitutes a great empire, with borders flung wide and far beyond the boundaries of the little kingdom which you have been considering as the entire area of the field of the forces, power, and activities of the Self.

The Self has often been likened to the king of a great mental kingdom; but, in view of the discovery of the new facts concerning the wonderful field of the unconscious, subconscious, and superconscious mental activities, the Self is now more properly to be represented as a mighty emperor of a vast empire of which only a comparatively small portion has as yet been explored. You are being called upon to appreciate more fully the ancient aphorism: "You are greater than you know." Your Self is like a new Columbus, gazing at a great new world, which it has discovered around itself, and of which it is the owner and the ruler.

Employing the term, "The Subconscious," to indicate the entire field of activities of the mind which are performed below, above, or in any way "outside of" the field or plane of the ordinary consciousness of the individual, we soon discover that the activities of the Subconscious extend over a very wide range of manifestation, and embrace a great variety of forms of expression.

In the first place, the Subconscious presides over the activities of your physical processes. It performs the manifold tasks of digestion, assimilation, nutrition, elimination, secretion, circulation, reproduction—in short, all of your vital processes. Your conscious mentality is thus relieved of these great tasks.

Again, the Subconscious supervises the performance of your instinctive actions. Every action that you perform automatically, instinctively, "by habit," "by heart," and without conscious employment of thought and will, is really performed by your subsconscious mentality. Your conscious mentality, thus relieved of this work, is able to concentrate upon those other tasks which it alone can perform. When you learn to perform an action "by heart," or "by habit," the conscious mentality has turned over this particular work to your Subconscious.

Again, the Subconscious is largely concerned with the activities of your emotional nature. Your emotions which rise to the plane or level of consciousness are but the surface manifestations of the more elemental activities performed in the depths of the ocean of the Subconscious. Your elemental and instinctive emotions have their source and home in the Subconscious; they have accumulated there by reason of habit, heredity or racial memory. Practically all the material of your emotional activities is stored on the planes and levels of the Subconscious.

Again, the Subconscious presides over the processes of Memory. The subconscious planes or levels of the mind constitute the great storehouse of the recorded impressions of memory. Moreover, on those planes or levels is performed the work of indexing and cross-indexing the memory-records, by means of which subsequent recollection, recognition and remembrance are rendered possible. These regions of your subconscious mentality contain not only the recorded impressions of your own personal experience, but also those racial memories or inherited memories which manifest in you as "instinct," and which play a very important part in your life.

Again, the Subconscious is able to, and frequently does, perform for you important work along the lines of actual "thinking." By means of "mental rumination" it digests and assimilates the materials furnished by your conscious mentality, and then proceeds to classify these, to compare them, and to proceed to form judgements and decisions upon them and from them—all below the levels of your ordinary consciousness. Careful psychologists have decided that by far the greater part of our reasoning processes are really performed on mental levels and planes outside of the field of the ordinary consciousness. Much of your creative mental work, particularly that of the constructive imagination, is performed in this way, the result afterward being raised to the levels of conscious thought.

Finally, there are levels and planes "above" those of the ordinary consciousness, just as there are those "below" the latter. Just as the lower levels are largely concerned with working over the stored-up materials of the past, so these higher levels are concerned with reporting that which may be considered to represent the future conscious activities of the human race. These higher regions of the Subconscious may be said to contain the seed or embryo of the higher faculties and powers which will unfold fully in the future stages of the mental evolution of the race; many of these higher faculties and powers are even now beginning to manifest in occasional flashes in the minds of certain individuals, and, as a consequence, such individuals are frequently regarded as "inspired" or as possessing that indefinable quality or power known as "genius."

On these higher planes of the Subconscious abide certain marvelous powers of the Self, which powers manifest and express themselves in that which we call genius, inspiration, illumination—the exceptional mental achievements of certain intellects which stamp them as above the average. On these high planes abide, and are manifested, those wonderful mental activities which we attempt to explain under the term "Intuition." These activities, however, are not contrary to reason, though they may seem to transcend it at times; it is better to consider them as the manifestation of a Higher Reason. The investigation and exploration of these higher realms of the Subconscious form one of the most interesting and fascinating tasks of modern psychology. Even now, the reports of the investigators and explorers are of surpassing interest; those which confidently may be looked for in the future, bid fair to constitute a marvelous contribution to the pages of the history of modern scientific research.

We shall ask you to accompany us in an exploration of the various regions of the Subconscious — those wonderful realms of your mind—from the highest to the lowest. In this new land there are valuable deposits of material useful to you and to all mankind. It is our purpose to point out these to you, and to instruct you in the most approved methods of mining and converting them to practical uses. You are interested in the matter of being led directly to the mines containing these rich deposits, and in being told just how to conduct the mining operations and the converting processes. In this spirit, then, our journey of exploration shall be conducted.

The Secret Forces of the Great Subconscious, like all other great natural forces, may be harnessed and pressed into service by you. Like electricity, they may be so managed and directed into the proper channels that they may be set to work by and for you. You have been employing these forces, to a greater or less extent, in very many of your mental activities; but, in all probability, you have been employing them instinctively and without a full knowledge of the laws and principles involved in them. When you understand just what these forces are, how they work, and the methods best calculated to produce efficient results and effects, then you may proceed to employ them intelligently, deliberately and with conscious purpose and intent, end and aim.

The average man employs but about 25 per cent of the Subconscious Power. The man who understands the principles and methods to which we have just referred will be able to employ 100 per cent of his available Subconscious Power. This means that he will be able to increase fourfold his Subconscious mental work and activity, with correspondingly increased results and effects. Inasmuch as at least 75 per cent of man's mental processes are performed on the plane or level of the Subconscious, it will be seen that the benefits arising from quadrupling his Subconscious mental activities and available power are almost beyond the power of adequate calculation. This increased power and efficiency, moreover, are not obtained at the cost of increased effort and mental wear and tear; on the contrary, the man effectively employing his Subconscious relieves himself of a great portion of the mental strain incident to the employment of the conscious mentality.

In addition to the offices and powers of the Superconscious which we have mentioned, there is another and a most important function of that phase of the mentality which may be called "the protective power." Many persons, most persons in fact, have at times experienced this beneficent power. They have felt strongly that they were in close contact with a force, power, or entity of some kind which was in some way higher than themselves, but which was concerned with their welfare. This beneficent presence has been interpreted in various ways in accordance with the trend of thought of those experiencing it. Some of the ancients called it "the kindly genius"; others termed it "the guardian angel"; still others have thought of it as "my spirit friend"; while many others, though quite vividly conscious of its presence and power, have failed to give it a special name.

But by whatever name it may have been thought of, or even when no name at all has been applied to it, the mysterious something has been recognized as a beneficent presence-power—a hovering and brooding Something or Somewhat animated by a warm, kindly interest in the individual, and seemingly devoted to his interests and disposed to render to him useful services.

This beneficent presence-owner has often acted as a warning guardian in the lives of many persons. In other cases it has been felt to have acted subtly to bring about advantageous results and conditions for the persons whom it protected. It has led some into circumstances and conditions calculated to be of advantage to them; it has drawn others away from conditions and circumstances calculated to bring harm to them. In short, it has played the part of the "kindly genius" or the "guardian angel" to many an individual.

The touch of this Unseen Hand has been felt by countless individuals—very likely by you who are now reading these lines. It has cheered men when the tide of circumstances seemed to be running against them; it has animated them with a new lively spirit, has encouraged them to renewed endeavor, has filled them with new courage when they needed it most. It has seemingly led persons into the presence of other persons and things, into conditions and environments, which have proved advantageous to them. Men of all ages—some of the most practical and "hard headed" men of affairs, among others—have felt the touch of this Unseen Hand, and have gratefully acknowledged its help in times of need, even though they have been perplexed concerning its real character.

To many careful thinkers who have earnestly investigated this phenomena, it has seemed that this beneficent presence-power — this Unseen Hand that has reached out in times of need—is not an external power, nor an entity outside of themselves, but rather a manifestation of that part of man's mental nature which we have here considered under the term "The Superconscious." Instead of being an entity outside of us, it is believed to be a part of ourselves—a phase, part or aspect of our Self that manifests above the levels or planes of the ordinary consciousness. In short, this "kindly genius" or "guardian angel" is your own Superconscious Self, manifesting on some of its higher levels or planes of activity or power.

In this Higher Self you have a friend far truer, more constant, and more loyal than can be any other friend—for it is Yourself, in its essence and substance. Your interests are its interests, for you are one with it in essential being and power. It will manifest a fidelity to you, and a watchfulness over your real interests which is amazing in its devotion and constancy. It will manifest toward you, in turns, the protecting care of a father; the brooding watchful, loving care of a mother; and the helpful, fraternal care of a brother. It will be all of these things to you—and more—if you will but give it the chance to unfold its presence and to manifest its power in your life.

This Higher Self—this phase of your Superconscious—needs but the encouragement of your recognition and realization in order to manifest its power in your behalf. It is seemingly discouraged, disheartened and abashed by your indifference, unbelief, and the failure to recognize its presence and to realize its power. It does not need "training" or "developing"—all that it asks is to be recognized and realized by you, and to have from you a kindly, sympathetic reception. It has done much for you in the past—it will do more for you in the future, if you will but meet it half-way.

This higher part of your Self is full of discernment, and of cold, keen-edged wisdom. It can see far ahead, and is able to discern and select the right road for you to travel, and then to lead you into that road and to keep your feet on its solid substance, in spite of your efforts to take a side path or to wander into the ditches which lie on either side of the road. You will do well to "get off by yourself" once in a while, then and there to commune with your Higher Self—to have a little "heart-to-heart" visit with it. You will find this Higher Self to be a wonderful companion—one closer to you than can be any human being—for it is Yourself, and nothing but Yourself, manifesting on the higher planes and levels of your being. You will emerge from these periods of self-communion with renewed strength and vigor, filled with new hope and faith, animated by new ambitions and purposive determination.

We have presented to you a view of your New Mental Empire—a view of its lowest and its highest planes and levels, of its highlands and its lowlands. It is your own empire—YOURS! Yours to rule and to govern, to explore and to cultivate. You are at home in it. The many wonderful phenomena manifested in its immense region are your phenomena—yours to control, direct, develop, cultivate; yours to restrict, restrain, inhibit; at your will, as you will, by your will.

Do not allow yourself to be tempted by the wonderful powers manifested by some of your subordinate mental machinery or instruments; do not allow yourself to fall under the spell of any of the phenomenal manifestations in your mental wonderland. View all; respect all; use all; demand and secure aid and work from all; but never lose sight of the fact that YOU, your Real Self—the "I am I"—is the Master of this land, the ruler of this Empire, and that you rightfully have power and dominion over it, all its inhabitants, and all contained in its realm.

Your "I am I," your Real Self—YOU—are a center of consciousness, subconsciousness, or superconsciousness; all these are but instruments or channels of expression of your Real Self, the "I AM I," of YOU.

PART II

SECRET NUMBER TWO AMBITION AND DESIRE— TWO KEYS TO SUCCESS

CHAPTER 2

How to Arouse Strong Ambition

"Ambition"—What a glorious word! How the very sound of it stirs one's energies, and makes one feel the inspiration to be up at work doing things, succeeding, creating, accomplishing!

And what does Ambition really mean, pray? It means more than a mere eagerness for things. It means the deep-seated desire to materalize certain ideals which exist in the mind as mental pictures. Before one can accomplish things he must be possessed of Ambition. And before he can feel Ambition he must have the preceding hunger which causes him to manifest Ambition with which to satisfy it. And so it follows, anything that will stimulate that mental hunger will arouse Ambition and thus create that eagerness for action and attainment. And how may that mental hunger be produced?

There is a psychological law underlying this mental hunger that manifests as Ambition. That law is:—*in order for mental hunger to be manifested it must have ideals presented to the mind's eye.* Just as the gastric juices of the stomach may be stimulated and caused to flow by the sight, smell, or thought of food, so is this mental hunger produced by the sight, thought or idea of the things needed for its satisfaction. If you are contented with your present life, and want nothing better, it is chiefly because you *know* nothing better—have seen nothing better—have heard of nothing better, or else you are mentally and physically lazy. The ignorant savage seeking to till his land by means of a sharpened stick, cannot desire a steel plow or other agricultural implements if he does not know of them. He simply keeps right at work in his old way—the way of his forefathers—and feels no desire for a better implement. But by-and-by some man comes along with a steel plow, and our savage opens his eyes in wide surprise at the wonderful thing. If he be a savage of discernment he begins to get up an interest and sees how much better it accomplishes the task than does his rude pointed stick. If he be a progressive savage, he begins to wish he had one of the strange new implements, and if *he wants it hard enough* he begins to experience a new, strange feeling of mental hunger for the thing, which if sufficiently strong, causes his Ambition to bud.

And this is the critical point. Up to this time he has felt the strong Desire preceding Ambition. But now with the dawn of Ambition comes the arousing of the Will. And this is what Ambition is, *A Strong Will* aroused by a *Strong Desire.*

Without these two elements there can be no Ambition. Desire without will is not Ambition. One may want a thing very much but if he does not arouse his Will strongly enough to actively cooperate with the Desire, his Ambition will "die a-borning." And though one's Will be as strong as steel, yet if there be not a strong Desire animating and inspiring it, it will not manifest as Ambition.

To manifest Ambition fully, one must first eagerly desire the thing—not a mere "wanting" or "wishing" for it, but a fierce, eager, consuming hunger which demands satisfaction. And then one must have a Will aroused sufficiently strong to go out and get that which Desire is demanding. These two elements constitute the activity of Ambition.

Look around you at the successful men of the world in any line of human effort and endeavor, and you will see that they all have Ambition strongly developed. They have the fierce craving of Desire for things, and the firm Will which will brook no interference with the satisfaction of the Desire. Study the lives of Caesar, Napoleon, and their modern counterparts, the Twentieth Century Captains of Industry, and you will see the glare of this fierce ambition burning brightly and hotly within them.

The trouble with the majority of the people is that they have been taught that one should take what was given him and be content. But this is not Nature's way. Nature implants in each living being a *strong desire* for that which is necessary for its well-being and nourishment, and a *strong will* to gratify that natural desire. On all sides in Nature, you may see this law in effect. The plant and the animal obey it, and are not afraid. But Man, as he ascended the scale of evolution, while seeing the necessity and advantage of curbing and restraining certain tendencies and desires which if freely gratified would work harm on himself and upon society, has swung to the other extreme. In cutting off the dead branches of Desire, he has lopped off some live ones at the same time—that is, the majority of men have—the few who haven't reach out and gather to themselves the good things of life, throwing the "cores" and leavings to the rest.

But the wise, the sane, the strong men of the day are now reaching out for the use of the LAW and are accomplishing great things by reason of it. When the Many use the LAW, the Few will cease to be the sole possessors of the good things of life, which alas! so many of them have misused. When the secret is generally known, the evil will be eradicated and good will supersede it.

Therefore, be not afraid to stand boldly out, crying: "I want this, and I am going to have it! It is my rightful heritage, and I demand it of the LAW!" Be ambitious to attain Financial Success because that is the goal for which you are striving.

How to Turn on the Fire of Desire

We may compare Desire with the fire that burns brightly beneath a receptacle containing water which later represents the mind. Unless the fire of Desire burns brightly and imparts its heat to the water, or mind, there will be nothing but water. But let the fire manifest its ardent energy and heat, and lo! the water is converted into steam which turns mighty wheels and drives powerful machinery, and in fact "makes things go." We are apt to forget the causes that have operated in order that the steam be produced in our wonder, amazement and admiration of the power and effect of the manifested steam. But, in order to get the right idea of the matter fixed in our mind, we must take into consideration the water of the mind and the fire of Desire.

The mind is well represented by water, for it is unstable, changeable, in motion, having eddies, storms, ripples and calms. And Desire is well represented by fire, for it is ardent, hot, strong, and burning, and when manifested properly invariably acts upon the water-mind and produces the will-steam which may be turned to the accomplishment of any task and the moving of the material necessary for our plans. By all means keep the fire of Desire burning brightly under the proper amount and degree of the steam of Will, then apply it to the accomplishment of your life tasks.

If you allow the fires of Desire to burn low, or to become clogged with the ashes of dead and gone things long since exhausted and useless, you will find that they will be in the position of the majority of people who are like tea kettles simmering over a faint fire, and accomplishing nothing.

Unless you want a certain thing "the worst way" and manifest that Desire in the shape of a strong impelling force, you will have no will with which to accomplish anything. You must not only "want" to do a thing, or to possess a thing, but you must "want to" hard. You must want it as the hungry man wants bread, as the smothering man wants air. And if you will but arouse in yourself this fierce, ardent, insatiate Desire, you will set in operation one of Nature's most potent mental forces.

What is that great impelling force that you have felt within yourself whenever you have made a mighty effort to accomplish something? Is it not that surging, restless, impelling force of your being that you know as Desire? Did you do the thing simply because you thought it best, or because you felt within yourself a strong feeling that you WANTED to do the thing, or to possess the thing, in the strongest possible way? Did you not feel this strong force of Desire rising within you and impelling you to deed and action?

Desire is the great moving power of the Mind—that which excites into action the will and powers of the individual. It is at the bottom of all action, feeling, emotion or expression. Before we reach out to do a thing or to possess a thing, we must first "want to," and in the degree that "want to" is felt, so will be our response thereto. Before we love, hate, like or dislike, there must be a Desire of some kind. Before we can arouse ambition, there must be a strong desire. Before we can manifest energy, there must be a strong impelling Desire.

Did you ever stop to think that the difference between the strong and the weak of the race is largely a matter of Desire? The degree of Desire manifests in the different degrees of strength and weakness. The strong men of the race are filled with strong desires to do this thing, or to possess that. They are filled with that strong creative Desire that makes them want to build up, create, modify, change, and shift around. It is not alone the fruits of their labor that urge them on, but that insistent urge from their Creative Desire that drives them.

Do not be afraid to allow your Desire for Financial Success to burn brightly. Keep the ashes of past failures, disappointments and discouragements well cleared away so that you may have a good draught. Keep the fire of Desire burning brightly, ardently and constantly. Do not be sidetracked by outside things, for remember, concentrated Desire is that which produces the greatest steam producing power. Keep your mind fixed on that which you want, and keep on demanding that which belongs to you, for it is your own. The Universal Supply is adequate for all the needs of everyone, but it responds only to the insistent demand and the earnest Desire. Learn to Desire things in earnest, and rest not content with a mere wanting and wishing.

Desire creates Mental Attitude-develops Faith-nourishes Ambition-unfolds Latent Powers-and tends directly and surely toward Success. Let the strong, dominant desire for Financial Independence possess you from the tips of your toes to the roots of your hair-feel it surging through every part of your body, and then don't stop until you reach your goal.

CHAPTER 3

Desire—The First Law of Gain

If YOU had a wishing ring, what one thing would you wish for? Wealth? Honor? Fame? Love? What one thing do you desire above everything else in life?

Whatever it is, you can have it. Whatever you desire wholeheartedly, with singleness of purpose—you can have. But the first and all-important essential is to know what this one thing is. Before you can win your heart's desire, you must get clearly fixed in your mind's eye what it is that you want.

It may sound paradoxical, but few people do know what they want. Most of them struggle along in a vague sort of way, hoping—like Micawber—for something to turn up. They are so taken up with the struggle that they have forgotten—if they ever knew—what it is they are struggling for. They are like a drowning man—they use up many times the energy it would take to get them somewhere, but they fritter it away in aimless struggles—without thought, without direction, exhausting themselves, while getting nowhere.

You have to know what you want before you stand much chance of getting it. You have an unfailing "Messenger to Garcia" in that Genie-of-your-Mind—but YOU must formulate the message. Aladdin would have stood a poor chance of getting anything from his Genie if he had not had clearly in mind the things he wanted the Genie to get.

In the realm of mind, the realm in which all is practical power, you can possess what you want at once. You have but to claim it, visualize it, believe in it, to bring it into actuality. It is yours for the taking. For the Genie-of-your-Mind can give you power over circumstances, health, happiness and prosperity. And all you need to put it to work is an earnest, intense desire.

Sounds too good to be true? Well, let us go back for a moment to the start. You are infected with that "divine dissatisfaction with things as they are" which has been responsible for all the great accomplishments of this world—else you would not have gotten thus far in this book. Your heart is hungering for something better. "Blessed are they which do hunger and thirst after righteousness (right-wiseness) for they shall be filled." You are tired of the worry and grind, tired of the deadly dull routine and daily tasks that lead nowhere. Tired of all the petty little ills and ailments that seemingly have become the lot of man here on earth.

Always there is something within you urging you on to bigger things, giving you no peace, no rest, no chance to be lazy. It is the same "something" that drove Columbus across the ocean; that drove Hannibal across the Alps; that drove Edison onward and upward from a train boy to the inventive wizard of the century; that drove Henry Ford from a poor mechanic at forty to probably the richest man in the world at sixty.

This "something" within you keeps telling you that you can do anything you want to do, be anything you want to be, have anything you want to have—and you have a sneaking suspicion that it may be right.

That "something" within you is your Higher Self, your part of Universal Mind, your Genie-of-the-brain. Men call it ambition, and "Lucky is the man" wrote Arthur Brisbane, "whom the Demon of Ambition harnesses and drives through life. This wonderful little coachman is the champion driver of all the world and of all history.

"Lucky you, if he is *your* driver.

"He will keep you going until you do something worthwhile—working, running and moving ahead.

"And that is how a real man ought to be driven.

"This is the little Demon that works in men's brains, that makes the blood tingle at the thought of achievement and that makes the face flush and grow white at the thought of failure.

"Every one of us has this Demon for a driver, IN YOUTH AT LEAST.

"Unfortunately the majority of us he gives up as very poor,

hopeless things, not worth driving, by the time we reach twenty-five or thirty.

"How many men look back to their teens, when they were harnessed to the wagon of life with Ambition for a driver? When they could not wait for the years to pass for opportunity to come?

"It is the duty of ambition to drive, and it is your duty to *keep Ambition alive and driving.*

"If you are doing nothing, if there is no driving, no hurrying, no working, *you may count upon it that there will be no results. Nothing much worth while in the years to come.*

"Those that are destined to be the big men twenty years from now, when the majority of us will be nobodies, *are those whom this demon is driving relentlessly, remorselessly, through the hot weather and the cold weather, through early hours and late hours.*

"Lucky YOU if you are in harness and driven by the Demon of Ambition."

Suppose you *have* had disappointments, disillusionments along the way. Suppose the fine point of your ambition has become blunted. Remember there is no obstacle that there is not some way around, or over, or through—and if you will depend less upon the 10 percent of your abilities that reside in your conscious mind, and leave more to the 90 percent that constitute your subconscious and superconscious, you can overcome all obstacles. Remember this—there is no condition so hopeless, no life so far gone, that mind cannot redeem it.

Every untoward condition is merely *a lack* of something. Darkness, you know, is not real. It is merely a lack of light. Turn on the light and the darkness will be seen to be nothing. It vanishes instantly. In the same way poverty is simply a lack of necessary supply. Find the avenue of supply and your poverty vanishes. Sickness is merely the absence of health. If you are in perfect health, sickness cannot hurt you. Doctors and nurses go about at will among the sick without fear—and suffer as a rule far less from sickness than does the average man or woman.

So there is nothing you have to *overcome.* You merely have to *acquire* something. And always Mind can show you the way. You can obtain from Mind anything you want, if you will learn how to do it. "I think we can rest assured that one can do and be practically what he desires to be," says Farnsworth in "Practical Psychology." And psychologists all over the world have put the same thought in a thousand different ways.

"It is not will, but desire," says Charles W. Mears, "that rules the world." "But," you will say, "I have had plenty of desires all my life. I've always wanted to be rich. How do you account for the difference between my wealth and position and power and that of the rich men all around me?"

The Magic Secret

The answer is simply that you have never focused your desires into one great dominating desire. You have a host of mild desires. You mildly wish you were rich, you wish you had a position of responsibility and influence, you wish you could travel at will. The wishes are so many and varied that they conflict with each other and you get nowhere in particular. You lack one *intense* desire, to the accomplishment of which you are willing to subordinate everything else.

Do you know how Napoleon so frequently won battles in the face of a numerically superior foe? By concentrating his men at the actual *point of contact!* His artillery was often greatly outnumbered, but it accomplished far more than the enemy's because instead of scattering his fire, he *concentrated it all on the point of attack!*

The time you put in aimlessly dreaming and wishing would accomplish marvels if it were concentrated on one definite object. If you have ever taken a magnifying glass and let the sun's rays play through it on some object, you know that as long as the rays are scattered they accomplish nothing. But focus them on one tiny spot and see how quickly they start something.

It is the same way with your mind. You have to concentrate *on one idea at a time.*

"But how can I learn to concentrate?" many people ask. Concentration is not a thing to be learned. It is merely a thing to do. You concentrate whenever you become sufficiently interested in anything. Get so interested in a ball game that you jump up and down on your hat, slap a man you have never seen before on the back, embrace your nearest neighbor—*that* is concentration. Become so absorbed in a thrilling play or movie that you no longer realize the orchestra is playing or there are people around you—*that* is concentration.

And that is all concentration ever is—getting so interested in some one thing that you pay no attention to anything else that is going on around you.

If you want a thing badly enough, you need have no worry about your ability to concentrate on it. Your thoughts will just naturally center on it like bees on honey.

In his experiments at Duke University, Dr. J.B. Rhine has shown that the mind can definitely influence inanimate objects, but only when there is intense interest or desire.

When the subject's interest was distracted, when he failed to concentrate his attention, he had no power over the object. It was only as he gave his entire attention to it, concentrated his every energy upon it, that he got successful results.

Dr. Rhine has proved through physical experiments what most of us have always believed—that there is a Power over and above the merely physical power of the mind or body, that through intense concentration or desire we can link up with that Power, and that once we do, nothing is impossible to us.

Man is no longer at the mercy of blind chance or Fate. He can control his own destiny. Science is at last proving what Religion has taught from the beginning—that God gave men *dominion,* and that we have only to understand and use this dominion to become the Masters of our Fate, the Captains of our Souls.

So hold in your mind the things you most desire. Affirm them. Believe them to be existing facts. Let me quote again the words of the Master, because there is nothing more important to remember in this whole book. "Therefore I say unto you, what things soever ye desire when ye pray, *believe that ye receive them* and ye shall have them."

And again I say, the most important part is the *"believe that ye receive them."* Your subconscious mind is exceedingly amenable to suggestion. If you can truly believe that you *have* received something, you impress that belief upon your subconscious mind, which in turn passes it along to the superconscious. Being a part of Universal Mind, sharing that Universal Mind's all-power, it has only to put the Creative Force all about it into the mold of your thought and bring the object into being. "The Father that is within me, He doeth the works." Your mind will respond to your desire in the exact proportion in which you believe. "As thy faith is, so be it unto thee."

The people who live in beautiful homes, who have plenty to spend, who travel about in yachts and fine cars, are for the most part people who started out to accomplish *some one definite thing.* They had one clear goal in mind, and everything they did centered on that goal.

Most men just jog along a rut, going through the same old routine day after day, ekeing out a bare livelihood, with no definite desire other than the vague hope that fortune will some day drop in their lap. Fortune doesn't often play such pranks. And a rut, you know, differs from a grave only in depth. A life such as that is no better than the animals live. Work all day for money to buy bread, to give you strength to work all the next day to buy more bread. There is nothing to it but the daily search for food and sustenance. No time for aught but worry and struggle. No hope of anything but the surcease of sorrow in death.

You can *have* anything you want—if you want it badly enough. You can *be* anything you want to be, *have* anything you desire, *accomplish* anything you set out to accomplish—if you will hold to that desire with singleness of purpose; if you will understand and BELIEVE in your own powers to accomplish.

What is it that you wish in life? Is it health? In the chapter on health we shall show you that you can be radiantly well—without drugs, without tedious exercises. It matters not if you are crippled or bedridden or infirm. Your body rebuilds itself largely every eleven months. You can start now rebuilding along perfect lines.

Is it wealth you wish? In the chapter on success we shall show you how you can increase your income, how you can forge rapidly ahead in your chosen business or profession.

Is it happiness you ask for? Follow the rules herein laid down and you will change your whole outlook on life. Doubts and uncertainty will vanish, to be followed by calm assurance and abiding peace. You will possess the things your heart desires. You will have love and companionship. You will win contentment and happiness.

But desire must be impressed upon the subconscious before it can be accomplished. Mere conscious desire seldom gets you anything. It is like the day-dreams that pass through your mind. Your desire must be vitalized, must be persisted in, must be concentrated upon, must be impressed upon your subconscious mind before it can reach the superconscious or *Creative Mind.* Don't bother about the means for accomplishing your desire—you can safely leave these to your superconscious mind. If you can visualize the thing you want, if you can impress upon your subconscious mind the *belief that you have it,* you can safely leave to your Higher Self the finding of the means of getting it. Trust the Universal Mind to show the way. The mind that provided everything in such profusion must find joy in seeing us take advantage of that profusion. "For herein is the Father glorified—that ye bear much fruit."

You do not have to wait until tomorrow, or next year, or the next world, for happiness. You do not have to die to be saved. "The Kingdom of Heaven is within you." That does not mean that it is up in the heavens or on some star or in the next world. It means *here* and *now!* All the possibilities of happiness are always here and always available. At the open door of every man's life there lies this pearl of great price—the understanding of man's dominion over the earth. With that understanding and conviction you can do everything which lies before you and you can do it to the satisfaction of everyone and the well-being of yourself. God and good are synonymous. And God—good—is absent only to those who believe He is absent.

Find your desire, impress it upon your thought, and you have opened the door for opportunity. And remember, in this new heaven and new earth which we are trying to show you, *the door of opportunity is never closed.* As a matter of fact, you constantly have *all that you will take.* So keep yourself in a state of receptivity. It is your business to receive abundantly and perpetually. The law of opportunity enforces its continuance and availability. *"Every good gift and every perfect gift is from above and cometh down from the Father of light, with whom is no variableness, neither shadow of turning."*

CHAPTER 4

Strong Desire Essential to Success

Desire Power is one of the many phases of Personal Power—of that Personal Power which flows into and through the individual from that great source of the All-Power of All-Things which in this instruction is known as POWER.

You do not create your own Personal Power of any kind, though you may modify it, adapt it, develop it, and direct it. POWER, the source of All-Power, has always existed and will always exist. You generate Personal Power by drawing upon the great Source and Fount of All-Power; by opening your natural channels to its inflow; and by supplying it with the proper physical and mental mechanism by means of which it is enabled to express and manifest itself efficiently.

An old writer once said: "Few speakers succeed who attempt merely to make people think—they want to be made to feel. People will pay liberally to be made to feel or to laugh, while they will begrudge a sixpence for instruction or talk that will make them think. The reasons are palpable and plain: it is heart against head; soul against logic; and soul is bound to win every time." Cardinal Newman once said: "The heart is commonly reached, not through reason, but through the imagination, by means of direct impressions, by descriptions. Persons influence us, voices melt us, deeds inflame us."

One has but to recall instances of the great influence exerted over the public mind by the emotional appeals to affection or dislike, to prejudices for or against, to desires, ambitions, aspiratons, cravings, longings and things eagerly wanted, made by orators, politicians, statesmen, actors, and preachers, in order to realize the potent effect of Emotion, Affection and Desire upon men's thoughts, opinions, beliefs and convictions.

A modern writer says: "A large part of the business of life consists in moving the emotions and desires of men so as to get them to act."

Another says: "The successful man is he who is able to persuade the crowd that he has something that they want, or that they want something that he has." The successful salesman, advertising man, or any other man who has things to sell other men, all bring into play the force of Desire in those whom they are seeking to interest in their projects. They appeal to the "want" or "want to" side of the mind of men. They play upon men's sympathies, their prejudices, their hopes, their fears, their desires, their aversions.

Men "do things" and "act" because of the motive power of their emotional nature, particularly in the form of Affection and Desire. This is the only reason impelling or influencing men to "do things." Were this motive power absent, there would be no action or doing of things; there would be no reason or cause for such action or doing, in that event. We act and do solely because we "like" and "want". Were the emotional element absent, there would be no element of volition. Without Desire we would make no choices, would exercise no decision, would perform no actions. Without the "want" and "want to" there would be no "will to do" and no "doing." Desire is the motive power of Action; take away the motive power and there cannot be and will not be any movement, activity or volition. Without the motive power of Desire, the machinery of voluntary action ceases to operate, and comes to a complete standstill.

An old writer, whose words have been preserved for us, though his name is unknown to the present writers, enunciates a profound truth in the following rather startling statement:

"Every deed that we do, good or bad, is prompted by Desire. We are charitable because we wish to relieve our inner distress at the sight of suffering; or from the urge of sympathy, with its desire to express its nature; or from the desire to be respected in this world, or to secure a comfortable place in the next one. One man is kind because he desires to be kind—because it gives him satisfaction and content to be kind. Another man is unkind because he desires to be so—because it gives him satisfaction and content to be so. One man does his duty because he desires to do it—he obtains a higher emotional satisfaction and content from duty well done than he would from neglecting it in accordance with some opposing desires.

Another man yields to the desire to shirk his duty—he obtains greater satisfaction and content from refraining from performing his duty, in favor of doing other and contrary things which possess a greater emotional value to himself.

" The religious man is religious in his actions, because his religious desire. are stronger than are his irreligious ones—he finds a greater satisfaction and content in religious actions than in the pursuits of the worldly-minded. The moral man is moral because his moral desires are stronger than his immoral ones—he obtains a greater degree of emotional satisfaction and content in being moral than in being immoral. Everything we do is prompted by Desire in some shape or form, high or low. Man cannot be Desireless, and still act in one way or another—or in any way whatsoever. Desire is the motive-power behind all action—it is a natural law of Life. Everything from the atom to the monad; from the monad to the insect; to man; from Man to Nature; and possibly from Nature to God; everything from lowest to highest and from highest to lowest—everything that is—is found to act and to do things, to manifest action and to perform work, by reason of the power and force of Desire. Desire is the animating power, the energizing force, and the motive-power in, under, and behind all natural processes, activities and events."

There is a general rule concerning Desire which is important that you should note and remember. The rule is as follows: *"The degree of force, energy, will, determination, persistence and continuous application manifested by an individual in his aspirations, ambitions, aims, performances, actions and work is determined primarily by the degree of 'want' and 'want to' concerning that object."*

So true is this principle that some who have studied its effects have announced the aphorism: *"You can have or be anything that you want—if you only want it hard enough."* To "want a thing hard enough" is equivalent to "paying the price" for it—the price of the sacrifice of lesser desires and "wants"; the casting off of the non-essentials; the concentration of Desire upon the one essential idea or thing; and the application of the will to its attainment or accomplishment.

Although we have been in the habit of ascribing to the possession and the manifestation of a "strong will", it has really been due to the element of Will which is called Conation (i.e., Desire tending toward expression in Will-action.) The man filled with an ardent, fierce, burning, craving and urge for and toward a certain object, will call to his aid the latent powers of his Will, and of his Intellect. These, under the motive power and stimulus of Desire, will manifest unusual activity and energy toward the accomplishment of the desired end. Desire has well been called the Flame which produces the heat which generates the Steam of Will.

Very few persons, comparatively, know how to Desire with sufficient intensity and insistence. They content themselves with mere "wishing" and mild "wanting." They fail to experience that Insistent Desire, which is one of the important elements of the Master Formula of Attainment. They do not know what it is to feel and manifest that intense, eager, longing, craving, insistent demanding, ravenous Desire which is akin to the persistent, insistent, ardent, overwhelming desire of the drowning man for a breath of air; of the shipwrecked or desert-lost man for a drink of water; of the famished man for bread and meat; of the fierce, wild creature for its mate; of the mother for the welfare of her children. Yet if the truth were known, the desire for success of the men who have accomplished great things has often been as great as these.

We are not necessarily slaves to our Desires; we may master the lower or disadvantageous desires by Will, under the Power of the "I AM I," or Master Self. We may transmute lower desires into higher; negatives into positives; hurtful into helpful in this way. We may become Masters of Desire, instead of being mastered by it. But before we may do so, we must first desire to do so, to accomplish and to attain this end. We may even rise to the heights of Will—the place where the "I AM I" may say truthfully, "I Will to Will" and "I Will to Desire", but even there we must first desire to so "Will to Will" and "Will to Desire."

Even at these sublime heights of Egohood, we find Desire to be the fundamental and elemental Motive Power: this because it abides at the very heart of things—the heart of ourself—the Heart of Life. Even there, we essay and accomplish the highest deeds and acts of Will solely and simply because they serve to "content our spirit" to give us the highest degree of "self satisfaction" and to gratify, satisfy and give expression and manifestation to our greatest, most insistent, most persistent and strongest "want" and "want to."

CHAPTER 5

Magnetic Power of Desire

The strongest and most persistent desires of the individual tend to attract to him (or him to) that which is closely related to or correlated with those desires. That is to say: the strong insistent desires of a person tend to attract to him those things which are closely related to such desires; and, at the same time, tend to attract him toward those related things. The Attractive Desire of Desire operates in two general ways, viz., (1) to attract to the individual the things closely related to his desires; and (2) to attract the individual to such related things.

In your own experience, in all probability, you have experienced many cases of the operation of this subtle law of Nature. You have become intensely interested in some particular subject, and your desire for further progress and attainment along the lines of that subject has been actively aroused. Then you have noticed the strange and peculiar way in which persons and things related to that subject have come under your observation and attention —sometimes even being apparently forced upon you apart from any act on your part. In the same way, you have found yourself attracted in certain directions in which, unknown to you, were to be found persons or things related to the subject of your desire, information concerning that subject, conditions in which the subject was involved or being manifested. In short, you have found that things happened "as if" you were either attracting persons, things, and circumstances to you, or else that you were being attracted, drawn, or "led" to such persons, things, or circumstances.

Under such conditions, you will find arising on all sides certain events connected with and related to the subject of your desire; books containing information concerning it; persons having some connection with it; conditions in which that subject plays an important part. You will find, on the one hand, that you seem to have become a centre of attraction for things, persons and circumstances related to that subject; or, on the other hand, that you are being attracted to certain centres of attraction related to that subject. In short, you will discover that you have set into operation certain subtle forces and principles which have "correlated" you with all matters related to that subject.

More than this, you will find that if you will maintain for a considerable time a continuous and persistent interest and desire in that particular subject, you will have established a vortex-centre of attraction for that which is related to the subject. You will have set into operation a mental whirlpool, steadily spreading its circumference of influence, which draws into itself and to your central point the related and correlated things, persons, and circumstances. This is one of the reasons why after you "get things going" in any particular line of interest and desire, things tend to "come easier" to and for you as time passes. In such cases, that which required enormous effort in the earlier stages seems to move almost automatically in the later ones. These are matters of common and almost universal experience with those who have been actively engaged in any particular line of work in which strong interest and insistent desire have been aroused and maintained.

So, you see, Desire Power tends not only to develop and evolve within you the qualities and powers necessary to enable you to manifest and express yourself along the lines of the desires persistently held by you; it also tends to attract to you, and you to them, the things, persons, circumstances and conditions related to or correlated with the subject of such desires. In other words, Desire Power employs every means at its disposal to express and manifest itself more fully, and through you, attain its objective—its greatest possible degree of satisfaction and realization. When you have thoroughly aroused Desire Power within you, and have created for it a strong, positive focal centre of influence, you have set into operation powerful forces of Nature, operating along subconscious and invisible lines of activity. In this connection, remember the adage: *"You may have anything you want—if you only want it hard enough."*

The attractive force of Desire Power operates in many different ways, in addition to the "drawing power." Operating along the lines of "something like telepathy" of which we have spoken, it also operates in other ways on the subconscious planes of the mind in order to influence, guide and direct the person to the other persons, things, conditions, and circumstances related or correlated to or with the particular desire which is being persistently and insistently held by that person. Under its influence, the subconscious mentality raises to the levels of consciousness new ideas, thoughts, plans, which if applied will tend to "lead" the person in the direction of the things which will serve to aid him in the realization of those desires which he is insistently harboring.

In this way, the person is led to the related things, just as the things in other ways are led to him. Desire Power pushes, as truly as it pulls—it urges you forward as truly as it attracts things to you. In some cases the process is entirely subconscious, and the person is amazed when he finds "by chance" that he has "stumbled upon" helpful things in places where he had least expected to find them, and in places where he had apparently been led by Chance. But there is no Chance about it. Persons are undoubtedly "led to" helpful things and conditions, but by Desire Power operating along the lines of the subconscious mentality, and not by Chance.

Many successful men could tell how often in their respective careers, at critical times, the most peculiar happenings have been experienced by them, seemingly "by chance" or "by accident," which served as the means of transforming defeat into victory. In this way they acquired "by chance" some important bit of information serving to supply the missing link in their mental chain, or else giving them a clue to that which had previously escaped their thought.

Of course, the subconscious mentality of the individual is the "helper," or "directing genius" in such cases, and the happenings are merely phases of the general phenomena of the Subconscious. But, nevertheless, Desire Power is the animating principle involved. The subconscious mentality, like the conscious mentality, is energized and aroused into activity by the urge of Desire Power. Desire Power employs every possible form of energy, activity and motive-power at its command; and also presses into service all kinds of machinery and instruments, mental and physical. The Fire of Desire kindles every faculty of the mind, on conscious and subconscious planes, and sets them all into some form or phase. None of these faculties would manifest activity; where activity is manifested by them, there is always implied the presence and urge of Desire Power.

Sometimes Desire Power will operate in strangely indirect ways in order to accomplish its results. By means of the "under the surface" perception of the subconscious faculties, Desire Power seemingly perceives that "the longest way 'round is the quickest way home," and it proceeds to cause the individual to pursue that "longest way 'round" in order to attain his desire in the shortest possible time. In such cases it often acts to upset and overturn the plans which one has carefully mapped out; the result makes it seem to one that failure and defeat, instead of victory and success, have come to him. It will sometimes tear the person away from his present comparatively satisfactory environment and conditions, and lead him over rock roads and hard trails, and *finally,* when he has almost despaired of attaining success, he finds it literally thrust upon him.

Such instances are not invariable, of course, but they occur sufficiently often and with such characteristically marked features that they must be recognized. It often happens like, as one who has experienced it has said, "It seems as if one were grabbed by the back of his neck, lifted out of his set environment and occupation, dragged roughly over a painful road, and then thrust forcibly but kindly upon the throne of success, or at least into the throne room with the throne in plain sight before him."

But, in the end, those who have experienced these strenuous activities of Desire Power operating through the subconscious nature in many other ways are found to agree universally in the statement, "The end justified the means; the thing is worth the price paid for it." It requires philosophy and faith to sustain one when he is undergoing experiences of this kind, but the knowledge of the law and principle in operation will of course greatly aid him. The right spirit to maintain in such cases is that expressed in the phrase, "it's a great life, if you don't weaken."

Desire Power employs freely the subconscious faculties in its work of Realization through Attraction. It employs these in man just as it employs them in the case of the homing pigeon, the migrating bird, the bee far from its hive. It supplies the "homing instinct" to the man seeking success, as well as to the animal seeking refuge. It is said that animals separated from their mates, seemingly are attracted to them over long distances. Lost animals find their way home, though many miles over strange country have to be traveled. Let a person establish a "refuge for birds, and the birds will soon begin to travel toward it—even strange species from long distances putting in an appearance. Water fowl travel unerringly toward water; just as the roots of trees manifest the same sense of direction toward water and rich soil.

In all matters, the Law of Desire Attraction manifests its power. Man is under the law, and may even cause the law to work for him when he understands its nature. Man may harness Desire Power and set it to work for him just as he has harnessed other great forces of Nature. Once set to work for him, this power will work "without haste, and without rest" toward the end impressed upon it. It will work for him while he is awake and working otherwise, and when he is asleep and resting from his conscious work. Desire is the "force of forces," because it is the inmost kernel of all the other forms of natural force—physical or mental. All force depends upon inner Attraction or Repulsion—and these are but the manifestation of Desire Power, positive or negative.

CHAPTER 6

The Master Formula for Getting What You Want

The Master Formula of Attainment, stated in popular form, is as follows:

"You may have anything you want, provided that you (1) know exactly what you want, (2) want it hard enough, (3) confidently expect to attain it, (4) persistently determine to obtain it, and (5) are willing to pay the price of its attainment."

When you consider the question, "Exactly what do I want? you will first regard it as one quite easy to answer. But after you begin to consider the question in detail, and in real earnest, you will discover two very troublesome obstacles in your way on the road to the correct answer. The two obstacles are as follows: (1) the difficulty in ascertaining a clear and full idea of your desires, aspirations, ambitions, and hopes; and (2) the difficulty in ascertaining which ones of a number of conflicting desires, aspirations, ambitions, and hopes you "want" more than you do those opposing them.

You will find yourself with "the divine discontent" of a general dissatisfaction with your present condition, circumstances, possessions, and limitations. You will feel, perhaps strongly, the "raw desire" of the elemental Desire Power within you, but you will not have clearly outlined in your mind the particular directions in which you wish that elemental force to proceed into manifestation and expression.

You will often feel that you wish that you were somewhere other than where you now are; that you were doing something different from what you are now doing; that you possessed things other and better than you now possess; or that your present limitations were removed, thus giving you a wider and fuller expression and manifestation of the power which you feel to be within you. All these general feelings will be experienced by you, but you will not be able to picture clearly to yourself just what "other things" you really want to take the place of those which are now your own.

Then, when you attempt to form the clear picture and definite idea of what you want, you will find you want **many** things. Some of them opposing each other, each offering attractive features, each bidding actively for your favor and acceptance, thus rendering a choice and definite decision very difficult. You find yourself suffering from an embarrassment of riches and like the perplexed lover in the song, you say, "How happy would I be with either, were t'other fair charmer away." Or, like the psychological donkey who was placed at an equidistant point between two equally tempting haystacks, and who died of hunger because he couldn't make up his mind which one he wanted most, you may remain inactive because of strong conflicting desire-motives.

It is because of one or both of the above-mentioned conditions that the great masses of people do not avail themselves of the great elemental urge of Desire Power. Although ready to exert its power, most people lack definite direction and power of decision. So they remain, like the vegetables or the lower animals, content to allow Nature to work along the instinctive lines of self-protection and propagation, without employing initiative or self-direction.

The few people who break these barriers, and who strike out for themselves, are found to have known very clearly "just what they wanted," and to have "wanted it hard," and to have been willing to pay the price of attainment. In order to set to work the forces of Desire Power in a special direction, individuals must make clear an ideal path over which they may travel, as well as to arouse the forces so as to cause them to travel over that path.

Self-Analysis

You will find that a scientific application of the principle of Self-Analysis, or mental stock-taking, will aid you materially in overcoming the two great obstacles in the Path of Attainment, which we have just mentioned. Self-Analysis in this case consists of a careful analysis of your elements of Desire, to the end that you may discover which of these elements are the strongest, and that you may clearly understand just what these strongest elements are really like in character. You are advised to "think with pencil and paper" in this work of self-analysis—it will greatly aid you in crystallizing your thought and, besides, will give a definite and logical pattern to the results of your work. The following suggestions and advice will aid you materially in this task.

Begin by asking yourself the question: *"What are my strongest desires? What do I 'want' and 'want to' over and above anything and everything else? What are my highest Desire-Values?"* Then proceed to "think with pencil and paper," and thus to answer this important question just stated. Take your pencil and begin to write down your strongest desires—your leading "wants" and "want tos"—as they come into your consciousness in response to your inquiry. Write down carefully the things and objects, the aims and ideals, the aspirations and ambitions, the hopes and confident expectations, which present themselves for notation in the course of your mental stock-taking. Note all of them, without regard to the question of whether or not you ever expect to be able to secure or attain them.

Put them all down on the list, no matter how ridiculous and unattainable they may seem to you at the time. Do not allow yourself to be overcome by the magnificent aims and ideals, aspirations and ambitions, which thus present themselves. Their very existence in your Desire-nature is, in a measure, the prophecy of their own fulfillment. As Napoleon once said: "Nothing is too magnificent for a soldier of France!" You are that soldier of France! Do not impose limitations on your Desire-nature in this way. If a magnificent desire is within you, it should be respected—so put it down on the list.

By this process of Self-Analysis you bring to the surface of your consciousness all the various feelings, desires, longings, and cravings which have been dwelling in your subconscious mind. Many of these deep desires are like sleeping giants and your exploration of your subconscious mental regions will arouse these; will cause them "to sit up and take notice," as it were. Do not be frightened by these awakening sleepers. Nothing that you find there is alien to you. Even though you may find it necessary to transmute them, or to inhibit them in favor of more advantageous desires at a later stage of your work, do not now deny them a place on your list—put them down on paper. The list must be an honest one, therefore be honest with yourself in the analysis.

At first, you will find that your list is a more or less higgledy-piggledy conglomeration of "wants" and "want tos," apparently having but little or no logical order or systematic relation. Do not let this disturb you, as all this will be taken care of as you proceed; order and arrangement will establish themselves almost automatically when the proper time arrives. The main thing at this stage is to get all of your stronger desires into the list. Be sure to exhaust your subconscious mind of strong desires—dig out of that mine anything and everything that has strength in it.

The next step is that of the cold-blooded, ruthless, elimination of the weakest desires, with the idea and purpose that in the end there will be a "survival of the fittest" on your list. Begin by running over your list, striking off the weaker and less insistent desires—the mere temporary and passing—and those which you clearly recognize as likely to bring you but little if any permanent satisfaction, continued happiness and lasting content.

In this way you will create a new list of the stronger desires, and those having a great permanent and satisfying value. Then, examining this list, you will find that some of the items will still stand out from the others by reason of their greater comparative strength and greater degree of permanent value. Make a new list of these successful candidates, including only those possessing the greatest strength and value to you, and dropping the others from the list. Then continue this process of elimination of the weakest and the least satisfying until you reach that point where you feel that any further elimination would result in cutting away live wood.

By this time you will have become aware of a most significant and important fact, namely, that as your list has grown smaller, the strength and value of the surviving desires has grown greater. As the old gold-miners expressed it you are now "getting down to pay dirt"—getting down to the region in which the nuggets and rich ore abide. When you have reached this stage, you will do well to stop work for the time being; this will give you a needed mental rest, and will also furnish your subconscious mentality with the opportunity to do some work for you along its own particular lines.

When you again take up your list for consideration, you will find a new general order and arrangement of its items pictured in your mind. You will find that these remaining desires have grouped themselves into several general classes. Your subconscious mental faculties will have performed an important task for you. Then you will be ready to compare these general classes, one with the other, until you are able to select certain classes which seem stronger than the others. Then you will be ready to proceed to the task of eliminating the weaker general classes, making a new list of the stronger ones.

After working along these general lines for a time, with intervals of rest and recuperation, and for subconscious digestion and elimination, you will find that you have before you a list composed of a comparatively few general classes of "wants" and "want tos"—each of which possesses a far greater degree of strength and value than you had previously suspected. Your subconscious mind has been working its power upon these classes of desires, and they have evolved to a higher stage of strength, definiteness, clearness and power. You are beginning at last to find out "just what you want," and are also well started on your way to "wanting it hard enough."

General Rules of Selection

In your task of selection, elimination, "boiling down," and chopping away the dead wood, et cetera, you will do well to observe the three following general Rules of Selection:

I. *The Imperative Requisite.* In selecting your strongest desires for your list, you are not required to pay attention to any fears lurking in your mind that any of the particular desires are apparently unattainable—that they are beyond your power of achievement, and are rendered impossible by apparently unsurmountable obstacles. You are not concerned with such questions at this time and place—ignore them for the present. You are merely concerned here with the question of whether or not your "want" or "want to" concerning a certain thing is felt "hard enough" for you to sacrifice other desirable things—whether you feel that the particular desire is of sufficient value for you to "pay the price" of its attainment, even though that price be very high. Remember the old adage: "Said the gods to man, 'Take what thou wilt—but pay for it!' " If you are not willing to "pay the price," and to pay it in full, then you do not "want it hard enough" to render it one of your Prime Desires.

II. The Test of Full Desire. We have told you that, *"Desire has for its object something that will bring pleasure or get rid of pain, immediately or remote, for the individual or for some one in whom he is interested."* Therefore, in passing upon the comparative strength and value of your respective desires, or general classes of desires, you must take into consideration all of the elements of Desire noted in the above definite statement—the indirect as well as the direct elements of personal satisfaction and contentment.

You must weigh and decide the value of any particular desire, or class of desires, not only in the light of your own *immediate* satisfaction and contentment, but also in the light of your own *future* satisfaction and contentment; not only in the light of your own *direct* satisfaction and contentment but also in the light of your *indirect* satisfaction and contentment derived from the satisfaction and contentment of others in whom you are interested. Your future satisfaction and contentment often depend upon the sacrifice of your present desire in favor of one bearing fruit in the future. You may be so interested in other persons that their satisfaction and contentment has a greater emotional value to you than the gratification of some desire concerned only with your own direct satisfaction and contentment. These Desires-values must be carefully weighed by you. If you leave out any of these elements of Desire, you run the risk of attaching a false value to certain sets of desires. You must weigh and measure the value of your desires by the use of the standard of the full content of Desire.

III. Seek Depth of Desire. You will find it advisable to omit from your list all purely superficial and transient feelings, emotions and desires. They have but a slight value in the case. Instead, plunge into the deep places of your mental being or soul; there you will find abiding certain deep, essential, basic, permanent feelings, emotions and desires. In those regions dwell the "wants" and the "want tos" which when aroused are as insistent and as imperative as are the want of the suffocating man for air; the want of the famished man for food; the want of the thirsting man for water; the want of the wild creature for its mate; the want of the mother for the welfare of her child.

These deep desires are your real emotional elements—the ones most firmly and permanently imbedded in the soil of your emotional being. These are the desires which will abide when the transient, ephemeral ones have passed and are forgotten. These are the desires for which you will be willing to "pay the price," be that price ever so high in the form of the sacrifice and relinquishment of every other desire, feeling or emotion. Measure your desires by their essential depth, as well as by their temporary weight. Select those which are embedded so deeply in the soil of your emotional being that they cannot be uprooted by the passing storms of conditions and circumstances.

The Struggle for Existence

You are now approaching the final stages of your discovery of "just what you want." You now have a list of Insistent Desires—the survivors in the Struggle for Existence on the part of your many desires and classes of desires. If you have proceeded earnestly and honestly in your work of Self-Analysis and Selection, you will have a group of sturdy Desire-giants before you for final judgment. By a strange psychological law these surviving candidates have taken on much of the strength and energy of those which they have defeated in the struggle; the victors will have absorbed the vitality of those whom they have defeated, just as the savage hopes to draw to himself the strength of the enemies killed by him in battle. Your Desire Power has now been concentrated upon a comparatively small group of desires, with a consequent focusing of power.

An Appeal to the Touchstone

In cases in which careful analysis, deliberation, tests of imagination and association, and all other means of weighing and measuring, trying and testing, fail to reveal the advantage of one set of desires over an opposing set, one must resort to the Touchstone of Positivity so often referred to in this instruction. The Touchstone by which the Positivity of a mental state, thought, feeling, desire, or action is determined, is as follows:

"Will this tend to make me better,

stronger and more efficient?"

In the degree that any mental state meets the requirements of this test, so is its degree of Positivity and consequent desirability.

You have now finally reached the stage in which you have on your list nothing but your Dominant Desires—the survivors in the Struggle for Existence—the Survival of the Fittest. These Dominant Desires must thereafter rule your emotional realm. Any newcomer must prove its worth by a test of strength with these Dominant Desires—if it shows its strength, and is able to hold its place very well, it may be added to the list. Those going down in defeat must be eliminated. This will require strength and determination on your part—but you are a strong and determined individual, or at least are becoming one.

The process of Self-Analysis and Selection which you just considered will furnish you with two classes of reports: (1) it will demonstrate to you your strongest classes of desires—your Dominant Desires; and (2) it will cause you clearly and definitely to picture and form a strong idea of each of such Dominant Desires.

In both reports it will cause you to "know exactly what you want," which is the first requisite of the Master Formula of Attainment.

CHAPTER 7

Putting Power into Your Desire

According to the Master Formula you must not only "know exactly what you want," but must also "want it hard enough," and be "willing to pay the price of its attainment." Having considered the first of the above stated three requisites for obtaining that which you want, we ask you now to consider the second requisite, i.e., that of "wanting it hard enough."

You may think that you "want it hard enough" when you have a rather keen desire or longing for anything but when you compare your feeling with that of people manifesting really strong, insistent desire, you will find that you are but merely manifesting a "wish" for that for which you have an inclination or an attachment. Compared to the insistent "want" or "want to" of thoroughly aroused Desire, your "wish" is but as a shadow. The chances are that you have been a mere amateur—a dilettante—in the art and science of "wanting" and "wanting to." Very few persons really know how to "want" or "want to" in such manner as to arouse fully the elemental forces of Desire Power.

An old Oriental fable illustrates the nature of Desire aroused to its fullest extent. The fable relates that a teacher took his pupil out on a deep lake, in a boat, and then suddenly pushed him overboard. The youth sank beneath the surface of the water, but rose in a few seconds, gasping for breath. Without giving him time to fill his lungs with air, the teacher forcibly pushed him under once more. The youth rose to the surface the second time, and was again pushed under. He rose for the third time, almost entirely exhausted; this time the teacher pulled him up over the side of the boat, and employed the usual methods to restore him to normal breathing.

When the youth had fully recovered from his severe ordeal,the teacher said to him: "Tell me what was the one thing that you desired above all other things before I pulled you in—the one desire to which all other desires seemed like tiny candles compared with the sun?" The youth replied, "Oh, sir, above all else I desired air to breath—for me, at that time, there existed no other desires!" Then said the teacher, " Let this, then, be the measure of your desire for those things to the attainment of which your life is devoted !'"

You will not fully realize the measure of Desire pointed out in this fable, unless you employ your imagination in the direction of feeling yourself in the drowning condition of the youth—until you do this, the fable is a mere matter of words. When you can realize in feeling, as well as recognize in thought, the strength of the desire for air present in that youth, then, and only then, will you be able to manifest in expression a similar degree of Desire for the objects of your prime "wants" and "want tos." Do not rest satisfied with the intellectual recognition of the condition—induce the corresponding emotional feeling in yourself to as great a degree as possible.

Varying the illustration, you will do well to induce in yourself (in imagination) the realization of the insistent, paramount desire for food experienced by the starving man lost in the dense forest in midwinter. The chances are that you never have been actually "hungry" in the true sense of the term; all that you have mistaken for hunger is merely the call of appetite or taste—the result of habit. When you are so hungry that an old, stale, dry crust of bread will be delicious to your taste, then you are beginning to know what real hunger is. Those men who, lost in the forest or shipwrecked, have tried to satisfy intense hunger by gnawing the bark of trees, or chewing bits of leather cut from their boots—could give you some interesting information concerning hunger. If you can imagine the feelings of men in this condition, then you may begin to understand what "insistent desire" really means.

Again, the shipwrecked sailors adrift at sea with their supply of water exhausted; or the desert-lost man wandering over the hot sands with a thirst almost inconceivable to the ordinary person; those men know what "insistent desire" means. Man can live many days without food; but only a few days without water; and only a few minutes without air. When these fundamental essentials of life are withdrawn temporarily, the living creature finds his strongest and most elemental feelings and desires aroused—they become transmuted into passions insistently demanding satisfaction and contentment. When these elemental emotions and desires are thoroughly aroused, all the derivative emotional states are forgotten. Imagine the emotional state of the starving man in sight of food, or the thirst-cursed man within reach of water, if some other person or thing intervenes and attempts to frustrate the suffering man's attainment of that which he wants above all else at that time.

Other examples of insistent desire may be found in the cases of wild animals in the mating season, in which they will risk life and defy their powerful rivals in order to secure the chosen mate. If you have ever come across a bull-moose in the mating season, you will have a vivid picture and idea of this phase of elemental desire raised to the point of "insistent demand."

Again, consider the intense emotional feeling, and the accompanying desires experienced by the mother creature in connection with the welfare and protection of her young when danger threatens them—this will show you the nature and character of elemental desire aroused to its fullest extent. Even tiny birds will fight against overwhelming odds in resisting the animal or man seeking to rob their nests. It is a poor spirited mother-animal which will not risk her life, and actually court death, in defense of her young. The female wild creature becomes doubly formidable when accompanied by her young. "The female of the species" is far "more deadly than the male" when the welfare of its young is involved. The Orientals have a proverb: "It is a very brave, or a very foolish, man who will try to steal a young tiger-cub while its mother is alive and free in the vicinity.

We have called your attention to the above several examples and illustrations of the force within strongly aroused elemental emotions and desires, not only to point out to you how powerful such desires and feeling become under the appropriate circumstances and conditions, but also to bring you to a realization of the existence within all living things of a latent emotional strength and power which is capable of being aroused into a strenuous activity under the proper stimulus; and of being directed toward certain definite ends and purposes indicated by the stimulus. That this strength and power is aroused by, and flows out toward, the particular forms of stimulus indicated above is a matter of common knowledge. But that it may be aroused to equal strength, power, and intensity by other forms of stimulus (such stimulus having been deliberately placed before it by the individual) is not known to the many; only the few have learned this secret.

We ask you to use your imagination here, once more, for a moment. Imagine an individual who has "his mind set upon" the attainment of a certain end or purpose to such a degree that he has aroused the latent Desire Power within him to that extent where he "wants" or "wants to" that end or purpose in the degree of strength, power, insistency, and fierceness, manifested by the drowning man who "wants" air; by the desert-lost man who "wants" water; by the starving man who "wants" food; by the wild creature who "wants" its mate; by the mother animal who "wants" the welfare of her young. This is the individual in whom the elemental Desire Power has been aroused to such an extent, and directed toward the attainment or achievement of his Dominant Desire. How would you like to compete with such a man for the attainment of that object of his Desire Power? How would you like to be the opposing obstacle standing directly in his path of progress and attainment? How would you like to play with him the part analogous to that of one who would try to snatch away the bone from a starving wolf, or pull the tiger cub from the paws of its savage mother?

This is an extreme case or illustration, of course. Very few individuals actually reach the stage indicated—though it is not impossible by any means.

Many travel a long way along that road. The strong, successful men who have "made good," who have "arrived," who have "done things," in any line of human endeavor, will be found to have travelled quite a distance in that direction, on the road of Desire. They have aroused within themselves the strong, elemental Desire Power which abides latently in the depths of the mental and emotional being—the "soul," if you will—of every human creature; and have caused that elemental force to pour through the channels of the particular Dominant Desires which they have brought to the surface of their nature from the depths of the subconscious self.

Look in any direction you wish, and you will find that the strong, masterful, dominant, successful men are those in whom Desire Power has been aroused and directed in this way. These men "know what they want"—just as the drowning man, the starving man, the thirst-cursed man, the wild mating creature, the mother creature, each knows what he or she wants—they have no doubts concerning their Dominant Desires. And these men also "want hard enough" that which represents their Dominant Desires—just as did the drowning man, the starving man, and the rest of our illustrative examples. And like those examples, these men were also "willing to pay the price."

Run over the list of the successful men and women with whose careers you are acquainted. Place on that list the great discoverers, inventors, explorers, military men, businessmen, artists, literary men and women, all those who have "done things" successfully. Then check off name after name, as you discover the biographical report of the Desire Power manifested by these individuals. You will find that in each and every case there was present the "Definite Ideals, Insistent Desire, Confident Expectation, Persistent Determination, and Balanced Compensation," which constitute the Master Formula of Attainment of our instruction. And this second requisite—the "Insistent Desire"—is found to be this elemental Desire Power directed into the appropriate channels of manifestation and expression. These individuals "knew just what they wanted"; they "wanted it hard enough", and they were "willing to pay the price."

It is this spirit of "wanting it hard enough" that distinguishes the men and women of strong purpose and determination from the common herd of persons who merely "wish for" things in a gentle, faint, conventional way—that distinguishes the true "wanters" from the dilettante "wishers." It was the recognition of this spirit in men that caused Disraeli to say that long meditation had brought him to the conviction that a human being with a settled purpose, and with a will which would stake even existence itself upon its fulfillment, must certainly accomplish that purpose.

"But," you may say, "admitting the truth of your premise, how am I to proceed in order to arouse the dormant latent Desire Power within me, and to cause it to flow forth in the direction of the attainment of my Dominant Desires?" Answering the question, we would say, "Begin at the very beginning, and proceed to arouse and draw forth the latent Desire Power, by presenting to it the stimulus of suggestive and inciting ideas and pictures." For, from beginning to end, there prevails the principle expressed in that axiom of psychology which says: *"Desire is aroused and flows forth toward things represented by ideas and mental pictures; the stronger and clearer the idea or mental picture, the stronger and more insistent is the aroused desire, all else being equal."*

You should proceed to apply this principle from the very beginning even at the stage of semi-awakened Desire Power. There abides within you a great store of latent, dormant Desire Power—a great reservoir of Desire Power which contains within itself the latent and nascent powers of wonderfully diversified manifestation and expression. You will do well to begin by "stirring up" this great reservoir of Desire Power—arousing it into activity in a general way, to the end that you may afterward direct its power and cause it to flow forth into and along the channels of expression and manifestation which you have provided for it.

In the great crater of a mighty volcano of Hawaii, in plain sight of the daring visitor to the rim of the abyss, there abides a large lake of molten lava, seething and bubbling, boiling and effervescing in a state of hissing ebullience—a lake of liquid fire, as it were. This great fiery lake is comparatively calm on its surface; however, the ebullition proceeds from its depths. The whole body of fiery liquid manifests a rhythmic tide-like rise and fall, and a swaying from side to side of the crater. The observer is impressed with the recognition of a latent and nascent power of almost immeasurable possibilities of manifestation and expression. He feels borne upon him the conviction that this seething, rising and falling, swaying, tremendous body of liquid fire, if once fully aroused into activity, would boil and seeth up to the edge of the crater, and overflowing, would pour down into the valleys beneath, carrying and destroying every obstacle in its path.

This great lake of molten lava—this great body of liquid fire—is a symbol of the great body of latent and nascent Desire Power abiding within every individual—within YOU. It rests there, comparatively inactive on the surface, but always manifesting a peculiar churning ebullition emanating from its great depths. It seethes and boils, effervesces and bubbles, rises and falls in tide-like rhythm, sways in rhythmic sequence from side to side. It seems ever to say to you, "I am here, restless and disturbed, ever longing, craving, hankering for, hungering and thirsting for, desiring for expression and manifestation in definite form and direction. Stir me up; arouse my inner force; set me into action; and I will rise and assert my power, and accomplish for you that which you direct!"

Of course, we realize that this stirring up or agitation of your latent Desire Power is apt to—in fact, certainly will—create additional Discontent on your part; but what of it? Some philosophers praise the Spirit of Contentment, and say that Happiness is to be found only therein. Be that as it may, it may be positively asserted that all Progress proceeds from Discontent.

While admitting the value of Content, at the same time we believe in preaching the "Gospel of Discontent" to a sane degree and extent. We believe that Discontent is the first step on the Path of Attainment. We believe that it is this very Divine Discontent that causes men and women to undertake the Divine Adventure of Life, and which is back of and under all human progress. Content may be carried too far. Absolute Content results in Apathy and Lethargy—it stops the wheels of Progress. Nature evidently is not Content, else it would cease to manifest the process of Evolution. Nature has evidently been ever-filled with the Spirit of Discontent, judging from her invariable manifestation of the Law of Change.

Without Discontent and the Desire to Change, there would be no Change in Nature. The Law of Change shows plainly Nature's opinion on the subject, and her prevailing feelings and desires in the matter.

You will do well to begin "treating" your great body of elemental Desire Power for increased activity, and for the transmutation of its static power into dynamic power—bringing it from its state of semi-rest into the state of increased restlessness and tendency to flow forth into action. You may do this in the same way that you will later employ in the case of specific, particular, and definite desires, i.e., *by presenting suggestive and inciting ideas and mental pictures!*

Begin by presenting to your elemental Desire Power the suggestive idea and mental picture of itself as akin to the great lake of molten lava, or liquid fire, filled with latent and nascent energy, power, and force; filled with the elemental urge toward expression and manifestation in outward form and action; able and willing to accomplish anything it desires to do with sufficient strength, providing a definite channel is provided for its flow of power. Show it the picture of itself as ready and willing to transmute its static energy into dynamic force, and to pour forth along the channels which you will provide for it—and above all else, quite *able* to do this if it will but arouse itself into dynamic action. In short, present to its gaze your idealistic and creative mental equipment in the form of the surface of a great mirror, reflecting the picture of the elemental Desire Power as it presents itself to that mirror—let Desire Power see itself as it is. Supply Desire with its complementary Idea.

You will do well to accompany this mental picture with a verbal statement or affirmation of the details of that picture. Treat your elemental Desire Power as if it were an entity—there is a valid psychological reason for this, by the way—and tell it in exact words just what it is, what are its powers, and what is its essential nature, displaying the disposition to express and manifest itself in outward form and activity. Pound these suggestive statements into it, as firmly, earnestly and persistently as you can. Supply the Desire

Power with the element of Idea and Mental Pictures. Give it the picture of what it is, and the pattern or diagram of what it can do if it will.

The result of this course of "treatment" applied to your elemental Desire Power will soon show itself in an increased feeling of more vigorous rhythmic tidal-movement and side-to-side movement, as previously described; and in an increased rate and vigor of its seething, boiling, effervescing ebullition. From its depths will arise mighty impulses and urges, upheavals and uprisings. The great molten-lake of Desire Power will begin to boil with increased vigor, and will show an inclination to produce the Steam of Will. You will experience new and strange evidences of the urge of Desire Power within you, seeking expression and manifestation along the channels which you have provided for it.

But before reaching this stage, you must have created the channels through and in which you wish the overflowing Desire Power to flow when it reaches the "boiling over" stage. These channels must be built along the lines of those desires which you have proven to be your Dominant Desires. Build these channels, deep, wide and strong. From them you can afterward build minor channels for your secondary and derivative desires arising from your Dominant Desires. At present, however, your main concern is with your main channels. Let each channel represent the clear, deep, strong idea and mental picture of "just what you want" as you clearly see and know it. You have found out exactly what you want, when you want it, and how you want it; let your channels represent as closely as possible just these ideas. Build the banks high, so as to obviate any waste; build the walls strong, so as to stand the strain; build the channel deep and wide, so as to carry the full force and quantity of the current.

By "creating the channels" of your Dominant Desires, we mean establishing the paths to be traversed by the overflowing current of Desire Power which you have aroused from its latent and nascent condition. These channels or paths are created mentally by the employment of Creative Imagination and Ideation. These mental forces proceed to manifest in the direction of creating and presenting to your consciousness the ideas and mental pictures of your Dominant Desires which you have discovered in your process of Self-Analysis. The work of creating these channels is really but a continuation of the mental work performed by you in the discovery of your Dominant Desires.

In creating these channels you should observe three general rules, as follows:

(I) *Make the Channels Clear and Clean* by creating and maintaining a clear, clean, distinct, and definite idea of each of your Dominant Desires, in which the entire thought concerning the Dominant Desire is condensed, and in which there is no foreign or non-essential material.

(2) *Make the Channels Deep and Wide* by forming mental pictures or suggestive ideas appealing to the emotional feelings associated with the Dominant Desires. Thus you tempt the appetites of those desires by the representation of the objects of their longing, and by the presentation of imaginative pictures of the joys which will attend their final achievement and attainment.

(3) *Make the Banks Strong* by means of the employment of the Persistent Determination of the Will, so that the powerful swift current may be confined within the limits of the Dominant Desire and not be permitted to escape and waste itself by scattering its energy and force over the surrounding land.

When your current is flowing freely, you will find it necessary to build minor channels serving to bring about the attainment of objects and ends helpful to the accomplishment of the objects and ends of the major channels. In building these minor channels, follow the same general rules and principles which we have given you. From the great main channels down to the tiniest canal the same principle is involved. *Always build clear and clean, by means of definite ideas and aims; always build deep and wide, by means of suggestive ideas and mental pictures; always build strong banks, by means of the determined will.*

In concluding this consideration of the second requisite, i.e., the element of "wanting it hard enough," we wish to impress upon your mind the tremendous vitalizing, and inciting power exerted by Suggestive Ideas and Mental Pictures upon Desire Power. Suggestive Ideas and Mental Pictures act upon Desire Power with a tremendous degree of effect in the direction of inciting, arousing, stirring, stimulating, exciting, spurring, goading, provoking, moving, encouraging, animating, and urging to expression and manifestation. There are no other incentives equal to these. All strong desires are aroused by such incentives, consciously or unconsciously applied.

For instance, you may have no desire to visit California. Then your interest in that part of the country is aroused by what you read or hear concerning it, and a vague desire to visit it is aroused in you. Later, information in the direction of giving you additional material for suggestive ideas and mental pictures serves to arouse your desire to "go to California." You begin to search eagerly for further ideas and pictures, and the more you obtain the stronger grows the flame of your desire. At last, you "want to hard enough," and brushing aside all obstacles you "pay the price" and take the trip across the plains. Had you not been furnished with the additional suggestive ideas and mental pictures, your original desire would soon have died out. You know by experience the truth of this principle; you also know how you would use it if you wished to induce a friend to visit California, do you not? Then start to work using it on your Desire Power when you wish to incite it into "wanting hard enough" something that you know to be advantageous to you!

It is customary to illustrate this principle by the figure of pouring the oil of Idea upon the flame of Desire, thereby keeping alive and strengthening the power of the latter. The figure of speech is a good one—the illustration serves well its purpose. But your memory and imagination, representing your experience, will furnish you with one a little nearer to home. All that you need do is imagine the effect which would be produced upon you if you were hungry and were able to form the mental picture or create the suggestive idea of a particularly appetizing meal. Even as it is, though you are not really hungry, the thought of such a meal will make your mouth water.

Again, you may readily imagine the effect produced upon you, when you are parched and intensely thirsty on a long ride, by the vivid mental picture or strong suggestive idea of a clear, cold spring of mountain water. Or, again, when in a stuffy, ill-ventilated office you think of the fresh air of the mountain camp where you went fishing last Summer,—when you picture plainly the joys of the experience—can you deny that your Desire Power is intensely aroused and excited, and that you feel like dropping everything and "taking to the woods" at once.

Raising the principle to its extreme form of manifestation, try to imagine the effect upon a famishing man in a dream of plentiful food; the dream of the thirst-cursed man in which is pictured flowing fountains of water. Try to imagine the effect upon the mate-seeking wild bull-moose of the far-off bellow from the sought-for mate. Would you like to impede his path on such an occasion? Finally, picture the emotional excitement and frenzy of desire on the part of the tigress when she comes in sight of food for her half-starved cubs; or her force of desire when she hears the far-off cry of distress from her young ones.

In order to "want" and "want to" as hard as do these human beings and wild things which we have employed as illustrations, you must feed your Desire Power with suggestive ideas and mental pictures similar in exciting power to those which rouse into action their dominant and paramount "want" and "want to." Of course, these are extreme cases, but they serve to illustrate the principle involved.

In short, in order to "want it hard enough," you must create a gnawing hunger and a parching thirst for the objects of your Dominant Desires. This you must intensify and render continuous by repeatedly presenting suggestive ideas and mental pictures of the Feast of Good Things and the Flowing Fountain which awaits the successful achievement or attainment of the desires.

Think strongly on this idea until you grasp its full meaning!

PART III

SECRET NUMBER THREE FIND YOUR GOAL AND PURPOSE IN LIFE

CHAPTER 8

The Law of Supply

"They do me wrong who say I come no more
  When once I knock and fail to find you in;
For every day I stand outside your door,
  And bid you wake, and rise to fight and win.

"Wail not for precious chances passed away,
  Weep not for golden ages on the wane!
Each night I burn the records of the day—
  At sunrise every soul is born again!"

—Walter Malone.

Have you ever run a race, or worked at utmost capacity for a protracted period, or swam a great distance? Remember how, soon after starting, you began to feel tired? Remember how, before you had gone any great distance, you thought you had reached your limit? But remember, too, how, when you kept going, you got your second wind, your tiredness vanished, your muscles throbbed with energy, you felt literally charged with speed and endurance?

Stored in every human being are great reserves of energy of which the average individual knows nothing. Most people are like a man who drives a car in low gear, not knowing that by the simple shift of a lever he can set it in high and not merely speed up the car, but do it with far less expenditure of power.

The law of the universe is the law of supply. You see it on every hand. Nature is lavish in everything she does.

Look at the heavens at night. There are millions of stars there—millions of worlds—millions of suns among them. Surely there is no lack of wealth or profusion in the Mind that could image all of these; no place for limitation there! Look at the vegetation in the country round about you. Nature supplies all that the shrubs or trees may need for their growth and sustenance! Look at the lower forms of animal life—the birds and wild animals, the reptiles and the insects, the fish in the sea. Nature supplies them bountifully with everything they need. They have but to help themselves to what she holds out to them with such lavish hand. Look at all the natural resources of the world—coal and iron and oil and metals. There is enough for everyone. We hear a lot about the exhaustion of our resources of coal and oil, but there is available coal enough to last mankind for thousands of years. There are vast oil fields practically untouched, probably others bigger still yet to be discovered, and when all these are exhausted, the extraction of oil from shale will keep the world supplied for countless more years.

There is abundance for everyone. But just as you must strain and labor to reach the resources of your "second wind," just so you must strive before you can make manifest the law of supply in nature.

The World Belongs to You

It is your estate. It owes you not merely a living, but everything of good you may desire. You must *demand* these things of it, though. You must fear naught, dread not, stop at naught. You must have the faith of Columbus, crossing an unknown sea, holding a mutinous crew to the task long after they had ceased to believe in themselves or in him—*and giving to the world a new hemisphere.* You must have the faith of Washington—defeated, discredited, almost wholly deserted by his followers, yet holding steadfast in spite of all—*and giving to America a new liberty.* You must *dominate*—not cringe. You must make the application of the law of supply.

"Consider the lilies how they grow." The flowers, the birds, all of creation, are incessantly active. The trees and flowers in their growth, the birds and wild creatures in building their nests and finding sustenance, are always working—*but never worrying.* "Your Father knoweth that ye have need of these things." "And all these things shall be added unto you."

If all would agree to give up worrying—to be industrious, but never anxious about the outcome—it would mean the beginning of a new era in human progress, an age of liberty, of freedom from bondage. Jesus set forth the universal law of supply when he said—"Therefore I say unto you, be not anxious for the morrow, what ye shall eat, or wherewithal ye shall be clothed—but seek first the kingdom of God, *and all those things shall be added unto you."*

What is this "Kingdom of God"?

Jesus tells us—"The Kingdom of God is within you." It is the "Father within you" to which He so frequently referred. It is Mind—your part of Universal Mind. "Seek first the Kingdom of God." Seek first an understanding of this Power within you—learn to contact it—to use it—"and all those things shall be added unto you."

All riches have their origin in Mind. Wealth is in ideas—not money. Money is merely the material medium of exchange for ideas. The paper money in your pockets is in itself worth no more than so many pieces of paper. It is the idea behind it that gives it value. Factory buildings, machinery, materials, are in themselves worthless without a manufacturing or a selling idea behind them. How often do you see a factory fall to pieces? Machinery rust away, after the idea behind them gave out? Factories and machines, are simply the tools of trade. It is the idea behind them that makes them go.

So don't go out seeking wealth. Look within you for ideas! "The Kingdom of God is within you." Use it—*purposefully!* Use it to THINK constructively. Don't say you are *thinking* when all you are doing is exercising your faculty of memory. As Dumont says in "*The Master Mind*": "They are simply allowing the stream of memory to flow through their field of consciousness, while the Ego stands on the banks and idly watches the passing waters of memory flow by. They call this 'thinking,' while in reality there is no process of Thought under way."

They are like the old mountaineer sitting in the shade alongside his cabin. Asked what he did to pass the long hours away, he said: "Waal, sometimes I set and think; and sometimes I just set."

Dumont goes on to say, in quoting another writer: "When I use the word 'thinking,' I mean *thinking with a purpose, with an end in view, thinking to solve a problem.* I mean the kind of thinking that is forced on us when we are deciding on a course to pursue, on a life work to take up perhaps; the kind of thinking that was forced upon us in our younger days when we had to find a solution to a problem in mathematics; or when we tackled psychology in college. I do not mean 'thinking' in snatches, or holding petty opinions on this subject and on that. I mean thought on significant questions which lie outside the bounds of your narrow personal welfare. This is the kind of thinking which is now so rare—so sadly needed!"

The Kingdom of God is the Kingdom of Thought, of Achievement, of Health, of Happiness and Prosperity. "I came that ye might have life and have it more abundantly."

But you have to *seek* it. You have to do more than ponder. You have to *think*—to think constructively—to seek how you may discover new worlds, new methods, new needs. The greatest discoveries, you know, have arisen out of things which everybody had *seen,* but only one man had NOTICED. The biggest fortunes have been made out of the opportunities which many men *had,* but only one man GRASPED.

Why is it that so many millions of men and women go through life in poverty and misery, in sickness and despair? Why? Primarily because they make a reality of poverty through their fear of it. They visualize poverty, misery and disease, and thus bring them into being. And secondly, they cannot demonstrate the law of supply for the same reason that so many millions cannot solve the first problem in algebra. The solution is simple—but they have never been shown the method. They do not understand the law.

The essence of this law is that you must *think* abundance, *see* abundance, *feel* abundance, *believe* abundance. Let no thought of limitation enter your mind. There is no lawful desire of yours for which, as far as mind is concerned, there is not abundant satisfaction. And if you can visualize it in mind, you can realize it in your daily world.

"Blessed is the man whose delight is in the *law* of the Lord: And he shall be like a tree planted by the rivers of water, that bringeth forth his fruit in his season: his leaf also shall not wither; and whatsoever he doeth shall prosper."

Don't worry. Don't doubt. Don't dig up the seeds of prosperity and success to see whether they have sprouted. Have faith! Nourish your seeds with renewed desire. Keep before your mind's eye the picture of the thing you want. BELIEVE IN IT! No matter if you seem to be in the clutch of misfortune, no matter if the future looks black and dreary—FORGET YOUR FEARS! Realize that the future is of your own making. There is no power that can keep you down but yourself. Set your goal. Forget the obstacles between. Forget the difficulties in the way. Keep only the goal before your mind's eye—*and you'll win it!* Judge Troward, in his Edinburgh Lectures on Mental Science, shows the way:

"The initial step, then, consists in determining to picture the Universal Mind as the ideal of all we could wish it to be, both to ourselves and to others, together with the endeavor to reproduce this ideal, however imperfectly, in our own life; and this step having been taken, we can then cheerfully look upon it as our ever-present Friend, providing all good, guarding us from all danger, and guiding us with all counsel. Similarly if we think of it as a great power devoted to supplying all our needs, we shall impress this character also upon it, and by the law of subjective mind, it will proceed to enact the part of that special providence which we have credited it with being; and if, beyond general care of our concerns, we would draw to ourselves some particular benefit, the same rule holds good of impressing our desire upon the universal subjective mind. And thus the deepest problems of philosophy bring us back to the old statement of the law: Ask and ye shall receive; seek and ye shall find; knock and it shall be opened unto you.' This is the summing-up of the natural law of the relation between us and the Divine Mind. It is thus no vain boast that mental science can enable us to make our lives what we will. And to this law there is no limit. What it can do for us today it can do tomorrow, and through all that procession of tomorrows that loses itself in the dim vistas of eternity. *Belief in limitation is the one and only thing that causes limitation,* because we thus impress limitation upon the creative principle; and in proportion as we lay that belief aside, our boundaries will expand, and increasing life and more abundant blessing will be ours."

You are not working for some firm merely for the pittance they pay you. You are part of the great scheme of things. And what you do has a bearing on the ultimate result. That being the case, you are working for Universal Mind, and Universal Mind is the most generous paymaster there is. Just remember that you can look to it for all good things. Supply is *where* you are and *what* you need.

Do you want a situation? Close your eyes and realize that somewhere is the position for which you of all people are best fitted, and which is best fitted to your ability. The position where you can do the utmost good, and where life, in turn, offers the most to you. Realize that this is YOUR position, that it NEEDS you, that it belongs to you, that it is right for you to have it, that you are entitled to it. Hold this thought in mind every night for just a moment. then go to sleep knowing that your subconscious mind HAS the necessary information as to where this position is and how to get in touch with it. Mind you—not WILL have, but HAS. The earnest realization of this will bring that position to you, and you to it, as surely as the morrow will bring the sun. Make the law of supply operative and you find that the things you seek are seeking you.

Get firmly fixed in your own mind the definite conviction that you can do anything you greatly want to do. There is no such thing as lack of opportunity. There is no such thing as only one opportunity. You are subject to a law of boundless and perpetual opportunity, and you can enforce that law in your behalf just as widely as you need. Opportunity is infinite and ever present.

Berton Braley has it well expressed in his poem on "Opportunity":

> "For the best verse hasn't been rhymed yet,
>   The best house hasn't been planned,
> The highest peak hasn't been climbed yet,
>   The mightiest rivers aren't spanned,
> Don't worry and fret, faint hearted,
>   The chances have just begun,
> For the Best jobs haven't been started,
>   The Best work hasn't been done."

Nothing stands in the way of a will which wants—an intelligence which knows. The great thing is to start. "Begin your work," says Ausonius. "To begin is to complete the first half. The second half remains. Begin again and the work is done."

It matters not how small or unimportant your task may seem to be. It may loom bigger in Universal Mind than that of your neighbor, whose position is so much greater in the eyes of the world. Do it well—and Universal Mind will work with you.

But don't feel limited to any one job or any one line of work. Man was given dominion over all the earth. "And God said, Let us make man in our image, after our likeness: and let them have dominion over the fish of the sea, and over the fowl of the air, and over the cattle, and over all the earth, and over every creeping thing that creepeth upon the earth."

All of energy, all of power, all that can exercise any influence over your life, is in your hands through the power of thought. God—good—is the only power there is. Your mind is part of His mind. He is "the Father that is within you that doeth the works."

So don't put any limit upon His power by trying to limit your capabilities. You are not in bondage to anything. All your hopes and dreams can come true. Were you not given dominion over all the earth? And can anyone else take this dominion from you?

All the mysterious psychic powers about which you hear so much today are perfectly natural. Professor Rhine of Duke University has demonstrated them in all manner of subjects. I have them. You have them. They only await the time when they shall be allowed to assert their vigor and prove themselves your faithful servitors.

"Be not afraid!" Claim your inheritance. The Universal Mind that supplies all wisdom and power is *your* mind. And to the extent that you are governed by your understanding of its infinite law of supply, you will be able to demonstrate plenty. "According to your faith, be it unto you."

"Analyze most of the great American fortunes of the past generation," says *Advertising and Selling Fortnightly,* "and you will find that they were founded on great faiths. One man's faith was in oil, another's in land, another's in minerals.

"The fortunes that are being built today are just as surely being built on great faiths, but there is this difference: the emphasis of the faith has been shifted. Today it takes faith in a product or an opportunity, as it always did, but it takes faith in the public, in addition. Those who have the greatest faith in the public—the kind of faith possessed by Henry Ford and H.J. Heinz—*and make that faith articulate*—build the biggest fortunes."

"Wanted"

There is one question that bothers many a man. Should he stick to the job he has, or cast about at once for a better one. The answer depends entirely upon what you are striving for. The first thing is to set your goal. What is it you want? A profession? A political appointment? An important executive position? A business of your own?

Every position should yield you three things:

1. Reasonable pay for the present.
2. Knowledge, training, or experience that will be worth money to you in the future.
3. Prestige or acquaintances that will be of assistance to you in attaining your goal.

Judge every opening by those three standards. But don't overlook chances for valuable training, merely because the pay is small. It is a pretty safe rule, that concern with up-to-the-minute methods would profit you to learn, for it also pays up-to-the-minute salaries.

Hold each job long enough to get from it every speck of information there is in it. Hold it long enough to learn the job ahead. Then if there seems no likelihood of a vacancy soon in that job ahead, find one that corresponds to it somewhere else.

Progress! Keep going ahead! Don't be satisfied merely because your salary is being boosted occasionally. Learn something every day. When you reach the point in your work that you are no longer adding to your store of knowledge or abilities, you are going backward, and it's time for you to move. Move upward in the organization you are with if you can—but MOVE!

Your actual salary is of slight importance compared with the knowledge and ability you add to your mind. Given a full storehouse there, the salary or the riches will speedily follow. But the biggest salary won't do you much good for long unless you have the knowledge inside you to back it up.

It is like a girl picking her husband. She can pick one with a lot of money and no brains, or she can pick one with no money but a lot of ability. In the former case, she will have a high time for a little while, ending in a divorce court or in her having a worthless young "rounder" on her hands and no money to pay the bills. In the other, the start will be hard, but she is likely to end up with a happy home she has helped to build, an earnest, hard-working husband who has "arrived"—*and happiness.*

Money ought to be a consideration in marriage—but never *the* consideration. Of course it is an easy matter to pick a man with neither money nor brains. But when it is a choice of money *or* brains—take the brains every time. Possessions are of slight importance compared to mind. Given the inquiring, alert type of mind—you can get any amount of possessions. But the possessions without the mind are nothing. Nine times out of ten the best thing that can happen to any young couple is to have to start with little or nothing and work out their salvation together.

What is it *you* want most from life? Is it riches?

Picture yourself with all the riches you could use, with all the abundance that Nature holds out with such lavish hand everywhere. What would you do with it?

Day-dream for a while. Believe that you *have* that abundance *now.* Practice being rich in your own mind. See yourself driving that expensive car you have always longed for, living in the sort of house you have often pictured, well-dressed, surrounded by everything to make life worth while. Picture yourself spending this money that is yours, lavishly, without a worry as to where more is coming from, knowing that there is no limit to the riches of Mind. Picture yourself doing all those things you would like to do, living the life you would like to live, providing for your loved ones as you would like to see them provided for. *See* all this in your mind's eye. *Believe* it to be true for the moment. *Know* that it will all be true in the not-very-distant future. Get from it all the pleasure and enjoyment you can.

It is the *first step* in making your dreams come true. You are creating the model in mind. And if you don't allow fear or worry to tear it down, Mind will re-create that model for you in your everyday life.

"All that the Father hath is yours," said Jesus. And a single glance at the heavens and the earth will show you that He has all riches in abundance. Reach out mentally and appropriate to yourself some of these good gifts. You have to do it mentally before you can enjoy it physically. " 'Tis mind that makes the body rich," as Shakespeare tells us.

See the things you want as *already yours.* Know that they will come to you at need. Then LET them come. Don't fret and worry about them. Don't think about your LACK of them. Think of them as YOURS, as *belonging* to you, as already in your possession.

Look upon money as water that runs the mill of your mind. You are constantly grinding out ideas that the world needs. Your thoughts, your plans, are necessary to the great scheme of things. Money provides the power. But *it* needs YOU, it needs your ideas, before it can be of any use to the world. The Falls of Niagara would be of no use without the power plants that line the banks. The Falls need these plants to turn their power to account. In the same way, money needs your ideas to become of use to the world.

So instead of thinking that you need money, realize that money needs YOU. Money is just so much wasted energy without work to do. Your ideas provide the outlet for it, the means by which money can do things. Develop your ideas, secure in the knowledge that money is always looking for such an outlet. When the ideas are perfected, money will gravitate your way without conscious effort on your part, if only you don't dam up the channels with doubts and fears.

First have something that the world needs, even if it be only faithful, interested service—then open up your channels of desire, and dollars will flow to you. "First have something good—then advertise!" said Horace Greeley.

And remember that the more you have to offer—the more of riches will flow to you. Dollars are of no value except as they are used.

You have seen the rich attacked time and again in newspapers and magazines. You have read numerous articles and editorials against them, you have heard agitators declaim against them by the hour. But did you ever hear one of them say a single word against the richest man of them all—Henry Ford? I did not. And why? Because Henry Ford's idea of money was that it was something to be *used*—something to provide more jobs, something to bring more comfort, more enjoyment, into an increasingly greater number of lives.

That is why money flowed to him so freely. That is why he got so much out of life. And that is how you, too, can get in touch with Infinite Supply. Realize that it is not money you have to seek, but a way to *use* money for the world's advantage. *Find the need!* Look at everything with the question—How could that be improved? To what new uses could this be put? Then set about supplying that need, in the absolute confidence that when you have found the way, money will flow freely to and through you. Do your part—and you can confidently look to Universal Mind to provide the means.

Get firmly in mind the definite conviction that YOU CAN DO ANYTHING RIGHT THAT YOU MAY WISH TO DO. Then set your goal and let everything you do, all your work, all your study, all your associations, be a step towards that goal. To quote Berton Braley again—

"If you want a thing bad enough
To go out and fight for it,
Work day and night for it,
Give up your time and your peace and your sleep for it,
If only desire of it
Makes you quite mad enough
Never to tire of it,
Makes you hold all other things tawdry and cheap for it,
If life seems all empty and useless without it
And all that you scheme and you dream is about it,
If gladly you'll sweat for it,
Fret for it,
Plan for it,

Lose all your terror of God or man for it,
If you'll simply go after that thing that you want,
With all your capacity,
Strength and sagacity,
Faith, hope and confidence, stern pertinacity,
If neither cold poverty, famished and gaunt,
Nor sickness nor pain
Of body or brain
Can turn you away from the thing that you want,
If dogged and grim you besiege and beset it,
You'll get it!'

A Father's Prayer

"BUILD me a son, O Lord, who will be strong enough to know when he is weak, and brave enough to face himself when he is afraid; one who will be proud and unbending in honest defeat, and humble and gentle in victory.

Build me a son whose wishbone will not be where his backbone should be; a son who will know Thee—and that to know himself is the foundation stone of knowledge.

"Lead him, I pray, not in the path of ease and comfort, but under the stress and spur of difficulties and challenge. Here let him learn to stand up in the storm; here let him learn compassion for those who fail.

"Build me a son whose heart will be clear, whose goal will be high; a son who will master himself before he seeks to master other men; one who will learn to laugh, yet never forget how to weep; one who will reach into the future, yet never forget the past.

"And after all these things are his, add, I pray, enough of a sense of humor, so that he may always be serious, yet never take himself too seriously. Give him humility, so that he may always remember the simplicity of true greatness, the open mind of true wisdom, the meekness of true strength.

"Then, I, his father, will dare to whisper, 'I have not lived in vain.' "

—General Douglas MacArthur

CHAPTER 9

Visualizing Your Goals Treasure Mapping for Supply

So many people have won success and happiness by making "Treasure Maps" to more easily visualize the things they wanted, that Nautilus Magazine recently ran a prize competition for the best article showing how a "Treasure Map" had helped to bring about one's heart's desire. Caroline J. Drake won the contest.

"I had been bookkeeper, in a large department store for seven years when the manager's niece, whose husband had just died, was put in my place.

"I felt stunned. My husband had died ten years previously, leaving a little home and some insurance. But sickness and hospital bills had long since taken both home and money. I had supported the family for eight years and kept the three children in school, but had not been able to save any money. The eldest child, a boy, had just finished high school but as yet had found nothing to do to help along.

"Day after day I looked for work of any kind to do which might pay rent and give us a living. I was thirty-five years old, strong, capable and willing; but there was absolutely no place for me. For the first time in my life I was afraid of the future. The thought that we might have to go on relief appalled me.

"Thus three months passed. I was behind two months with the rent when the landlord told me I would have to move. I asked him to give me a few days longer in which to try and find work. This he agreed to do.

"The next morning I started out again on my rounds. In passing a magazine stand I stopped and glanced over the papers and magazines. It must have been the answer to my many prayers that led me to pick up the copy of a magazine which stared me in the face. Idly I opened it and glanced at the table of contents.

My mind was in such a turmoil that I was barely conscious of the words which my eyes saw.

Suddenly my eye was caught by a title about 'treasure-mapping' for success and supply. Something impelled me to buy a copy of the magazine which proved to be the turning point in our lives.

"Instead of looking for work, I went home. Still under the influence of that 'Something' (which I did not then understand) I began to read the magazine. Strange and unreal as it then seemed, still I did not doubt. I read each article eagerly and in its order and when I came to the article about treasure-mapping bringing success and supply, something about the idea seemed to hold me in its grip. As a child I had always loved games, and this idea of making a treasure-map reawakened the old desire.

"I read the article several times. Then, with a bunch of papers which I hunted up, I set to work to make my treasure-map of success and supply. So many things came into my mind to put on that treasure-map! First, there was the little cottage at the edge of town. Then there was a little dress and millinery shop which I had always longed for. Then, of course, a car. And in that cottage would be a piano for the girls; a yard in the back where we could work among the flowers of an evening or a morning. My enthusiasm grew by leaps and bounds. From magazines and papers I cut pictures and words and sentences—all connected with the idea of success and abundance.

How I Made the "Treasure-Map"

"Next I found a large wheel of heavy white paper and began building that map. In the center I pasted a picture of a lovely little cottage with wide porches and trees and shrubbery around it. In one corner of the map I put a picture of a little storeroom and underneath I pasted the words, 'Betty's Style Shop.' Close to this I pasted pictures of a few stylish dresses and hats.

"At different places on the map I placed sentiments and mottoes—all carrying out the idea of success, abundance, happiness and harmony.

"I do not know how long I worked on that treasure-map which was to be the means of attracting into our lives the things which we had need of and desired. I could already feel myself living in that cottage and working in the little dress shop. Never had I felt so completely fascinated and thrilled with an idea as with that treasure-map and what I was sure it would bring us. I tacked the map on the wall of my bedroom, right in front of my bed, so that the first thing I saw in the morning and the last thing at night would be that treasure-map of my desires.

"Every night and morning I would go over every detail of that map until it fairly seemed to become part of my very being. It became so clear that I could call it instantly to mind at any moment in the day. Then in my Silence period I would see myself and the children going through the rooms of the cottage, laughing and talking, arranging the furniture and curtains. I would picture my daughters at the piano singing and playing; I would see my son sitting in the library with books and papers all around him. Then I would picture myself walking about my shop, proud and happy; people coming in and going out. I would see them buying the lovely hats and dresses, paying me for them and going out smiling.

"During all this time, I was learning more and more of the power of the mind to draw to us the things and conditions like unto our thoughts. I understood that this treasure-map was but the means of impressing upon my subconscious mind the pattern from which to build the conditions of success and harmony into our lives. Always, after each of my Silence periods, I would lovingly thank God that the abundance and harmony and love were already ours. I believed that I *had* received; for mentally living in the cottage and working in the shop was to me the certain fact that I would take possession of them in the material world, just as in the mental.

"When the children found out what I was doing, they entered heartily into the spirit of the game and each of them soon had a treasure-map of his own.

"It was not many weeks before things began to happen. One day I met an old friend of my husband's and he told me that he and his wife were going west for several months and asked if we would come out and take care of their house for the rent. A week later we were settled in that cottage, which was almost the very picture of the one I had on my treasure-map. A little later my son was offered work evenings and Saturdays in an engineering office, which proved the means of his entering college that fall.

"We had been in the cottage nearly two months when I saw an advertisement in the local paper for a woman to take charge of a lady's dress shop. I answered the ad and found that the owner was having to give up the shop for several months, perhaps permanently, on account of her health. Arrangements were quickly made so that I was to run the business and share half the expenses and the profits.

"Within six months after we started treasure-mapping for supply, we had accomplished practically everything that map called for. When the owner of the cottage came back several months later, he made it possible for us to buy the place and we are still here.

"The business, too, is mine now. The lady decided not to come back, so I bought the business, paying her so much a month. It is a much larger and more thriving business now—thanks to the understanding of the power of thought which I gained through my study and practice."

In another article in Nautilus, Helen M. Kitchel told how she used a "Treasure Map" to sell her property. She pasted an attractive picture of her house on a large sheet of paper, put a description of it underneath and then surrounded picture and description with such mottoes as—"Love, the Divine Magnet, attracts all that is good"—and others of a similar nature. She hung her map where she could see and study it several times a day, and repeated some of the affirmations or mottoes whenever the thought of making a sale occurred to her.

She also started a little private letter box which she called "God's Box" and in it, whenever the thought occurred to her, she placed a letter written to God telling of her needs and desires. Then each month she went over the letters, taking out and giving thanks for those that had been answered.

Within a year her house was sold, on the very plan she herself had outlined in one of her "Letters to God," on the exact basis and for the exact price she had asked in that letter.

Another method is to "Talk with God." Go somewhere where you can be alone and undisturbed for a little while, and talk aloud to God exactly as you would to a loving and understanding Father. Tell Him your ambitions and desires. Describe in detail just what you want. Then thank Him just as you would an earthly father with whom you had had a similar talk and who had promised you the things you asked for. You will be amazed at the result of such sincere talks.

"My word shall not come back to me void, but shall accomplish that whereunto it was sent." Whatever you can visualize—and BELIEVE in—you can accomplish. Whatever you can see as yours in your mind's eye, you can get. "In the beginning was the Word." In the beginning is the mental image.

Corinne Updegraff Wells had an article in her little magazine "Through Rose Colored Glasses" that illustrates the power of visualizing your ambitions and desires. "Many years ago," she says, "a young girl who lived in a New York tenement was employed by a fasionable Fifth Avenue modiste to run errands, match samples and pull basting threads.

"Annie loved her job. From an environment of poverty she had become suddenly and miraculously an inhabitant of an amazing new world of beauty, wealth and fashion. It was thrilling to see ladies arrive in fine cars, to watch the social elite preen before Madam's big gold framed mirrors.

"The little errand girl, in her starched gingham, soon became filled with desire and fired with ambition. She began imagining herself as head of the establishment instead of its most lowly employee. Whenever she passed before mirrors she smiled at a secret reflection she saw of herself, older and more beautiful, a person of charm and importance.

"Of course, nobody even suspected the secret existence of this make-believe person. Hugging her precious secret, Annie smiled confidently at that dazzling reflection in the mirror and began playing an exciting game, 'I'll pretend I'm already Madam. I'll be polite and look my best and have grand manners and learn something new each day. I'll work as hard and take as much interest as though the shop were really and truly mine.'

"Soon fashionable ladies began whispering to Madam: 'Annie's the smartest girl you've ever had!' Madam herself began to smile and say: 'Annie, you may fold Mrs. Vandergilt's gown if you'll be very careful,' or 'I'm going to let you deliver this wedding dress,' or, 'My dear, you're developing a real gift for color and line,' and, finally, 'I'm promoting you to the work-room.'

"The years passed quickly. Each day Annie came more and more to resemble the image she alone had seen of herself. Gradually the little errand girl became Annette, an individual; then Annette, stylist; and finally, Madam Annette, renowned costume designer for a rich and famous clientele.

"The images we hold steadfastly in our minds over the years are not illusions; they are patterns by which we are able to mould our own destinies."

"You never can tell when you do an act
Just what the result will be,
But with every deed you are sowing a seed,
Though the harvest you may not see.
Each kindly act is an acorn dropped
In God's productive soil;
You may not know, but the tree shall grow
With shelter for those who toil.

"You never can tell what your thought will do
In bringing you hate or love,
For thoughts are things and their airy wings
Are swifter than carrier doves.
They follow the law of the universe—
Each thing must create its kind,
And they speed o'er the track to bring you back
Whatever went out from your mind."

—Ella Wheeler Wilcox

Part IV

SECRET NUMBER FOUR
FAITH IN YOURSELF AND IN YOUR INNER MIND

CHAPTER 10

The Formula of Success

"One ship drives east, and another drives west,
With the self-same winds that blow.
'Tis the set of the sails, and not the gales
Which tells us the way they go.

"Like the waves of the sea are the ways of fate
As we voyage along thru life.
'Tis the set of the soul which decides its goal
And not the calm or the strife."
—ELLA WHEELER WILCOX.

What is the eternal question which stands up and looks you and every sincere man squarely in the eye every morning?

"How can I better my condition?" That is the real life question which confronts you, and will haunt you every day till you solve it.

Read this chapter carefully and I think you will find the answer to this important life question which you and every man must solve if he ever expects to have more each Monday morning, after payday, than he had the week before.

To begin with, all wealth depends upon a clear understanding of the fact that mind—thought—is the only creator. The great business of life is thinking. Control your thoughts and you control circumstance.

Just as the first law of gain is desire, so the formula of success is FAITH. Believe that you have it—see it as an existent fact—and anything you can rightly wish for is yours.

Faith is "the substance of things hoped for, the evidence of things not seen."

It is now a good many years since Professor Henry made his famous experiment with a charged magnet, which revolutionized the electrical practice of his age.

First he took an ordinary magnet of large size, suspended it from a rafter, and with it lifted a few hundred pounds of iron.

Then he wrapped the magnet with wire and charged it with the current from a small battery. Instead of only a few hundred, *the now highly charged magnet lifted 3,000 pounds!*

Your magnet is your subconscious mind. Impelled by strong desire, it can bring you a reasonable amount of the good things of life. But charge it with a strong current of faith, of belief in its power, *and there is no limit to the good things it will bring to you.*

You have seen men, inwardly no more capable than yourself, accomplish the seemingly impossible. You have seen others, after years of hopeless struggle, suddenly win their most cherished dreams. And you have probably wondered, "What is the power that gives new life to their dying ambitions, that supplies new impetus to their jaded desires, that gives them a new start on the road to success?"

That power is belief—*faith.* Someone, something, gave them a new belief in themselves, a new faith in their power to win—and they leaped ahead and wrested success from seemingly certain defeat.

Do you remember the picture Harold Lloyd was in some years ago, showing a country boy who was afraid of his shadow? Every boy in the countryside bedeviled him. Until one day his grandmother gave him a talisman that she assured him his grandfather had carried through the Civil War and which, so she said, had the property of making its owner invincible. Nothing could hurt him, she told him, while he wore this talisman. Nothing could stand up against him. He believed her. And the next time the bully of the town started to cuff him around, he wiped up the earth with him. And that was only the start. Before the year was out he had made a reputation as the most daring soul in the community.

Then, when his grandmother felt that he was thoroughly cured, she told him the truth—that the "talisman" was merely a piece of old junk she had picked up by the roadside—that she knew all he needed was *faith in himself,* belief that he could do these things.

The Talisman of Napoleon

Stories like that are common. It is such a well-established truth that you can do only what you think you can, that the theme is a favorite one with authors. I remember reading a story years ago of an artist—a mediocre sort of artist— who was visiting the field of Waterloo and happened upon a curious lump of metal half-buried in the dirt, which so attracted him that he picked it up and put it in his pocket. Soon thereafter he noticed a sudden increase in confidence, an absolute faith in himself, not only as to his own chosen line of work, but in his ability to handle any situation that might present itself. He painted a great picture—just to show that he *could* do it. Not content with that, he visioned an empire with Mexico as its basis, actually led a revolt that carried all before it—until one day he lost his talisman. *And immediately his bubble burst.*

I instance this just to illustrate the point that it is *your own belief in yourself* that counts. It is consciousness of dominant power within you that makes all things attainable. *You can do anything you think you can.* This knowledge is literally the gift of the gods, for through it you can solve every human problem. It should make of you an incurable optimist. It is the open door to welfare. *Keep it open*—by expecting to gain everything that is right.

You are entitled to every good thing. Therefore expect nothing but good. Defeat does not *need* to follow victory. You don't have to "knock wood" every time you congratulate yourself that things have been going well with you. Victory should follow victory—and it will if you "let this mind be in you which was also in Christ Jesus." It is the mind that means health and life and boundless opportunity and recompense. No limitation rests upon you. So don't let any enter your life. Remember that Mind will do every good thing for you. It will remove mountains for you.

"Bring ye all the tithes into the storehouse, and prove me now herewith, saith the Lord of hosts, if I will not open you the windows of heaven, and pour you out a blessing, that there shall not be room enough to receive it."

Bring all your thoughts, your desires, your aims, your talents, into the Storehouse—the Consciousness of Good, the Law of Infinite supply—and prove these blessings. There is every reason to know that you are entitled to adequate provision. Everything that is involved in supply is a thing of thought. Now reach out, stretch your mind, try to comprehend *unlimited thought, unlimited supply.*

Do not think that supply must come through one or two channels. It is not for you to dictate to Universal Mind the means through which It shall send Its gifts to you. There are millions of channels through which It can reach you. Your part is to impress upon Mind your need, your earnest desire, your boundless belief in the resources and the willingness of Universal Mind to help you. Plant the seed of desire. Nourish it with a clear visualization of the ripened fruit. Water it with sincere faith. But leave the means to Universal Mind.

Open up your mind. Clear out the channels of thought. Keep yourself in a state of receptivity. Gain a mental attitude in which you are constantly *expecting good.* You have the fundamental right to all good, you know. "According to your faith, be it unto you."

The trouble with most of us is that we are mentally lazy. It is so much easier to go along with the crowd than to break trail for ourselves. But the great discoverers, the great inventors, the great geniuses in all lines have been men who dared to break with tradition, who defied precedent, who believed that there is no limit to what Mind can do—and who stuck to that belief until their goal was won, in spite of all the sneers and ridicule of the wiseacres and to those who said "It-can't-be-done."

Not only that, but they were never satisfied with achieving just one success. They knew that the first success is like the first olive out of the bottle. All the others come the more easily for it. They realized that they were a part of the Creative Intelligence of the Universe, and that the "part" shares all the properties of the "whole". That realization gave them the faith to strive for any right thing, the knowledge that the only limit upon their capabilities was the limit of their desires. Knowing that, they couldn't be satisfied with any ordinary success. They had to keep on and on and on.

Edison didn't sit down and fold his hands when he gave us the talking machine. Or the electric light. These great achievements merely opened the way to new fields of accomplishment.

Open the channels between your mind and Universal Mind, and there is no limit to the riches that will come pouring in. Concentrate your thoughts on the particular thing you are most interested in, and ideas in abundance will come flooding down, opening a dozen ways of winning the goal you are striving for.

Don't let one success—no matter how great—satisfy you. The Law of Creation, you know, is the Law of Growth. You can't stand still. You must go forward—or be passed by. Complacency—self-satisfaction—is the greatest enemy of achievement. You must keep looking forward. Like Alexander, you must be constantly seeking new worlds to conquer. Depend upon it, the power will come to meet the need. There is no such thing as failing powers, if we look to Mind for our source of supply. The only failure of mind comes from worry and fear—or from disuse.

William James, the famous psychologist, taught that "The more mind does, the more it can do." For ideas release energy. You can *do* more and better work than you have ever done. You can *know* more than you know now. You know from your own experience that under proper mental conditions of joy or enthusiasm, you can do three or four times the work without fatigue that you can ordinarily. Tiredness is more boredom than actual physical fatigue. You can work almost indefinitely when the work is a pleasure.

You have seen sickly persons, frail persons, who couldn't do an hour's light work without exhaustion, suddenly buckle down when heavy responsibilities were thrown upon them, and grow strong and rugged under the load. Crises not only draw upon the reserve power you have, but they help to create new power.

"It Couldn't Be Done"

It may be that you have been deluded by the thought of incompetence. It may be that you have been told so often that you cannot do certain things that you've come to believe you can't. Remember that success or failure is merely a state of mind. Believe you cannot do a thing—and you can't. Know that you *can* do it—and you *will.* You must *see yourself doing it.*

"If you think you are beaten, you are;
If you think you dare not, you don't;
If you'd like to win, but you think you can't,
It's almost a cinch you won't;
If you think you'll lose, you've lost,
For out in the world you'll find
Success begins with a fellow's will—
It's all in the state of mind.

"Full many a race is lost
Ere even a race is run,
And many a coward fails
Ere even his work's begun.
Think big, and your deeds will grow,
Think small and you fall behind,
Think that you can, and you will;
It's all in the state of mind.

"If you think you are outclassed, you are;
You've got to think high to rise;
You've got to be sure of yourself before
You can ever win a prize.
Life's battle doesn't always go
To the stronger or faster man;
But sooner or later, the man who wins
Is the fellow who thinks he can."

There is a vast difference between a proper understanding of one's own ability and a determination to make the best of it—and offensive egotism. It is absolutely necessary for every man to believe in himself, before he can make the most of himself. All of us have something to sell. It may be our goods, it may be our abilities, it may be our services. You have to believe in yourself to make your buyer take stock in you at par and accrued interest. You have to feel the same personal solicitude over a customer lost, as a revivalist over a backslider, and hold special services to bring him back into the fold. You have to get up every morning with determination, if you are going to go to bed that night with satisfaction.

There is mighty sound sense in the saying that all the world loves a booster. The one and only thing you have to win success with is MIND. For your mind to function at its highest capacity, you have to be charged with good cheer and optimism. No one ever did a good piece of work while in a negative frame of mind. Your best work is always done when you are feeling happy and optimistic.

And a happy disposition is the *result*—not the *cause*—of happy, cheery thinking. Health and prosperity are the *results* primarily of optimistic thoughts. *You* make the pattern. If the impression you have left on the world about you seems faint and weak, don't blame fate—blame your pattern! You will never cultivate a brave, courageous demeanor by thinking cowardly thoughts. You cannot gather figs from thistles. You will never make your dreams come true by choking them with doubts and fears. You must put foundations under your air castles, foundations of UNDERSTANDING and BELIEF. Your chances of success in any undertaking can always be measured by your BELIEF in yourself.

Are your surroundings discouraging? Do you feel that if you were in another place success would be easier? Just bear in mind that your real environment is within you. All the factors of success or failure are in your inner world. *You* make your own inner world—and through it your outer world. You can choose the material from which to build. If you have not chosen wisely in the past, you can choose again now the material you want to rebuild it.

The richness of life is within you. No one has failed so long as he can begin again.

Start right in and *do* all those things you feel you have it in you to do. Ask permission of no man. Concentrating your thought upon any proper undertaking will make its achievement possible. Your belief that you *can* do the thing gives your thought forces their power. Fortune waits upon you. Seize her boldly, hold her—she is yours. She belongs rightfully to you. But if you cringe to her, if you go up to her doubtfully, timidly, she will pass you in scorn. For she is a fickle jade who must be mastered, who loves boldness, who admires confidence.

A Roman boasted that it was sufficient for him to strike the ground with his foot and legions would spring up. And his very boldness cowed his opponents. It is the same with your mind. Take the first step, and your mind will mobilize all its forces to your aid. But the first essential is that you *begin.* Once the battle is started, all that is within and without you will come to your assistance, if you attack in earnest and meet each obstacle with resolution. But *you* have to start things.

"The Lord helps them that help themselves" is a truth as old as man. It is, in fact, plain common sense. Your superconscious mind has all power, but your conscious mind is the watchman at the gate. *It* has to open the door. *It* has to press the spring that releases the infinite energy. No failure is possible in the accomplishment of any right object you may have in life, if you but understand your power and will perseveringly try to use it in the proper way.

The men who have made their mark in this world all had one trait in common—*they believed in themselves!* "But," you may say, "how can I believe in myself when I have never done anything worth while, when everything I put my hand to seems to fail?" You can't, of course. That is, you couldn't if you had to depend upon your conscious mind alone. But just remember what one far greater than you said—"I can of mine own self do nothing. The Father that is within me—He doeth the works."

That same "Father" is within you. And it is by knowing that He *is* in you, and that through Him you can do anything that is right, that you can acquire the belief in yourself which is so necessary. Certainly the Mind that imaged the heavens and the earth and all that they contain has all wisdom, all power, all abundance. With this Mind to call upon, you know there is no problem too difficult for you to undertake. The *knowing* of this is the first step. *Faith.* But St. James tells us—"Faith without works is dead." So go on to the next step. Decide on the one thing you want most from life. No matter what it may be. There is no limit, you know, to Mind. Visualize this thing that you want. See it, feel it, BELIEVE in it. Make your mental blueprint, and *begin to build!*

Suppose people DO laugh at your idea. Suppose Reason does say—"It can't be done!" People laughed at Galileo. They laughed at Henry Ford. Reason contended for countless ages that the earth was flat. Reason said—or so numerous automotive engineers argued—that the original Ford motor wouldn't run. But the earth *is* round—and many of those millions of Model T Fords are still running.

Let us start right now putting into practice some of these truths that you have learned. What do you want most of life right now? Take that one desire, concentrate on it, impress it upon your subconscious mind, and through it upon the superconscious.

Psychologists have discovered that the best time to make suggestions to your subconscious mind is just before going to sleep, when the senses are quiet and the body is relaxed. So let us take your desire and suggest it to your subconscious mind tonight. The two prerequisites are the earnest DESIRE, and an intelligent, understanding BELIEF. Someone has said, you know, that education is three-fourths encouragement, and the encouragement is the suggestion that the thing can be done.

You know that you can have what you want, if you want it badly enough and can believe in it earnestly enough. So tonight, just before you drop off to sleep, concentrate your thought on this thing that you most desire from life. BELIEVE that you have it. SEE YOURSELF possessing it. FEEL yourself using it.

Do that every night until you ACTUALLY DO BELIEVE that you have the thing you want. When you reach that point, YOU WILL HAVE IT!

Even better than making such suggestions to yourself is to put them on a record and have them played to you while you are asleep. That is the most successful method yet discovered. We have been told that the Army used this method with great success during the war in teaching languages. Certainly it would be the quickest way to learn any diffcult subject.

CHAPTER 11

A Positive Mental Attitude Wins Success

You remember the saying of the sacred writer: "As a man thinketh in his heart, so is he." A truer statement never was uttered. For every man or woman is what he or she is, by reason of what he or she has thought. We have thought ourselves into what we are. One's place in life is largely determined by his Mental Attitude.

Mental attitude is the result of the current of one's thoughts, ideas, ideals, feelings, and beliefs. You are constantly at work building up a Mental Attitude, which is not only making your character but which is also having its influence upon the outside world, both in the direction of your effect upon other people, as well as your quality of attracting toward yourself that which is in harmony with the prevailing mental state held by you. Is it not most important, then, that this building should be done with the best possible materials—according to the best plan—with the best tools?

"A positive Mental Attitude Wins Financial Success." Before going any further, let us define the word "Positive" and its opposite, "Negative," and then see how the former wins success and the latter attracts failure. In the sense in which I use the terms, "Positive" means Confident Expectation, Self-Confidence, Courage, Initiative, Energy, Optimism, Expectation of Good, not Evil—of Wealth, not Poverty—Belief in One's Self and in the LAW, etc.; "Negative," means Fear, Worry Expectation of Undesirable Things, Lack of Confidence in One's Self and the LAW, etc.

In the first place Mental Attitude tends towards success by its power in the direction of "making us over" into individuals possessing qualities conductive to success. Many people go through the world bemoaning their lack of the faculties, qualities or temperament that they instinctively recognize are active factors in the attainment of success. They see others possessing these desirable qualities moving steadily forward to their goal, and they also feel if they themselves were but possessed of these same qualities they, too, might attain the same desirable results. Now, so far, their reasoning is all right—but they do not go far enough. They fail here because they imagine that since they have not the desired qualities at the moment, they can never expect to possess them. They regard their minds as something that once fixed and built can never be improved upon, repaired, rebuilt, or enlarged. Right here is where the majority of people "fall down."

As a matter of fact, the great scientific authorities of the present time distinctly teach that a man by diligent care and practice, may completely change his character, temperament, and habits. He may kill out undesirable traits of character, and replace them by new and desirable traits, qualities and faculties. The brain is now known to be but the instrument and tool of something called Mind, which uses the brain as its instrument of expression.

And the brain is also now known to be composed of millions of tiny cells, the majority of which are not in use. It is also known that if one turns his attention and interest in certain directions, the unused cells in the area of his brain which is the center of such subject, will be stimulated into action and will begin to manifest actively. Not only this, but the stimulated sections of cells will begin also to actively manifest their reproductive qualities and *new brain cells* will be evolved, grown and developed in order to furnish proper mental tools with which to manifest the new desires, qualities and feelings pressing forward for expression.

Scientific Character Building is not a mere idle theory, but a live, vital, actual, practical fact, being put into operation in the psychological laboratories of the country, and by thousands of private individuals all over the world who are rapidly "making themselves over" by this method. *And the prevailing Mental Attitude is the pattern upon which the brain cells build.* If you can but grasp this truth you have the key to success in your hands.

Now, let us consider the second phase of the action of Mental Attitude toward Financial Success. I allude to the effect upon others of one's Mental Attitude. Did you ever stop long enough to think that we are constantly giving other people suggestive impressions of ourselves and qualities?

Do you not know that, if you go about with the Mental Attitude of Discouragement, Fear, Lack of Self-Confidence, and all the other Negative qualities of mind, other people are sure to catch the impression and govern themselves toward you accordingly?

Let a man come into your presence for the purpose of doing business with you and if he lacks confidence in himself and in the things he wishes to sell you, you will at once catch his spirit and will feel that you have no confidence in him or the things he is offering. You will catch his mental atmosphere at once, and he will suffer thereby. But let this same man fill himself up with thoughts, feelings, and ideals of Enthusiasm, Success, Self-Confidence, Confidence in his proposition, etc., and you will unconsciously "Take stock" in him and interest in his goods, and the chances are that you will be willing and glad to do business with him.

Do you not know men who radiate Failure, Discouragement and "I Can't"? Are you not affected by their manifested Mental Attitude to their hurt? And, on the other hand, do you not know men who are so filled with Confidence, Courage, Enthusiasm, Fearlessness, and Energy, that the moment you come into their presence, or they into yours, you at once catch their spirit, and respond thereto? I contend that there is an actual atmosphere surrounding each of these men—Which if you are sensitive enough you can feel—one of replusion, and the other of attraction. And further, that these atmospheres are the result of the constant daily thought of these men or the Mental Attitude of each toward life. Think this over a bit, and you will see at once just how the LAW works.

The third phase of the action of Mental Attitude towards Financial Success may be called the working of the Law of Attraction. Now, without attempting to advance any wild theories, I still must assert that all thinking, observing men have noticed the operation of a mental Law of Attraction, whereby "Like attracts like."

I state the general principle that a man's Mental Attitude acts as a *magnet,* attracting to him the things, objects, circumstances, environments, and people in harmony with that Mental Attitude. If we think Success firmly and hold it properly before us, it tends to build up a constant Mental Attitude which invariably attracts to us the things conducive to its attainment and materialization. If we hold the ideal of Financial Success—in short, Money—our Mental Attitude will gradually form and crystallize the MONEY ideal. And the things pertaining to Money—people calculated to help us win Money—circumstances tending to bring us Money—opportunities for making Money—in fact, all sorts of Money-things—will be attracted toward us.

You think this visionary talk, do you? Well, then, just make a careful study of any man who has attained Financial Success and see whether or not his prevailing attitude is not that of *expectation of money.* He holds this Mental Attitude as an idea, and he is constantly realizing that ideal.

Fix your mind firmly upon anything, good or bad, in the world, and you attract it to you or are attracted to it in obedience to the LAW. You attract to you the things you expect, think about and hold in your Mental Attitude. This is no superstitious idea, but a firmly established, scientific, psychological fact.

To further illustrate the workings of the above LAW, there are thought currents in the mental realm just as there are air currents in the atmosphere, and ocean currents in the seas. For instance there are thought currents of vice and others of virtue; thought currents of fear and others of courage; thought currents of hate and others of love; thought currents of poverty and others of wealth. And, further than this, the person who thinks and talks and expects poverty is drawn into the poverty thought currents of the world and attracts to himself others who think and talk along the same lines; and vice versa: the person who thinks, talks and expects wealth and prosperity attracts, or is attracted to, people of wealth and comes, in time, to share their prosperity with them. It behooves each one of us to watch our thought and talk, getting rid of the poverty thought, and in its place substituting the wealth and prosperity thought.

Sweep out from the chambers of your mind all these miserable negative thoughts like "I can't," "That's just my luck," "I knew I'd do it," "Poor me," etc, and then fill up the mind with the positive, invigorating, helpful, forceful, compelling ideals of Success, Confidence, and expectation of that which you desire; and just as the steel filings fly to the magnet, so will that which you need fly to you in response to this great natural principle of mental action—the Law of Attraction. Begin this very moment and build up a new ideal—that of Financial Success—see it mentally—expect it—demand it! This is the way to create it in your Mental Attitude.

Believe in Your Ability

"FAITH" is a word that has been often misused, misapplied and misunderstood. To many it means simply that attitude of mind which will accept anything that is told it, merely because someone else has said it—credulity, in fact. But those who have penetrated within the shell of the word know that it means something far more real than this—something imbedded deep down in the Heart of Things. To those who understand the Law, Faith is the contact which one raises to meet the Great Forces of Life and Nature, and by means of which one receives the inflow of the Power which is behind, and in all things, and is enabled to apply that Power to the running of his own affairs.

To some, it may seem a far cry from Faith to Financial Success, but the two are closely interwoven. For one to attain Financial Success he must first have Faith in himself; second, Faith in his fellowman; and third, Faith in the LAW.

Faith in one's self is of primary importance, for unless one has it he can never accomplish anything; can never influence any other person's opinion of him; can never attract to himself the things, persons and circumstances necessary for his welfare. A man must first learn to believe in himself before he will be able to make others believe in him. People are prone to take a person at his own estimate. If one is weak, negative and lacking in self-confidence, he surrounds himself with an atmosphere of negativity which unfavorably impresses those with whom he comes in contact. If one be strong, confident and positive, he radiates like qualities, and those coming in contact with him receive an impression of these qualities. The world believes in those who believe in themselves. And so you see, it is of the utmost importance to you that you cultivate this faith in yourself.

And not only does Faith in yourself operate in the direction of influencing others with whom you come in contact, but it also has a most positive bearing upon your own mental status and thoughts. If you deaden your mind with a negative attitude toward yourself, you stifle budding ideas, thoughts and plans—you choke the budding plants of your mentality. But, if you let pour forth a full, abiding, confident Faith in yourself—your abilities, your qualities, your latent powers, your desires, your plans and your Success, you will find that the whole mental garden responds to the stimulating influence; and ideas, thoughts, plans and other mental flowers will spring up rapidly. There is nothing so stimulating as a strong, positive "I Can and I Will" attitude toward oneself.

And you remember what has been said about the Law of Attraction—you remember how "like attracts like" and how one's Mental Attitude tends to draw toward him the things in harmony with his thoughts. Well, this being so, can you not see that a Mental Attitude of Faith or Confidence in Oneself is calculated to attract to you that which fits in with such Faith—that will tend to materialize your ideal?

CHAPTER 12

How to Develop Faith Power for Successful Living

To you, Faith has no doubt been a term properly applied in sermons and theological books, but which has little or no practical place or meaning in the world of action and deeds—in the world in which most of us live most of our time, and perform most of our actions.

We assure you that Faith Power is something having a most intimate and important relation to Personal Power along practical lines, and is something which, in the current phrase, "you need in your business."

Mr. Leon Jolson, president of the huge Necchi Sewing Machine Company, is today worth many millions of dollars. A few years ago he was a poor Polish immigrant who couldn't even speak English. The newspaper account of his spectacular rise to success quoted him as saying, "I had unfaltering faith. I prayed for guidance every step of the way. I used head and foot work."

The general conception of Faith—the idea of Faith held by most persons—is that it is an emotional state independent of, if not indeed actually contrary to Reason. However, we believe that the most important reasoning of practical everyday life is based on Faith. We do not know positively that the sun will rise tomorrow morning—all that we know is that in the history of the race the sun always has risen in the morning, and we "believe" that it will continue the practice on the morrow; but we do not "know" absolutely that such will be the case, we cannot prove it absolutely by argument—even by mathematics—unless we admit the existence of Universal Law, or the law of Causation, whereby "the same causes, under the same conditions will produce the same effects."

You may object to this as being silly—but it is the strictest application of the rules and laws of practical thought. Of course, you say that we "know" that the sun will rise tomorrow morning, and can even tell to a second the time of its rising. Certainly we "know" this, but we know it only by an act of Faith. That Faith, moreover, is the belief that there exists Universal Law—that "natural things act and move under Law"—that "the same causes, under the same conditions, produce the same results."

In the ordinary affairs of life and action you act according to Faith. You do this so naturally and instinctively, so constantly and habitually, that you are not aware of it. As an example, you start on an airline flight. You buy your ticket, having faith that the plane will start from the airport named on the ticket, and approximately on the time noted in it. You have faith that it will proceed to the destination promised. You do not "know" these things from actual experience so you cannot know what lies in the future: you take them for granted, you assume them to be true, you act upon Faith.

You take your seat. You do not know the pilot or the co-pilot—you have never seen them, nor do you even know their names. You do not know whether or not they are competent, reliable, or experienced. All that you know is that it is reasonable to suppose that the plane company will select the right kind of men for the task—you act upon Faith, upon Faith rationally interpreted. You have Faith in the company, in the management, in the system of flights, in the equipment, etc. and you stake your life and wholeness of body upon that Faith. You may say that you only "take a chance" in the matter; but, even so, you manifest Faith in that "chance," or else you wouldn't take it. You wouldn't "take a chance" of standing in the path of a rushing express train, or of leaping from the Empire State Building, would you? You manifest Faith in something—even if that something be no more than the Law of Averages.

You place your money in a bank; here again you manifest Faith—Faith rationally interpreted. You sell goods on credit to your customers—Faith again. You have Faith in your grocer, your butcher, your lawyer, your physician, your clerks, your insurance company. That is to say Faith of some kind, or of some degree—else you would not trust anything whatsoever to them. If you "believe" that a man is dishonest, incompetent, or insane, you do not place confidence in him, nor trust your affairs or interests to him; your Faith is in his "wrongness," and not in his "rightness"—but it is Faith, nevertheless. Every "belief" short of actual, positive knowledge, is a form or phase of Faith.

You have the Faith that if you step off a high building into space, you will fall and be injured, perhaps killed: this is your Faith in the Law of Gravitation. You have a similar Faith in certain other physical laws—you have the Confident Expectation that evil results to you will follow certain courses of action concerning these physical laws. You have Faith that poisons will injure or destroy your physical body, and you avoid such. You may object that you "know" these things, not merely "believe" them; but you don't "know" anything directly and immediately until you experience it and you cannot experience a future happening before its time. All that you can do concerning each and every future experience is to "believe" certain things concerning it—and that "belief" is nothing else but Faith, interpreted more or less rationally and correctly.

You do not "know" certainly and positively, by direct experience, or by pure reason, a single thing about the happenings of tomorrow, or of some day next week, or of the corresponding day of next year. Yet you act as if you did possess such knowledge—but why? Simply because of your Faith in the Law and Order of the Universe; of the operation of the Law of Causation; whereby effects follow causes; of the Law of Probabilities, or of the Law of Average; or of some other Natural Law. But your knowledge of and belief in such Laws are but forms of your Faith, i.e., Confident Expectation that "things will work out according to the rule observed in past actions." You cannot get away from Faith in your thoughts and beliefs concerning the present and the future, any more than you can run away from your shadow in the bright daylight.

From the foregoing, and the reflections aroused in your mind by the consideration of it, you will perceive that Faith has as true and as sound a position and place in the psychology of the human being as have Reason and Intellect.

Without the Confident Expectation of Faith, there will be no kindling of the flame of Insistent Desire—no application of the steel of

Persistent Determination. Unless Faith expresses itself in the Confident Expectation of the obtaining or attainment of the thing desired and willed, will Desire then find it difficult to "want it hard enough," and Will will find it impossible to "persistently determine to obtain it." Desire and Will depend upon Faith for their Inspirational Forces and by means of the latter, the Energizing forces of Desires and Dynamic Forces of Will are inspired and vitalized, and have the Breath of Life breathed into them.

How Sickness Is Cured by Faith

Among the many phases and forms of the application and manifestation of the mental principle of Faith Power is that important segment known generally as "Faith-Cure."

Faith-Cure is a term applied to the practice of curing disease by an appeal to the hope, belief, or expectation of the patient, and without the use of drugs or other material means. Formerly, Faith-Cure was confined to methods requiring the exercise of religious faith, such as the "prayer-cure" and "divine healing," but has now come to be used in the broader sense, and includes the cures of Mental Science.

It is now generally agreed that the cures made by the various practitioners of the numerous schools and forms of Faith-Cure have as their underlying effective principle the mental condition or state of Faith; this principle operating so as to call forth the innate power of the mental-physical organism to resist and to overcome the abnormal conditions which manifest as disease. Thus, all cures wrought by the mental forces of the individual, under whatever name or method, are, at the last, Faith Cures.

This innate power of the organism so lodged in the subconscious mentality, is found to respond readily to the ideas accepted as true by the individual—to his "beliefs." These beliefs are forms of Faith, at the last.

From the psychological point of view, all these different kinds of faith-healing, as indeed all kinds of mind-cure, depend upon suggestion. In proper faith-healing not only are powerful direct suggestions used, but the religious atmosphere and the autosuggestions of the patient are utilized, especially when the cures take place during a period of religious revival or at other times when large assemblies and strong emotions are found. The suggestibility of large crowds is markedly greater than that of individuals, and to this greater faith—must be attributed the greater success of the fashionable places of pilgrimage."

Analyzing the phenomena attributed to Suggestion, and reducing the idea of Suggestion to its essential elements, we find that Suggestions consist of: (1) placing a strong idea in the mind—grafting it on the mind, as it were; (2) arousing the Expectant Attention of the results implied or indicated in the suggested idea; and (3) setting into operation the activities of the subconscious mentality in the direction of bringing about the result pictured by the Expectant Attention, which in turn has been aroused by the suggested idea. There you have the whole idea of Suggestion in a nutshell!

Now then, all phenomena of Faith-Cure, and or Suggestion as well, are seen to depend upon the presence and action of the element or principle of Faith Power in the mentality of the individual.

By an application of the first of the above stated elements of this greater principle of your being, and of Nature as a whole, you may keep yourself in health, strength, and general desirable physical well-being; or you may bring about by it a gradual return to health and physical well-being if you have lost these; again, if you allow this principle to be directed wrongly and abnormally, you may lose your physical well-being and health, and may start on the downward path of disease, the end of which is an untimely death. Your physical condition is very largely dependent upon the character and kind of the Ideas and Ideals which you permit to be planted in your mind and by the degree of Expectant Attention, or Faith, which you permit to vitalize these Ideas and Ideals.

Briefly stated, the course to be followed by you in this matter is as follows: (1) Encourage Ideas and Ideals of Health, Strength, and Vitality—the ideas of Physical Well-Being—to take lodgment in your mind, there to send forth their roots, sprouts, blossoms, and fruit; cultivate these Ideas and Ideals and vitalize them with a goodly amount of Expectant Attention, Confident Expectation and Faith along the lines of these conditions which you desire to be present in yourself; see yourself "in your mind's eye" as you wish to be, and "confidently expect" to have these conditions manifested in you by your subconscious mentality; (2) never allow yourself to hold the ideas of diseased abnormal conditions, and, above all, never allow yourself to cultivate the mental habit of "expecting" such conditions to manifest in your body—cultivate the attitude of Faith and Hope, and discard that of Fear; (3) if your mind has been filled with these negative, harmful and destructive mental Ideas and Expectancy, and if your body has manifested Disease in response to them, you should proceed to "kill out" these noxious mental weeds by a deliberate, determined and confident cultivation of the right kind of Ideas and Ideals and states of "Expectancy"; it is an axiom of advanced psychology that "the positives tend to inhibit and to destroy the negatives"—the weeds in the mental garden may be "killed out" by the careful and determined cultivation of the positive plants of Hope, Faith and Confident Expectation of the Good and Desirable.

Faith Power is present and active, is potent and powerful and is friendly to you if you recognize and realize its existence; it is ready to serve you, and to serve you well, provided that you call upon it properly and furnish it with the proper channels through which to flow in its efforts to manifest itself. This is the great truth back of the special lesson of Faith-Cure!

The Mighty Subconscious Mind

The Subconscious—that great field or plane of mental activity—is the seat of far greater power, and the source of far deeper and broader streams of mental force, than the average person even begins to realize. In that field, or on that plane, are performed over seventy-five percent of man's mental activities.

Our mental world is far more extensive than we usually conceive it to be. It has great comparatively unsounded depths, and equally grand comparatively unscaled heights. The explored and charted areas of our conscious mentality are incidental and subordinate to those broad areas of which even the brightest minds of our race have merely explored the borderland; the expanded uncharted interior of the strange country still awaiting the exploring expeditions of the future. Our position in relation to this great *Terra Incognita* of the mind is similar to that of the ancient civilized world toward the earth as a whole. We are as yet awaiting the Columbus who will explore the Western Continent of the mind, and the Livingstones and Stanleys who will furnish us with maps of the mental Darkest Africa.

Yet, even the comparatively small explored areas of the Subconscious have revealed to us a wonderful land—a land filled with the richest raw materials, precious metals, wonderful species of animal and plant life. And our daring investigators have discovered means of applying and using some of the wonderful things which have been discovered in even that borderland of the new mental world.

The Subconscious entertains deep-rooted convictions and beliefs concerning the general success or non-success of the individual. The person who has constantly impressed upon his subconscious mentality that he is "unlucky" and that "Fate is against me," has created a tremendous power within himself which acts as a brake or obstacle to his successful achievement. He has created an enemy within himself which serves to hold him back, and which fights against every inner effort in the direction of success. This hidden enemy hampers his full efforts and cripples his activities.

On the contrary, the person who believes that "luck is running my way," and that "things are working in my favor," not only releases all of his latent energies but also actually stimulates his full powers—along subconscious lines as well as conscious.

Many men have become so convinced of their propitious Destiny that they have overcome obstacles which would have blocked the progress of one holding the opposite conviction. In fact, most of the men who have used their failures as stepping-stones to subsequent success have felt within themselves the conviction that they would triumph in the end, and that the disappointments and temporary failures were but incidents of the games.

Men have believed in their "stars" or in the presence and power of something outside of themselves which was operating in the direction of their ultimate triumph. This has given to them an indomitable will and an unconquerable spirit. Had these same men allowed the conviction of the operation of adverse and antagonistic influences to take possession of their souls, they would have gone down in the struggle—and would have stayed down. In either case, however, the real "something" which they have believed to be an outside thing or entity, has been nothing more nor less than the influence and power of their own Subconscious—in one case pulling with them, and in the other pulling against them.

The man with his Subconscious filled with belief and Faith in his non-success, and in the inevitable failure of his efforts—the man whose Confident Expectation is that of non-success, failure and inability, and whose Expectant Attention is directed toward such an outcome and the incidents and circumstances leading up to it—is like a man in the water who is swimming against the stream. He is opposing the strong current, and his every effort is counteracted and overcome by the adverse forces of the stream. Likewise, the man whose Subconscious is saturated with the conviction of ultimate victory and final success—whose Confident Expectation is directed toward that end, and whose Expectant Attention is ever on the look-out for things tending to realize his inner beliefs—is like the swimmer who is moving in the direction of the current. Such a man not only is not really opposed by the forces of the stream, but, instead has these forces at work aiding him.

The importance of having the Faith, Confident Expectation and Expectant Attention of the Subconscious directed toward your success, achievement and successful ultimate accomplishment—and the importance of not having these mighty forces operate against yourself—may be realized when you stop to consider that in the one case you have three-quarters of your mental equipment and power operating in your favor, and in the other case you have that three-quarters operating against you. And that three-quarters, in either case, not only is working actively during your waking hours, but also "works while you sleep." To lose the assistance of that three-quarters would be a serious matter would it not? But far more serious is it to have that three-quarters actually working against you—having it on the side of the enemy! This is just what happens when the Subconscious gets into action under the influence of wrongly directed Faith, Expectant Attention and Confident Expectation.

Get busy with your Subconscious. Train it, educate it, re-educate it, direct it, incline it, teach it, suggest to it, along the lines of the Faith in Success and Power and not those of the Faith in failure and weakness. Set it to work swimming with that current. The Subconscious is much given to Faith—it lives on Faith, it acts upon Faith. Then see that you supply it with the right kind of Faith, and avoid as a pestilence that Faith which is based on fear and is grounded in failure and despair. Think carefully—and act!

How to Develop Enthusiasm for your Work

Faith is the underlying principle of that remarkable quality of the human mind which is known as Enthusiasm. It is its essence, it is its substance, it is its actuating principle. Without Faith there can be no manifestation of Enthusiasm. Without Faith there can be no expression of the activities of Enthusiasm. Without Faith there can be no exhibition of the energies of Enthusiasm. Without Faith the quality of Enthusiasm remains dormant, latent and static—Faith is needed to arouse it, to render it active, to cause it to become dynamic.

Moreover, the Faith required for the manifestation and expression of Enthusiasm must be positive Faith; Faith in the successful outcome of the undertaking; Faith exhibiting its positive phases; Faith in the attainment of that which is desirable and which is regarded as good. You can never manifest Enthusiasm toward that which you confidently expect to be a failure, nor toward that which you feel will bring undesirable results and effects. Negative Faith has no power to arouse Enthusiasm; the presence of Positive Faith is necessary to awaken this wonderful latent mental or spiritual force.

Enthusiasm is a mental or spiritual force which has always been regarded by mankind with respect—often with a respect mingled with awe. To the ancients it seemed to be a special gift of the gods, and by them it was regarded as animating the individual with almost divine attributes of power, and causing him to absorb a portion of the essence of the divine nature. Recognizing the fact that men under the influence of Enthusiasm often accomplish almost superhuman tasks, the ancients came to believe that this added power and capacity arose from the superimposition of power from planes of being above that of humanity. Hence, they employed terms to define it which clearly indicated their belief in its transcendent nature.

The term "Enthusiasm," is directly derived from the ancient Greek term meaning, "to be inspired by the gods." The two compositive elements of the original term are, respectively, a term denoting "inspiration," and one denoting "the gods" or "divinity," the two terms in combination meaning literally "inspired by the gods."

You have found that when you become quite intensely interested in a subject, object, study, pursuit, or cause, so that your Enthusiasm is thoroughly aroused, then there comes to you a highly increased and greatly intensified degree and amount of mental energy and power. At such times your mind seems to work with lightning-like rapidity, and with a wonderful sense of ease and efficiency. Your mental powers seem to be quadrupled. Your mental machinery seems to have some miraculous oil poured into the proper place, thus removing all friction and allowing every part of the mechanism to move smoothly and easily and with wonderful speed. At such times you feel, indeed, actually "inspired." You feel that a new world of attainment would be opened to you if you could make this mental condition a permanent one.

Looking around you in your world of practical everyday work and effort, you will see why businessmen and other men of affairs regard as an important factor of successful work that mental quality known as "enthusiastic interest" on the part of the persons performing that work. This "enthusiastic interest" in the work or task is found to call forth all the mental and physical powers of the worker. He not only puts into his task every ounce of his ordinary capacity, but he also draws upon that hidden reserve force of his Subconscious mentality and adds that to his ordinary full energy. When he approaches the fatigue limit his "enthusiastic interest" carries him on, and before long he has "caught his second wind" and obtained his fresh start.

Ask any successful sales-manager for a list of the essential characteristics of the successful salesman, and on that list you will find this capacity for or habit of "enthusiastic interest" occupying a prominent place. This, not only because of its highly important effect upon the work of the salesman himself, but also because "Enthusiasm is contagious," and the lively, quickened interest of the salesman tends to communicate itself to the subconscious mentality of his customer.

In the same way the Enthusiasm of the public speaker, orator, advocate or statesman energizes and quickens his entire intellectual and emotional nature, thus causing him to do his best, likewise communicating it to his audience by means of "mental contagion," The man with "his soul afire" tends to fire the souls and hearts of those around him. The spirit of the enthusiastic leader, foreman, or "boss" is "caught" by those under him.

Enthusiasm is clearly a manifestation of the emotional phase of man's mentality, and it appeals directly and immediately to the emotional nature of others. Likewise, it is clearly a product of the subconscious mentality, and accordingly it appeals directly and immediately to the subconscious mentality of others. Its effect is characteristically animating, energizing, inspiring, "quickening." It not only stirs the feelings and sets fire to the spiritual nature but it also stimulates and vivifies the intellectual faculties. The "live wires" in the world of men are those individuals who possess the quality of "enthusiastic interest" highly developed and habitually manifested when the occasion calls for it. Overdone, it defeats its object—the Golden Mean must be observed; but lacking it, the man is what is known in the idiom of practical men as a "dead one."

The man of true Enthusiasim is characterized by his abiding Faith in his proposition or subject; by his lively interest in it; by his earnestness in presenting it and working toward its accomplishment; by his untiring, indefatigable efforts on its behalf. Faith, however, is the foundation upon which all the rest is built; lacking Faith, the structure of Enthusiasm falls like a house of cards.

The more Faith a man has in that which he is doing, toward which he is working, or that which he is presenting to others, the greater will be the manifestation of his own powers and capacity. The more efficient his performance of the work, the greater will be his ability to influence others and to cause them to see things in the light of his own belief and interest. Faith arouses and sustains Enthusiasm; lack of Faith deadens and inhibits it; Unfaith and positive disbelief kill it. It is clear that the first step toward the cultivation and development of Enthusiasm is that of the creation of Faith in the subject or object toward which you wish to manifest and express Enthusiasm.

If you have no Faith in the subject or object of your activities, then you will never be able to manifest Enthusiasm concerning that subject or object.

Life without Faith and Enthusiasm is a living death and persons living that life are mere walking corpses. If you would be a "live wire" instead of a "dead one," you must begin to arouse and develop Enthusiasm in your heart and soul. You must cultivate that keen and quickened Interest, and that lively and earnest Faith in what you are doing, and in the things to which you are giving your time and work. You must mentally "breathe in" and inspire that Spirit of Life which men for many centuries have called "Enthusiasm" and which is the twin-sister of Inspiration. Then will you know the exhilaration of that "enkindled and kindling fervor of soul"—that "ardent and lively zeal"—the mark of true Enthusiasm.

The Flame of Desire Essential to Faith

Desire is the second factor of Mental Power. You must not only "know definitely exactly what you want," and manifest it by means of Idealization; you must also "want it hard enough," and manifest it in Insistent Desire. Desire is the flame and fire which create the steam of Will. The Will never goes out into effective action except when drawn forth by active and sufficiently strong Desire. Desire furnishes the "motive" for Will; Will never becomes active in absence of a "motive". When we speak of a man having a — "strong will" — we often really mean that he has strong desire—Desire strong enough to cause him to exert every ounce of power and energy in him toward the attainment or accomplishment of the object of Desire.

Desire exerts a tremendous influence upon all of the mental

faculties, causing them to put forth their full energies and powers and to perform their work efficiently. It stimulates the intellect, inspires the emotions and quickens the imagination. Without the urge of Desire there would be little mental work performed. The keynote of Desire is "I Want" and to gratify and satisfy that "want" the mind puts forth its best energies. Without Desire you would do little thinking, for there would be no motive for such action. Without Desire you would perform no actions, for there would be no moving-reason for such. Desire is ever the "mover to action"—mental as well as physical.

Moreover, the degree and intensity of your work, mental or physical, is determined by the degree of Desire manifested in you concerning the object or end of such work. The more you want a thing, the harder you will work for it, and the easier will such work seem to you to be. The task performed under the influence and incentive of strong Desire will seem much easier than would be the same task performed without such influence and incentive. Infinitely harder would the same task appear if its end and object were contrary to your Desire. No argument is needed to establish these facts—they are matters of common knowledge and are proven by the experience of everyday life.

The degree of force, energy, will, determination, persistence and continuous application manifested by an individual in his aspirations, ambitions, aims, performances, actions, and work, is determined primarily by the degree of his Desire for the attainment of these objects—his degree of "want" and "want to" concerning that object. So true is this principle that some who have studied its effects have announced the aphorism: "You can have or be anything you want—if you only want it hard enough."

Without Faith it is practically impossible for you to manifest strong, ardent, insistent Desire. If you are filled with doubt, distrust, or disbelief in a thing, or concerning the successful accomplishment or attainment of anything, you will not be able to arouse the proper degree of desire for that thing or for its accomplishment and attainment. Lack of Faith or better yet, positive disbelief, tends to paralyze the Desire Power; it acts as a brake or as a damper upon its power.

You create environment, conditions, circumstances, events, assistance and means to ends, by Mental Power operating along the lines of the Law of Mental Attraction. Mental Attraction, like all forms or phases of Mental Power, is the transformation of the subjective Ideal into objective Reality—thought taking form in action; the mental form taking on objective materiality and substance. The ideal is represented by the clear, strong, definite, mental picture or ideal form manifested in Idealization. Desire furnishes the flame and heat which generate the steam of Will needed in the creative process; but the Idealization is impaired and weakened, the Desire dies away and the Will loses its determination, unless Faith be there to create the Confident Expectation. The less the Faith and Confident Expectation, or the greater the doubt, disbelief, distrust, and lack of confidence, the weaker is the Idealization, Desire, and the Will Power manifested.

Without Faith there can be no Confident Expectation; without Faith, the Fires of Desire die away; without Faith, the Steam of Will ceases to be generated; and thus Attainment becomes impossible. Whenever you think of the Law of Mental Attraction, think of Faith—for Faith is its very soul—its inspiration.

Believe in Yourself

Among the many characteristics and qualities which make for success of the individual there is none more fundamental, essential and basic than that of Self Confidence and Self Reliance—both of these terms being but expressions of the idea of Faith in Oneself. The man who has Faith in himself not only brings under his control and direction those wonderful powers of his subconscious mentality, and the full power of his conscious mental faculties and instruments, but also tends to inspire a similar feeling in the minds and hearts of those other individuals with whom he comes in contact in the course of his pursuit of the objects of his endeavors. An intuitive perception and realization of one's own powers and energies, capacity, and efficiency, possibilities and capabilities, is an essential attribute of the individual who is destined to success.

A study of the world of men will disclose the fact that those men who eventually succeed, who "arrive" ultimately, who "do things," are marked by this deep intuitive Faith in themselves, and by their Confident Expectation of Ultimate success. These men rise superior to the incidents of temporary defeat; they use these failures as stepping-stones to ultimate victory. They are living expressions of Henley's *Invictus*—they, indeed, are the Masters of their Fate, the Captains of their Souls! Such men are never Really defeated; like rubber balls, they have that "bounce" which causes them to rise triumphantly after each fall—the harder they are "thrown down," the higher do they rise on the rebound. Such men are always possible—nay, probable and certain—victors, so long as they maintain this intuitive Faith in self or Self Confidence; it is only when this is lost that they are really defeated or destroyed.

The failures in life are discovered usually to be either (1) those who have never manifested this Faith in Self, or Self Confidence; or else (2) those who have permitted themselves to lose the same under the "Bludgeonings of Chance."

Those who have never felt the thrill of Faith in Self, or of Self Confidence, are soon labeled by their fellows as lacking the elements of successful achievement—the world soon "gets their number" and places them where they belong. Their lack of Self Faith and Self Confidence is felt by those with whom they come in contact; the world lacks Faith in them and has no Confident Expectation of their success.

The study of the life-story of the successful men in all walks of life will illustrate this principle to you so forcibly that, having perceived it, you will never again doubt its absolute truth. In practically every case you will find that these successful men have been knocked down, and bowled out, many times in the early days of their careers—often even later on in life. But the knock-out, though perhaps dazing them for a short time, never robbed them of their gameness, their will-to-succeed. They always arose to their feet before they were counted out and firmly, but resolutely, faced Fate. Though their "heads were bloody, they were unbowed," as Henley triumphantly chants. Fate cannot defeat such a spirit; in time, Destiny recognizes the fact that "here is a man"—and being feminine, she falls in love with him and bestows her favors upon him.

When you have found your Real Self—That "Something" within this "I AM I"—then you have found that Inner and Real Self which has constituted the subject and object of that Faith and Confident Expectation which has inspired, animated, enthused, and sustained the thousands of men who have reached the Heights of Attainment by the Path of Definite Ideals, Insistent Desire, Confident Expectation, Persistent Determination, and Balanced Compensation. It is this Intuitive perception and consciousness of the Real Self which has caused men to live out the ideal of *Invictus* in the spirit of that glorious poem of Henley. Nothing but this inner realization would have been sufficient to fill the soul of man with this indomitable spirit and unconquerable will.

Invictus

By W.E. Henley

Out of the night that covers me,
   Black as the pit from pole to pole,
I thank whatever gods there be
   For my unconquerable soul.

In the fell clutch of circumstance
   I have not winced or cried aloud;
Under the bludgeonings of chance
   My head is bloody but unbowed.

Beyond this vale of doubt and fear
   Looms but the terror of the Shade
And, yet, the passing of the years
   Finds, and shall find me, unafraid.

It matters not how straight the gate,
   How charged with punishments the scroll
I am the Master of my Fate,
   I am the Captain of my Soul.

The wise teachers of our race have for centuries taught that this Faith in the Real Self, in the "I AM I," will enable the individual to convert into the instruments of his success even those circumstances which apparently are destined to defeat his purposes; and to transmute into beneficent agencies even those inimical forces which beset him on all sides. They have discovered, and passed on to their followers, the knowledge that such a Faith is a spiritual Power, a living force, which when trusted and rightly employed will annihilate the opposition of outward circumstances, or else convert them into workers for good.

Your Real Self is a ray from the great Sun of Spirit—a spark from the great Flame of Spirit—a focal point of expression of that infinite SELF OF SPIRIT.

The earnest Faith in your Real Self and your Confident Expectation concerning its manifestation and expression in your work, your endeavors, your plans, your purposes all serve to bring into action your full mental and spiritual power, energy, and force. It quickens your intellectual powers; it employs your emotional powers efficiently and under full control; it sets into effective action your creative imagination; it places the powers of your will under your mastery and direction. It draws upon your subconscious faculties for inspiration and for intuitive reports; it opens up your mind to the inflow of the illumination of your superconscious spiritual faculties and powers. It sets into operation the Law of Mental Attraction under your direct control and direction, whereby you attract to yourself, or you to them, the circumstances, events, conditions, things and persons needed for the manifestation of your ideals in objective reality. More than this, it brushes away the obstacles which have clogged the channels of your contact with and communication with SPIRIT itself—that great source of Infinite Power which in this instruction is called POWER.

Discover your Real Self, your "I AM I"—then manifest your full faith in and toward it; and cultivate your full Confident Expectation concerning the beneficent results of that Faith.

CHAPTER 13

The Infinite Loves You

Become an Invincible Soul

The Message of Truth: You, yourself, in your essential and real being, nature, and entity, are Spirit, and naught but Spirit; in and of SPIRIT; spiritual and not material. Materiality is your instrument of expression, the stuff created for your use and service in your expression of Life, Consciousness and Will. It is your servant, not your master. You condition, limit and form it, not it you. When you recognize and realize your real nature, you will awaken to a perception of its real relation to you and you to it. The report of SPIRIT received by its accredited individual centers of expression, and by them transmitted to you is this:

In the degree that you perceive, recognize, and realize your essential identity with ME, the Supreme Presence-Power, the Ultimate Reality, in that degree will you be able to manifest My Spiritual Power. I AM over and above you, under and beneath you, I surround you on all sides. I AM also within you, and you are in ME; from ME you proceed and in Me you live and move and have your being. Seek Me by looking within your own being, and likewise by looking for Me in Infinity, for I abide both within and without your being. If, and when, you will adopt and live according to this Truth, then will you be able to manifest that Truth—in and by it alone are Freedom and Invincibility, and true and real Presence and Power, to be found, perceived, realized and manifested.

Francis Thompson, in his mystic poem entitled *The Hound of Heaven* describes with a tremendous power, and often with an almost terrible intensity, the hunt of Reality for the unwilling individual Self. He pictures Divinity as engaged in a remorseless, tireless quest—a seeking, following, tracking-down of the unwilling individual soul. He pictures the separated spirit as a "strange, piteous, futile thing" that flees from the pursuing Divinity "down the nights and down the days." The individual spirit, not knowing its relation to and identity with the pursuing Absolute, rushes in a panic of terror away from its own good. But, as Emerson says, "You cannot escape your own Good', and so the fleeing soul is captured at last. By Faith in the Infinite, however, the individual soul overcomes its terror of the Infinite and recognizing it as its Supreme Good, turns and moves toward it. Such is the mystic conception of the effect and action of Faith in the Infinite.

The complete poem, *The Hound of Heaven,* covers five pages. Presented here is a condensed version of these beautiful and gripping lines by Francis Thompson. If you are not reciprocating the Great Love of God, you may have a feeling of remorse and resolve to do better. If this feeling does not come to you—you must have a heart of stone.

THE HOUND OF HEAVEN
By Francis Thompson

I fled Him, down the nights and down the days;
I fled Him, down the arches of the years;
I fled Him, down the labyrinthine ways
Of my own mind; and in the mist of tears

I hid from Him, and under running laughter.
Up vistaed hopes I sped;
And shot, precipitated,
Adown Titanic glooms of chasmed fears,
From those strong Feet that followed, followed after.
But with unhurrying chase,
And unperturbed pace,
Deliberate speed, majestic instancy,
They beat—and a Voice beat
More instant that the Feet—
"All things betray thee, who betrayest Me."

I said to Dawn: Be sudden—to Eve: Be soon;
With thy young skiey blossoms heap me over
From this tremendous Lover—

Still with unhurrying chase,
And unperturbed pace,
Deliberate speed, majestic instancy,
Came on the following Feet,
And a voice above their beat—
"Naught shelters thee, who wilt not shelter Me."

In the rush lustihead of my young powers,
I shook the pillaring hours
And pulled my life upon me; grimed with smears,
I stand amid the dust of the mounded years—
My mangled youth lies dead beneath the heap.
My days have crackled and gone up in smoke.
Designer Infinite!—
Ah! must Thou char the wood ere Thou canst limn with it?
My freshness spent its wavering shower in the dust;
And now my heart is as a broken fount.

Now of that long pursuit
Comes on at hand the bruit;
That Voice is round me like a bursting sea:

How little worthy of any love thou are!
Whom wilt thou find to love ignoble thee
Save Me, save only Me?
All which I took from thee I did but take,
Not for thy harms,
But just that thou mightest seek it in My arms.
All which thy child's mistake
Francis as lost, I have stored for thee at home:
Rise, clasp My hand, and come!"

Halts by me that footfall:
Is my gloom, after all,
Shade of His hand, outstretched caressingly?
"Ah, fondest, blindest, weakest,
I am He Whom thou seekest!
Thou dravest love from thee, who dravest Me."

Prentice Mulford said: "A Supreme Power and Wisdom governs the Universe. The Supreme Mind is measureless and pervades all space. The Supreme Wisdom, Power, and Intelligence are in everything that exists, from the atom to the planet. The Supreme Power has us in its charge, as it has the suns and endless system of worlds in space. As we grow to recognize this sublime and exhaustless Wisdom, we shall learn more and more to demand that Wisdom, draw it to ourselves, and thereby be ever making ourselves newer and newer. This means ever perfecting health, greater power to enjoy all that exists, gradual transition into a higher state of being, and the development of powers which we do not now realize as belonging to us. Let us then daily demand Faith, for Faith is power to believe and power to see that all things are parts of the Infinite Spirit of God, that all things have Good or God in them, and that all things, when recognized by us as parts of God, must work for our good."

To sum up:

I. There exists a greater underlying Something that is beneficent and well-disposed toward you, and which tries to help, aid, and assist you whenever and wherever It can do so.

2. Faith and Confident Expectation regarding the beneficent power of that Something tends to open the channels of Its influence in your life; while doubt, unbelief, distrust, and fear, tend to dam up the channel of its influence in your life, and rob it of the power to help you.

3. To a great extent, at least, you determine your own life by the character of your thought. By the nature and character of your thoughts you furnish the pattern or mold which determines or modifies the efforts of the Something to aid you, either in the direction of producing desirable results or else in bringing about undesirable results by reason of your damming up the sources of your Good.

In the *Book of Psalms* in our own Scriptures, are to be found several of the great masterpieces of the esoteric teachings concerning Faith Power—in them is given the essence of the Secret Doctrine concerning Faith in the Infinite. Chief among these are the Twenty-Third Psalm, and the Ninety-first Psalm, respectively. So important are these two great esoteric poems—so filled with practical helpful information are they—that we deem it advisable to reproduce them here that you may avail yourself of their virtue and power at this particular stage of this instruction.

The Psalm of Faith
Psalm 23

The Lord is my shepherd; I shall not want. He maketh me to lie down in the green pastures; he leadeth me beside the still waters. He restoreth my soul; he leadeth me in the paths of righteousness for His name's sake. Yea, though I walk through the valley of the shadow of death, I will fear no evil; for thou art with me; Thy rod and Thy staff they comfort me. Thou preparest a table before me in the presence of mine enemies; Thou anointest my head with oil; my cup runneth over. Surely goodness and mercy will follow me all the days of my life, and I will dwell in the house of the Lord forever.

The Psalm of Security
Psalm 91

He that dwelleth in the secret place of the most High shall abide under the shadow of the Almighty. I will say of the Lord, He is my refuge and my fortress: my God in Him will I trust. Surely He shall deliver thee from the snare of the fowler, and from the noisome pestilence. He shall cover thee with His feathers, and under His wings shalt thou trust: His truth shall be thy shield and buckler. Thou shalt not be afraid for the terror by night; nor for the arrow that flieth by day; nor for the pestilence that walketh in darkness; nor for the destruction that wasteth at noonday. A thousand shall fall at thy side, and ten thousand at thy right hand; but it shall not come nigh thee. Only with thine eyes shalt thou behold and see the reward of the wicked. Because thou hast made the Lord, which is my refuge, even the most high, thy habitation. There shall no evil befall thee, neither shall any plague come nigh thy dwelling. For He shall give His angels charge over thee, to keep thee in all thy ways. They shall bear thee up in their hands, lest thou dash thy foot against a stone. Thou shalt tread upon the lion and the adder: the young lion and the dragon shalt thou trample under feet. Because he hath set his love upon Me, and therefore will I deliver him; I will set him on high, because he hath known My name. He shall call upon Me, and I will answer him and honor him. With long life will I satisfy him, and show him my salvation.

Lead Kindly Light

The teachers and students of the Inner teachings, the Ancient Wisdom, the Secret Doctrine, are also aware of the esoteric spiritual significance of the lines of the well-known hymn "Lead Kindly Light,' written by Newman in a period of spiritual stress. Few who read or sing this hymn realize its esoteric spirit and meaning—none but "those who know" perceive and recognize that which dwells under the surface of those wonderful words and lines.

The Chant of Faith Power
(Lead Kindly Light)

Lead kindly Light, amid the encircling gloom; Lead Thou me on.
The night is dark, and I am far from home; Lead Thou me on.

Keep Thou my feet; I do not ask to see the distant scene; one step enough for me,
Lead Thou me on.

*****

Carry with you ever the spirit of the ancient aphorism of the wise sage, which is; "Faith is the White Magic of Power."

PART V

SECRET NUMBER FIVE CREATIVE IMAGINATION BRINGS FINANCIAL REWARDS

CHAPTER 14

The Master Mind

The connecting link between the human and the Divine, between the formed universe and formless energy, lies in your imagining faculty. It is, of all things human, the most God-like. It is our part of Divinity. Through it we share in the creative power of the Heaven Mind. Through it we can turn the most drab existence into a thing of life and beauty. It is the means by which we avail ourselves of all the good which God is constantly offering to us in such profusion. It is the means by which we can reach any goal, win any prize.

Do you want happiness? Do you want success? Do you want position, power, riches? *Image* them! How did God first make man? "In his image created He him." He "*imaged*" man in His Mind.

And that is the way everything has been made since time began. It was first imaged in Mind. That is the way everything you want must start—with a mental image.

So use your imagination! Picture in it your Heart's Desire. Imagine it! Day-dream it so vividly, so clearly, that you will actually BELIEVE you HAVE it. In the moment that you carry this conviction to your subconscious mind, in that moment, your dream will become a reality. It may be a while before you realize it, but the important part is done. You have created the model. You can safely leave it to your subconscious mind to do the rest.

Every man wants to get out of the rut, to grow, to develop into something better. Here is the open road—open to you whether you have schooling, training, position, wealth, or not. Remember this: Your subconscious mind knew more from the time you were a baby than is in all the books in all the colleges and libraries of the world.

So don't let lack of training, lack of education, hold you back. Your mind can meet every need—and will do so if you give it the chance. The Apostles were almost all poor men, uneducated men, yet they did a work that is unequalled in historical annals. Joan of Arc was a poor peasant girl, unable to read or write—yet she saved France! The pages of history are dotted with poor men, uneducated men, who thought great thoughts, who used their imaginations to master circumstances and became rulers of men. Most great dynasties started with some poor, obscure man. Napoleon came of a poor, humble family. He got his appointment to the Military Academy only through very hard work and the pulling of many political strings. Even as a Captain of Artillery he was so poverty-stricken that he was unable to buy his equipment when offered an appointment to India. Business today is full of successful men who have scarcely the rudiments of ordinary education. It was only after he had made his millions that Andrew Carnegie hired a tutor to give him the essentials of an education.

So it isn't training and it isn't education that make you successful. These help, but the thing that really counts is that gift of the Gods—Creative Imagination!

You have that gift. Use it! Make every thought, every fact, that comes into your mind pay you a profit. Make it work and produce for you. Think of things—not as they are but as they MIGHT be. Make them real, live and interesting. Don't merely dream—but CREATE! Then use your imagination to make that CREATION an advantage to mankind—and, incidentally, yourself.

Get *above* your circumstances, your surroundings. Get above your troubles—no matter what they may be. Remember, the Law is that Power flows only from a higher to the lower potential. Use your imaging faculty to put yourself and keep yourself on a higher plane, *above* trouble and adversity. "Circumstances?" exclaimed Napoleon when at the height of his power. "I make circumstances!" And that is what you too must do.

"As the rain cometh down and the snow from heaven, and returneth not thither, but watereth the earth, and maketh it bring forth and bud, and giveth seed to the sower and bread to the eater; so shall my word be that goeth forth out of my mouth: it shall not return unto me void, but it shall accomplish that which I please, and it shall prosper in the thing whereto I sent it."—Isaiah.

Do You Have Money Worries?

Say to yourself and believe—"There is no lack in the Kingdom of Heaven." Then make a Treasure Map as suggested in The Magic Word, showing all the riches and supply you may long for. All this must start, you know, with an idea, a mental image.

"All that the Father hath is mine," said Jesus. And all that the Father hath is yours, too, for all He has to begin with is IDEAS, *mental images,* and you can create these as easily as He. Make your mental image of the thing you want, picture it on paper as much as you can to make it more real and vivid to you, then have FAITH!

Faith starts you DOING the things you need to do to bring your ideas into realities. Faith brings to you the opportunities and people and things you need to make your images realities.

All that the Father hath is yours—all the ideas, all the mental images, all the power to make them manifest.

Do you want riches? They are yours for the making. The ancient Alchemists who spent their lives trying to turn base metals into gold were trying and working from the bottom up. Power does not flow that way. You must start ABOVE the thing you want, working from the higher potential to the lower.

Riches, health, happiness, power, all are yours if you work for them in the right way—if you make them yours in Heaven first and then use your faith and your abilities to make them manifest here on earth.

"Thy will be done on earth as it is in Heaven," God's will for you is for riches, for happiness, for health. If you haven't these now, deny the lack. Deny the wrong conditions. Say to yourself: "There is no lack in Heaven. There is no disease there, no weakness, no trouble or conflict, no worries of any kind. There is only love and plenty."

Then take your beliefs out of the images around you, which are merely the result of your previous belief objectified and put all your faith, all your hopes, all your strength and abilities into making your new Heaven images come true.

You CAN do it. But you must believe so firmly that you can actually ACT the part. As the Prophet Noel told us, "Let the weak say—I am strong!" And the poor say, I am rich. And the sick say, I am well. And the miserable say, I am happy. Say it, repeat it until you believe it—then ACT *the part!*

In one of Edgar Rice Burroughs' Martian stories, he told of a great walled city that had outlived its usefulness and was now peopled by only a few old men. But every time an invading army appeared before this city, it was driven away by hordes of archers that manned every foot of the walls and even swarmed out through the gates to meet the enemy in the open. When the enemy fled, the archers disappeared!

Where did the archers come from? According to the story, they came entirely from the minds of the old men who still lived in that almost-deserted city. These old men remembered the huge armies that had garrisoned the town in its heyday. They remembered former invasions when their soldiers had repelled every assault and then dashed out through the gates and swept the invaders into the sea. And by gathering together and visualizing those mighty armies of theirs as once more existent, they brought them into being so that their enemies too could see them and be driven into flight by them.

Does that sound far-fetched? Then remember that you have only to go back to the Bible to find a parallel. Just turn to II Kings, Chapter 6, and you will read how the King of Syria sent his horses and chariots and a great host to capture the Prophet Elisha, and how in the night they compassed him around.

"And when the servant of the man of God was risen early,

and gone forth, behold, an host compassed the city both with horses and chariots. And his servant said unto him, Alas, my master, what shall we do?

"And he answered, Fear not! For they that be with us are more than they that be with them.

"And Elisha prayed, and said, Lord, I pray thee, open his eyes, that he may see. And the Lord opened the eyes of the young man; and he saw: and behold, the mountain was full of horses and chariots of fire around Elisha."

Again, when the High Priest sent his soldiers to seize Jesus, and Peter struck one of the soldiers with his sword, Jesus rebuked him, saying: 'Thinkest thou that I cannot now pray to My Father, and He shall presently give Me more than twelve legions of angels?"

CHAPTER 15

My Precious Gift From Conan Doyle

by Selwyn James

"To the world, Sir Arthur Conan Doyle was the creator of Sherlock Holmes, master detective and brilliant, razor-sharp brain. To me, when I was seven, he was the gentle-hearted man who led me through his garden one summer twilight and taught me to believe in Imagination. I soared with him into a magical world where fantasy is real, where anything is possible. I saw pixies and fairies. With my kindly teacher at my side, I discovered the limitless quality of the human imagination. For what is true imagination but a belief in the impossible—and what is that but a launching site for creativity? Somerset Maugham, who made millions from his writings, said, "Man consists of body, mind and imagination. His body is faulty, his mind untrustworthy, but his imagination has made him remarkable.

"The world Sir Arthur showed me, was visited by the great composers, poets, and painters, who return to us with their uniquely beautiful patterns of sound and sight. Leonardo da Vinci visited that world, for he saw the vision of man flying like a bird in the sky. It must have been visited by the mad scientists of the past who knew the moon was within our grasp centuries before its conquest became a matter of exotic fuels and heat-resistant alloys, and by all the great inventors and creators of every age.

"Is this wonderful world of the imagination the private preserve of children and geniuses? It need not be. But many of us are so burdened by the mechanics of plain living that we never pause to hear angels singing to a Brahms symphony or see cherubs sliding down a rainbow.

"A businessman I know hikes off alone deep into the Maine woods for a week every summer. He neither hunts nor fishes. He arms himself only with knapsack and pup tent. What on earth do you find to do there? To me he confessed, 'I eat and drink with the Seven Dwarfs. I walk with Hansel and Gretel. And I come out of that wonderful place feeling ten years younger and strong enough in spirit to accomplish anything.' "

CHAPTER 16

Your Creative Power*

by Alex Osborn

How to use IMAGINATION to get ahead on your job, build a happier marriage, find success in business and public affairs, and turn your daydreams into reality.

"Since my newspaper days, my work has been in advertising: and that means ideas. Starting from scratch, I became the head of an organization of about 1000 people, many of whom were blessed with more inborn talent than I. Whatever creative success I gained was due to my belief that creative power can be stepped up by *effort,* and that there are ways in which we can guide our creative thinking.

"It is only recently that the *value* of imagination has been fully recognized in America. The Chrysler Corporation hailed imagination as 'the directing force' which 'lights tomorrow's roads, explores today for clues to tomorrow, hunts better ways for you to live and travel.' The Aluminum Company coined a new word, 'Imagineering,' which means that 'you let your imagination soar and then engineer it down to earth. You think about the things you used to make, and decide that if you don't find out some way to make them immeasurably better, you may never be asked by your customers to make them again.'

"Competition has forced American business to recognize the importance of conscious creative effort. Now the heart and center of every successful manufacturing company is its creative research. The new research not only takes things apart in order to find out what caused what and why, but adds a definite and conscious creative function aimed to discover *new* facts, arrive at *new* combinations, find *new* applications.

"How true it is that, in our own private lives, Micawber-like we wait for things to turn out well, and meanwhile fail to make conscious use of our imagination—despite the fact that, in most cases, with enough creative effort, each of us could find the ideas that would smooth our rocky roads!

*Published by Dell Pub. Co. Inc., New York, N.Y. Copyright 1948 by Alex F. Osborn.

"Creative effort pays in more coins than cash." That little idea of yours will bring in $5,000,000 a year.' Sanford Cluett laughed at such a forecast when he first found a way to stop cloth from shrinking. But as it turned out, the Cluett Peabody Company actually did make as much as five million dollars a year from royalties on Mr. Cluett's *Sanforizing* process. Some people sneered at Henry Ford as having had only *one* idea in all his life. Yes, but that was a big idea—how to make cars cheap enough for the millions. From that idea he gained more riches than any man, not excepting Midas. There are still opportunities for inventive effort. Raymond Yates has recently listed 2,100 inventions urgently needed.

"Every day, in store, office, and factory, millions of men resign themselves to sterile drudgery by thoughtlessly ignoring, or blandly defaulting, the marvelous faculty of imagination. The most valuable motto these should have is 'Use your imagination.'

"In the store and on the road, the best selling is *helpful* selling; and this kind calls for *ideas.* A salesman has to use his imagination, deliberately and consciously, to think up just what little thing he can do to be helpful to each customer. Every case calls for a different strategy. Resourcefulness can turn a peddler into a star.

"During the last war," said John Collyer of B. F. Goodrich, "suggestions came in from our employees at the rate of 3000 per year. And we found that about one third of these were good enough to deserve cash awards."

"Clarence Budington Kelland has turned out more fiction than even Alexandre Dumas. Even when on vacation, Kelland would arise from an early breakfast, chain himself to his typewriter and force his creative wheels to spin. He made his success by living up to the law laid down by Elbert Hubbard; 'the way to write is to write and write and write and write.' "

CHAPTER 17

Are You Creative?*

Following a few simple rules can help turn the average executive into a true "idea man."

"Imagination," Albert Einstein once said, "is more important than knowledge. For knowledge is limited, whereas imagination embraces the whole world, stimulating progress, giving birth to evolution." What is true of science holds equally well for American business. One need only recall Samuel Colt's idea of mass-producing revolvers or Henry Ford's five-dollar day to see the power that imagination has had.

And never has business been more aware than today of the hard profits to be gained from the soaring world of the mind. In proof, one need only look at the welter of suggestion plans that bombard even the plant janitor, or the cost-reduction committees and work-simplification groups that have proliferated through American industry. With competition so fiercely intense, every individual corporation desperately needs new ideas—ideas in marketing, production, transportation and every other phase of business.

But is the corporation getting those ideas? More to the point, is it getting them from the executives it hires not only to manage its affairs but to point them in new directions?

Psychologist Eugene Raudsepp, well-known writer and authority on creativity, does not think that it is. "A mere handful of executives in America," says Raudsepp bluntly, "are exercising their ideaing powers. The reservoirs are full, but they are not being tapped."

"There are," say Raudsepp and other authorities, "reasons why those reservoirs are not being tapped." And the executive cannot hope to open up his own imagination until he understands what they are. The first: the very simple fact that many executives do not realize that they may well be "idea men." In other words, they feel that only persons in, say, the

*Dun's Review and Modern Industry, Published by Dun & Bradstreet Publishing Corp., 99 Church Street, New York City, May 1962.

arts are truly creative and that the ability to generate ideas does not lie in themselves.

No less an authority than Professor J. P. Guilford, former president of the American Psychological Association, has scotched this notion that creativity is the exclusive preserve of the writer and the poet. "Creative acts," he says, "can be expected of almost *all* individuals. Those persons who are recognized as creative merely have more of what all of us have."

How to tap the reservoir of creativity in the mind

The executive can easily do that, but to do it he must first understand what that nebulous thing called creativity really is.

New York University's Dr. Morris I. Stein calls it: "That process which results in a novel work that is accepted as useful or satisfying by a group at some period in time." Professor John E. Arnold of Stanford University; "Creativity is that mental process by which man combines and recombines his past experience, possibly with some distortion, in such a way that he arrives at new patterns, new configurations and new arrangements that better solve some needs of mankind."

Creativity can be broken into three elements, on which most experts agree. The three: sensitivity to the existence of problems; fluency in offering solutions; flexibility in solving problems (which is also known as "imagination").

The way to become creative, then, is to stimulate these three basic elements.

But how is that done? Look first at problem sensitivity. Its meaning can best be summed up in the old cliche' of the company suggestion programs: "What can I do to improve my job?" Characteristically, the creative executive thinks along such lines, day in and day out. For him the question has become so ingrained that he habitually seeks out new programs and new fields to conquer, often without even being aware of it.

The executive who does not have that built-in sensitivity,

however, can acquire it by making himself dissatisfied. First of all, he should plot out what would make his job ideal. Then he sorts out the factors that are preventing it from being that and devises ways to overcome them. This can be done by studying each element and zeroing in on the fundamentals to separate cause from effect. As an aid, he can call on the brain's primitive faculty for picture-making to conjure up an image of the elements. Visualizing the bottlenecks in work flow, for example, helps to define the problem areas.

Developing this sensitivity is no easy task. Usually it requires considerable time and effort since it involves a conscious effort to develop new habits of expression and adjustment. Fortunately, though, concentrated effort will pay off in the long run, for those dormant faculties in the mind will ultimately rise to the challenge and begin generating their own challenges.

How to brainstorm

Perhaps as a form of compensation, fluency in solving problems can be developed fairly easily. One way to ideate is by "brainstorming," a technique which swept U.S. corporations some five years ago. In brainstorming, which was invented by advertising man Alexander F. Osborn (the "O" in BBD&O), some eight to twelve people are assembled in a room, given a problem and told to rapid-fire their solutions. The executive can adopt this technique to his own use by simply filling his mind with a tumbling flow of ideas for the problem at hand—even fantastic ideas. Disregard the quality of the ideas, and do not criticize them until you have finished. Let the ideas build one on the other, and do not discard one merely because it overlaps another. Finally, when you have assembled a number of ideas, dissect each one for its value.

Psychologist Raudsepp offers one way to make the most of private brainstorming sessions. "Set aside a regular time and place for ideating," he says, "and stick to it. Give yourself a quota. For example, demand six ideas for a new marketing program. And specify a deadline. After a while, jack up the quota, or shorten the time span for thinking."

The executive should also ideate in his spare time. On trains, for example, or when waiting for buses or elevators. If ideating seems to come hard in the beginning, the executive might try taking a page from the psychiatrist's notebook. He uses a couch to put his patient at ease and draw him out. So the executive might well try his ideating in some favored, relaxed place such as the bathtub, den or parlor.

He must, however, adhere strictly to his time limit. After a while, ideation will occur as a reflex action, coming in anticipation of the scheduled time and will spill over afterwards. But with steady practice, the executive will be able to ideate at will, even under severe pressure.

The businessman should, however, note one vital point: mere quantity of ideas, while a virtue in itself, is useless if quality is lacking. The theory behind fluency, of course, is that at least some ideas out of a whole host of them will have merit. But meritorious ideas generally have quality because they extend beyond the conventional. And this, in turn, springs from that intellectual nimbleness known as flexibility, or imagination.

Curiosity & imagination

Perhaps the most glamorous of the creative factors, imagination is also the most vital. Happily, though, developing the imagination can be one of the most enjoyable exercises in developing the creative faculties. For its basic exercise follows one simple rule: never suppress curiosity. As most psychologists see it, there is a close relation between curiosity and imagination. And since solutions in one field are often suggested by techniques in another, curiosity about any field outside of your own should be gratified by finding out all about it.

A fantastic idea? Consider the experience of a storekeeper

from Dayton, Ohio named Jacob Ritty. While on a transatlantic voyage, Ritty kept staring with fascination at the device that recorded the propeller revolutions of the ship. Eventually, Ritty saw that the same principle could be used to register the amount of money rung up in a storekeeper's till. The result was the cash register, which even today follows Ritty's basic principles.

In stretching the mind to become more sensitive, fluent and flexible, the executive who is advanced in years might well wonder whether all the effort is worthwhile. After all, won't age wash out the gains?

Many examples prove that it will not. Benjamin Franklin, Leonardo da Vinci and Albert Einstein, for example, remained highly creative right up to the end of their lives. Indeed, octogenarian Somerset Maugham asserts that creativity grows by exercise. "Contrary to common belief," says Maugham, "it is more powerful in the mature than in the young."

The final quality

But all the creativeness in the world adds up to little if another quality is lacking: perseverance. Good ideas, spewed forth in abundance, and responsive to the most critical problems, are of no value until they are carried out. And the execution of even great ideas can call for perseverance on a heroic scale.

Thomas Edison found that out. The Wizard of Menlo Park tried over 6000 different materials in a search for the conductive filament that was the heart of his electric bulb. Though each material failed, Edison would not give up. And to a discouraged assistant he cheerily commanded: "Try everything—even Limburger cheese."

—J.J.F.

CHAPTER 18

The Builder & the Plan

IMAGINATION

Now you are asked to consider a wonderful phase of Personal Power which is latent, inherent and abiding within you—the Power of Imagination. This power is a phase of your Personal Power. Your Personal Power, in turn, is a phase of the manifestation of that POWER which is the source of All-Power, and which is expressed, manifested, and employed in all phases of Power of which you have, or can possibly have, any cognizance.

The struggle for existence is still underway. The survival of the fittest is a fact of modern human existence, as well as of the past history of the race—and of the world in general. But now, more than ever, Constructive Imagination is the great element of the struggle—the great standard of the fitness to survive, succeed and accomplish. The people, the race, the nation, and the individual possessing the greatest degree of development and application of continuous and persistent Constructive Imagination will be found to be the "fittest" to survive, all else being equal, and will prove to be the ultimate winner in the struggle for existence. If man is ever succeeded by the Superman, as some have predicted, it will be found that the Superman is possessed of superior powers of Constructive Imagination, and of a greater faculty of exercising and applying them. Such is the Law of Evolution—of Progress—of Life.

THE BUILDER AND THE PLAN

In the processes of Efficient Constructive Imagination, directed by a definite purpose and toward a determined end, you will find it advantageous to follow the general rule given below.

General Rule

I. Create a clear mental picture of the general idea representing your Definite Purpose.

II. Form a comprehensive picture of the whole field of the proposed undertaking.

III. Make a written list of all the probable factors involved in the problem or undertaking.

IV. Classify these ideas, elements and factors according to their general nature, their general uses.

V. Weigh the various factors one against the other, taking into consideration the associated and related values of each in the general idea, plan or purpose.

VI. Having reached at least a fairly satisfactory working plan, idea, invention, or solution of your problem, you should then carefully detach yourself from it; you should move from your personal point of view, and try to see it as others will see it. Try to imagine the effect it will have on the persons whom you wish to be interested in your finished product; how it will meet their requirements, satisfy their wants, arouse their desires for it.

Your own created conjunction, plan, method, design, or invention naturally will seem to you as the infant appears to its mother, as no mother is an unprejudiced critic of her own baby. You must see the thing as others will see it, in order to arrive at an intelligent idea of the actual degree of utility possessed by your invention, creation, composition, or contrivance. You must employ past experience, reason, judgment, discrimination and cool decision in this final testing process.

In the General Rule of Efficient Constructive Imagination, the first step is that of: "Creating a clear mental picture of the general idea representing your Definite Purpose, i.e., the particular end which you wish to accomplish; the particular obstacle which you wish to overcome; the particular result which you wish to obtain; the particular desire which you wish to satisfy; the particular ideal which you wish to make real; the particular idea which you wish to materialize in objective form."

Halleck says of this characteristic of the Creative Imagination:

> "The Constructive Imagination is always characterized by a definite purpose, which is never lost sight of until the image is complete. A child starts to build a house out of blocks. These are often changed and taken down many times, before the form in

which they are built is such as to fix the growing, purposive image in the child's mind. Before an architect builds a house, he must form successive images, which he alters whenever they conflict with the general plan of that special dwelling. An inventor often spends years in changing and recombining the images of parts of his machine, but he is all the while dominated by a Definite Purpose. The images must be altered until matter poured into their mold fulfills the aim of the inventor."

The Creative Ideal arises in the inventor and proceeds through him. Its life is a becoming process, and not an unchangeable fixed form. Its 'fixed' character consists of its Continuity and Definite Purpose. If we liken creative imagination to physiological generation, this Creative Ideal is the ovum awaiting fertilization in order to begin its development. The Creative Ideal is a creative image tending to become real.

Before you may expect to accomplish creative mental work successfully, you must know, at least in a general way, just what you wish to create. You must select at least the general goal toward which you desire to journey. You must not be content to sing, in the words of the familiar ballad, "I don't know where I'm going, but I'm on the way." You must sketch at least the general map of the country over which you wish to travel, and to indicate with at least a fair degree of definiteness the place at which you hope to arrive at your journey's end.

All true exercise of the Constructive Imagination is inspired by a want, a lack, an obstacle, a problem, or a "thwarted purpose"—the latter being stated by an eminent psychologist to be "the occasion for all reasoning." If your every want were satisfied; if you suffered no lack; if there were no problem requiring solution, no obstacles to be overcome, no "thwarted purposes" present in your experience; then you would never be called upon to exercise your powers of Constructive Imagination. Your want, your lack, your unsatisfied desire, your "thwarted purpose" all call into activity the creative powers of your mind.

It may not be always quite clear to you what constitutes the prime factors of your want, desire, lack, problem, or "thwarted purpose"; you may find it necessary to "boil down" the thing, evaporating the excess fluid in which this essence is dissolved. You must get to the real essential elements of the problem—get "down to brass tacks." Here, as in many other instances and cases, you will find it helpful to "think with your pencil," i.e., to express in written words the essence of the somewhat hazy general idea which is present in your mind as representing your problem or want. Unless you have practiced this plan, you can have no adequate conception of its value to you in thinking and planning.

Continue the task of analyzing and dissecting the subject until you finally reduce it to its ultimate elements of Definite Purpose. That Definite Purpose is always there, though usually hidden by a mass of comparatively non-essential ideas.

It is your work to clear away the mass of encumbering material of thought, so that you may bring into plain view the precious thing at the centre of the mass. Or, employing another figure, it is "up to you" to carve away the mass of stone which hides the figure of your ideal, just as the sculptor with his chisel releases the hidden form of his ideal creation—that ideal which is crying for release from the encumbering material.

Your Definite Purpose, once discovered, becomes your Definite Ideal—the focal point around which is built the entire structure of your creation. The Definite Ideal is like the grain of sand which exists at the centre of every pearl, and about which the pearly material has gathered. It is "the big idea" around which your Constructive Imagination builds, deposits, and accumulates its wealth of material. Your Definite Ideal represents your desire, need, want, purpose, plan, design—it is the vital germ of the entire future organism—it is the seed from which will spring the downward-pressing roots and the upward-pressing stalk. Without it there would be no creative growth. In the degree of its strength, definiteness, and clearness of form, so will be the degree of perfection and vigor in that which springs from it.

(I) *"Think with your pencil."* Write down all of the ideas concerning the general field and plan, and then compare these for the purpose of selection. Eliminate the non-essentials, cancel the duplications and contradictories, and arrange the selected items in a logical and orderly classification. In short, make a chart or diagram of the general field and plan, showing the ground to be covered, the obstacles to be overcome, the strong places, the weak points, et cetera. You will do well to bestow sufficient care and attention upon this task, for your chart will be to you what his map of the battlefield is to the commanding officer.

(2) *"Visualize your Map."* Study your map until you can easily visualize it. Learn it "by heart" so that it will become as familiar as your "A, B, C's," or your Multiplication Table of childhood days. Impress your map upon your memory, so that you can bring it at will into conscious representation or recollection.

CHAPTER 19

The Mental Laboratory

The third section of the General Rule tells you to: "*Make a written list of all of the probable factors involved in the problem or undertaking; compile a list of all of the probable elements involved in the working out of the matter; gather together all of the ideas of the things at all likely to be called into the creative process; have within easy reach the ideas of all of the materials likely to be employed in the construction of the ideal form which you wish to materialize.*

Here you proceed to supply the Constructive Imagination with the raw materials for its creative processes. You have seen that the Constructive Imagination does not, and cannot, create "something out of nothing." Instead, it creates by combination, adaptation, adjustment, transformation—always employing the material which you furnish it for the purpose. Therefore, you must supply it with the kind of mental images which are best adapted for the creation of the new forms, images or ideas which contribute to the manifestation of your Definite Purpose—your Definite Central Ideal. This material (composed of mental images) is then employed both by your conscious mentality and by your subconscious mentality, in their work of weaving or fusing the fabric or form of the necessary new images.

In the first place, you must fairly saturate yourself with the subject represented by your Definite Purpose and Definite Ideal, the achievement of which is so insistently desired, so confidently expected, and so persistently willed by you. You must learn at least the name and general character of everything connected with or related to that subject—even if remotely related to it. Because the images or ideas of these related things are precisely the "stuff" upon which your Constructive Imagination must depend for the materials which it must weave or fuse into newer and more efficient images.

But just how are you to saturate yourself with such knowledge? Just how are you going to know at least the name and general character of everything connected with or related to that particular subject?

Consider this proposition: "Mr. Blank, I want someone to prepare for me the fullest and most complete list possible of the things concerning or related to this particular subject (Here naming the subject of your Definite Purpose and Definite Ideal). I will give you a salary of double the amount you are now earning, and also pay all your expenses, while you are conducting the search and preparing the list. When you have completed the list, if it is found to meet the requirements of reasonable completeness and perfection, I will make you a present of one hundred thousand dollars. Will you undertake the task?" If some very wealthy man were to call you into his office and make you that offer, you would accept it at once, and would proceed to devise the proper means to accomplish the task without hesitancy and win the reward.

Then, what would be the first steps in your preparation of the list? Well, you would begin by reading the best textbooks covering the general subject—starting off with the descriptive articles dealing with it which you would find in the best encyclopedias. You would saturate yourself with the subject. You would consult with persons employed in occupations necessitating at least a working knowledge of the subject. You would read the trade journals circulating among those engaged in such callings—not forgetting to read the advertisements. You would carefully consider the price-lists and catalogues of houses dealing in the supplies required in those branches of work. In short, you would seek in every possible direction, and from every possible source, the names of the things concerning or related to that special subject.

You would seek every possible "association" of that subject—the subjects closely associated with it, and having some practical relation to it. You would discover these associations by asking yourself:

(1) What is this thing?
(2) Of what is it composed?
(3) What is its purpose?
(4) For whose use is it intended?
(5) What is its past history—its evolutionary story?

(6) What are the things most resembling it?
(7) What thing is most unlike it—its "opposite?"

and many more questions of that sort. You would seek to fill your mind with all the essential images connected with or related to your subject.

Briefly, you would fill your mind with the "mental images," concepts, or ideas of each and every thing connected with or related to that subject. Of course, you would use your pencil in noting down these names and their meaning—you would "think with your pencil." You would arrange your facts into classes—minor classes forming greater classes and so on. You would have on your list every important element involved in the matter. You would know what each of these meant—an adequate conception of each and every one of these elements. You would not be satisfied until your list was made as complete and as comprehensive as possible for the one hundred thousand dollar reward would inspire you. But, as you worked, the growing interest in the task itself would urge you on to awaken the "creative instinct" which had been lying dormant within you.

Well then, this is just the way for you to go to work concerning the subject of your Definite Purpose and Definite Ideal. What you would do for the millionaire, you must do for yourself. You must work for yourself just as faithfully as you would work for such an employer. The same spirit must inspire you—the same interest must urge you on—the same "creative instinct" must be awakened. Here is what you must accomplish in this stage: *You must make an inventory of all the essential elements involved in your special subject; and each name on that inventory must be so well understood by you that it constitutes a definite mental image, concept, or idea.*

The ideal inventory of "important elements" must include (1) every discoverable important thing employed or used in connection with the subject; (2) every discoverable important fact concerning that subject; (3) every discoverable important item of information concerning the essential application of that subject; (4) every discoverable important event or experience in the history of that subject; (5) every discoverable important cause affecting that subject; (6) every discoverable important effect produced by that subject; and (7) every discoverable important law, principle, or method employed in the processes connected with that subject.

You must know (1) of what the thing is made; (2) how it is made; (3) who makes it; (4) who uses it or may use it; (5) what the users need it for, and how they use it—and how others may use it, and the other ways in which persons may use it; (6) how it is sold (or may be sold) to those who use it; (7) the general methods of its distribution, and the extent of such. The above are but general suggestions: you must adapt them and add to them according to the special requirements of the case.

The fourth section of the General Rule tells you to: "*Classify these ideas, elements and factors according to their general nature, their general uses, their known relations and associations; cross-indexing them under appropriate headings, and referring to the lesser elements, parts or factors of which each is composed. Diagram and chart these ideas according to your system of classification, so as to have the whole matter under your mind's eye, and that you may be able to grasp the arrangement at a glance without having to hunt for scattered items.*"

By following this method, after having accumulated your materials of Constructive Imagination, i.e., your concepts, ideas, or mental images of the elements involved in the future creation of new images, you will arrange them according to some logical system of classification. In this way you file away each particular concept or idea according to its proper place in a more general class, and thereby you are more easily able to find it when you need it. This plan, as compared with that of simply piling your ideas and concepts in a miscellaneous heap, is akin to the scientific method of filing away correspondence in a filing cabinet as compared with that of simply throwing the letters together in a barrel, box, or large drawer.

A businessman is able to find the letter he needs, simply by going to his file and placing his hand on the proper compartment. He has an immense advantage over the one who has to hunt through a large mass of unfiled correspondence. *It is not enough to have the idea of a thing—it is necessary to know where to find that idea when you want it.* Psychology informs us that one may far more easily remember facts filed in the memory records according to some system of logical classification, than where the facts simply exist "somewhere in the mind."

The ideal for practical use would be a classification showing: *(1) every possible use or end to which a certain thing might be applied, employed or directed; and (2) every possible thing which might be applied, employed, or directed to a certain use or end.* The nearer you approach this ideal, in your work of classification of the things concerned with, connected with or related to the general subject of your Definite Purpose and Definite Ideal, the better will be your chances of the successful achievement of that purpose; the successful realization of that ideal.

It is said that a certain eminent inventor possesses a very complete index, and series of cross-indexes, of *nearly everything concerned with the general field in which he is working.* For instance, he has lists showing (1) all the discovered uses to which each and every such thing has been put; the discovered effects of its combinations with other things; the things most nearly related to or resembling it; and (2) each and every such thing which has been discovered to be of possible use, employment and effect in the direction of producing or effecting a certain result, effect, combination or composition. In short, he has the *cause-relations* and the *effect-relations* of every object on his list, noted and classified, indexed and cross-indexed.

When this inventor wishes to know the possible *causes* of a desired effect, he turns to his indexes, and the information is at hand. Likewise, when he wishes to know the possible *results and effects* related to a particular thing, he puts his hand on the information in the same way. The list is kept current and posted by a corps of assistants who note the reports contained in the scientific journals, et al, and also the results of their employer's own original experiments. He has built up, and maintained, a veritable encyclopaedia of information relating to the things concerned with his own particular line of work. Consequently, he not only has a wealth of valuable information on hand, but he also saves an immense amount of time and labor when he is engaged in actual experimental and inventive work.

While the illustrated instances cited above represent extreme cases, they serve to bring out the principle involved. It is not expected that you should undertake any such elaborate system of classification; yet you should not fail to employ its general principle to the highest degree of which you are capable, or which you find possible under the circumstances. All else being equal, the person who has (1) the greatest store of concepts or mental images concerning the general subject of his Definite Purpose and Definite Ideal; and who has (2) that material most thoroughly classified and indexed, either in his memory or mechanically; that person will manifest the highest degree of success in his work of Constructive Imagination.

You will do well to impress upon your memory all new facts arranged according to their logical classification. You will do well also to use your pencil in making written lists of the things involved in your creative work. In short, in every possible manner and by every possible method seek to *(1) Acquire concepts, ideas, or mental images related to your Definite Purpose and Definite Ideals; and then (2) Classify these concepts, ideas, or mental images according to a definite, logical scientific plan, so that you may find them easily and quickly when you need them in the work of Constructive Imagination.* With well-selected materials in sufficient amount and stored away systematically so that you may "put your hand on them" when needed, you will have progressed very far on the road to the achievement of your Definite Purpose and Definite Ideal by the processes of the Constructive Imagination.

Employing another illustrative figure of speech, we may say that by following the previously mentioned plan of the collection and classification of the materials of image-ideas, you have built and stocked for yourself a great and valuable Mental Laboratory. You have proceeded upon the same general plan as that employed by scientists in the creation of their experimental laboratories. In these laboratories—their workshops in which these scientists perform their experimental work—are to be found the various elements which, when combined in certain arrangements and proportions, produce the sought-for synthetic compositions. The scientist in his laboratory, and in his actual work, follows the same general plan which you are to follow in your experimental work along the lines of Constructive Imagination, i.e., he tries first this combination, and then that one, until he reaches the best working combination—the most satisfactory composition.

Edison perfected a similar laboratory, which he employed in his work of creative invention. He tested out every conceivable substance which seemed possible of being used as a filament for the electric-light bulb. Then step by step, by experiment after experiment, employing the process of test, trial, elimination, and selection, he finally settled upon the best possible known substance for that special purpose.

Luther Burbank conducted his experimental work in Plant Creation in a similar way: he tested, tried, experimented, combined, separated, eliminated, and finally, selected and preserved the "fittest."

Moreover, Nature, herself, in her creative evolutionary processes, is discovered to proceed along the same general lines. The history of Natural Evolution is but a record of ages-long series of experiments, tests, combinations, adaptations, and "natural selection," ending in the "survival of the fittest" for the particular purpose at each particular stage of the process. The plan is but the taking of a leaf from the Book of Nature—it is based upon the sound, fundamental principles of Natural Creation.

Elmer Gates, the psychologist-inventor, made many of his important discoveries and inventions in precisely the way indicated in our preceding consideration of Effective Constructive Imagination—the method of combining the elements of previously classified concepts and images. In fact, he attributed his success in his inventive work directly to the psychological methods based upon this general principle, which he had previously worked out and systematized.

It is stated that Professor Gates secured practically all of his many important discoveries and inventions in electricity and acoustics—his special branches of inventive work—in just this way. He spent several years and much money in acquiring the materials for his list of concept-images which formed the elements of his constructive work in these branches. He worked with a list of about 2,000 *simple* concept-images in electricity alone, from which he has produced about 15,000 *complex* idea-images. In acoustics, he worked with over 3,000 *simple* concept-images, from which he has evolved nearly 10,000 *complex* idea-images.

The general plan of the Mental Laboratory, or of the Mental Thesaurus, which we have outlined for you in this section of this book, is applicable not only for the inventor, the investigator, the researcher, but for the businessman, the clerk, the salesman, the stenographer, or the worker in each and every line of business, trade or profession. The principle is universal and may be applied in every field of human endeavor and industry. In fact, it is not too much to say that some of the elements of this plan have been consciously or unconsciously employed by every individual who has worked his way up from a subordinate position to one of authority and command.

The essence and substance of the general idea is the gathering up and storing away of as many facts as possible associated with the work in which you are engaged—the ideas of the things likely to be needed at some time in that work—so that you may have them within each mental reach at such times in which you have need for them. The task is twofold: (1) the task of acquiring the necessary concepts, ideas and mental images in question; and (2) the logical, scientific classification and filing away of these facts, concepts and ideas, so that you may be able to "put your finger on them" easily and quickly when you have need for them. The individual who will saturate himself with these essential facts, and who will classify and store them away for future use, is certain to reap his reward of success, appreciation and achievement in his particular line of work.

CHAPTER 20

Creative Composition

In Creative Composition, you begin with the building materials of mental image-ideas which you have gathered together and arranged according to a convenient and efficient classification. For the purpose of a familiar illustration of the scientific principle involved, let us ask you to think of these building materials of mental image-ideas as resembling the familiar building-blocks of childhood.

You have the general idea of your Definite Purpose and Definite Ideal before you. You perceive clearly the obstacle which you wish to overcome; the new means to an old end, or new ends for old means: the bridge which you wish to build over the space separating the two sides of the stream of Ideas. How shall you proceed to accomplish these ends by means of your imaginative building-blocks? The answer is as simple as the way a child proceeds when he wishes to build the structure which he has in mind—by taking up the various building blocks of various sizes and forms, and *experimenting with them.* The child puts *this block* alongside of *that* block, and finding that the combination will not answer, he continues to *make* new and still newer combinations, *until* at last he discovers the combination that *will* work.

In working toward the achievement of your Definite Purpose and Definite Ideal through the Constructive Imagination, you must *"put this and that together,"* along the lines of experiment, trial and test. You must arrange your imaginative building-blocks, first in *this* new combination, and then in *that* one. You must at times even break apart some of the blocks, using portions of them to add to others, and thus forming new combinations. You must proceed with the idea that:*"Somewhere in these blocks there abides the certainty of a successful combination; and it is 'up to me' to find it."* In your imaginative building-blocks there is hidden the secret of the exact combination which you are seeking. You can discover this only by experiment; and if you continue to experiment faithfully and intelligently you will surely discover the solution of the problems.

Every contrivance of Man, every tool, every instrument, every utensil, every article designed for use, evolved from very simple beginnings along the line of experimentation and Creative Composition. Everything made by Man is "put together," made up of material parts; and the idea of every such thing is "made up" of simpler and more elemental ideas, united and combined in Creative Composition. This is the only way in which Man has ever invented or contrived anything; and this is always the way in which you must proceed in your work of Constructive Imagination. The truth of the matter is so simple that most persons entirely overlook it; you have possibly never thought of it until you now have it presented to you in this book.

But here is an important point. While Man has always employed this principle in his inventive and creative work, he has done so almost entirely using his conscious mind. Now that modern psychology has uncovered the subconscious mind for us—has taken off the cover so that we may see "how the thing works," and "how the wheels go 'round"—we may hope for much more effective and efficient exercise of the power of the Constructive Imagination in the future. Already a number of great inventors and scientific investigators have taken advantage of the new teaching of psychology concerning this phase of mental operation, and they have thereby attained results far superior to those possible under the old hit-or-miss methods.

Artists and writers also employ the same general methods of Creative Composition, though in most cases in a more or less haphazard and instinctive way. The various characters, situations, scenes and combinations of pictures, stories and plays, are gathered together from a comparatively small list of elements—the great variety of results arising from the many possible combinations and arrangements of these few elements. If this seems incredible to you, you have but to remember the almost infinite number of possible combinations of the 26 letters of the alphabet—the largest dictionary contains only a small proportion of the possible word-creations by such combinations. Again, from 52 playing cards, are derived all of the numerous combinations of "hands" dealt out in card games—in many games, in fact, a smaller number of cards are used.

That modern writers are turning this principle of Creative Composition to practical account is evident to those who study the advertising columns of magazines devoted to the writing craft. For instance, there is advertised a book for story-writers called *"The 36 Dramatic Situations,"* which is described as follows: "A catalogue of all the possible situations that the many relations of life offer to the writer. The author has read and analyzed thousands of plays and novels, and resolved their basic story material into fundamental categories. A true philosophic consideration, but practical in every respect, that makes available to every writer all the possible material that life offers him."

Again, there is advertised a book called *"The Fiction Factory,"* which is described as follows: "A writer who wrote thousands of stories and made thousands of dollars by setting up a story-mill, tells how he did it, and gives a record of his work in this instructive stimulating book. It should be in the hands of everyone interested in how authors do their work."

You may smile at these advertisements, and shrug your shoulders—but you buy and read the stories so composed.

Jack London, in his story of "Martin Eden" (which many regard as being largely autobiographical) pictured his hero as busily engaged in writing "newspaper storiettes" for the syndicates which supply them to newspapers in all parts of the country. These productions were what are known as "pot boilers," written hastily to meet the popular demand and to gratify the popular taste.

London pictured Martin busily engaged in reading over his rejected storiettes, and thus finding out how *not* to write such productions, as well as *"just how" to write them.* He found out *what to put in, and what to leave out.* In this way he *worked out a perfect formula.* This formula consisted of three parts: (1) A pair of lovers jarred apart; (2) They are united by some deed or event; (3) Wedding bells. He reached the conclusion that the third part was an unvarying quantity; but that the first and second parts could be varied an infinite number of times.

The application of the formula, in London's own words, was as follows: "Thus, the pair of lovers could be jarred apart by misunderstood motives; by accident or fate; by jealous rivals; by irate parents; by crafty guardians; by scheming relatives; and so on and so forth. They could be reunited by the brave deed of the man-lover; by a similar deed of the woman-lover; by change of heart in one lover or the other; by forced confessions of a crafty guardian, scheming relative, or jealous rival; by a voluntary confession of same; by lover storming girl's heart; by lover making long and noble self-sacrifices; and so on, endlessly. It was very fetching to make the girl propose in the course of being united, and Martin discovered, bit by bit, other decidedly piquant and fetching ruses. But marriage bells at the end was the one thing that he could take no liberties with."

The author related that Martin soon worked out half a dozen stock forms, which he always consulted when constructing storiettes. "These forms," he adds, "were like the cunning tables used by the mathematicians, which may be entered from top, bottom, right, and left, which entrances consist of scores of lines and dozens of columns, and from which may be drawn, without reasoning or thinking, thousands of different conclusions, all unchallengably precise and true. Thus, in the course of half an hour, with his forms, Martin could frame up a dozen or more storiettes, which he put aside and filled in at his convenience. The real work was in constructing the frames and that was merely mechanical. He had no doubt whatever of the efficacy of his formula. His machine-made storiettes, were successful."

We shall close our consideration of the methods of Efficient Constructive Imagination by reminding you that the General Rule finally tells you: *"Having reached at least a fairly satisfactory working plan, idea, invention, or solution of your problem, you should then carefully detach yourself from it—you should move from your personal point of view, and try to see it as others will see it. Try to imagine the effect it will have on the persons whom you wish to be interested in your finished product; how it will meet with their requirements, satisfy their wants, arouse their desires for it, et cetera. Your own created conjunction, plan, method, design, or invention naturally will seem to you as the infant does to its mother, as no mother is an unprejudiced critic of her own baby. You must see the thing as others see it, in order to arrive at an intelligent idea of the utility of your idea. You must use past experience, reason, judgment, discrimination and cool decision in this latter testing process.*

The above statement speaks for itself, and is sufficiently comprehensive to stand alone. All that we wish to add are these few words: if your detached inspection and survey convinces you that your work will not fill the requirements of those for whom it is intended, then, back to the mental workshop with it. You will be able to cure the defects, strengthen the weak points, and to reshape the form in accordance with "the heart's desire" of Those-Who-Must-Be-Satisfied, by precisely the same methods already employed. Find out first what is required, then adapt these new factors to the old form by the same old method, and the desired result will be obtained. The principle is universal in its application, and will fit any case to which it is applied. It is as invariable as the Laws of Mathematics; but, like those Laws, it requires skill, patience, work and determination to apply it to difficult problems.

Without the power of Constructive Imagination, man will never be all that there is in him to be; never do all that is in him to do; never reach all that is in him to reach. "It lights up the whole horizon of thought—as the sunrise flashing along the mountaintop lights the world."

CHAPTER 21

The Art of Creation

Passing on from the consideration of the more familiar forms of the application of Efficient Constructive Imagination, you are now asked to enter into a consideration of a still higher phase of that Creative Power which is a mode of manifestation of your Personal Power. Your Personal Power, in turn, is but a phase of the All-Power—that POWER in which you live and move and have your being, and which is that All which is in All-Things, and in which All-Things are. You are now asked to consider the subject of your Creative Power in its higher phase of manifestation.

Creation is an attribute of the highest Power of which you can have any knowledge, or of which you may dream. Whatever else the Supreme Power may be, or may not be, it must be conceived as Creative Power. The fact that the Power behind Creation must be Creative; and the fact that Creation must be the result of Power; must bring to the mind of the true thinker the conviction that in Creative Power is to be found Power in its most essential and elemental aspect. In Creation you participate with the Supreme Power!

To "create" is to "bring into being; to cause, to produce." Man may be said apparently to create in several ways, yet at the last he is found to be able to create in only one essential way. And that one essential way in which he can create is found to be the way in which the Ultimate Creative Power proceeds in its own creative work. It will be well for you to become convinced of the essential and elemental nature of your own Creative Power, in order that you may realize the majesty and dignity of the forces and energies which you call into play and operation in your own creative activities.

Many persons are disposed to regard as more or less unreal and unsubstantial anything that is purely ideal and mental in its nature. To such we would cite the celebrated rule of Spinoza: "A thing has only so much reality as it posesses power." Applying this rule to the ideal forms or mental images underlying material forms, you will discover that such possess a very high degree of reality and substantiality. Ideal forms and creative mental images are not merely such stuff as dreams are made of, but in reality are strong, powerful forces. In fact, many manifestations of natural forces are really efforts toward the expression of the Creative Idea. The inner form striving to manifest in the outer form often exercises a tremendous force. The inner form of a growing plant has been known to crack a heavy concrete block; and the power of growing roots, arising from the inner urge of the ideal form, has been known to tear asunder heavy foundation stones.

John Burroughs, the great naturalist, said concerning this force of the inner form striving for outward expression:

> "We know that the roots of trees insert themselves into seams in the rocks, and force the rocks asunder. This force is measurable, and often is very great. Its seat seems to be in the soft milky substance called the cambium layer under the bark. These many minute cells, when their force is combined, become regular rock-splitters. One of the most remarkable exhibitions of plant force I ever saw was in a Western city where I observed a species of wild sunflower forcing its way up through the asphalt pavement. The folded and compressed leaves of the plant, like a man's fist, had pushed against the hard but flexible concrete until it had bulged up and then split, and let the irrepressible plant through. The force exerted must have been many pounds. I think it doubtful if the strongest man could have pushed his fist through such a resisting medium. If it was not Life which exerted this force, what was it?"

In the same way, the great giants of the forest have pushed their way up toward the skies, counteracting the pull of gravitation, and lifting weights which it would have required mighty machinery to move. The mental pattern in the giant redwood trees proceeds to the materialization of the gigantic outer form of the tree, and the "inner urge" of the idea form calls to its aid the mighty latent forces of Nature in order to materialize that which is contained in the idea form or mental image of the living organism of the tree. Nature seems ready to furnish such power to the inner urge, provided that such is sufficiently needed, insistently desired, and persistently demanded, and provided that it is called for in the right way. If man ever obtains the inner secret of this demand, he will have the creative powers and forces of Nature in his hands. Already he has acquired a portion of this secret, and is able to perform mighty creative work by directing his mental powers toward the physical plane. In this instruction we seek to disclose the principles of this process to you.

It is a fact acknowledged by many very careful observers and reasoners that the man of strong ideals—he whose mind contains strong, clear mental pictures of that which he hopes to accomplish—actually sets into operation the forces, powers and energies of his entire mental and physical being. These, in turn, draw upon the common source of Nature for their nourishment and subsistence, and all the power so generated tends toward manifestation and expression in the material form which is being built upon the mental framework or pattern of the Creative Idea. Just as the oak is able to draw upon Nature for power with which it may lift itself far above the surface of the earth, and to send forth mighty limbs and branches; just as the growing plant is able to secure from Nature sufficient force to enable it to push aside, or break through the obstacles in the path of its progress—even through concrete blocks as we have seen—so may the Creative Idea of the "man who knows" be able to draw upon Nature for the still more subtle forces of her laboratory needed to materialize his idea forms, to make his ideas become real.

We are fast approaching the place in which we shall see the inner meaning of the ancient philosophers who asserted that in Will and Imagination—combined and harmonized—are to be found the Secret of Power.

CHAPTER 22

Dynamic Idealization

"The Master Formula of Attainment"

I. Definite Ideals
II. Insistent Desire
III. Confident Expectation
IV. Persistent Determination
V. Balanced Compensation

The spirit of the Master Formula is expressed in popular phrasing as follows:

"You may have anything you want, provided that you (1) know exactly what you want; (2) want it hard enough; (3) confidently expect to obtain it; (4) persistently determine to obtain it; and (5) are willing to pay the price of its attainment."

"You are the creator of your own world of experience. Consciously or unconsciously, you are molding your world of experience and determining your own destiny. In ignorance or in wisdom, for good or for evil, you are creating, building, constructing the scenery of that world in which you live, and move, and have your being. For weal or for woe, you are thus building. For better or for worse you are thus constructing. Your personal world of experience is largely what you, yourself, have made it. Your Ideals ever tend to become Real. You are always realizing your Ideals. What you have been doing unconsciously, you may now proceed to do consciously. By creating and controlling your Ideals, you create and control your world of experience. You may become an active master of Creation, instead of a passive slave."

The strong, definite Dynamic Creative Ideal will call forth the full powers of your body, of your mind, and of your spirit. Reason, Imagination, Invention, will perform their best work under its influence; Desire will energize more intensely, and Will will determine more persistently, under its influence. The wonderful storehouse of the Subconscious will open wide its doors when the Creative Ideal gives "the right knock." The still higher realm of the Superconscious will superimpose its wisdom and knowledge upon the conscious mind, when this be demanded by the Dynamic Ideal. All things will work together for good for him in whom the Dynamic Creative Ideal is manifesting its power. "I call them all forth; and forth come they in answer to my call," says the Spirit of the Ideal in the old allegory of the Orient, "and chief of all, and the first to come forth, is my twin brother WILL!" concludes that Ideal Spirit.

Definite Ideal and Concentrated Will—these are the Twin-Giants of your Creative Power. Cultivate and develop both of them, to an equal extent. Do not let your Definite Ideals suffer by reason of the lack of pulling and pushing power of your Concentrated Will. Neither let your Concentrated Will become static and inert, by reason of the lack of the directing and guiding power of your Definite Ideals. Grasp the hands of the Twin-Giants, one on the right of you, one on your left; and then let the "I AM I" give the command, "Forward March!" Naught can oppose the phalanx composed of your Definite Ideals, your Real Self, your Concentrated Will. Rightly may such a combination shout its battlecry: *"I Can, I Will; I Dare, I Do!"*

The "Will that Can" is the "Will that Knows." The ancient Buddhists had an old aphorism which ran something like this: "To Know rightly, is to Think rightly; to Think rightly, is to Will rightly; to Will rightly, is to Act rightly: the root of Action is Knowledge; the fruit of Knowledge is Action." The ancient Chaldeans had a similar proverb: "He who Knows, is able to Will effectively; he who Wills effectively, Creates his World!" All through the Secret Doctrines runs this song of "Ideal-Will"—of Knowing and Doing; and the most practical thinkers of our own times and lands echo the ancient reports.

Whatever may be the Ultimate Truth, it is certain that Man has at his disposal a mighty Creative Power, which in its more familiar phase is called "Constructive Imagination" and which in its less familiar esoteric, transcendental phase is called Man. For in his own realm he is a Creator and the limits of his realm are determined by himself, by his Imagination, by his Will!

PART VI

SECRET NUMBER SIX THE POWER OF WILL

CHAPTER 23

Most Failures in Life Due to Weak Wills

How to Consciously Cultivate the Will to Win Life's Battles as Thousands of Others Have Done

The reason that only one man succeeds to every ten that fail in business must be due to some vital characteristic lacking in those who do not succeed in their undertaking and a trait possessed by the comparatively few who do.

In making an analysis of the attributes of great men in every field of endeavor, the one predominating characteristic seems to be an indomitable Will. Personally, I have never heard of a man succeeding without a Will of his own, and I know of no failures who did not lack Will power.

These facts any man can verify to his own satisfaction by merely recalling the predominating characteristics of both classes of men of his own acquantance.

Anyone Can Have a Strong Will

Everyone knows what can be accomplished by exercising the brain. Our whole educational system is founded upon the theory that the brain can be developed in proportion to the amount of intelligent exercise and use to which it is put. For years scientists have known that the same is true of the Will—that the Will can be made indomitable by intelligent exercise and use. The trouble has been that until now no one has ever devoted their attention to the cultivation of the Will. And since we have never been taught to use it, most of us don't know how. We float along carrying out other people's Will simply because our own Will has become scotched and dormant from lack of use. The authors of this section on "THE POWER OF WILL", have devoted years to the most profound analysis of the Will in human beings. Yet every step in the fascinating lessons is written so simply that anyone can understand them and apply the principles, methods and rules set down with noticeable results almost from the very start.

Will Power the Key to the Door of Success

"O Well for him whose will is strong!" wrote Tennyson, and the poets of all nations and times have sung the same song. Tennyson voices this human regard and admiration for the power of the Will. He tells us again: "O living Will, thou shalt endure, when all that seems shall suffer shock."

The Will of man is strange, subtle, intangible, and yet a very real thing that is closely connected with the inmost essence of his "I." When the "I" acts, it acts through the Will. The Will is the immediate expression of the Ego, or "I" in Man, which rests at the very seat of his being. This Ego, or "I" within each of us—that inmost self of each one of us—expresses itself in two ways. It first asserts "I AM" by which it expresses its existence and reality; then it asserts "I WILL" by which it expresses its desire to act, and its determination to do so. The "I WILL" comes right from the center of your being, and is the strongest expression of the Great Life Force within you. And in the degree that you cultivate and express it, is the degree of positivity that you manifest. The person of weak Will is a negative cringing weakling, while he of strong Will is the positive, courageous, masterful individual in whom Nature delights and whom she rewards.

The human Will is an actual living force. It is just as much an active force of Nature as is Electricity, Magnetism, or any other form of natural force. Will is as real as Energy, as is gravitation. From atom to man, desire and Will are in evidence—first comes the desire to do a thing, and then comes the Will that does it. It is an invariable law pervading all natural forms, shapes, degrees of things—animate and inanimate.

Nothing is impossible to the man who can Will—providing he can Will sufficiently strong. And as Will depends so very much upon one's belief in his ability, it may be said that all action depends upon belief. One does not Will unless he believes that he has a Will. And many a man of inherent strong Will does not express it or exert it, simply because he does not realize that he possesses it. It is only when the necessity arises from some new unexpected demand for the exercise of the Will, that many men realize that they really possess such a Will. To many, alas, such a necessity never comes.

In speaking about the Will, I do not mean stubbornness. The man with the strong Will knows when to recede from his position as well as when to go forward; he never stands still. When the occasion warrants it, he steps back, but only for the purpose of getting a better start, for he always has a definite goal in view. When the command from within calls him to go forward, he drives right ahead like the mighty ocean steamer, majestic in his power and stopping for nothing. This frame of mind is best illustrated by the following quotation written of Howard, the philanthropost:

> "The energy of his determination was so great, that if instead of being habitual, it had been shown only for a short time on particular occasions, it would have appeared a vehement impetuosity; but, by being unintermitted, it had an equality of manner which scarcely appeared to exceed the tone of a calm constancy, it was so totally the reverse of anything like turbulence or agitation. It was the calmness of an intensity, kept uniform by the nature of the human mind forbidding it to be more, and by the character of the individual forbidding it to be less."

The writer believes that the basis of all personal power resides in the Will and that if one intends to accomplish anything in this world he must acquire a powerful Will. The best way to do this is to first recognize your lack, and then by constant affirmations of "I can and I will accomplish this thing," and by the repetition of selections on the Will, taken from the best literature, build up within yourself, little by little, an invincible power and energy that will overcome every temptation to side-track you from your life purpose. At the end of this chapter I have appended some excellent selections which can be memorized and then repeated in times of trial and discouragement and they will prove invigorating tonic for the depressed mind.

The proper attitude of the student of the Law of Financial Success is that mental attitude which may be best expressed as the "I CAN AND I WILL" state of mind. In this mental attitude there are combined the two primary elements of the accomplishment of things. First, there comes that belief in one's ability, powers, and force which begets confidence, and which causes one to make a clear mental channel over which the Will flows. Then, second, comes the assertion of the Will itself—the "I WILL" part of it. When a man says "I WILL" with all the force and energy and determination of his character being poured into it, then does his Will become a very Dynamic Force which sweeps away obstacles before it in its mighty onrush.

Not only does this expression of the Will stir into activity the latent powers and dormant energies of the man's mind, bringing to the accomplishment of the task all his reserve force, power and strength, but it does much more. It impresses those around him with a mighty psychical power which compels attention to his words and demands recognition for himself. In all conflicts between men, the strongest Will wins the day. The struggle may be short, or it may be long, but the end is always the same—the man of the strongest Will wins.

And not only does the awakened Will do this, but it also acts in the direction of affecting those at a distance from the person. It sets in motion certain natural laws which tend to compel things toward the center occupied by a mighty Will. Look around you, and you will see that the men of giant Wills set up a strong center of influence, which extends on all sides in all directions, affecting this one and that one, and drawing and compelling others to fall in with the movements instigated by that Will. There are men who set up great whirlpools or whirwinds of Will, which are felt by persons far and near. And, in fact, all persons who exert Will at all, do this to a greater or lesser extent, depending upon the degree of Will expressed.

Read, study and absorb the following selections:

> "The education of the Will is the object of our existence."

*****

> "They can who think they can. Character is a perfectly educated Will."

*****

> "Nothing can resist the Will of a man who knows what is true and wills what is good."

*****

> "In all difficulties, advance and Will, for within you is a power, a living Force which, the more you trust and learn to use, will annihilate the opposition of matter."

*****

WILL POWER

"The star of the unconquered Will,
He rises in my breast,
Serene and resolute and still,
And calm and self-possessed.

"So nigh is grandeur to our dust,
So near is God to man,
When Duty whispers low, 'Thou must!'
The youth replies, 'I can.' "

* * *

"I will to will with energy and decision! I will to persist in willing! I will to will intelligently and for a goal! I will to exercise the will in accordance with the dictates of reason and of morals."

* * *

In this world, the human spirit with its dominating force, the WILL may be, and ought to be, superior to all bodily sensations and all accidents of environment. *Kennan*

* * *

When you get into a tight place and everything goes against you until it seems that you cannot hold on for a minute longer, never give up then; for that is just the place and time that the tide will turn.
Harriet Beecher Stowe

* * *

Go on, sir, go on! The difficulties you meet with will resolve themselves as you advance. Proceed, and the light will dawn, and shine with increasing clearness on your path. *D'Alembert*

* * *

It is defeat that turns bone to flint, and gristle to muscle and makes men invincible, and forms those heroic natures that are now in ascendency in the world. Do not be afraid of defeat. You are never so near victory as when defeated in a good cause. *Henry Ward Beecher*

* * *

It is astonishing how many men lack the power of "holding on" until they reach the goal. They can make a sudden dash, but they lack grit. They are easily discouraged. They get on as long as everything moves smoothly, but when there is friction they lose heart. They depend upon stronger personalities for their spirit and strength. They lack independence or originality. They only dare to do what others do. They do not step boldly from the crowd and act fearlessly. *Cuyler*

* * *

I know no such unquestionable badge and ensign of a sovereign mind as that of tenacity of purpose, which, through all changes of companions or parties or fortunes, changes never, bates no jot of heart or hope, but wearies out opposition and arrives at its port. *Emerson*

* * *

Is there one whom difficulties dishearten, who bends to the storm? He will do little. Is there one who wills to conquer? That kind of man never fails. *John Hunter*

* * *

The truest wisdom is a Resolute Determination. *Napoleon Bonaparte*

* * *

A strong defiant purpose is many-handed, and lays hold on whatever is near that can serve it; it has a magnetic power that draws to itself whatever is kindred. *Munger*

* * *

The man who is perpetually hesitating which of two things he will do first, will do neither. The man who resolves, but suffers his resolution to be changed by the first counter-suggestion of a friend—who fluctuates from opinion to opinion, from plan to plan, and veers like a weather-cock to every point of the compass, with every breath of caprice that blows—can never accomplish anything real or useful. It is only the man who first consults well, then resolves firmly, and then executes his purposes with inflexible perseverance, undismayed by those petty difficulties which daunt a weaker spirit—that man can advance to eminence in any line. *Wirt*

* * *

Great souls have wills; feeble ones have only wishes. *Chinese Proverb*

* * *

In the schools of the wrestling master, when a boy falls he is bidden to get up again, and to go on wrestling day by day till he has acquired strength; and we must do the same, and not after one failure suffer ourselves to be swept along as by a torrent. You need but will, and it is done; but if you relax your efforts you will be ruined; for ruin and recovery are both from within. *Epictetus*

* * *

He who has a firm will molds the world to himself. *Goethe*

* * *

In the world there is nothing impossible if we can bring a thorough will to do it. *W. Humboldt*

* * *

The saddest failures in life are those that come from not putting forth the power and will to succeed. *E. P. Whipple*

* * *

People do not lack strength; they lack will. *Victor Hugo*

* * *

In idle wishes fools supinely stay; be there a will, and wisdom finds a way. *Crabbe*

* * *

All the grand agencies which the progress of mankind evolves are the aggregate result of countless wills, each of which, thinking merely of its own end, and perhaps fully gaining it, is at the same time enlisted by Providence in the secret service of the world. *James Marineau.*

* * *

"The human will, that force unseen,
The offspring of a deathless soul,
Can hew a way to any goal,
Though walls of granite intervene.

"You will be what you will to be,
Let failure find its false content
In that poor word environment,
But spirit scorns it and is free.

"It masters time, it conquers space,
It cows that boastful trickster, chance,
And bids the tyrant circumstance
Uncrown and fill a servant's place.
There is no chance, no destiny, no fate,
Can circumvent, or hinder, or control
The firm resolve of a determined soul.

"Gifts count for nothing, will alone is great;
All things give way before it soon or late.
What obstacle can stay the mighty force
Of the sea-seeking river in its course,
Or cause the ascending orb of day to wait?
Each well-born soul must win what it deserves,
Let the fools prate of luck. The fortunate
Is he, whose earnest purpose never swerves
Whose slightest action, or inaction serves
The one great aim. Why, Even Death himself
Stands still and waits an hour sometimes
For such a will."

CHAPTER 24

You Can Do It

Try to be somebody with all your might.
Find your purpose and fling your life into it.
"The iron will of one stout heart shall make a thousand quail."
" 'Impossible,' is a word to be found only in the dictionary of fools."
"He who has resolved to conquer or die is seldom conquered."

I AM constantly asked by men and women whether I think they really have enough in them to make much of a success in life, anything that will be distinctive or worth while, and I answer, "Yes, you have. I know you have the ability to succeed, but I do not know that you will. That rests entirely with you. You can, but will you?"

It is one thing to have the ability to do something distinctive, something individual, but doing it is a very different thing. There is a tremendous amount of unproductive ability in the great failure army today. Why did not the men who have it make something of themselves? Many of those men could be prosperous, successful men of standing in their community, instead of the dregs of society. They had the opportunity to make good. Why didn't they?

You say you long to make your life count; that you are ambitious to get on. Why don't you? What are you waiting for? What holds you down? Who is keeping you back? Answer these questions and you will find the reason. There is only one—yourself. Nothing else keeps you back. The opportunities are on every hand, infinitely better ones than thousands of men and women who have made their lives count ever had.

It is up to you to find where and what the trouble is. Is it physical or mental? Do you lack physical vigor? If you do, your vitality and your will power are depleted. Is your education deficient? Is your training for your vocation inadequate? Do you know what shortcomings are responsible for your failure to accomplish what you dream of and long to do? Very often some apparently trivial personal trait or defect proves strong as iron bonds to hold a man back from the attainment of a worthy ambition.

Now, if your achievement does not begin to match your ambition there is something wrong. If you are dissatisfied with the result of your efforts up to the present time examine yourself carefully, take stock of your mental and physical assets, and see where you have been slipping, falling down, where you have made your greatest mistakes or failures. You know the strength of a chain doesn't lie in its strongest link, no matter how strong, but in its weakest. Find your weak link, and then strengthen it.

Many Lack the Will to Succeed

Do not hide behind such silly excuses as that you have no chance, nobody to help, nobody to boost you, to give you a pull, to help you to capital, nobody to show you the way. If there is something in you, if you are worth your salt, you will make a way if you cannot find one.

"Despite all the cries of lack of opportunity which are being so frequently voiced in various ways, the hardest task today for us employers of labor is to get in sufficient numbers, boys and girls—with a *thorough* knowledge of three R's."

This is the recent utterance of the manager of one of the large department stores in New York City. He puts the blame for the state of things he describes partly on our public school system, and partly on the boys and girls themselves. Indeed, the most serious part of his indictment deals with them. His conclusion, based on experience with thousands of public school graduates, is that they are not only poorly equipped for business, but that they are also *"lacking in energy and the will to succeed."*

Now, without the energy and the will to succeed, no amount of education, no power on earth outside of one's self can push or lead or boost a person into success.

It is the difficult things in life that develop our mental and moral muscle, that build up courage and stamina. In tropical countries, where man's food practically grows on trees ready to eat, and where there is little or no housing or clothing problem, the people are naturally indolent, slipshod, and slovenly. They are brutal in their passions. They know little of self-mastery or mastery of conditions, adaptation to a severe climate, or the conquest of a hard and stubborn soil. Consequently these people have contributed but little to civilization. The things which make life worth living are the achievements, the inventions and discoveries, the noble deeds, the advancement of industry, science, and art, which have been contributed by men who have struggled with hard conditions of Nature; who have fought and conquered obstacles; who have lived in the temperature zones; and have experienced the rigors of cold and the enervation of heat.

It is doubtful whether any territory in the world ever generated more noble qualities, more sterling character, more civilizing forces than has the stubborn, hard soil and severe inhospitable climate of New England. It was the surmounting of obstacles strewn in the path of these sons of New England, which earlier bred fortitude, persistence, and those allied traits which led to preeminence and success.

The man who waits for favorable conditions and favorable circumstances will find that success in any field is never a walkover. It is the man who wins in spite of circumstances, in spite of adverse conditions, the man who wins when other people say he cannot, the man who does the "impossible," the man who rides over obstacles, who gets on in this world. And why? Because the very struggle to overcome the obstacles in his way develops the power that carries him step by step to his goal.

William of Orange

"As well can the Prince of Orange pluck the stars from the sky as bring the ocean to the wall of Leyden for your relief," was the derisive shout of the Spanish soldiers when told that the Dutch fleet would raise that terrible four months' seige of 1574. But from the parched lips of William, tossing on his bed of fever at Rotterdam, had issued the command: *"Break down the dikes: give Holland back to the ocean"*; and the people had replied: "Better a drowned land than a lost land." They began to demolish dike after dike of the strong lines, ranged one within another for fifteen miles to their city of the interior. It was an enormous task. The garrison was starving. The besiegers laughed in scorn at the slow progress of the puny insects who sought to rule the waves of the sea. But ever, as of old, heaven aids those who help themselves. On the first and second of October a violent equinoctial gale rolled the ocean inland, and swept the fleet on the rising waters almost to the camp of the Spaniards. The next morning the garrison sallied out to attack their enemies, but the besïegers had fled in terror under cover of the darkness. The next day the winds changed, and a counter tempest brushed the water, with the fleet upon it, from the surface of Holland. The outer dikes were replaced at once, leaving the North Sea within its old bounds. When the flowers bloomed the following spring, a joyous procession marched through the streets to found the University of Leyden, in commemoration of the wonderful deliverance of the city.

Who can keep a determined man from success and how can it be done? Place stumbling-blocks in his way and he uses them as stepping-stones on his climb to greatness. Take his money away, and he makes spurs of his poverty to urge him on. Cripple him, and he writes the Waverly Novels. Lock him up in prison, and he writes the "Pilgrim's Progress"; leave him in a cradle in a log cabin in the wilderness, and in a few years, you'll find him in the White House.

"All the performances of human art, at which we look with praise and wonder," say Johnson, "are instances of the resistless force of perserverance."

Adverse circumstances spur a determined man to success.

The degree in which a man sees insurmountable obstacles and impossible situations in his path will measure his success ability. To some people the way ahead of them is so full of obstacles, so full of difficulties and impossible situations that they never get anywhere; while another man feels so much bigger than the things which try to hinder him, so much stronger than the obstacles which try to down him, the stumbling-blocks which try to trip him, that he does not even notice them.

We are all familiar with men who are continually up against something that they think is impossible, they are sure cannot be done; and yet there is generally somebody near them who manages to do this very impossible thing.

I have in mind a man who has such a habit of thinking that things cannot be done that almost any kind of a difficulty downs him. Unless he can see the road clear to his destination he is afraid to move a foot forward. If he sees any obstruction ahead he loses courage, even to undertake what he longs to do. If you ask him to do anything which is at all difficult he will say, "Well, now, I don't believe I can do it. In fact, it simply cannot be done." The result is he makes no progress in any direction and he never will.

If our ambition is merely a weak desire to obtain a certain thing provided it does not cost much effort, or if we would merely "*like* to have" a certain thing, then there is no magnetism in such a milk-and-water purpose. The ambition must be backed by the willingness and the determination to do anything that is within human power to accomplish the aim. This is the mental attitude that wins.

The habit of being a quitter before the battle begins is fatal to all distinctiveness. It is the death-blow to the development of originality and strength of character; and without these no man can be a leader. He must remain a trailer always; he must follow someone else's lead.

Your Obstacles Melt Away

If you are trying to get a start in the world but don't feel able to remove the many barriers that block your way, do not get discouraged. The obstacles that looked so formidable at a distance will grow smaller and smaller as you approach. Have courage and confidence in yourself and the road will clear before you as you advance. Read the life stories of great men who from the start have cleared their pathway of obstructions which make yours look puny. Magnify your faith in yourself and you will minimize the obstacles in your way.

The whole science of efficiency and success in life consists of the vigorous, persistent affirmation of our determination and our ability to do the thing we have set our heart on. It consists of setting our face like a flint toward our goal, turning neither to the right nor the left, though a Paradise tempt us, our failure and disaster threaten us.

If your determination is easily deflected, if any persuasion can separate you from your life resolve, you may be pretty sure that you are on the wrong track.

Ill health or personal deformity may sometimes hold one back—-though there are numerous instances of success in spite of them—but in the vast majority of cases where people fail in getting a good start in life or in ultimately reaching their goal is because there is no energy in their resolution, no grit in their determination. They peter out after a few rebuffs. Two or three setbacks take the edge off their determination. They do not realize that success in anything worthwhile is the result of tremendous resolution, vigorous self-faith, and work, work, work—steady, conscientious, wholehearted, unremitting work. Light resolve, half-hearted efforts, indifferent, intermittent work have never yet accomplished anything and never will.

"Mere wishes and desires but engender a sort of green sickness in people's minds, unless they are promptly embodied in act and deed," says Samuel Smiles. "It will not avail merely to wait, as so many do, 'until Blucher comes up,' but they must struggle on and persevere in the meantime, as Wellington did. The good purpose, once formed, must be carried out with alacrity and without swerving. He who allows his application to falter, or shirks his work on frivolous pretexts, is on the sure road to ultimate failure."

Get busy, then, and work with all your might. There is no such thing as failure for the willing, ambitious worker.

Work, which many have called a curse, is really the salvation of the race. It is the greatest educator. There is no other way of developing power, calling out the resources, building stamina and breadth of character. Work is the great saviour of the race. Without it we should be a backboneless and staminaless, characterless race.

Emerson says: "Men talk of victory as of something fortunate. Work is victory. Wherever work is done victory is obtained."

The man

"Who breaks his birth's invidious bar,
And grasps the skirts of happy chance,
And breasts the billows of circumstance
And grapples with his evil star"

will tower above his fellows.

Energy of will distinguishes such a man as surely as muscular power distinguishes a lion.

"He who has a firm will," says Goethe, "molds the world to himself."

"People do not lack strength," says Victor Hugo, "they lack will."

Julius Caesar

Of Julius Caesar it was said by a contemporary that it was his activity and giant determination, rather than his military skill, that won his victories. The man who starts out in life determined to make the most of his eyes and let nothing escape him which he can possibly use for his own advancement; who keeps his ears open for every sound that can help him on his way; who keeps his hands open that he may clutch every opportunity; who is ever on the alert for everything which can help him to get on in the world; who seizes every experience in life and grinds it up into paint for his great life's picture; who keeps his heart open that he may catch every noble impulse, and everything which may inspire him—that man will be sure to make his life successful. There are no "ifs" or "ands" about it. If he has his health, nothing can keep him from final success.

No tyranny of circumstances can permanently imprison a determined will.

The world always stands aside for the determined man. Will makes a way, even through seeming impossibilities. "It is the half a neck nearer that shows the blood and wins the race; the one march more that wins the campaign; the five minutes more of unyielding courage that wins the fight."

Emerson said, "Man was born to be rich, or grows rich by the use of his faculties, by the unison of thought with nature. Property is an intellectual production. The game requires coolness, right reasoning, promptness, and patience in the players."

* * * *

Donald G. Mitchell said, "Ambition is the spur that makes man struggle with destiny. It is heaven's own incentive to make purpose great and achievement greater."

* * * *

Rowe said, "Great souls, by nature half divine, soar to the stars, and hold a near acquaintance with the gods."

CHAPTER 25

Yesterday Ended Last Night

What do you want from life? Whatever it is, you can have it—and you have the word of no less an authority than Jesus for that.

Does that mean that you must become saintly in order to amass material possessions? Experience would seem to indicate that it seldom works out that way. The saintly are not often burdened with worldly goods. No, saintliness is not the answer. Then what is?

Let us examine the meaning of "righteousness" and see if the answer does not lie in it. The word used for "righteousness" in the ancient Greek text of the original Gospels is "dikaiosune," which, literally translated, means the absolute dictatorship of the spirit within you.

Translated thus the passage reads—"Seek ye first the Kingdom of God and His absolute dictatorship of the spirit within you, and all these things shall be added unto you." In other words, put the problem up to God in You, the pat of Divinity that is the Creative Force in you, and leave it to Him to work out while you rest in serene faith that it IS done.

How would this work out in practice? There was an article in UNITY recently that exemplified the idea so well that I quote it here:

> "Let us say we are planning a business venture, or a social event, or a religious meeting, or the recovery of the sick. We are ready to pray over the situation. Now instead of futurizing our prayers and asking for something to take place tomorrow, let us imagine (imagination is an aid to the release of faith power) that everything has turned out just as we desired it. Let us write it all down as if it were all past history. Many of the Bible predictions are written in the past tense. Let us try listing our desires as if they had already been given to us.
>
> "Of course we shall want to write down a note of thanksgiving to God for all that He has given us. He has had it for us all the time or else we should not have received it. More than this, God has it for us or we could not even desire it now or picture it in our imagination.

"What happens? After we have written down our desires in the past tense, read them over carefully, praised God for them, let us then put away our paper and go on about our business. It will not be long before we actually see the desired events taking place in ways so natural that we may even forget that God is answering our prayers.

"Imagination helps us to have faith, for it pictures the thing desired and helps make it real. After we have tried this experience a few times we shall find that our imagination has increased our faith, and faith has turned to praise, and praise has opened our eyes to see what God has for us."

The habit of thanking God ahead of time for benefits about to be received has its firm basis in past experience. We can safely look upon it as a sure formula for successful prayer because Christ used it. David always praised and thanked God when he was in trouble. Daniel was saved from the lions through the praise of God. Paul sang songs of praise and liberated himself from prison. And don't you, and everyone else, find satisfaction in being praised for a task well done?

Wrote William Law:

"If anyone could tell you the shortest, surest way to all happiness and all perfection, he must tell you to make it a rule yourself to thank and praise God for everything that happens to you. For it is certain that whatever seeming calamity happens to you, if you thank and praise God for it, you turn it into a blessing. Could you therefore work miracles, you could not do more for yourself than by this thankful spirit; for it... turns all that it touches into happiness."

And Charles Fillmore adds:

"Praise is closely related to prayer; it is one of the avenues through which spirituality expresses itself. Through an inherent law of mind, we increase whatever we praise. The whole creation responds to praise, and is glad. Animal trainers pet and reward their charges with delicacies for acts of obedience; children glow with joy and gladness when they are praised. Even vegetation grows better for those who love it. We can praise our own ability, and the very grain cells will expand and increase in capacity and intelligence, when we speak words of encouragement and appreciation to them."

So don't let anything that has happened in your life discourage you. Don't let poverty or lack of education or past failures hold you back. There is only one power—the I AM in you—and it can do anything. If in the past you have not used that power, that is too bad as far as the past is concerned; but it is not too late. You can start NOW. "Be still, and know that I AM God." What more are you waiting for? God can do for you only what you allow Him to do through you, but if you will do your part, He can use you as a channel for unlimited power and good.

The difference between failure and success is measured only by your patience and faith—sometimes by inches, sometimes by minutes, sometimes by the merest flash of time.

Take Lincoln. He went into the Black Hawk War a Captain and came out a private. His store failed and his surveyor's instruments, on which he depended to eke out a livelihood, were sold for part of the debts. He was defeated in his first try for the Legislature. Defeated in his first attempt for Congress. Defeated in his application for Commissioner of the General Land Office. Defeated for the Senate. Defeated for the nomination for the Vice Presidency in 1856. But did he let that long succession of defeats discourage him? Not he. He held the faith—and made perhaps the greatest President we have ever had.

Then there was Grant: He failed of advancement in the army. Failed as a farmer. Failed as a businessman. At 39, he was chopping and delivering cordwood to keep body and soul together. Nine years later he was President of the United States and had won a martial renown second in this country only to Washington's.

Search the pages of history. You will find them dotted with the names of men whom the world had given up as failures, but who held on to their faith, who kept themselves prepared and when their chance came they were ready and seized it with both hands.

Napoleon, Cromwell, Patrick Henry, Paul Jones—these are only a few out of thousands.

When Caesar was sent to conquer Gaul, his friends found him one day in a fit of utter despondency. Asked what the matter was, he told them he had just been comparing his accomplishments with Alexander's. At his age, Alexander had conquered the entire known world—and what had Caesar done to compare with that? But he presently roused himself from his discouragement by resolving to make up as quickly as possible his lost time. The result? He became the head of the Roman Empire.

The records of business are crowded with the names of middle-aged nobodies who lived to build great fortunes, vast institutions. No man has failed as long as he has faith in the Father, faith in the great scheme of things, faith in himself.

Yesterday Ended Last Night

When Robert Bruce faced the English at the battle of Bannockburn, he had behind him years of failure, years of fruitless efforts to drive the English out of Scotland, years of heart-breaking toil in trying to unite the warring elements among the Scots themselves. True, at the moment a large part of Scotland was in his hands, but so had it been several times before, only to be wrested from him as soon as the English brought together a large enough army.

And now in front of him stood the greatest army England ever gathered to her banners–troops from all the dominions of Edward II, over 100,000 men. There were hardy veterans from the French provinces, all the great English nobles with their armored followers, wild Irish and Welsh bowmen.

To defend Scotland, Bruce had only been able to muster 30,000 men, brave and hardy, it is true, but lacking the training and discipline of the English.

Was Bruce discouraged? Not he. Even though the English had the better archers. Even though they were better armed, better trained, better disciplined. He was fighting for freedom—and he believed in himself, he believed in his men, he believed in the God of battles.

And, as always, weight, numbers, armament, proved of no avail when confronted with determination and faith. The vast English host was completely defeated and dispersed. Bruce was firmly seated upon the throne of Scotland, and never more did an invading English army cross its borders.

It matters not how many defeats you have suffered in the past, how great the odds may be against you. Bulow put it well when he said—"It's not the size of the dog in the fight that counts, so much as the size of the fight in the dog." And the size of fight in you depends upon your faith—faith in yourself, in the Creative Force working through you and in your cause. Just remember that yesterday ended last night, and yesterday's defeats with it.

Time after time throughout the Bible we are told that the battle is not ours—but the Lord's. But like all children, we know better than our Father how our affairs should be handled, so we insist upon running them ourselves.

Is it any wonder they get so tangled as to leave us in the depths of discouragement?

Like the Black Prince when his little army was penned in by Philip of France. Most men would have felt discouraged, for the hosts of France seemed as numerous as the leaves on the trees. The English were few and mostly archers. And archers, in that day, were believed to stand no chance against such armored knights as rode behind the banners of Philip.

The French came forward in a great mass, thinking to ride right over the little band of English. But did the Black Prince give way? Not he. He showed the world that a new force had come into warfare, a force that would soon make the armored knight as extinct as the dodo. That force was the common soldier—the archer.

Just as the Scot spearmen overthrew the chivalry of England on the field of Bannockburn, just as infantry have overthrown both cavalry and artillery in many a latter battle, so did the "common men" of

England—the archers—decide the fate of the French at Crecy. From being despised and looked down upon by every young upstart with armor upon his back, the "common men"—the spearmen and archers—became the backbone of every successful army. And from what looked like certain annihilation, the Black Prince by his faith in himself and his men became one of the greatest conquerors of his day.

Troubles flocked to him, but he didn't recognize them as troubles—he thought them opportunities. And used them to raise himself and his soldiers to the pinnacle of success.

There are just as many prizes in business as in war; just as many opportunities to turn seeming troubles into blessings. But those prizes go to men like the Black Prince who don't know a trouble when they meet it; who welcome it, take it to their bosoms, and get from it their greatest blessings.

What is the use of holding on to life—unless at the same time you hold on to your faith? What is the use of going through the daily grind, the wearisome drudgery—if you have given up hoping for the rewards, and unseeing, let them pass you by?

Suppose business and industry did that? How far would they get? Success is simply holding on hopefully, believingly, watchfully. As Kipling put it:

> "Forcing heart and nerve and sinew to serve your
> turn long after they are gone, and so hold on
> when there is nothing in you except the will
> which says to them: 'Hold on'!" From that many
> a business man has worked out his salvation.

It is not enough to work. The horse and the ox do that. And when we work without thought, without hope, we are not better then they. It is not enough to merely hold on. The poorest creatures often do that mechanically, for lack of the courage to let go.

If you are to gain the reward of your labors, if you are to find relief from your drudgery, you must hold on hopefully, believingly, confidently—knowing that the answer is in the great heart of God, knowing that the Creative Force working through you will give it to you, the moment you have prepared yourself to receive it.

It is never the gifts that are lacking. It is never the Creative Force that is backward in fulfilling our desires. It is we who are unable to see, who fail to recognize the good, because our thoughts are of discouragement and lack.

So never let yesterday's failure discourage you. As T.C. Howard wrote in Forbes Magazine:

> "Yesterday's gone—it was only a dream;
> Of the past there is naught but remembrance.
> Tomorrow's a vision thrown on Hope's screen,
> A will-o'-the-wisp, a mere semblance.
>
> "Why mourn and grieve over yesterdays ills
> And paint memory's pictures with sorrow?
> Why worry and fret—for worrying kills—
> Over things that won't happen tomorrow?
>
> "Yesterday's gone—it has never returned—
> Peace to its ashes, and calm;
> Tomorrow no human has ever discerned,
> Still hope, trust, and faith are its balm.
>
> "This moment is all that I have as my own,
> To use well, or waste, as I may;
> But I know that my future depends alone
> On the way that I live today.
>
> "This moment my past and future I form;
> I make them whatever I choose
> By the deeds and the acts that I now perform,
> By the words and thoughts that I use.
>
> "So I fear not the future nor mourn o'er the past
> For I do all I'm able today,

Living each present moment as though 'twere my last;
Perhaps it is! Who knows! Who shall say?"

"Duty and today are ours," a great man once wrote. "Results and the future belong to God." And wise old Emerson echoed the same thought. "All that I have seen," he said, "teaches me to trust the Creator for all I have not seen." In short, a good daily prayer might be one I read in a magazine recently—"Lord, I will keep on rowing. YOU steer the boat!"

Easy enough to say, perhaps you are thinking, but you never knew such disaster as has befallen me. I am broken down with sickness, or crippled by accident, or ruined financially, or something else equally tragic. Shakespeare wrote the answer to your case when he told us—"When Fortune means to man most good, she looks upon him with a threatening eye."

In the town of Enterprise, Alabama, there is a monument erected by its citizens for services done them. And you could never guess to whom it is dedicated. To the Boll Weevil!

In olden days, the planters living thereabouts raised only cotton. When cotton boomed, business boomed. When the cotton market was off—or the crop proved poor—business suffered correspondingly.

Then came the Boll Weevil. And instead of merely a poor crop, left no crop at all. The Boll Weevil ruined everything. Debt and discouragement were all it left in its wake.

But the men of that town must have been lineal descendants of those hardy fighters who stuck to the bitter end in that long-drawn-out struggle between North and South. They got together and decided that what their town and their section needed was to stop putting all their eggs into one basket.

Instead of standing or falling by the cotton crop, diversify their products! Plant a dozen different kinds of crops. Even though one did fail, even though the market for two or three products happened to be off, the average would always be good.

Correct in theory, certainly. But, as one of their number pointed out, how were the planters to start? They were over their heads in debt already. It would take money for seeds and equipment, to say nothing of the fact that they had to live until the new crops came in.

So the townsfolk raised the money—at personal sacrifices only the Lord knows—and financed the planters.

The result? Such increased prosperity that they erected a monument to the Boll Weevil, and on it they put this inscription:

> "In profound appreciation of the Boll Weevil, this monument is erected by the citizens of Enterprise, Coffee Co., Ala."

Many a man can look back and see where some Boll Weevil—some catastrophe that seemed tragic at the time—was the basis of his whole success in life. Certainly that has been the case with one man I know.

When he was a tot of five, he fell into a fountain and all but drowned. A passing workman pulled him out as he was going down for the last time. The water in his lungs brought on asthma, which, as the years went on, kept growing worse and worse, until the doctors announced that death was only a matter of months. Meantime, he couldn't run, he couldn't play like other children, he couldn't even climb the stairs!

A sufficiently tragic outlook, one would say. Yet out of it came the key to fortune and success.

Since he could not play with the other children, he developed a taste for reading. And as it seemed so certain that he could never do anything worthwhile for himself, what could be more natural than that he should long to read the deeds of men who had done great things. Starting with the usual boy heroes, he came to have a particular fondness for true stories of such men as Lincoln, Edison, Carnegie, Hill and Ford—men who started out as poor boys, without any special qualifications or advantages, and built up great names solely by their own energy and grit and determination.

Eventually he cured himself completely of his asthma—but that is another story. The part that is pertinent to this tale is that from the time he could first read until he was seventeen, he was dependent for amusement almost entirely upon books. And from his reading of the stories of men who had made successes, he acquired not only the ambition to make a like success of himself, but the basic principles on which to build it.

Today, as a monument to his Boll Weevil, there stands a constantly growing, successful business, worth millions, with a vast list of customers that swear by—not at—its founder.

And he is still a comparatively young man, healthy, active, putting in eight or ten hours at work every day, an enthusiastic horseman, a lover of all sports.

"There is no handicap, either hereditary or environmental, which cannot be compensated, if you are not afraid to try." Thus wrote one of New York's greatest psychiatrists. "No situation in our heredity or in our environment can compel us to remain unhappy. No situation need discourage one or hold him back from finding a degree of happiness and success."

Age, poverty, ill-health—none of these things can hold back the really determined soul. To him they are merely stepping stones to success; spurs that urge him on to greater things. There is no limit upon you, except the one you put upon yourself.

> "Ships sail east, and ships sail west,
> By the very same breezes that blow;
> It's the set of the sails,
> And not the gales,
> That determine where they go."

Men thought they had silenced John Bunyan when they threw him into prison. But he produced "Pilgrim's Progress" on twisted paper used as a cork for the milk jug.

Men thought that blind Milton was done. But he dictated "Paradise Lost."

Like the revolutionist of whom Tolstoy wrote—"You can imprison my body, but you cannot so much as approach my ideas."

You cannot build walls around a thought. You cannot imprison an idea. You cannot cage the energy, the enthusiasm, the enterprise of an ambitious spirit.

This is what distinguishes us from the animals. This is what makes us in very truth Sons of God.

> "Waste no tears
> Upon the blotted record of lost years,
> But turn the leaf
> And smile, oh, smile to see
> The fair, white pages that remain for thee."
>
> —Ella Wheeler Wilcox

CHAPTER 26

Don't Put It Off and Don't Give Up

How "Putting Off" Lost a War

The British War Office has made an important decision. In order to crush the American colonies, it is decided that General Burgoyne, in Canada, shall march south to meet, at Albany, the forces of General Howe, who is to march north from New York. Through the union of these two forces the American colonies will be cut in two and further resistance will be impossible. The letter of instructions to Burgoyne has been forwarded by Lord George Germain, the British Secretary of State for the American colonies, and the letter to Howe is in preparation.

The weekend comes. Lord Germain has planned to make a visit to his country estate.

On his way out of London—by horse and carriage—he stops at his office to take care of important last-minute business. The most important business is to sign the letter of instructions to General Howe. He finds, however, that his under-secretary, D'Oyly, has forgotten to write these instructions.

"If you will wait just five minutes," says D'Oyly apologetically, "I'll write a few lines."

"So!" cries Lord Germain angrily, "my poor horses must stand in the street all the time, and I can never do anything as I plan it. The letter will just have to wait till I get back."

And with these words he leaves in a huff—to take care of his poor horses— and to get to his country place.

Not only are the instructions not sent on time, but they are never sent—for upon Lord Germain's return to town both he and his secretary D'Oyly have completely forgotten the matter.

Howe never gets these instructions, and not knowing what else to do marches southward.

Largely because of lack of Howe's aid Burgoyne suffers total defeat and the capture of his entire army by the Americans at Saratoga.

Because of this great and decisive victory Benjamin Franklin is able to induce the French king to send aid to the American colonies.

Because of this aid Washington is able to bottle up Cornwallis at Yorktown and force his surrender. With this surrender England has forever lost her American colonies.

The American colonies won their independence because of their own courage and love of freedom—but it is also true that Britain lost the colonies because of stupidity and blundering on the part of her generals and statesmen. Had it not been for Lord Germain's procrastination regarding Howe's instructions, the result of the war might have been far different.

Among those who have the ability to succeed, the one greatest cause of failure is procrastination. Through waste of time:

Duties go unperformed.
Important decisions are never made.
Opportunities fly by ungrasped.
Engagements go unmet.
Trains are missed.
Life itself slips by unlived.

Whatever is being done—*all* that is being done—in this vast teeming world of ours is being done *now. Today.* Nothing has ever happened *tomorrow.* What you are going to be—what success you will reach—is being decided by the action you are taking *now.*

The procrastinator fools himself into thinking he has more time than he has. He puts off deciding until it's time to act; because of fear decides to do that important job next week; forgets to keep accurate check on his time; tries to solve a big problem without enough facts or without analysis and ends up by not solving it at all; postpones unpleasant tasks until tomorrow.

The smart man has a definite schedule and follows it. He keeps a fresh list of jobs to do and then does today the things that need doing today. He makes a definite decision to keep all engagements on time. He starts preparation early enough so that when the time arrives to act he will be ready. He has an accurate timepiece and keeps an eye on it. He divides his big problem into little problems and solves them one at a time in order. He knows beforehand so thoroughly what he is going to do that he starts unafraid.

Cut out procrastination today.

Below are listed several suggested courses of action. Choose the one that fits you best and follow it out *now.*

1. Schedule your routine duties.
2. Set down the things (outside of routine) that you have to do and want to do—and set a definite time to give them your serious attention.
3. If you are undecided whether or not to do a certain thing, sit down and figure out the situation honestly. *Decide whether* you will do it or not. If you decide *not* to do it, *forget it.* If you decide to do it—*fix a definite time to do it.*
4. Plan to take up only one problem at a time till completion.
5. If your procrastination is the result of fear—*put fear aside—risk failure.* Put fear aside by telling yourself that while you *may* fail if you make the move you desire, your failure is certain and automatic if you *don't* make the move.
6. If you procrastinate when faced with a big difficult problem, *analyze,* break the problem into parts, and handle one part at a time.

Answer These Questions

1. *Is there something I know I ought to do, and haven't done?*
2. *Is there any good reason why I don't do it right now?*
3. *Do I have and follow a schedule of my daily routine duties—so as to avoid procrastination because of petty indecisions?*
4. *Do I crowd my calendar with so many appointments that I cannot possibly meet them on time?*
5. *Do I wait till 10 o'clock to prepare for a 10 o'clock appointment?*
6. *Do I waste time by inability to decide which of two courses of action to take?*

7. *Do I let small problems pile up on me while wasting time trying to decide on some big problem?*
8. *Do I waste time thinking vaguely about courses of action I will probably never take up?*
9. *Do I procrastinate because of some big problem which, because of my failure to analyze, seems impossible to solve?*
10. *Do I procrastinate in important matters because I let fear or distaste turn me aside from decision and action?*

Break through the cobwebs of indecision. Whenever you are faced with these questions:

Shall I do this or not?
Which of these courses shall I take?

and similar questions, remember that perhaps the biggest danger is in the *procrastination* resulting from your indecision. *Decide, act,* and you have a fighting chance for success—while indecision and procrastination can have no possible result but failure.

The Value of Persistence

A serene moon shines down on a calm sea.

But a roar fills the air, and the salt odor of the sea is smothered under the acrid fumes of gunpowder.

Broken masts, and spars, and fragments of sail float about—with here and there a man struggling frantically.

There is a lull in the firing from one of the ships—the one whose sails are nearly all gone, whose masts are jagged stumps, whose hull is shattered below the waterline. Has her captain decided to surrender? After all, with nothing but a sinking ship between him and the bottom of the ocean, he may well think it time to surrender.

The captain of the other ship notes the sudden quiet. Have the rebels decided to give up? he asks himself. If they have surrendered, their flag ought to be down, but through the smoke he cannot see what they are doing. He therefore cries out across the water:

HAVE YOU STRUCK YOUR COLORS?

And from the shattered ship the reply comes back, a defiant shout:

I HAVE NOT YET BEGUN TO FIGHT!

It is John Paul Jones, hero of the American navy. Far from admitting defeat, he is working out a new plan of attack.

Since his own ship, the *Bon Homme Richard,* is slowly sinking, the only way he can win is to *board the enemy ship* and fight the British on their own decks!

Slowly he maneuvers his unwieldy sinking ship closer to the enemy. Side scrapes side, and then drifts away again. John Paul's men make several attempts to grapple the enemy, but without success. Then, by chance, an anchor-fluke of the *Bon Homme Richard* catches in a chain attached to the other ship. The enemy is caught! A little quick deft work with ropes and the two ships are lashed firmly together.

"Board her! board her!" shouts John Paul, and indomitable American seamen swarm across to the decks of the British frigate—*and start their fighting.*

Soon, almost alone among his dead and dying, the British captain strikes his own colors, and John Paul and his exultant Americans sail away, masters of the *Serapis,* while the *Bon Homme Richard,* a hopeless wreck, slowly sinks.

Without *persistence,* John Paul, instead of sailing back to France in command of the *Serapis,* might well have gone to a watery grave with the *Bon Homme Richard* or have been captured by the British and dangled from a yard-arm as a pirate.

You know, there's a peculiar thing about persistence. Most of us have much more persistence than we realize. We have great persistence—but do not exert that persistence in the *right direction. Persistence* is the expression of a man's *will to live.* We can either exert our persistence by pushing the world out of our way till we reach freedom or *success*—or we can exert it by *running away* from our problems and difficulties—and let the world crush us the first time we stumble. But persistence must be combined with intelligence. If at first you don't succeed, try, try again—but in different ways! Many a man, who objects that his persistence does no good in doing difficult jobs, fails because of persisting with the wrong method instead of using his persistence to find and use new and better methods until he *does* succeed.

Of two men, one brilliant and with little persistence, the other of average intelligence but great persistence, the second is far more likely to achieve great results—in science, in art, in the professions, in *business.* The Law of Averages will favor the man who persists. All of us have bad luck and good luck. The man who persists through the bad luck—who keeps right on going—is the man who is *there* when the good luck comes—and is ready to receive it.

Which way do you persist? If your heart ticks off the normal number of beats per minute, you have plenty of persistence. The question is, are you exerting that persistence in the RIGHT DIRECTION in connection with your work?

Here are a number of questions that will enable you to check on yourself. Answer these questions honestly, and thereby learn in what parts of your work you are lacking in the RIGHT KIND OF PERSISTENCE.

Man fortunately has it in his own power to change the direction of his persistence if he will only make an honest, intelligent effort to do so. Change the direction of your persistence where you are now using the wrong kind, and you will be able to make many gains you are now losing.

1. *Reviewing my own life, can I cite definite cases in which I have achieved something I wanted just because of unusual persistence on my part?*
2. *Since I achieved success in those instances simply because of my PERSISTENCE, isn't it logical to believe that the steady use of persistence in my work, day in and day out, will pay me real dividends?*
3. Do I *persist doing the work every day that I know I ought to do to achieve the ends I desire?*

4. Do I *persist more in running away from difficulties—or in overcoming them?*
5. Do I *persist in studying my business or work to try to better my knowledge of it?*
6. Do I *persist in studying my work to try to improve it?*
7. Do I *have people who I KNOW need my work—and will possibly suffer loss if I don't persist until I see them?*

DON'T GIVE UP! Many men who have achieved great success modestly disclaim the possession of genius, brilliance, or unusual intelligence, attributing their success to an average intelligence coupled with great persistence and will-power.

Others, still more modest, attribute their success to luck.

When John Paul Jones was attempting to lash the *Bon Homme Richard* to the *Serapis* so he could board the latter, it was pure luck that an anchor-fluke of his ship caught in a chain of the British frigate. But if he had not persisted in fighting *long after apparent defeat,* this "luck" would not have come to him.

Luck is chance, and most of us have an equal share of both good and bad luck. But many of us fail to enjoy the good luck that ought to be ours simply because we do not have the necessary positive persistence to carry us through the bad luck that happens to hit us first.

"They are fools whose hearts are set on riches but whose souls admit defeat."

217

Consecration

Laid on Thy altar, my Lord divine
Accept my gift this day for Jesus' sake;
I have no jewels to adorn Thy shrine,
Nor any world-famed sacrifice to make.
But here I bring within my trembling hands
This will of mine—a thing that seemeth small
And only Thou, dear Lord, canst understand
How, when I yield Thee this, I yield mine all.

Hidden therein Thy searching eyes can see
Struggles of passion, visions of delight,
All that I love or am, or fain would be—
Deep loves, fond hope, and longing infinite.
It hath been wet with tears and dimmed with sighs:
Clinched in my grasp till beauty it hath none.
Now, from Thy footstool, where it vanquished lies,
The prayer ascendeth, O, may Thy will be done.

Take it, Oh, Father, ere my courage fail:
And merge it so in Thine own will that e'en
If in some desperate hour my cries prevail
And thou give back my gift, it may have been
So changed, so purified, so fair have grown,
So one with Thee, so filled with peace divine,
I may not know, or feel it as my own,
But gaining back my will, may find it Thine.

—AUTHOR UNKNOWN

PART VII

SECRET NUMBER SEVEN THE MASTER PILOT TO STEER THRU LIFE'S STORMS

CHAPTER 27

How to Get a Daily Blueprint to Help Plan Your Life

Faith is an ever-growing tree, more long-lived than the giant redwoods of California. The growth of Christian wisdom did not cease when the last book of the Bible had been written and received with love and esteem by the early church fathers. In each age the great tree of faith puts forth new branches; Luther, Calvin, Knox, Wesley—these are names that testify to its constant vitality. Our own time, too, has seen the birth of powerful religious movements. Not the least important of them is one identified with the initials MRA.

MRA—the letters stand for Moral Re-Armament—has swept like a tidal wave over many lands. This flood of faith has washed countless thousands clean of sin and borne them onward to a better existence. Many prominent persons in different walks of life have testified to its great value for the modern world; it was highly praised by Henry Ford, Richard E. Byrd, Harry S. Truman, and Joe DiMaggio. The president of Norway's Parliament, C. J. Hambro, declared MRA has made a new man of him.

MRA supporters are confident that their movement will make the brotherhood of man a reality. "Out of a million homes in touch with God will come a nation's peace," they say. "Nationalism can unite a nation. Supernationalism can unite a world. God-controlled supernationalism is the only sure foundation for world peace."

How does Moral Re-Armament hope to achieve this great goal of world peace where hard-headed statesmen and planners have failed?

The answer is: By living according to the Word of God. Covenants between nations may fail, but not covenants between man and his Maker. People must accept the ethic of fair play and make it an integral part of their lives. Once they put hatred out and let God in, all major human problems can readily be solved.

Of course religious persons have been saying this almost since the beginning of time. The novelty of MRA is that it is doing something about it.

Moral Re-Armament has recovered some of the crusading zeal of the Apostles who carried Christ's message far from the tiny land of His birth. Not a sect or a cult with churches of its own, but working through all churches, it has succeeded in teaching people to live together and act together, to share their heartaches and their happiness, and to renew their spirit by a full acceptance of God and the principle of honesty. The quest for wealth and the pursuit of sensual pleasure have come to seem idle things to these persons, weighed against the pure delight of putting their energies to work in the service of the Lord.

Sometimes you will hear the members of MRA—there are thousands of them—organized in lively, informal circles around the globe and referred to as the Oxford Group or Fellowship. The great University of Oxford, the home of Newman and Keble, is also the home of this modern religious movement. Oddly enough, however, the man behind the movement is not an Englishman.

MRA's Founder

Frank N. Buchman first saw the light of day in a small town of Pennsylvania, where his father ran a hotel. His mother was a woman deeply confirmed in the Lutheran faith, and it seemed natural to her that her son should become a minister when he came of age. Young Frank was glad to go along with her wishes.

But this earnest youth could see his mission as no routine one. He gave up his first pastorate early, and moved on to Philadelphia. Not only was he active in guiding the development of the Church of the Good Shepherd, his enormous zeal drove him on to establish a

Lutheran settlement house, the first in the city.

After about five years of this valuable work, Frank found himself in conflict with his church's committeemen. These gentlemen wanted him to reduce expenditures that went to provide food and shelter for the needy. But to Frank, his godly labors came first. He could not compromise on such a vital matter. Harboring more ill will than he felt was fitting in a good Christian, particularly a clergyman, he shook the dust of Philadelphia from his feet and set out for Europe.

The Call Comes

It was in a small church in the village of Keswick, England, that Frank's call came to him. Mind you, up till now he had been a pious man. But he had been one among many, a rank-and-filer, not a general, in the Army of the Lord.

Sitting in the little church one afternoon, amid a congregation of but sixteen people, Frank listened to a woman preacher. She spoke of Christ and how He had taken the sins of the world upon His shoulders and died.

Before Frank's eyes there appeared a vision of Jesus on the cross. There was a look of infinite suffering on His face.

"I realized for the first time the great abyss separating myself from Him," says Buchman.

A sudden wind blew through the American minister's soul, sweeping from it all pettiness, ill will, and insecurity, and leaving in their place an overpowering feeling of love and selflessness. A great force seemed to drive him on to communicate this wonderful sensation to others.

After this spiritual upheaval, one of Buchman's very first deeds was to sit down and write letters to the six economy-minded board members of the church in Philadelphia, confessing the ill will he had nursed against them, and asking their forgiveness. They never replied, but Frank felt a burden had been lifted from his shoulders. He had relearned the ancient truth that confession is good for the soul, and henceforth he was to make this, as well as the practice of restitution, cardinal principles for himself and those who sought to find God under his leadership.

A New Kind of Faith

Frank returned to the United States. For seven years afterward, he worked at Penn State College with the YMCA. If he had been vigorous before, he was now a man inspired.

Faith, Frank taught the students who came to him, can be no passive thing. We must show by concrete acts how seriously we take our religion. He emphasized the importance of direct communion with God. His zeal touched off a spark in his listeners. Students who had cheated in examinations confessed their dishonesty and promised they would never be guilty of such an act again. Some who had stolen, came forward to make a clean breast of their crimes and return the things they had taken. Frank became widely known as a "life-changer," and soon his influence was felt on other campuses.

The Oxford Group Makes Headway

Buchman's success with the youths in American colleges was repeated as he traveled elsewhere. He seemed to have a special skill in working with the young. When he began his activities at Oxford, he skyrocketed to fame. Students who had succumbed to materialism to such an extent that life's values had lost all meaning were able to find themselves again under the minister's guidance.

Full of his mission, Frank sought not just to turn people back to God, but to make of each convert an apostle of godly living as well. He introduced a new wrinkle into the old business of saving souls. At his suggestion, his disciples gave parties for their classmates; the main business here, however, was not funmaking but confession and purifying one's heart.

Next, Frank went out into the world and around it, and his collegiate disciples did likewise. They found older men and women only too eager to confess, put away their sins, and gain a faith—the mighty One the Oxford Group had to offer. The movement spread like a fire in a dry forest.

Messages from the Holy Spirit

One reason the Oxford Fellowship has such power is that it speaks directly to God, and not just on Sundays. A member of the Group makes contact with his Lord every day. Each morning, the member sets aside fifteen minutes for direct communion with the Holy Spirit. This period is called "the quiet time." For a quarter of an hour the member rests peacefully, either sitting or on his knees in an attitude of prayer. Nearby he keeps a pad and pencil handy. Groupers call the pad their "guidance book."

A devout frame of mind opens the channel to God. Soon the person praying receives a message from God that has immediate bearing on some urgent problem or some question of everyday conduct. The counsel or order received in this way is often very specific. For example, it may tell a person to go and see somebody or do something; it may name names and give addresses or other precise information.

Following out the instructions they get in these messages, members of the Oxford Group have achieved fabulous results in life's endeavors. Some have found jobs, others have learned to better their position in business; still others have been led to the solution of serious difficulties in marriage, parenthood, and relationships with friends and associates. On the other hand, when they do not approach this communion in the right spirit, their efforts to tune in on the Infinite meet with no response.

According to the Oxford Groupers, one may tune in alone or in a group, so long as all are silent and receptive. If there is a need for guidance, the message will come through. The person who has fully given himself into God's hands will find the messages blaze a trail through the labyrinth of everyday living. God has a plan for all of us and this is one method by which it is made manifest.

How the Messages Are Tested

No doubt you are wondering: What about thoughts that seep in from the mortal mind? Isn't it possible for these to be mistaken for messages from the Holy Spirit?

Groupers have found a way to prevent errors of this kind. They give us touchstones which we may use to check the authenticity of the message. For one thing, it should not conflict with the teachings of Christ as revealed in the Bible. Four "absolutes" gives us an absolute test for the spiritual communication: absolute honesty, absolute purity, absolute love, and absolute unselfishness. If the message has all these qualities, and does not run counter to our real duties, we may safely follow it through.

If, however, we are not sure that the guidance we have received fully meets these requirements, we must go on praying until certainty comes. It is also possible to seek the opinion of another believer, or a group of believers, who can resolve the doubts one way or the other.

The Groupers tell us we may be guided throughout the day as well as at the quiet time. By reading the Bible and praying, by listening to our conscience and reasoning, or by talking to other Christ-minded persons in a church or group, we may find the light shed upon our path.

Guidance in Action

A. J. Russell, an outstanding London editor and author, as well as a man of profound religious impulse, became one of Frank Buchman's followers after he had made a careful inquiry into the purposes and methods of the Group. As part of his investigation, Mr. Russell relates in his book *For Sinners Only*, he called on Canon L. W. Grensted, one of the Church of England's most outstanding scholars and psychologists. Dr. Grensted was Oriel Professor of the Philosophy of the Christian Religion and a member of the Archbishop's Committee on Doctrine and on Spiritual Healing, besides being Canon of Liverpool. One of the queries Mr. Russell posed to the Canon concerned the guidance we have been speaking of.

" 'You think everybody needs this guidance?' "

" 'Unquestionably. Especially those who ascend in the world. As men climb to more important jobs, they find the difficulty of preserving a sense of proportion becomes far greater. By constantly referring their work back to God, it does put them into proportion for all sorts of situations, and helps them to adjust the difficulties of others. One does not like to make claims for oneself, but in so far as I have been able to make spiritual progress, it has been largely through the insight which has come from these Quiet Times of listening to God.

" 'Of course, nobody pretends that all one's thoughts are guidance. There is no knack about it. Guidance often comes in the form of good impulses—the work of the Holy Spirit in human life. I get strong and certain guidance about some things, and then some guidance which is not so clear. Often I get guidance on how best to handle people who come to me for advice in trouble. Yet the guidance that comes to one person is not very different from what comes to anyone else. It is simple and elemental. If one compared guidance-books, there would not be much difference, save that each contains things applicable to the person who wrote it for the time it was written.

" 'Guidance is often getting a new sanction for what we know already. Once it came to me in guidance to take a certain text, "Go into the City and it shall be shown you what you must do"—a text I had no wish to preach on, but I did, and three persons came to me afterwards to thank me for the special help which they had received. I often get guidance to speak on a subject that I have not prepared and to abandon the prepared subject. I always follow such guidance. A great advantage of guidance is that with it you have to make only one decision on one subject, whereas otherwise you might make twenty. For a while guidance may differ in a group of several persons, but eventually it is clearly shown that no real duties in life conflict. Which shows that the leading is part of the plan of God.' "

Losing His Life Every Day

Mr. Russell soon discovered that Frank Buchman himself is as much dependent on the Lord's guidance as is any other member of the Oxford Group. The English writer explains:

"It is impossible to understand Frank at all unless he is thought of as always in God's presence, listening for direction and accepting power, which he says is the normal way for a sane human being to live. Frank is an example of the psychologically mature man, thoroughly integrated round the highest relationship possible to man. The interesting part of this is the amazingly practical way his guidance works out.

"If a man's life is thoroughly integrated in God, he finds a dominant purpose in which everything fits. It does not mean rigidity, but being so flexible as to be responsive to unexpected opportunities giving further opportunities to serve God, Whose ways are not men's ways, as Paul found when he was going his roundabout way to Rome.

"Frank is perfectly disciplined. He does not wander voluntarily in his spiritual life: he goes direct to the Source all the time, and expects the Source to come direct to him. Whatever he does he feels must be right, since he is doing what is the guided thing for him to do.

"Through his constant practice of losing his life daily, he had come to find himself. He awakes in the morning with the idea that today is not his day, but God's day. Losing his life, he finds it all the time. The result of his discipline is abounding energy—which he is confident comes from the Holy Spirit. This discipline at the heart of the movement means complete freedom. The paradox of Christianity.

"Frank is a child listening to God and obeying Him implicity, and getting all those around him to do the same. And no one will ever understand this movement who does not accept this as a working hypothesis, whether he believes it or not at the start. After a time he begins to see it is true.

"As I thought of Frank living this listening-in life, I felt that it was excellent in theory, but impossible in general practice. And then the former Master of Selwyn (Dr. Murray) lent me the notes of one of his lectures on Prayer, in which I found this paragraph, which gave me a better understanding of Frank:

" 'For our life here is not meant to be a monotonous and lonely tramp on a treadmill. It is meant to be a brisk, an intelligent and adventurous march onward towards a goal which, however distant and however dimly discerned, is certain because God has appointed it. But it can only become this in proportion as we hear and respond to the call of God, to cooperate with Him in the bringing in of His Kingdom. And when you come to look under the surface of our Lord's teaching on Prayer, you see that it is all directed to secure just this harmonious and effective cooperation.' "

The Value of Confession

I have already given a general picture of the Oxford Group, but I should fill in some of the details, particularly on the value of confession. To lead the good life, we have seen, we must first surrender to the will of God. One approach to this is through public confession and restitution. "We must hate sin and expose it at every turn", says Frank Buchman. "Otherwise, it will continually drag us down."

If we confess to sin as soon as we become aware of it, a heavy weight is lifted from us and we gain a sense of freedom. Avowing our transgressions is no pleasant matter, and the simple memory of the act of confession will often serve to keep us from being guilty of sin, or at least the same sin, again. Then, too, when our friends listen to our confession, they get a keener awareness of the traps that they, too, must shy away from if they wish to possess a clear conscience. If we are strong in our love of God, it cannot be difficult to put sin from us.

Cleansed of sin by confession, and having fully accepted the Holy Spirit, we may gain guidance from on high, and learn what the Lord's plan is. We share our experiences with our fellows, and find a new kind of meaning and joy in human existence. Life is quite changed when it is guided by the four absolutes—love, purity, honesty and unselfishness, which should be the four points of our compass.

A Happier Family Life

Frank Buchman's teachings on family life hold great interest for us. We learn from him that people should not be too possessive, either toward their children or their mates. Our dear ones belong to God more than to ourselves, and we should inquire about His wishes for them before we allow our own full play.

Too often there is disagreement between husband and wife as their wills clash. One tries to bend the other to his wishes, and neither is happy with the disharmony that results.

The answer to this problem is to realize that the true meaning of love is surrender. In giving ourselves fully to those we love, we find deep happiness and so do they.

Still, so long as we are cased in flesh and subject to mortal weaknesses, we cannot free ourselves of the will to be independent to some degree. Full surrender is possible for us only when we give ourselves to God. Only when we belong to Him can we really learn to love one another in the finest and most satisfying sense. United in God's will, marriage partners may bring their union to genuine perfection.

These are some of the aims the Oxford Group has for the individual. That it has brought loving understanding and wonderful harmony into the lives of many cannot be doubted. If it could but prevail in the wide world, we would see the Golden Age in our own time.

Guided by this higher morality, husband and wife and mother and child could live peacefully together. Businessman and laborer would no longer squabble over the division of the fruits of their toil. Chinese, Russian, American, and German, mindful of their brotherhood under God, would see their interests as identical and not separate. Each man would stop wanting to change the other fellow, each nation would cease saying the other is at fault.

To make the world better, says the Oxford Group, the place to start is with ourselves. As men change, so will the nations.

CHAPTER 28

Your Problem Can Be Answered

Dreamland

Q: SOME time ago I purchased a little set of books—"The Secret of the Ages." I want to take this opportunity to tell you how much I enjoyed reading your books. Whatever your advice to the public, whatever you write, seems to instill so much courage and assurance that life is really worth living. You shine out like a light urging me to have heart and forge ahead."

Miss A.L.T., New York, N.Y.

A: That's a mighty nice letter of yours and I appreciate it. Did you ever see the movie called "Peter Ibbetson"? It was the story of a man unjustly convicted of murder, who had to serve all his life in prison. Physically, he led a miserable routine existence, but mentally he lived in dreamland—the happiest dreamland imaginable.

It's a beautiful picture and there's only one thing wrong with it—if one can live in that realm of dreamland, he presently finds that the dreamland becomes a reality, and the drab reality vanishes.

The great thing to realize is that wealth is just as plentiful, just as free as the air you breathe. For what is gold made of? Electrons and protons, just like the air about you, only in gold they are differently and more densely arranged.

God—the Father—has all this wealth, and you are His son—not only heir to Infinite supply, but He definitely gave you dominion over the earth.

What you must do is realize your sonship, realize the power it gives you; then command this Man inside You to turn to gold whatever amount of electrons may be necessary for your present need, leaving to Him the channel through which He will bring it to you.

In your business deals, don't worry about the commission end of it. Think rather of what you can do to serve your customers best.

There are always new and better ways of developing districts. Try to find these rather than struggle with your competitors over the little business that seems now available.

And when difficulties confront you, baptize them OPPORTUNITY and set the Man Inside You to finding the way to turn them from difficulties into opportunities.

Question: How can I rout out the devils of doubt and fear from my mind?

Answer: The worst thing about Fear and Worry is that while they exhaust a great part of the energy of the average person, they give nothing good in return. Nobody ever accomplished a single thing by reason of Fear and Worry. Fear and Worry never helped one along a single inch on the road to Success. And they never will, because their whole tendency is to retard progress, and not to advance it. The majority of things that we fear and worry about *never come to pass at all,* and the few that actually do materialize are never as bad as we feared they would be. It is not the cares, trials and troubles that we fear may come some time in the future. Everyone is able to bear the burdens of today, but when he heaps on the burdens of tomorrow, the next day, and the day after that, he is doing his mind an injustice, and it is no wonder that after a bit he heaps on the last straw that breaks the back of the mental camel.

The energy, work, activity and thought that we expend on these imaginary troubles of the future would enable us to master and conquer the troubles of each as they arise. Nature gives each of us a reserve supply of strength and energy upon which to draw and oppose unexpected troubles and problems as they come upon us each day. But we poor silly mortals draw upon this reserve force and dissipate it in combating the imaginary troubles of next week, or next year; the majority of which never really put in an appearance. And when we have need of the force to oppose some real trouble of the day, we find ourselves bankrupt of power and energy, and are apt to go down in defeat.

I tell you that if once you learn the secret of killing off this vampire of fear, and prevent the rearing of her hateful brook of reptile emotions, life will seem a different thing to you. You will begin to realize what it is to live. You will learn what it is to have a mind cleared of weeds, and fresh to grow healthy thoughts, feelings, emotions and ambitions.

How can you kill it out? Very easily! Suppose you had a roomful of darkness. Would you start to shovel or sweep out the darkness? Or would you not throw open the windows and admit the light? When the light pours in, the darkness disappears. And so with the darkness of Fear. Throw open the windows, and let a little sunshine in. Let the thoughts, feelings, and ideals of Courage, Confidence, and Fearlessness pour into your mind, and Fear will vanish. Whenever Fear shows itself in your mind, administer the antidote of Fearlessness immediately. Say to yourself: "I am Fearless; I fear nothing; I am Courageous." Let the sunshine pour in.

Question: I work in a big advertising agency. Sometimes I seem to be completely lacking in ideas for copy, and am overcome with nervous tension in trying to meet "deadlines." How can I open myself to the Universal Mind as the source of all ideas and wisdom?

Answer: Remember that "in quietness there is strength." Every person who is ambitious and has a definite object in life should take a few minutes off each day and sit alone, giving himself a chance to think, meditate, and allow the great rhythmic harmony of Nature to flow through his cleared mind, and thus gain renewed strength and energy. It is in these quiet moments, when the outer mind is relaxed and resting, that the inner mind flashes to us that which is best for us to do. We should cultivate this habit in moments of meditation, when we may escape from the people and the crowd, and thus be able to listen to the voice that sounds from within. By doing this, we place ourselves in harmony with the Great Universal Power from which all original ideas spring into our mental organism ready for use a few moments later when we re-emerge into the world of action and of men.

Here are a few directions for entering into harmony with the Universal Rhythm of Nature. First, your mental attitude must be right. You must have gained control of our thoughts and words, so that your mind is open and receptive to the great good of the world.

There must be no hate there, no discouragement, no pessimism, no negative, cringing, worm-of-the-dust or poverty thought. Your frame of mind must be that of good-will, encouragement, optimism; with positive thoughts expectant of wealth, prosperity, and all the good things that man, heir of the universe, is entitled to by right of his sonship. This latter mental attitude will surround you with a personal thought atmosphere which repels from you the negative or evil things and attracts to you the positive or good things of life.

Take a few deep breaths, which will tend to relax your body and mind. Then detach your thoughts from the outer world, and things, and turn the mind inward upon yourself. Shut out all the material cares, worries, and problems of the day and sink into a mental state of peaceful calm. Think, "I open myself to the inflow of the Universal Rhythmic Harmony," and you will soon begin to feel a sense of relationship with that Harmony coming to you, filling your mind and body with a feeling of rest and peace, and latent power. Then shortly after will come to you a sense of new strength and energy, and a desire to once more emerge upon the scene of your duties. Now go forth with your new energy, filled with the vibrations of the Universal, and you will see how refreshed and vigorous you are, and how your mind leaps eagerly and enthusiastically to the tasks before it.

A few moments spent with your inner self and the Great Universal Power each day, as described above, if practiced faithfully, will establish within you the Creative Mind—that wonderful thing which marks the difference between the ditch digger and the man at the top who does things—the capitalist who creates and builds. The more you practice, the more you will open up that great subconscious reservoir of yours which is overflowing with original ideas. In time you will gain the power to get in touch with your inner mind and tap the reservoir wherever you may be—in a car; out for a walk; while you are shaving— and there will flash through to your conscious mind, in vivid outlines, ideas that when worked out will mean for you Money and Financial Independence.

Question: Dear Mr. Collier: Can you please tell me your own Secrets of Success that have brought you wealth and prosperity?

Answer: It is told of Thomas Lawson, of Boston—he of *Frenzied Finance* fame—that when he was a youth, he painted a mental picture of a large estate with a swimming pool and beautiful gardens and trees and a home furnished with valuable objects of art and fine furniture. He has said that his successive steps toward the acquirement of that home—the gaining of the wealth necessary for its purchase—was like the filling of the details of the picture, the image of which faded away from his mind.

And so it is with Financial Success. You must form a mental picture of what you want, and then bend every effort to fill in the picture. Every person should have a purpose in life. To win anything one should have a definite goal for which to strive. We should have a picture in our mind of what we want to own or attain. If we want money, we should create a mental picture of money—see ourselves using it, spending it, acquiring more, and in short going through all the motions of the man of money. One should paint a great mental picture of wealth, and then start to work to fill in the picture, and to materialize it.

The majority of people say, "I want money—I want money," and that is all there is to it. They do not use their imaginations sufficiently to mentally create money, and then proceed to materialize it. You must first know just *what you want,* before you will be able to materialize it. Unless you know what you want, you will never get anything. The great successful men of the world have used their imaginations, instead of ignoring them. They *think ahead* and create their mental picture, and then go to work materializing that picture in all its details, filling in here, adding a little there, altering this a bit and that a bit, but steadily building—steadily building.

If you would attain Financial Success, you must become a mental creator and designer of that which you long for as well as a material builder. The two go hand in hand and work for Financial Success.

PART VIII

GO YOU AND PROFIT BY THEIR EXAMPLE

CHAPTER 29

Albert Lewis Pelton

How Pelton Gained 900,000 Customers Through Mail Order

SOME years ago there was a young man in a small Connecticut town with a book—and an idea. The book was written for ambitious men—to help show them the way to succes. This young man had an idea that he could sell it to every man who was willing to study and work for success. But selling takes time—and money. *And he had only a couple of hundred dollars to his name!*

In such case, what would you have done? Many a man, in the same circumstances, rails against fate—and does nothing. But above all else, this young man had courage. He believed in the book, he believed in his idea, and he was willing to stake his all on his judgment.

The question was—how to use his $200 so as to get the most of of it? As an appropriation for a publicity campaign, it was a joke. Bookstores? Posters? Circulars? Mail order! It would just pay for a page ad in one of the Current Events Magazines that was largely read by a high type of serious-minded man.

He took his problem to this magazine, and got its help and that of a good advertising agent in laying out his ad. Book men themselves, they knew the kind of copy that would most appeal to the book-buyer. And they helped him to put that kind of copy into his ad.

The magazine came out—and *nothing happened!* Two or three days passed—and still not an order. Can you imagine the suspense, with his last penny staked in the venture? He had almost concluded that he must bid his $200 "Goodbye!" Then a single order came straggling in. He welcomed it like a long-lost brother. Next day three or four. Then they started coming in bunches.

From that first ad, costing him $200, he got $2,000 worth of orders for his books!

The young man was A. L. Pelton, of Meriden, Connecticut, and that $200 was the start of his fortune. With the $2,000 received from his orders, he immediately placed more ads, and as the orders kept rolling in, branched out into other magazines. In the subsequent ten years this young man sold $7,000,000 *worth of books!*

And to show the quality of the books, more than half of that $7,000,000 represented *repeat* orders from pleased customers. After he staked his all on an idea, A. L. Pelton built up a list of over 900,000 customers and published more than 75 great inspirational works.

And all this from only $200 and an idea!

Of course, there will be some to attribute his success to luck, but if you have ever sold goods by mail (as I have), you know how small a share luck has in its success, and how great a part consists of careful planning, intensive thinking and hard work.

It was like the man who got up a dinner for Dr. Alexis Carrel and ascribed the success of this famous surgeon to genius. Dr. Carrel looked at him sadly. "Here I work heart and soul for twenty years to get where I am," he answered, "and all the credit I get for my effort is to be told I am a born genius." Genius is not born. Genius is acquired. And as Edison put it—it is 98% perspiration and 2% inspiration.

What is the lesson of Pelton's success? Simply this—that material capital is the least important of all the elements that go to make up success. The biggest successes have been built up from little or no money. The thing that counts—the thing without which any amount of money is useless—is the idea. And that can be the product only of mind.

You have a mind—as good a mind as Pelton or Ford or any other man who has built his fortune through his own unaided efforts. What are you doing with it? Are you developing ideas that will make men better or richer or more comfortable? Are you thinking in terms of service? Or are you just wondering how you can make more money?

There is only one man who will pay you money, you know—and that is the man for whom you do something—be that something the shining of his shoes, the writing of a book, the repairing of his car or the filling of his stomach. And the better you do it, the more he will pay you.

So think first in terms of service. What can you offer that people must have done for them?

Find the service—get the idea—then put into it everything you have—money and time and thought. In a few years, you also will be able to look upon your hundreds or your hundreds of thousands of satisfied customers.

How Pelton Built Up His Business by Mail

The career of Albert Lewis Pelton is a success story whose elements are a mixure of talent, energy, persistence, and the WILL to achieve.

Power of Will was the basis of Mr. Pelton's career. That is the title of the book which started him on a world-wide publishing enterprise which brought personal fortune to him. Today, Mr. Pelton lives in pleasant retirement at his home in Meriden, Connecticut, enjoying the fruits of his labor. His health is fine, and the same nervous restlessness, acumen, and persistence which helped him to the top in business success, characterize him today. *Power of Will* is now published by Robert Collier Publications, Inc.

For most of 35 years, Mr. Pelton operated the Pelton Publishing Company which maintained offices on Church street. From these quarters, thanks to the United States mails, his business stretched to every part of the nation, and to lands overseas. It is remarkable that very few Meriden people knew what he did or how he made his money.

"Most of them assumed we were a job printing affair," snorted Mr. Pelton. "I never had any printing equipment other than a letter duplicating machine and about 40 typewriters. My offices were for handling book orders, mailing millions of circulars offering the books for sale, a shipping department, and a collection department for tens of thousands of charge accounts."

"During my 35 years in publishing, I spent about $500,000 in national magazine advertising; and much more for the mailing of descriptive circulars seeking customers. I paid wages in Meriden of $700,000, counting my own office employees. Thus, our business benefited the local township, but practically all of the money received in sales came from the outside world. In 35 years of business I sold less than $50.00 worth of books locally. 'A prophet is not without honor, save in his own country, you know,' he observed with a wry smile.

Mr. Pelton's success is a striking tribute to the power of direct mail advertising. Not only did he build his fortune upon adroit advertising of fine books but he prepared the advertising himself.

Mr. Pelton was city advertising man for the *Meriden Morning Record.* The advertising instinct ran strong and deep in Mr. Pelton, whose ability as an ad writer was quickly proven on the *Record.* He studied ad writing on the side, and determined to try his talents in another direction and for his own exclusive gain. About this time, too, he was mulling over a book which he read and reread many times. The Book was *The Power of Will* by Frank Channing Haddock.

"I still have my first copy of the book," said Mr. Pelton, as he leafed through a worn volume bound in green cloth. "This book has travelled thousands of miles with me. During the year that I attended business college and later worked in Hartford, I read it going back and forth on the train. The book helped me so much that I thought it would help other people too. I got in touch with the author, Frank Channing Haddock. We entered into a contract and I began to try to sell it.

"While I was still at the *Record,* I rented a small upstairs room on West Main Street for an office. I had a girl address envelopes for mailing circulars advertising my books in response to ads which I had written and placed modestly in some magazines, and to such mailing lists as I could rent.

"After I had been with the *Record* for about six years, I rented a large room on the third floor of Wilcox Block and left the *Record.* I remember that E. E. Smith told me that he thought I was making a mistake, that the *Record* was an established business, and that it was pretty risky for a young fellow to try to start a business of his own. But I had made up my mind to leave.

"Because of much increased advertising and circularizing of prospects, I soon had several employees, and it was not long before I occupied six rooms in Wilcox Block and employed more than 60 office clerks. And in six years from leaving the *Record,* I had completed paying cash on the line for a 16 room house in Bradley Park, long known as the showplace of Meriden.

"During the busy years of my book publishing, a truck drove up to Wilcox Block five nights a week and loaded ten to twenty sacks of mail, circulars, and books, which skyrocketed the postage sales at the local post office. I think we had more incoming and outgoing mail than any other Meriden concern. The first books made for the Pelton Publishing Company were produced by a local printer, but soon they were unable to make them fast enough to meet increasing demand, and the book making was transferred to the Kingsport Press, of Kingsport, Tennesee, the largest book production concern in the country."

Mr. Pelton took over publication of the *Ralston Books,* written by Edmond Shaftsbury, the pen name of Webster Edgerly, who was a one-time president of the Ralston University in Washington, D.C. Shaftsbury was quite a fellow in his day; he had a wide acquaintance among the leading political figures of the day. Shaftsbury was no slouch himself as a promoter. He got fancy prices for his books. Several of them sold for $25 each, and one sold for $50.

The initial leader which Mr. Pelton used to promote the *Ralston Books* was *Instantaneous Personal Magnetism.* He sold more than 500,000 copies of this title alone. The Ralston history runs back many years, stemming from the "Ralston Health Club," an agency devoted to disseminating information on how to become healthy and stay healthy. There were Ralston Health Clubs all over the country which used as a testbook, *Life Building Methods.* This book went through more than 100 editions, and it is published today by the Ralston Publishing Company, under the direction of Mr. Martin Kohe. Present title of the book is *Complete Life Building of Nature's Doctors.*

Besides the *Personal Power Books* and the *Ralston Books,* the Pelton Publishing Company took on the sales of the *Napoleon Hill Books.* The sales of the 'leader' in this group was the famous *Think and Grow Rich* of which he sold 120,000 copies. Since then Mr. Kohe has sold nearly 100,000 more copies. In addition to the *Think and Grow Rich* book, there was an eight-volume *Law of Success* library. In promoting his books, Napoleon Hill made use of testimonials by such leading public figures as Andrew Carnegie, Thomas A. Edison, and four presidents of the United States—Theodore Roosevelt, Taft, Wilson and Harding—also university presidents, and such business leaders as F. W. Woolworth, king of the 5 & 10 cent stores, and George Eastman of the Eastman Kodak Co. They all praised Hill's simplification of the principles of a philosophy of success and wished him well.

"MY BOOK BUSINESS was no 'fad idea', offering some quickly forgotten books to light-minded people. Among my far-flung clientele, I was honored by the patronage of hard-headed, keen-minded high executives in scores of the greatest industries of the country," said Mr. Pelton.

"More than two million men and women of America have been helped by the approximately 75 different 'self-improvement' books which the Pelton Publishing Co. distributed.

"Looking back, I believe that in my 35 years as an inspirational book publisher, with huge sums spent in magazine advertising and millions of direct mail circulars, I did make it known throughout the United States that there was a city in Connecticut named Meriden."

Mr. Pelton's adroitness as a businessman and his exceptional knack in using advertising to advantage contributed in large measure to making his fortune from the very start of his career.

"ALL PUBLISHING was on a royalty basis, so far as payment to the authors was concerned," explained Mr. Pelton. "Eight per cent was the royalty rate. This meant that on a $3 book, the author got 15 cents on cash received."

Mr. Pelton's reference to "cash received" is significant.

"I WAS ONE of the first to advertise 'Send no money; read five days free; then pay $3 or return the book'." said Mr. Pelton. "On this basis over half a million books were sent out. During several years we carried from 15,000 to 20,000 such open accounts. We found that about 90 per cent of the people were honest and kept their agreement. Of course, it required an elaborate collection system to handle so many accounts.

Part of the Pelton technique lay in getting a single volume, "the leader" into the hands of a customer, then persuading him to buy a set of books along the same line.

"THE FOLLOW-UP was the juice, not the original sale," said Mr. Pelton. "If we broke even on single book sales, there was no complaint. Because to such buyers we sold on installment accounts tens of thousands of sets of books ranging from $16 to $36 per set. This was the real profit of the book business."

As for hobbies, Mr. Pelton has never had any except his work.

"MY HOBBY was working like the devil writing sales literature," he said. The Cleveland firm which todav publishes about 30 of the books which were formerly issued by the Pelton Publishing Co. still uses some of Mr. Pelton's pieces.

Mr. Pelton married Louise Benker of Meriden. They have two sons, Charles Pelton of Dorchester, Mass., and Roger Pelton of San Francisco and a daughter, Gloria.

Looking back over his career of 35 years, Pelton commented:

"I feel that through the many instructive and inspirational books of the Pelton Publishing Co., I have helped bring health, happiness and success to millions of men and women."

THE CAREER of Albert Pelton presents the amazing phenomenon of a "mail order medicine man" who took his own medicine and achieved in abundance the success which he offered to those who bought his wares.

Albert Pelton's record is a most amazing one and an inspiration to all of us. Almost single-handedly, he built up a huge business solely by mail. He rang up over seven million dollars in sales of his books and courses; all from circulars sent to customers through the post office. He had no agents and very little was done through bookstores. He started with virtually nothing in a money way. But he was willing to devote long hours, days and evenings, to keep up a steady flow of direct mail advertising circulars. He was a one man business and had only himself and his wife to be accountable to.

Pelton's books have sold millions of copies and awakened the urge to manifest Personal Power in many thousands of ambitious Americans. Some of these thousands have attained enormous wealth and outstanding success from an application of the principles outlined in Pelton's books. His courses have been "incubators" of men who "do things." These men have been inspired to go to the top in the business, professional and political worlds.

CHAPTER 30

The Creed of the Conquering Chief

By Albert Lewis Pelton

How to Become a Genius

MAN is the crowning work of the Maker of all created things.

He gains his greatness and maintains his position of supremacy solely because he possesses that wonderful endowment: MIND—the ability to think and reason; and having thought—to forge ahead along such lines as he chooses.

He is forever separated from—and superior to—all other orders of creation, because no other has this "Mind" attribute.

For many years I have been an investigator in that great field of phenomena known as Psychology—the study of the Human mind.

In my studies and researches into the Science of mental power, my experiments had been largely in the realm commonly termed Genius.

Genius is the classification given certain men who exhibit rare qualities of mind-power. It is used to describe the sort of men who concentrate and intensify, to the *nth* degree, phases of brain energy which the mass of men use only in a weak, scattering way.

"The highest form of creation, whether in art or life, is genius," says Wingfield-Stratford. "Genius is natural to man, and in no way more mysterious than any other faculty of the mind. It may be defined as subconscious activity functioning rightly."

Men of Genius are unmistakable guide-posts where History records man's passage from the beginning to the end of world-life. Men of genius are stately peaks rising above the foothills covered by the submerged multitudes.

I had sought to discover the causes or secret—the foundation principle, as it were—of the great men. Time after time I had mentally asked myself:

1. *Are there any definite laws which the superior man applies?*
2. *Is "Genius" a divine endowment—the despair of all to whom it*

does not come early and clearly in life?

3. Are men of genius a "race apart'—each one struck off from the Great Center only at odd intervals?

Those were some of the questions for which I tried to find answers in my mind. They caused much thought and meditation. In whatever direction I pursued my quest for some tangible result—always was it made manifest that the genius-mind exemplified these deep truths:

1. Thought *intensified.*
2. Vision *made concrete.*
3. Clear observation *frozen into fact.*

In short—it is Mind-power turned into ACTION. Genius is energy-charged, Will-directed, Thought-force *vitalized into life.* This is the turning point at which the man of genius separates himself from the humdrum crowd.

Thought is Power!

Again and again declare that great truth. Believe it. Dream it. Go forth and PUT IT INTO ACTION.

Ah yes!—ability to *think*—that is the great man's chief characteristic. It is Brain-energy harnessed and made productive; it is the trait which infallibly makes men masters.

I have watched men at work and men at play. I have studied the mass—the so-called "submerged millions"—and their minds grow little more than weeds. Their brains are giving them scant harvests. Something has blighted and stunted their productiveness. Their brain plants seem to have scarcely enough depth or root to save them from blowing across the sands—withering and disappearing.

And they constitute the bulk of mankind!

Yet again—here and there I have seen men whose minds were productive to a remarkable degree. Deep, fertile, steadily reaching upwards—self-centered, sturdy and strong. They owned brains which were yielding rich fruits of thought—a Mind in all its greatness.

The Mind has two levels or phases of action. The upper or surface level which often reveals beautiful creations and hangs heavy with rich and luscious fruits—those wonderful products of mental growth and harvest. The lower level—that deep, unfathomable sea—is where the surface life roots down and from which it draws its nourishment and power.

These two levels of the Mind are given the names *conscious* and *sub-conscious.* The mind-life of which we are aware in the round of the day's duties, is the Conscious phase of mind. Deep down below the surface, there exists a vast mental life of which we are not aware. It is the sub-conscious realm—the powerhouse of Thought-energy.

It is from these depths that men of genius draw a brimming measure of creative power. It is from this unfailing spring the great man brings up into conscious use the huge stores of thought or idea-force which he turns into visible ACTION or RESULTS. Then men call him "genius."

The relation of the conscious mind to the sub-conscious (under) mind might be illustrated in this way: after a heavy rain storm you will find the ground still damp or wet on the surface. But deeper and deeper down—trickling through the grains of sand—the *bulk* of the rain has passed, finally to accumulate far below the surface, awaiting the call of the artesian drill.

Such a reservoir is your sub-conscious mind. During your waking hours it is incessantly receiving a supply of thought material from the upper or conscious mind. It is storing, combining, mixing, increasing and amassing BRAIN-POWER. All that you have ever seen, heard or felt has sunk down into your subconscious storehouse.

Great is he who has learned the secret of making the subconscious yield up its unlimited wealth. HE IS A GENIUS.

I asked of many I met: *"What is the secret of reaching this great reservoir of Power? How can this subconscious mind be tapped in the way the genius draws upon it? How can the average man command this creative force in a masterly fashion?"*

And always did those who had given the subject any thought reply *"O, genius is just 'inspiration', that's all,"* or words to that effect. Others said: *"Genius is the result of hard work."*

To be a genius one need only study hard enough to be able to tell the people what they already think. The superiority of genius is therefore no different from that of any educated person; *except in the degree of application.* Anyone might possess this superiority.

People seem to hold the common belief that the great man is a peculiar personality, unsolvable excepting on the ground of a divine "inspiration" having aroused his every cell and fibre and nerve—and made him what he is.

Therefore my problem resolved into this question: "What is 'inspiration,' so called?"

I say: *Inspiration is a Mind a-flame.*
Inspiration is a Heart a-glow.
Inspiration is a Body a-tingle.

Inspiration, as explaining the great man's secret, is nothing else than energy from the subconscious mind flaring up into the field of the conscious mind—and rapidly ripening fruits or products which astonish the average person.

I have seen men at their work—dull, listless, mentally asleep. "Nobody at home" as the expression is. And again, here and there I have seen another kind of man, in whom was pulsating a vibrant Life-energy—a Mind-energy—a Creative-energy. He is eager, ambitious, alert, and alive in every cell. His very soul seems to be peering out of his eye-windows—beaming in every action and effort to express his true Self. It is to men of this type that "inspiration" comes as a spark which flashes into action the gift of greatness.

"God creates by intuition; man creates by inspiration, strengthened by observation. This second creation, which is nothing else but divine action carried out by man, is what is called genius."

What, then, is the secret of this inspirational spark?

Most of us, alas, allow this quality of genius to slumber, to weaken, and to fade away. We go through life unaware of what we might do, of the high goals we might reach, of the brilliant accomplishments really open to us, of the masses of men we might lead—and the success-heights to which we might rise.

All, in the last analysis, because we are too "indolent" to make the glorious attempt.

The Creed of the Conquering Chief

Behold! I address this message to men of courage and ambition.

I bid you to fearlessly look upon the inner shrine wherein you hold dear your ambition of ambitions—that guarded secret which is nothing less than your desire to BE SUPERIOR—to be supreme in your life-sphere—to be dominant and TO LEAD.

In short—it is your *self* calling for CONQUEST.

I know my own heart in this respect. I know the fundamental traits of other men's hearts.

Unafraid, I express my self. I speak that which is within me. I talk of natural, inexorable laws. I set forth my own instinct. You will come to agree with much that I say.

If I advance opinions and tenets which surprise you—which you have never thought of before—which possibly "cut in"—then I ask you: *"Why should I be shackled by the cottony bands which most men allow to hold them in everlasting subjection? Why may I not dispel these gossamer threads of foolish tradition and maudlin sentiment which a mere breath of intellectual effort will scatter to the skies?"*

We live in an artificial state of society. There is not the rugged, vital, agressive type of man now, as of old. Members of the civilized social order are emasculated, as it were, if comparison is made with the *natural man.* We see foppery, vanity, and effeminacy on all sides. There is a fawning attitude, and a sinking of individuality.

If you could silently, quietly, clearly, peer into the hearts of the sad failures in life—if you could once learn the never-revealed sombre secret of men and women who merely serve as the background mass of humanity—the dark wall which sets forth in added brilliance the splendor of the successful—THERE, in that closed chamber, would be read the Tale of FEAR—cringing, hesitating, shrinking, servile COWARDICE.

It is a tragedy.

For it's the story of bright hopes blasted—the record of things hoped for, but never gained.

It's the life history of a good soul seeking higher levels of power and unfoldment, but bound and shackled and scared by an ever present: *"Oh, I dare not."*

It's the chronicle of youth's fine faith in a golden future, filled with health, happiness and financial ease—all gradually dimmed and blotted and finally sunk into oblivion. All because the race struggle for supremacy requires MEN WHO DARE.

In other words—men who are fired with the spirit of The Conquering Chief.

There are FOUR stages through which you mentally pass in establishing firmly the mood or tendency for conquest. These steps are:

1. I *wish* for Conquest.
2. I *desire* to conquer.
3. I am *resolved* upon conquest.
4. I DEMAND and INSIST that I become a conqueror.

If you are to go on with me, you must have the Open Mind.

Hundreds of millions grind out their grist of human grief in a never-changing, never widening, soul-stunting narrowness of mental vision.

CHAPTER 31

Pelton's Seven Essential Points For Success

Point One: PLOT WITH YOURSELF TO WIN.

To crush obstacles—whether of personal weaknesses, opposition of others, unexpected developments. Plan out what you must do to GAIN YOUR GOAL. MASS YOUR UTMOST POWERS to crush each obstacle that bars your way to what you desire.

Go forward with just as definite, a detailed, prearranged plan as Napoleon prepared a battle map months ahead of the encounter. Most people drift—and the fickle tide of fate ebbs and flows. One day is the same as another to them so far as any definite plan, strategy, attack upon fortune, power, fame and success is concerned.

Strategy, brain-work, thought, speed, decisiveness— all these are your chief weapons.

Remember, to falter, hesitate, and back down on your plans—to give up—to weaken and lazily quit, is to dissipate the conquest power within you.

Make great plans—but forever fight forward for their consummation. Make plans at first well within your power of accomplishment. Stick to them. Achieve them.

When you have risen a degree—view from aloft the incline up which you have come. It creates confidence. It develops power. It instills courage. It steels the sinews for greater effort. Then gradually brave steeper ascents—try the larger task. Go upwards. Dominate. CONQUER—until you reach and master the big things. Some day in your career you will assay the Grand Ascent—your Life's Ambition; your Crowning Achievement in Life. Up, up you go, with adequate ability, clear sight, sure steps, iron grip, unfailing energy.

For so do the World's Great rise.

Emerson, in his clear, precise way, tells us:

"Life is a search for Power; and this is an element with which the earth is so saturated there is no chink or crevice in which it is not lodged—that no honest seeking goes unrewarded."

You should interpret his use of the word "Power" as meaning an intangible force, influence, medium or *"something"* which man can control and make use of to attain his legitimate goals.

All the Power you can ever use now exists potentially within you and awaits your intelligent mastery.

What people commonly call Fate is, as a general rule, nothing but their own stupid and foolish conduct.

Life is one long battle; we have to fight at every step.

It is a cowardly soul that shrinks or grows faint and despondent as soon as the storm begins to gather, or even when the first cloud appears on the horizon. Our motto should be *No surrender.* As long as the issue of any matter fraught with peril is still in doubt, and there is yet some possibility left that all may not come right, no one should ever tremble or think of anything but resistance.

The pathway to Power calls for everlasting vigilance, to the end that your own natural weak tendencies may be overcome by never yielding to their solicitations.

Point Two: THE POWER OF AN IDEA. The Conquering Chief, from the day of the cave man's discovery of the sling as a weapon superior to his arm-hurled rock, up to the present-day giants of conquest—whether in war, finance, science, thought—have all progressed through the POWER OF AN IDEA.

Says someone: *"the most potent, powerful, revolutionizing thing in the world is AN IDEA."*

Idea is Power!

Ideas rule the world.

An idea built the Universe.

A single idea—the sudden flash of a thought—may be worth a million dollars, and one trained mind can be the sponsor of a momentous plan. In your brain are real "ideas of power" awaiting the miracle of birth.

One idea birthed America.

Edison had an idea—and gave man the incandescent light.

Carnegie's brain flashed an idea into steel—and it paid him multimillions.

Woolworth had just a 5 and 10 cent idea—but the stores he

sprinkled over the country have made many fortunes.

Single ideas issuing from the recesses of gray matter have made men immortal.

Ideas are conceived in the brain cells, are nurtured in their depths, and pass on to the miracle of birth.

Enshrouded in them is the marvel of divine creation.

Wonderful mental fruits grow in the fertile fields of the master intellects of a race.

Rich, virile, power-fraught ideas fairly overflow as they rush forth from the man-type termed "genius."

Your brain, so Science says, has a possible capacity for producing *over three billion ideas.*

How many of this uncountable number of ideas, hidden in your thought-cells, are you bringing into living and breathing existence?

Are you creating forceful thoughts?

Do feasible ideas fairly flash from your brain as sparks leap the gap in a static electric machine?

Are they making you bigger and better and more powerful in your life's sphere?

There are millions of thought-cells in the human brain which are never used. Each individual has capacities that are never realized; powers that are never unfolded.

Why?

Largely because of sheer laziness to delve into the treasure vaults of the mind.

Most men go from cradle to the grave, unaware of the vast "acres of diamonds" locked in their own brains. "What a tremendous power lies coiled in the mind of man!" says Emerson.

In 1810 the world watched with bated breath as a crowning example of the power of ideas held sway.

One small man toppled kings off their thrones and made over the Map of Europe to suit his whims.

Why?

Sharp and clear comes the answer.—

SIMPLY BECAUSE HE HAD AN IDEA.

And when Napoleon applied his strategy—he stood towering

above the crowd, a Superman headed for world domination.

It was the "power of an idea."

That's all.

And so, every man who is making his mark; every leader of men, yes every living human being who is going two-rounds-at-a-time to dazzling heights on the ladder of success, is doing it—

HOW?

Solely by means of the IDEAS which he makes his own brain produce.

What are you doing to open the way for the "three billion capacity" of your brain?

As a Conquering Chief you must learn where ideas are started, how to have more and better ideas. You must learn how your brain works. You must become skilled in getting greater values from it. You must learn how to get the power out of ideas.

"There is no limit to the capacity of the mind for holding ideas. An overloaded mind is an ill-arranged mind. It may confidently be affirmed that there is nobody who is incapable of developing genius in the right direction, for genius is as natural to man as is the flower to the seed."

Point Three: ALWAYS WILL I STRIVE TO BE GREATER THAN I AM. I Must SURPASS MYSELF. In each successive act, test, encounter, thought, I will BE GREATER than in the one previous. I am what I am now; but in an hour I must be MORE than I am now. In everything must I exert MORE POWER TO SURPASS MYSELF.

The spirit of the foregoing theme is well-illustrated by Stewart Edward White in the "Blazed Trail" where he says:

"Of these men Thorpe demanded one thing—success. He never tried to ask of them anything he did not believe to be thoroughly possible; but he expected always that in some manner, by hook or crook, they would carry the affair through. No matter how good the excuse, it was never accepted. Accidents would happen, there as elsewhere; *a way to arrive in spite of them always exists, if only a man is willing to use his wits, unflagging energy and time.* Bad luck is a reality; but much of what is called bad luck is nothing but a want of careful foresight."

Surpassing of *self* is the first aim; surpassing of *others* is the second. This is the substance of Emerson's *"Every man believes he has a greater possibility."* You draw a circle to the utmost of your ability today, but on the morrow, lo—you must still draw one *outside* of that. You must *surpass yourself.*

This is involved philosophy, bordering perhaps upon mysticism. But—STOP AND THINK!

"Whatever cannot obey itself is commanded" says the great writer on "surpassing self." The failures in life are the men who could not or would not obey themselves; they became commanded by others. They could not hold to the course; they lost their grip. They did not do as they promised their own hearts they would do.

They failed to surpass themselves.

For such is the nature of things—he who cannot obey himself, in an ever-increasing degree is commanded by others.

The Conquering Chief MUST OBEY HIMSELF if he is to command others.

It is here that I would have you work into your plan of action this declaration:

From now on I vow I will try to act the part of a man TEN TIMES BIGGER THAN I AM NOW; for by so doing, I construct greater powers in my own brain which will actually build me into such a leader. I refuse to be confined by the shadowy walls which heretofore have cramped me into a narrow sphere. From this day forth the word "limit" is banished from my mind.

Point Four: BE A MINUTE BUILDER. WASTE NOT ONE MOMENT IN YOUR CLIMB TO SUCCESS.

You and I are architects of the minutes.

We build ourselves every moment.

What you are this minute is the result of what you were building during the thousands of minutes that already have passed.

What you will be a minute from now depends upon what you are now, *plus* what you are mentally demanding that this present moment shall add. With every turn of the second hand, are you building yourself anew? Are you changing, altering, revising, remaking, INCREASING?

Just as surely as the pilot of a vessel deliberately moves his wheel one way, and swings the huge conveyance to the east; or moves it the other way and swings it toward the setting sun: he so pursues his course as he elects, and finally reaches his port if his steering has been correct. So can you deliberately direct your own course toward any goal.

I repeat: You are the product of minutes. Each minute is an opportunity to build—for growth, advance, gain, supremacy, CONQUEST.

It all rests with you.

Keep your eyes on the minutes.

The minute makes the man.

The Creed of the Conquest calls for the everlastingly aggressive, watchful mind, which reasons, plans and forges ahead as the moments pass.

Stop a minute, in the quiet, and see the logic of this. In your own inner sanctum YOU know what you are building—or not building. YOU know whether you are increasing your power. YOU know if you are gradually shrinking smaller and smaller in the life scale. YOU know what effectiveness or lack of it is evident in your building plans.

There's no limit to your building possibilities, if you will persist. One of the surest principles in the material world is this: *Nature achieves the grandest results by the simplest means—the constant adding together of atoms.*

A gigantic planet is but molecules assembled.

Your life, your power, your fortune, is the addition of minutes. From this, draw a law of Conquest.

In the eternal flow of moments, each one contains a measure of power and success which I CAN add to my store. I resolve that never will I be found unmindful of this principle of conquest. I will gather power from every living minute. Alertness and ACTION are the qualities which secure this value.

Again we find the author of the "Blazed Trail" saying:

"It is a drama, a struggle, a battle. We are fighting always with Time. When we gain a day we have scored a victory; when the wilderness puts us back an hour, we have suffered defeat. *Our ammunition is Time;* our small shot the minutes, our heavy ordnance the hours."

Be a Builder of Minutes.

"The Spirit of the Day"

As a companion thought to the "minute builders," the Conquering Chief will find great help in practicing the "Spirit of the Day" plan here outlined, which I introduce by asking:

Do you want buoyancy for the day? Do you want power? Do you want zest and activity and personality and happy accomplishment of the day's tasks? Do you want a bit of strategy applied in the morning that will carry you successfully through the hurly-burly of the day? Then learn to use the "Spirit of the Day" based upon the following:

Going to one's work in the morning is rarely done with mental preparation. The body is started right by giving it a supply of food. The more important ally, the mind, is usually left to hit-or-miss conditions. Herein lies a *major cause* for lost motion, loss of time and accomplishment, lack of pleasure, waste of nervous forces, et cetera.

The "Spirit of the Day" is of tremendous importance and a few minutes given to its practice in the morning while preparing for the day's activities, will pay extraordinary dividends in accomplishment and happiness.

The idea is to make up your mind before you start out, what predominant state you wish to carry through the day with you. Shall it be Courage? Health? Energy? Feeling of power? Confidence? Rapid Thinking? Financial Skill? What?

Determine each morning, WHAT "spirit" you wish to be uppermost for that day. Select a different quality each day. INTEND the mind to build that quality all day long. And the mind *will do it.*

The Conquering Chief says, before the day's duties begin: "Today I CONQUER. I am strong, brilliant, magnetic."

Always positively assert your own mental superiority. Be not a worm of the dust nor a meek follower and yielder to others. With vigorous, clear, swift mentality boldly attack the problems confronting you. Remember that the main difference between the submerged millions and the towering leaders is largely one of Brave Self-assertion.

Point Five: SECRET OF SUPREMACY IS TO BUILD A STRONG WILL. The code of nature and man is:

1. Nature asserts—and infallibly demonstrates—that the man who leads and succeeds and takes the richest prizes, must be calm, cool, confident and COURAGEOUS.
2. The "survival of the fittest" is the deepest, soundest, most clearly evident LAW of Nature relating to the coming and going of life on this planet.
3. Nature, with an object in view—a result to be accomplished—-never hesitates, dawdles or delays. Neither does she ask permission to perform, but strikes out boldly and intrepidly, STRAIGHT FOR THE FINAL GOAL.

With the foregoing in mind, I have observed that men can be divided into three main classes:

1. The men of *Will-power* (the leaders).
2. The men of *Desire* (those whose intentions are good but who fail to put forth the necessary Dominance and Action to win out. They are the men who "wish" instead of DEMAND).
3. The men of *Fate* (those who give up all the glory of human achievement because they say *it's all no use—things will never come my way.*" This remark is correct: they certainly will never "come" but they can be APPROPRIATED—and that is what the Men of Will-power do).

The Conquering Chief naturally belongs to the first class—the dynamic personality *asserting* its own; *claiming* its own; and invariably striving to make ACTION of the particular character required to *win* its own.

Look to the biography of the world's great men, living or dead, and in nearly every instance one masterful trait stands out more prominent than all others. It is the real *secret* of their supremacy. And this I term indomitable, unconquerable WILL—self-declared refusal to yield an inch to the external forces which seek to thwart progress.

Napoleon was a superlative example of it; Bismarck had it; Grant illustrated it splendidly; Morgan mastered it; Roosevelt in action was a whirlwind example of it; Edison owes his famous concentration and persistence to it. Yes—the captains of Industry, Finance, Invention, Art, Science—all built their immortal achievements upon invincible Power of Will.

" '*I will*' is the Sovereign state of Mind—the most intense attitude of Self towards all external forces. Your *Self* with *Will* in action has for servants the Body, Intellect and the Feelings. And with these servants fully disciplined, the sovereign Self goes forth to conquer a World, a Universe."

And for this reason, I would play up strong:

Knowing that only as I enter the ranks of the First Grade of men—THOSE OF WILL POWER—can I expect to be a Conquering Chief, I do pledge myself to the large development of this Prime Quality. I will neither passively wish for things, nor drop back to the third grade of those who abdicate their realms under the delusion that Life is a matter of pre-arranged destiny.

You must make every encounter, every new deal, every plan, every idea, every desire for greater success—greater power and greater wealth—the concentrated, all-absorbing thought and aim for the time being. Bring every legitimate force you can command into the fray. Strike the heaviest possible blows against the obstacles, and constantly hold in mind the unbeatable resolution to FIGHT IT OUT TO A SUCCESSFUL FINISH.

Point Six: "THE GREATEST SUCCESSES HAVE BEEN FOR THOSE WHO HAVE ACCEPTED THE HEAVIEST RISKS." Mull over that for some time. It's the "whole thing" to the Conquering Chief. The daring to reach for the biggest attainable prizes before which the multitude stand in awe—this is a central law.

The world is filled with cowards who dare not attempt big things. Convention, and ridicule and "what will people say!" are ghosts which take the starch from them. Forget these bugaboos. Kick'em into the scrap heap. These best successes are open to you if only you take the heaviest risks—ever balanced by cool, discerning judgment.

"Dare what no other man will dare. Seek to accomplish what no other man would attempt, is the way to display yourself as a superior being in your own and in others' eyes." Every phenomenal conquest but testifies to the abandoning of tradition in the man's inner mind. It is sheer decisive, dazzling DARING that wins out for scores of big men of the present day.

Oh! I ask you: *"What is life worth if it be not filled with a wonderful effort toward great accomplishment?"*

The business philosopher Louis Balsam, writing on the subject of "Self-Made Slaves," said:

> "We have such strange, little, craving bodies, capable of such stupendous joys, such magnificent expression—and of such dreary, monotonous, fear-governed routine. How wistfully each of us regard the other and how fervent is our envy of those who seem to have happiness, dimly troubled by the stirrings of our own possibilities, we go along inhibited by our dismal, unnecessary, but thoroughly human fears.
>
> "The possibilities of life are bounded only by the skies. Everywhere about us, if we listen carefully, is movement and vibration that is in lyric rhythm with the motion of the universe. Rich, beyond the dizzied dreams of mankind, in opportunities for a bigger, fuller, more creative and joyous existence, life beckons us alluringly."

What is a man's frame and vesture worth as a home for his soul and intellect, if his veins are not filled with a fire and an energy that gives no peace when lazy loafing seeks to lull him to sleep?

Grant me the right to a life of strife and attainment.

Refuse the dead stare of standing still—of accepting as final anything whatsoever. Man has erred for ages. We have found supposed truths to be errors. One device is succeeded by a better. Creeds and religions arise—then better ones are born. Things of today will change—so will those of tomorrow.

The whole progress of man attests to the glory and grandeur of agitation caused by the desire for constant conquest and change and for success rising to higher levels. "To augment, to increase, to win strength, to march forward, to be worth more today than yesterday—that is at once glory and life" says the philosopher.

It is said that in Athens every man represented himself. Be your own representative and *make good to the last ounce of energy possessed.*

Point Seven: PLAY WITH MASTERLY SKILL EVERY ACT. PLAY FOR THE CHIEF GOALS YOU SEEK. PLAY WITH YOUR MIND CLEAR AND YOUR EYE OPEN. PLAY WITH THE CONSCIOUSNESS OF POWER AND ABILILTY AND ABUNDANT ENERGY FOR WINNING WHAT YOU WANT.

What do you want most in life RIGHT NOW? Is it Money, Personal Influence, Social Recognition, Brain Power? Lay a strategic plan leading to what you want. Put the weight of your ENTIRE BEING—the white hot flame of intense desire—the WILLINGNESS TO PAY THE PRICE in intelligent effort into your spirit of Conquest—and it is won!

I know what I say. I have experienced this thing with blood rushing through my veins; with energies unexplainably multiplied; with nerves a-tingle with a sensation as though charged with vitality unmeasurable; with brain tensed and aroused to a rare readiness for creative thinking—thoughts flashing out over the whole world and experiencing a sense of touching the realm of genius. My eyes were opened to big financial vision and a courage-confidence for startling phases of practical ability awaited my command.

In short, it was a sure grip upon the Art of Conquest.

The Conquering Chief MUST have huge endowment of Perseverance, unwavering decision, daring, and the fearless holding to the pathway of his goal—unswayed by the cheers or jeers of the mediocre multitude.

"Turn about. Take courage. Nature has a place for you if you are made of the right stuff. The masses that come and go, are melted over in the great melting-pot of nature; but those who rise up in their might with hearts of steel and souls of iron are never lost."

If you will try to combine all that I have thus far said into an energetic, agressive, intrepid plan of Action, you will experience the thrill of Power as you read the following classic from the great Victor Hugo (which you may interpret VICTOR, YOU GO).

"Human thought attains in certain men its maximum intensity."

The human mind has a summit.

This summit is the ideal.

"In each age men of genius undertake the ascent. From below, the world follows them with their eyes. These men go up the mountain, enter the clouds, disappear, reappear. People watch them, mark them. They walk by the side of precipices. They daringly pursue their road. See them aloft, see them in the distance; they are but black specks. On they go. The road is uneven, its difficulties constant. At each step a wall, at each step a trap. As they rise, the cold increases. They must make their ladder, cut the ice and walk on it, hewing the steps in haste. A storm is raging. Nevertheless they go forward in their madness. The air becomes difficult to breathe. The abyss yawns below them. Some fall. Others stop and retrace their steps; there is a sad weariness.

"The bold ones continue. They are eyed by the eagles; the lightning plays about them; the hurricane is furious. No matter, they persevere."

They reach the pinnacle.

They are Super-men.

They are Conquering Chiefs.

Go you and profit by their example.

I Believe

I believe in the supreme worth of the individual and in his right to life, liberty, and the pursuit of happiness.

I believe that every right implies a responsibility; every opportunity, an obligation; every possession, a duty.

I believe that the law was made for man and not man for the law; that government is the servant of the people and not their master.

I believe in the dignity of labor, whether with head or hand; that the world owes no man a living but that it owes every man an opportunity to make a living.

I believe that thrift is essential to well ordered living and that economy is a prime requisite of a sound financial structure, whether in government, business or personal affairs.

I believe that truth and justice are fundamental to an enduring social order.

I believe in the sacredness of a promise, that a man's word should be as good as his bond; that character—not wealth or power or position—is of supreme worth.

I believe that the rendering of useful service is the common duty of mankind and that only in the purifying fire of sacrifice is the dross of selfishness consumed and the greatness of the human soul set free.

I believe in an all-wise and all-loving God, named by whatever name, and that the individual's highest fulfillment, greatest happiness, and widest usefulness are to be found in living in harmony with His will.

I believe that love is the greatest thing in the world; that it alone can overcome hate; that right can and will triumph over might.

—John D. Rockefeller, Jr.

CHAPTER 32

Stories of Success

The Most Famous March in History

In 401 B.C. an army of Greek Mercenaries are hired by Prince Cyrus of Persia to help overthrow his reigning brother, King Artaxerxes. Upon reaching the center of Persia, all the high officers of the Greek contingent are invited to a huge banquet at which they are foully and treacherously murdered.

Here are ten thousand Greek soldiers, leaderless, deserted by the allies they had come to help, lost in the middle of the vast Persian Empire, and surrounded by enemies.

The Persians demand their unconditional surrender. But the freedom-loving Greeks would rather die than become slaves. Artaxerxes smiles disdainfully. The Greeks have 1500 miles of enemy territory and vast deserts and high mountains to traverse. Without leaders, they will soon disintegrate into a mob of hungry vagrants willing to surrender at any price. Artaxerxes feels that there is no need to waste the lives of his soldiers in attacking the Greeks.

But the king reckons without taking into account the high spirit and strong Will Power of the Greeks. These ingredients and a *goal* to reach—their homeland—makes a pot that is to keep the Greeks going though harried by roving bands, hunger, and disease through 1500 miles of trackless wilderness. They choose their own leaders, including one Xenophon, who later writes down for posterity of their incredible hardships and their indomitable fortitude in meeting them. This epic is known as *Xenophon's Anabasis.*

After many months of struggle, a scout on a hill waves his arms in wild exultation. "The Sea! The Sea!" joyously swells down the ranks, and the troops lose all weariness as they rush to the top to view the glorious water across which lies their beloved homeland. A voyage by sea and the soldiers are home at last to relate their experiences during the most famous march in history.

Ten thousand soldiers, without a leader, might well have become a disorganized mob. In this glorious instance, they did not. By employing self-discipline, will power, and a fixed goal, they were able to overcome deserts and mountains, forage for food, and drive off hostile marauders.

Without the Generals of Will Power and Self Discipline, a man is like a leaderless army. It takes these Generals to set up and conform to a daily schedule of work and play.

It is especially important for the executive, the merchant, the salesman, and the housewife—as classes—to set up a schedule and then give themselves orders to follow. The reason for this is that too much time can be wasted on worries over trivial matters or deciding on unimportant things. In the end, they become bundles of indecisions. They never get anything done.

Most housewives feel harassed by the unending duties and chores of household and family. They have a feeling of never getting caught up with their tasks. It has been found by research that if they set up a daily routine or schedule, they will eliminate much useless scurrying hither and thither and worrying, and have much more time to enjoy life.

Self-Discipline—The General Within—is a boss they will like to obey when they get used to him and find how much easier he makes things for them. He adds facility to each action every time they accomplish it.

By making routine duties automatic through the use of a daily schedule, not requiring thought or decision, a man finds his conscious mind far freer to deal with real problems that *do* require thought. He will find that in emergencies, too, he will have more freedom of thought and action.

A flywheel on a machine keeps the machine going if the power is shut off for a minute. A fixed schedule and good working habits act as a flywheel to carry a man through emergencies, difficulties, discouragements, without lessening his pace, without requiring an additional output of will power.

The procrastinator says to his friend: "What are you working at so hard, old man? Let's go to the show."

The friend, who realizes the value of a planned routine, replies, "Not yet. I'm planning my work for tomorrow. Let me finish this, and then I'll think of recreation."

The first man says, "I ought to do that too. I've tried ever since supper to get around to it, but I'm tired. I've done a hard day's work. I deserve a little rest. I'll map out my work in the morning when I'm fresh."

"Yes—and have it worrying you all night. You've got yourself all sour—finding reasons why you shouldn't do it *now.* I'm enjoying myself doing my work and you're grouchy *not* doing yours. I'll enjoy myself at the show, and you'll stay grouchy, knowing that you haven't finished your day's work. You'll go to bed grouchy and get up grouchy. You've got it to do; why not do it *now*—and like it? Make a habit of doing it at the right time and get out of the habit of looking for reasons for *not* doing it."

Benefits of a Planned Life

The benefits of a planned daily schedule are as follows: *Dependability*—your associates and customers will find that you do everything you promise to do. *Regularity*—You will be as regular as clockwork in your business or work hours; a great boon to your prospects, your company, and your bankroll. *Ease of Work*—Establishing a daily schedule is like buying a home, or any other long-term investment. You have to put out great effort and money for the purchase; but when you have made the purchase you have all its advantages at no further cost except for relatively small incidentals. So, once a daily schedule is established as a habit, it takes only a minimum of caution and effort to keep from losing it. *Time for More Work*—The time formerly spent in making useless or unnecessary decisions can now be spent in meeting important problems. *Greater Productivity*—in short, a bigger bankroll.

To acquire good working habits, all that is needed is: *Analysis*—to discover what necessary daily actions you want to make automatic. *Planning*—to place each action in its proper order and to set for yourself the one best method. *Decision*—to follow that plan; to make it permanent, and *Will Power.*

To launch new habits, you *must* start with the greatest possible effort of *Will.* A flywheel requires a comparatively large amount of power to start it. Once it has reached its speed, the power it requires is relatively negligible.

If you honestly and faithfully follow a Daily Schedule suited to your needs, you do more work in less time, find your work interesting and enjoyable, increase your earning power, and have more time for recreation, mental development, and other activities. In short, you pave the way to a fuller, more enjoyable life.

One of the fundamental rules in establishing a habit is not to permit a *single exception* to take place. Knowing this, and having decided on a daily schedule that suits your needs, you should adhere to it strictly until you are confident that you have created the Generals or Leaders in yourself that you need to achieve consistent success under all conditions.

Can you answer the following questions in the affirmative?

Do you have certain hours for arising in the morning and retiring at night?

Do you take time every night to analyze your day's work? Figure out what mistakes you made, if any, and how to avoid them in the future? Plan the next day's work?

Do you set yourself a daily quota of work? George Bernard Shaw, the celebrated Irish playwright, set himself a quota of five written pages every day. For nine years he followed this routine with barely a pittance in remuneration; and then he hit the jackpot in royalties for plays.

Have you made your decisions the night before so that you will not waste time deliberating during your precious work hours?

Do you put off your recreation and relaxation until all the day's work is done and off your mind?

Good Books Can Help You Get Ahead

A good book on self-improvement is like a friend who can help guide you over the rough spots in life and help you face the problems of every day living. My greatest joy is in finding a truly inspirational book and recommending it to over 300,000 customers all over the country and the world. The people read the books and then write me telling me of benefits received from applying the principles in the books: fortunes made, homes saved, illnesses corrected or healed, love found, friends made, et cetera. Many have blessed me for telling them of these worthwhile books.

Meeting new people in a business or social way, you are judged by your manner of diction and your vocabulary. And many times, this can mean a better job or a promotion. We are evaluated by what we say and how we say it. You can speak words of beauty and accuracy. Lincoln learned how to use words and became President of the United States. He had less than a year of schooling but he made companions of some of the best literature of the age. Lincoln could recite from Burns, Browning and Byron. He wrote, "I have gone over some of Shakespeare's plays perhaps as frequently as any unprofessional reader - Lear, Richard III, Henry VIII, Hamlet, and especially Macbeth - I think nothing equals Macbeth. It is wonderful!"

"This self-educated man," writes Robinson in his book, *Lincoln as a Man of Letters*, "clothed his mind with the materials of genuine culture. Call it genius or talent, the process of his attainment was that described by Professor Emerton in speaking of the education of Erasmus: 'He no longer was at school, but was simply educating himself by the only pedagogical method which ever yet produced any results anywhere; namely by the method of his own tireless energy in continuous study and practice.' "

At Gettysburg, Lincoln delivered one of the most beautiful addresses ever spoken by mortal man. His years of painstaking study resulted in a speech that is engraved in history—one that every school child recites by heart. How much the great speakers owe to their reading and to their association with books!

Dale Carnegie says in his book, *Public Speaking and Influencing Men in Business*, published by the International Committee of Young Men's Christian Associations: "Books! There is the secret! He who would enrich and enlarge his stock of words must soak and tan his mind constantly in the vats of literature."

"The only lamentation that I always feel in the presence of a library," says John Bright, "is that life is too short and I have no hope of a full enjoyment of the ample repast spread before me." Bright left school at 15, and went to work in a cotton mill, and he never had the chance of schooling again. Yet he became one of the most brilliant speakers of the generation, famous for his superb command of the English language. He read and studied and copied in note books and committed to memory long passages of poetry of Byron and Milton, and Wadsworth and Whittier, and Shakespeare and Shelley. He went through 'Paradise Lost' each year to enrich his stock of words.

Gladstone, Premiere of England, called his study a "Temple of Peace," and in it he kept 15,000 books. He was helped most, he confessed, by reading the works of St. Augustine, Bishop Butler, Dante, Aristotle, and Homer. The *Iliad* and the *Odyssey* enthralled him. He wrote six books on Homeric poetry and Homeric times.

You are classified by what you say. So follow Lincoln's example and keep company with the Masters of literature. Spend your evenings with Shakespeare and other great poets and masters of prose. Read with a dictionary at your side and look up unfamiliar words. Study their derivation and history. Don't use worn-out words. Be exact and precise in your meaning. Roget's *Thesaurus* can be a great help to you. Stand out from the crowd.

We Hear from a Man Who Reads

"We need to do all we can in this era to encourage people to read more—particularly our young people. I think the information you have included in this publication will stimulate them to do so." This is what a university president had to say about our campaign.

Letters such as this may explain why we have received requests for more than a million reprints since this series started a little over a year ago. To us, they confirm the idea with which we started out—the power and vitality of the printed word.

International Paper

The role of the legislator is an exacting one. At any given moment he must be many men: historian, lawyer, orator, public servant.

Our Congressmen know that information—complete and concise—is indispensable to their jobs. To get this information, they put in long hours. They attend meetings, they travel, and they *read.*

We studied the reading habits of 50 Congressmen. In a month, they read an average of 4.2 books per man. In a week, they averaged 3.3 magazines apiece. They also read the amazing total of 1461 newspapers in a single week. Over 29 each! The implication is as clear as print:

Men who read more achieve more.

Grass-roots Reading

In the case of our Congressmen, the New York and Washington press will not suffice. To stay within the mainstream of events, they must read their *hometown* newspapers.

Our Congressmen set their watches by the thump of the morning newspaper on their porches. Here is the latest information—quick and concise yet comprehensive. In a job like theirs, nothing less will do.

Literary Whistle-stops

Books, too, are exerting a strong impact on both statesmen and their constituents. In 1957, John F. Kennedy's best-selling *Profiles in Courage* was awarded the Pulitzer Prize.

Equal time for the Republicans. Senator Barry Goldwater's *The Conscience of a Conservative* also made the best seller list in its hard-bound form. And, as of last Election Day, there were 320,000 papberback copies in print.

The case for reading can be summed up in a joint, nonpartisan statement by two former presidents, Herbert Hoover and Harry S. Truman. This is it:

"Men die; devices change; success and fame run their course. But within the walls of even the smallest library in our land lie the treasures, the wisdom and the wonder of man's greatest adventures on this earth."

"The World of Books is the most remarkable creation of man. Nothing else that he builds ever lasts. Monuments fall, Nations perish, civilizations grow old and die out and after an era of darkness, new races build others. But in the world of books are volumes that have seen this happen again and again; and yet live on still young, still as fresh as the day they were written, still telling men's hearts of the hearts of men centuries dead."

CLARENCE DAY

What Are We Here For?

The average person thinks he is here for a good time and the world owes him everything. He never thinks of what he can contribute to the world. The common attitude seems to be "What's in it for me?"

Life is not going to hand us everything on a silver platter. Let's not kid ourselves. There's a lot of hard work involved in achieving the important things of life. The person who can't set aside an hour or so a day, week in and week out, to reach his goals, really isn't that much interested. The shrewdest advice, the most carefully planned goals, the best intentions, and all the surefire techniques—none of these will work if YOU don't get out and WORK. No one can do more than inspire you, inform you, and show you the way. A good book can outline an easier, shorter, or more effective way to achieve your desires. But the ultimate outcome is up to YOU. The magic wand of Success is contained inside you.

We only get out of life what we put into it. For a great majority of people, life has that empty, hollow feeling. And in spite of sincere intentions, lofty aspirations, and a knowledge of how to achieve what they want, these people cast a disillusioned glance back over the years. Instead of a rich, full life, they begin to see that their true accomplishments have amounted to little more than nothing.

Success is seldom an accident or a lucky break. Even Thomas Edison said, "I never did anything worthwhile by accident, nor did any of my inventions come by accident; they came by work." Stephen Leacock summed it up by saying, "I am a great believer in luck, and I find that the harder I work, the more I have of it." The industrialist Henry Ford said: "There is no man living who isn't capable of doing more than he thinks he can." William James said: "Compared with what we ought to be, we are only half awake. We are making use of only a small part of our physical and mental resources. The human individual lives far within his limits." The first of Henry Kaiser's Seven Keys to Success is this: "Most people use only one tenth of their total capacity for work and original thought. Harness your full powers and you will be amazed at the results."

Before we can figure out how to make better use of our time, we have to take a look at where our time really goes. The average person spends 7 hours a day working, 7 hours sleeping, one hour dressing, one hour in going to and from work, and two hours eating. This leaves 6 hours a day, besides weekends, for leisure. Here is a veritable jackpot of time waiting to be displaced for more important things. Frankly it is amazing how much of this time people are wasting. How much of this time could be put into helping you achieve the things you really want in life. How much of this time could be spent in planning, or reading up on subjects that will help you reach your goals.

The booklet *Forging Ahead in Business,* published by the Alexander Hamilton Institute in New York, says:

> "Up to a certain point, all men are interested in their business future. They will read about it and talk about it. But at that point, they divide sharply into two classes: One group talks, the other group acts. Men who are determined to get ahead usually accomplish their purpose. For they are the inspired, resolute workers who disdain failures and cheerfully accept the challenging obligations of success. Often, their progress is so rapid, it surprises even them. They find, to their amazement, that they

need to know only a little more than the average man in order to go a lot further, just as a man has to be only a few inches taller than others to stand out in a crowd. The man who makes twice as much money as you do does not have twice your brain power. An executive who earns $50,000 a year is not necessarily ten times smarter than a person whose salary is $5,000.

It's simply that once a man begins to exert himself a little more than his co-workers, his progress multiplies itself out of all proportion to the amount of effort he has to put forth. Reflect for a moment on your case. Are YOU lapsing into that large and pathetic category of men who plod along making little or no progress? Are the dreams you harbored, the plans you made, growing dimmer and unrealized with the passing years? Are your natural talents being wasted in blind concentration on mere routine tasks?

This is the fate of every man who neglects to "follow thru" on his early momentum—who thinks he can coast to the top. We call these men 80 percenters. They are not failures, neither are they successful. They go so far and no farther.

And the tragedy of this situation is that, with a little added knowledge, these men would not be stopped at the most critical stage of their careers. For most men, this crucial stage comes when their salaries are somewhere between five and ten thousand dollars a year. Men in that salary range are potentially worth at least twice the amount they are being paid. But it is up to them to prove it. The eighty percenters never do. They may mean to, but they never quite get around to adding that extra knowledge—that extra equipment—that would make them stand out from other men. The difference between the champion and the "also ran" is small indeed.

I am indebted to the Prentice-Hall, Inc. book, *Dynamic Thinking*, published in 1963, by Robert J. O'Reilly for these facts, figures and quotations.

*Tap Your Powers**

Happiness and Success are the eternal goals of men. All of us look for success, but only a few know how to achieve it. Among these few, Henry J. Kaiser towers as outstanding. His life is a living testimony that there is opportunity in America for the man who will grasp it. Here is his philosophy of a happy and successful life. Here is Mr. Kaiser's own down-to-earth, practical formula of success:

> "Know yourself and decide what you want most of all to make out of your life. Then write down your goals and a plan to reach them. Your plan for work and happiness should be big, imaginative, and daring. The mistake is to put your sights too low, not to raise them too high.
>
> "Use the great powers that you can tap through faith in God and the hidden energies of your soul and subconscious mind. Faith is the key to unlocking limitless powers of the mind, the heart, the soul. Faith and belief that smash fear, Faith and belief in the ultimate realization of your hopes that are right.
>
> "Love people and serve them. In a job, a business or profession, you simply are filling human wants. The opportunities to develop new products and services are as boundless as the ideas and desires of mankind.
>
> "Develop your positive traits of character and personality. You don't need to blow the top off an IQ test or be the son or daughter of genius to succeed. A number of surveys prove that attributes of personality are far more important than technical skills in winning and keeping a job.
>
> "Work! Put your life's plan into determined action and go after what you want with all that's in you."

*From *Opportunity* magazine. A. H. Kulikow, Sr., editor and publisher.

To succeed, Kaiser suggested this pledge:

I will make and put into action a plan to reach a definite goal. I will practice faith in myself, my fellowman, and God. I will tap the hidden powers within and above me. I will love and help people. I will work with all the energies of mind and body. I will know that I can achieve real happiness and success.

Mr. Kaiser is an outstanding man, not because he is rich. But he is rich because he is outstanding in his character and philosophy. His philosophy is positive, constructive, dynamic. He does not say: "Try, and maybe you will succeed," but he says, "Act and you will."

Know yourself; use your great powers; love and serve; develop your positive traits; work! These are the commandments which as - sure success in life.

*A Billionaire's Rules for Success**

Jean Paul Getty, one of the richest men in the world, says: "Making a million is work—hard work. There are no surefire formulas for getting rich. There are, however, fundamental rules to the game:"

1. To all intents and purposes, there is only one way to make a great deal of money—in one's own business. It must be a business the individual knows and understands well. He may not know all about it in the beginning, but he must start with a thorough, basic knowledge.

2. He must be a "Saver", willing to practice economy both in his business and in his personal life. He must be patient, and permit his enterprise to grow gradually. He must be willing to take risks.

3. What I call the "Nine-to-Five Complex" is another factor that contributes to the defeat of many budding businessmen. Being in business for yourself isn't the same as working for a firm that opens its doors at 9 in the morning and closes them at 5 in the afternoon. The successful executive puts in overtime at nights and weekends.

*Reprinted from *True, The Man's Magazine*, June, 1958.

*How E. W. Scripps Built His Newspaper Empire**

Among some of the success pointers given by the late E. W. Scripps:

"If circumstances compel you to pursue some other occupation or to follow some line of business which is being pursued by some other person, then do your work in some other way than that in which it is done by the other. There is always a good, better, and best way. If you take the best way, then the other fellow has no chance of competing with you.

"It is far more important to learn what not to do than what to do. You can learn this invaluable lesson in two ways, the first of which and most inspired is by your own mistakes. The second is by observing the mistakes of others. Any man who learns all the things that he ought not to do cannot help doing the things he ought to do.

"A man can do anything he wants to do in this world, at least if he wants to do it badly enough. Therefore, I say that any of you who want to become rich can become rich if you live long enough.

"There are two cardinal sins in the economic world; one is giving something for nothing, and the other is getting something for nothing. And the greater sin of these is getting something for nothing, or trying to do so. I really doubt if anyone ever does get something for nothing.

"The hardest labor of all labor performed by man is that of thinking. If you have become rich, train your mind to hard thinking and hold it well in leash so that your thinking will all be with one object in view, that of accumulating more wealth."

*From *Damned Old Crank*—a self portrait of E. W. Scripps, edited by Charles R. McCabe, copyright 1951 by Harper and Brothers. Reprinted in *How to Increase your Money-Making Power* by John Alan Appleman. Pub. by Frederick Fell, Inc., New York City, 1959.

CHAPTER 33

How Many Modern Men Make Money Millions

What are your chances of making a million dollars today? The chances are pretty good, if you go about it in the right way, apply certain principles, and live long enough to do it. It can be done, inspite of heavy taxes, fierce competition, and gigantic corporations. Believe it or not, there is more opportunity to make a million in this country than anywhere else in the world. According to the Federal Tax Office, ther are 95,000 millionaires in the U. S. A. today, and more added every year. Such men as: John D. MacArthur, Howard Ahmanson, John Mecom, W. Clement Stone, Henry Crown, are today worth *hundreds of millions.*

Most of these men do not like to show off their wealth. They do not live in gorgeous marble palaces like the old Rockefellers, Vanderbilts, Carnegies and Harrimans. Where the old multimillionaires made their money in oil, steel, and railroads, the new multi-millionaires make their money in the new technology, science, services, real estate.

What is the secret of their success? In a recent article by Stewart Alsop, *America's New Big Rich,* * he tells how he managed to interview the multi-millionaires and uncover from them their closely-guarded secrets. Their formula boils down to the following six points:

1. "Use money to make money." The idea is to borrow to build up a business, enterprise, or asset. As an asset is added to and increased, the growth means more collateral, against which more money can be borrowed, and thus the business is pyramided. Money can be borrowed, if the owner is stable,

**The Saturday Evening Post,* July 17, 1965, published by the Curtis Pub., Co., Philadelphia, Penna., 19105.

from the neighborhood bank, from friends, or from the Federal Government. Write to the SMALL BUSINESS ADMINISTRATION, Washington, D. C., for booklets, *Management Aids for Small Business: Annual No. 2,* and *Starting and Managing a Small Business of Your Own,* which contains information on Federal loans.

2. "Have a Good Idea and gamble on it". This essential for success is to discover a common need, and then find a way to fill it. Fortunes have been made on such simple things as: the zipper, the safety pin, razor blades, clothes, and paper clips. The modern entrepreneur finds a newer or better or more economical way to do a thing which brings to the market something that people want to buy. He is daring, energetic, keen, positive, and alert to opportunity. He is inspired by the vision of an idea, and he has the persistence and boldness to carry it out. He makes mistakes and fails often, but he bounces right back. Nothing keeps him down.

3. "Hire good brains, but run a one-man show." The multimillionaires make men who work for them rich too, but they don't want others telling them what to do. They run a tight ship. There have to be too many instantaneous decisions, as an opportunity presents itself, and they can't wait around for a board of directors to meet and ponder on it and argue and make concessions and amendments. They don't want a lot of stockholders telling them what to do either.

4. "Don't throw your money around, at least until you've made it." These men mostly live in unpretentious homes. They only spend money to make more money. They are very careful in their personal expenses. Getty had pay telephones installed in his guest houses, so he wouldn't be charged for long distance calls. John D. Rockefeller gave dime tips to his caddies and saved money on such things as bunghole stoppers for his oil barrels. Most of the new rich live in shacks compared to the palatial mansions of the old rich. Most of them did not get married until their late thirties, and picked women who were ambitious for

their husbands, were not too demanding of their time, and did not mind sharing their marriage with the business.

5. "Shun taxable income like poison". The really rich pay little or no taxes, or else they would be only in the moderate income group. The oil man has his 27½% depletion allowance, and deductions for drilling expenses, and this often cancels out any taxes. In real estate, they buy an apartment house, building, or hotel, write off the cost at more than normal rate, accelerated depreciation, save the taxes, sell it to another rich man at the rising rate on real estate, and then repeat the process all over again, making more each time.

Longfellow said, "The divine insanity of noble minds, that never falters nor abates, but labors, endures, and waits, till all that it foresees it finds, or what it cannot find, creates."

* * *

Napoleon said, "Victory belongs to the most persevering."

* * *

Milton said, "I argue not against heaven's hand or will, nor bate a jot of heart or hope, but still bear up, and steer right onward."

* * *

Shakespeare said, "See first that the design is wise and just; that ascertained, pursue it resolutely; do not for one repulse forego the purpose that you resolved to effect. Perseverence, dear lord, keeps honor bright. To have none, is to hang quite out of fashion, like a rusty nail."

*****

*How to Become a Millionaire**

"This country is loaded with opportunities. The trick is to discover a need and find a way to fill it. There is a gold mine in the rapidly changing technology, the shift to a service economy, and the insatiable appetite for a new and better way of doing things. It is easier to get ahead now than it was twenty years ago, on account of the population growth and rise in personal income. It is easier to borrow money.

"America's newly wealthy entrepreneurs have made tremendous sacrifices, taking meager salaries at first and pouring the profits back into the business. Many made their millions by manufacturing uncomplicated products and marketing them with single-minded concentration. They were often discouraged by the experts, and they failed frequently, only to rebound.

"Though small manufacturing and consulting services contribute many millionaires, real estate has probably produced more than any other field. Former carpenters Jordon Perlmutter, 34, and Samuel Primak, 39, have put up more than 8000 houses in the Denver area. Gerald Blakely, 45, earns close to 100 million constructing Industrial parks from Boston to San Francisco.

"Atlanta's Alvin Weeks, 41, began mixing divinity fudge on his mother-in-law's stove. With the profits he branched into baking. He saw the potential in the marketing of sweet rolls in easy-to-heat foil pans. This year he will sell 6 million dollars worth of Aunt Fanny's sweet rolls to supermarkets, airlines, and other large buyers."

What do today's millionaires have in common? They are not always domineering but they know how to influence other men and get them to fall in with their ideas and suggestions. They are organizers, builders, creators. They may tear down; but they build better on the foundations. Their mission seems to be to

**Time (December 3, 1965) copyright 1965 Time, Inc., Time & Life Bldg., Rockefeller Center, New York, N.Y., 10020.*

manifest their creative energies. They are not completely attached to money or possessions; these are but cards or pawns in the great game they have played so successfully; the game itself was the real thing to them. They are ambitious, determined, self-reliant, bold, enthusiastic, audacious, positive, keen, and energetic. They set out with a definite set objective in life, that of accumulating Wealth; and they made that their aim, and they did it! By making themselves richer, they have made their country richer and all of us richer, because they are here.

Rothschild said, "It requires a great deal of boldness and a great deal of caution to make a great fortune; and when you have got it, it requires ten times as much wit to keep it."

* * *

Ben Franklin sid, "The way to Wealth is as plain as the way to market. It depends chiefly on two words, industry and frugality; that is, waste neither time nor money, but make the best use of both. Without industry and frugality, nothing will do; and with them, everything."

CHAPTER 34

You, Too, Can Make a Million

America is still the land of Golden Opportunity. It is still easier for the average man to make a million dollars here than in any other place in the world.

During the Industrial Revolution and between the Civil War and First World War, men came up from poor families and made multimillion fortunes. Rockefeller made his money in oil, Gould made his in railroads, Morgan in banking, Carnegie in Steel, Ford in cars, Hearst in newspapers, and Edison in electricity. They lived in vast feudal-type estates with castles on the Hudson and summer homes in Newport that equaled the chateaux of King Louis.

Despite the competition from huge corporations, the bite of ever-increasing taxation from Federal, State and Township, it is still possible for any man to make a million if he is able to work and if he follows certain procedures and grabs the right opportunities. The changes and trends of Business, Technology, Economics, Politics, Science, and Population shifts, are so mercurial that Opportunity ever presents itself to the right person at the right time who is in a position to take advantage of it, and ready to receive it. Every day, new things come out which are making a fortune for someone.

The tremendous population explosion is ever opening up new fields and markets and services. Women, who do 80% of the buying of goods in the market, are ever demanding new services, luxuries, conveniences, foods, clothes, and pleasures. The home is becoming completely mechanized, relieving the housewife of labor and drudgery. She now has more time for social life, clubs, parties, restaurants, travel, etc. and all these services are making fortunes. Millions of women can now spend hours watching Television and this is reflected in the two billion dollar profit made by the TV Industry last year.

The men are ever demanding new comforts, shortcuts and efficiencies in business, transportation, cars, airlines, and customer entertainment. They are getting computers and IBM machines to take the work and drudgery out of business.

Elderly people are a large segment of the population and they have more money to spend than ever before; from pensions, old age benefits, Medicare, social security, etc. Their wants are for retirement developments, travel, nursing homes, cottages in Florida or California or the Southwest, Acapulco, Mexico, and the Caribbean. Doctors find the Oldsters a big source of income as the old chassis needs an occasional overhauling or new parts.

The teenage market is a tremendous field for the entrepreneur to make money with any product that can capture the imagination of the young, no matter how simple the product may be. The teenager is sure to fall for: new fads in clothing, musical instruments, stereos, recordings, girls' make-up, sports equipment, etc. On the serious side, Business Schools, Training Schools, Universities, are expanding all the time in order to take care of the growing tide of youth seeking education. To fill the teenage stomach, Drive-Ins, Hamburger Joints, Coffee Shops, and Ice Cream Parlors, are doing a thriving business.

In foreign countries, there is a great demand for American institutions like Cafeterias, Laundromats, Motels, Hot Dog stands, et cetera. There are opportunities in Africa, Europe, Asia, and South America. You can write to the United States Agency of International Development in Washington, D.C.

Millionaires find there are opportunities wherever there are problems to solve. If you can come up with a workable solution to a problem that is vexing many people, you can probably make a million. There is certainly no shortage of problems these days.

Secrets Of The Millionaires

Some of todays millionaires have divulged their secrets and are willing to give out certain pointers to those who wish to follow in their footsteps. Many people who aspire to be rich waste and fritter their lives away and end up poor because they fail to follow certain precepts. It is a fact that very few people really know how to go about making a fortune.

The millionaires agree that you should start out young, if possible, to make a million because most men have only about 40 productive years to work before they get too old and get dumped into the waste heap. However, some, such as Michelangelo, Dante, Ford, Edison, have been most productive in their 60's, 70's, and even 80's.

A College Degree is desirable but not essential. It is easier to make a million by working for yourself rather than a big corporation.

Look for a demand or market where there is little or no competition—a new field or endeavor. Then a big company may come along and buy you out and with the profits you can start another business. We had a neighbor, Harrison Minick, who invented a new plastic in a little shack in his backyard in Philipse Manor, Tarrytown, New York. After he died, his son sold the huge plant that was producing *tensolite* for twenty million dollars.

Timing is important and you should look out for population shifts, technological changes, new laws and the Economy.

Among the many fields where millionaires are making millions today in the U.S.A.:*

1. Department stores. New methods of display and merchandising have created fortunes for owners of stores like Marshall Fields in Chicago and Wanamakers, Macys, Altmanns, Korvettes, Gimbels, Sears Roebuck, Alexanders, Bloomingdales, in New York. Korvette's Eugene Kerkauf became a millionaire in his early 30's and is now worth 55 million.

**Millionaires under 40.* TIME, the weekly News magazine, Dec. 3, 1965. Published by Time, Inc., Rockefeller Center, N.Y.C. 10020

2. Land. Speculation in real estate is still one of the oldest and yet newest goldmines in the world. Miami Beach was once a sand dune. It was filled in and built up with fabulously expensive hotels and now worth billions. Swamps have been filled in and made into profitable areas. Formerly inaccessible places like mountains and islands can now be reached by plane or helicopter and people can live there.

Arthur Carlsberg of Los Angeles has earned over 5 million in real estate. He began by renovating old houses and investing in land. He found that 99% of real estate brokers did not understand the economics of real estate booms.

He initiated research into the factors that make land values fluctuate and what increases investment in land. He collected information on all kinds of items that would influence land value such as population shifts which can either blight an area or increase demands for better class home sections or suburbs, and nearness of the land to transportation facilities such as railroads, airports, harbors. All this information can be computerized and evaluated and made use of. Carlsberg now manages $50 million worth of land in California.

3. Homes. Arthur Decio is worth five million because he filled a need for low cost house trailers for a highly mobile and fast moving society. Although he entered a very competitive field, he copied the Auto Industry by coming out with new models every year. He started with a couple of thousand dollars and three friends and, like Henry Ford with his model 'T", Decio built a smaller, cheaper, more maneuverable model trailer home. He instituted a research department to find out trailer owners' needs and wanted styles, colors, and dimensions. He now has 2000 dealers throughout the country.

4. Auto Replacement Parts. Many people have made money in manufacturing and supplying auto parts to replace stolen, broken, or worn-out parts of cars and they have outlets and dealers all over the country. They also carry sidelines such as: paints, toys, hardware, sports and camping equipment, etc.

There is a high turnover in tires, hub caps, aerials, car radios, as millions of these are stolen out of cars every year.

5. Business Consultant. Using computers and data processing, the Business consultant of today is making millions by showing Corporations how to make money and even introducing American business techniques to Foreign firms and Foreign governments. They even give courses to Foreign executives on new business methods and new technology. Many bureaus of the U.S. Government are now employing Business Advisors who are also Efficiency Experts, to cut costs and institute economies and increase work production in the heavily staffed offices of our Bureaucrats.

6. Investment Banking and Stock Firms. Many tellers and clerks who started at the bottom and worked up through study and hard work are now millionaires. And of course there is the easy way up; marry the Banker's daughter.

7. Computers, Data Processing, IBM Machines, and National Cash Register. Merlyn Michelson was born on a washed-out farm in Minnesota. As a young man, he became interested in radio and electronics from serving in the merchant marine as a radio operator. After the war, there was a crying need for Memory Cores for Computers. Merlyn set up a laboratory in his basement where he worked nights while he held down a daytime job with Remington Rand. His total investment was for a couple of tools and pliers which you can buy at Woolworths. He soon had to employ neighborhood housewives to help assemble parts in order to fill the demand.

Through ambition and hard work and some Government subsidies and financing through stocks, he now has four big plants and employs over 2000 workers and turns out intricate memory systems that sell for up to $180,000 each.

8. Inventions to combat air and water pollution. Charles Gelman, Michigan Chemist, contrived a small air pollution machine contraption put together from parts he bought at a hardware store, and made a million from the sale of the invention.

Are Millionaires Really Happy?

It is fairly easy for the entrepreneur to borrow capital now. The Banks are dying to loan you money if you have a good idea. Most of today's millionaires started with little or no capital but they all had ideas and were Success motivated. They used Creative Imagination, worked hard, salted their earnings, knew how to influence and manage other men, were willing to take a chance on a good risk.

Most millionaires enjoy their work. They like to collect money just like people like to collect stamps, firearms, antiques, butterflies, paintings, etc. They are just as creative as writers, artists, except that they create business empires, buildings, plants, factories, fortunes. Pulling off a wheeler dealer is to them as satisfying and creative as Shakespeare writing a play or Da Vinci painting a Mona Lisa.

How They Found Their Dream Castle On An Island Paradise Thru Finding Dream Castles For Other People. *

Starting with practically no money and a good idea, this ingenious couple worked a financial miracle and were able to retire to the island of all their golden dreams before they even reached middle age:

> Dick and Susan Beamish were, at heart, writers and artists, so when they got married, they talked and dreamed about an island hideaway where they could write, read, paint, and swim before they were too old to enjoy it. Most people, when they reach retirement, about all they can do is sit in the rocking chair.
>
> The Beamishes married the summer after Dick's graduation from Columbia's School of Journalism. They moved to San Fransisco where Dick got a job in Public Relations and she worked for an interior decorator.

**We Retired at Age 30* by Susan Beamish. Condensed from *Redbook* magazine. Aug. 1966, copyright by McGail Corp., 220 Park Ave., New York, 10017.

They wore out the pavements looking for a place to live, but it seemed like everything was rented including hollow tree trunks. The best they could find for living quarters was a dingy, grimy, cramped apartment. When Susan discovered that she was pregnant, they began thinking of a larger place. After driving all over, the best they could find for any half-way decent house was $10,000.

So they scanned through the classified ads and found their dream cottage, with the babbling brook to top it off. When they went to see it, they just about dropped dead. It looked like a shanty from old shanty town. It needed everything: new roof, new walls, new foundation, new heating system. In fact, it needed a new house. However, there was a certain charm about the place; a big old stone fireplace, oak panelling in the lving room, and the running brook through the dells and giant redwood trees surrounding the house.

They wangled the owner down to $7000. The hitch was that they had no money left to pay carpenters, masons and painters; and they had never hammered a nail or stroked a paint brush in their lives. So they had to use the old fireplace for cooking food and heating the drafty old house and set out pots, pails, and pans to catch the rainwater which leaked in places like Niagara Falls. During the winter, they were able to brighten up some of the rooms with a little paint.

Susan finally had to give up her job as she was expecting. One night her husband came home from work and was amazed to find that his wife had made an attractive bookcase from some boards she had sawed up, nailed together and painted. Seeing in her a potential carpenter, and not wishing to be outdone by a female, Dick began sawing and hammering too, and before long the house looked like new. Before they knew it, someone came along and offered them $14,000 for the place, or twice what they paid for it. It took a little arm-twisting as they had come to love their home sweet home, but they figured they made $5000 clear profit over cost of repairs.

This opened up a whole new field of thinking along the lines of repeating the deal and making more spare-time money moonlighting with houses. They scoured the countryside for more broken-down houses and looked at over a hundred in all. Of course they were smart enough to know that it was essential to have basically sound structure and foundation, and a roof that would not fall down on your head. Also it was a prime importance not to buy in depressed, high-crime neighborhoods.

They bought a larger house for $11,500; paid a down payment and took a mortgage loan for the balance. They paid some masons and plumbers to do heavy and basic repair work and then set to work refinishing the house themselves. The baby daughter amused herself with a brush and paint and making real surrealistic, impressionist, and abstract paintings on boards.

Then another avenue opened up; a real bargain of a house for $12,000. It happened that the owner had two houses, so he settled with them on a package deal of $20,000 for the two houses. They were able to handle the cost thru refinancing and increasing mortgage loans. Now it took every spare moment and all their energy to fix up two houses at once.

In a few months they had the two houses remodeled and rented and a nice income from both. But they didn't get to enjoy the second house long because someone came along and grabbed it for $18,500—a net profit of $4000.

Tiring of shady hillsides for three and a half years, they longed for a sunny spot for a change. An agent showed them a roomy three bedroom house with a ballroom for a living room, but the house needed a lot of work. They shaved the owner down to $21,500 and after working on the house for a year and a half, had it looking like brand new.

The tenant who was renting the first house offered to buy for $14,500 and they took the money and bought another house for $15,500. Now Dick had been doing mountains of work all in his spare time and finally found it was too much for him unless he wanted to give up eating and sleeping to work 24 hrs. a day. So he resigned his job to devote full time to playing with houses.

They sold the $21,500 house for $31,500 at a tidy profit of $10,000. Then they sold the two houses that cost $20,000 for a total of $34,500 at a clear profit of $14,500. Finally, the last house sold for $24,500, with a net profit of $9,000.

With all this money they made in a few years, they were able to retire at the early age of thirty. After traveling nearly all over the world, they decided on their dream island. Their island paradise turned out to be the Isle of Tenerife in Spain's Canary Islands. Tenerife is a semi-tropical island of high mountains, lush valleys, deserts, beaches, art galleries, rambling villas and haciendas, and a University.

They live in a charming three bedroom house on a mountainside; surrounded by bouganvillea, green lawn, banana trees. Looking out of the window, one sees the sun sparkling on the deep purple of the ocean. It is a dream castle come true.

Dick is writing and Susan is taking art and painting at the university. They eat delicious Spanish dishes of fresh shrimp, mussels, chicken, tender young suckling pig barbequed, and all kinds of fish straight off the boats, and drink the unequaled red wine of Spain. They do reading, sunning, skin diving, and mountain climbing. The daughters go to school and learn French and Spanish, among other things.

After some years, they plan to return to the United States. They still get an occasional urge to look at an old house. They could pick up a real, authentic Spanish Castle for a couple of thousand, but many of them need plumbing and wiring. However, sunning and swimming are much less strenuous in a warm climate than undertaking a twenty to thirty room palace.

*****

*N. H. Moos, In His Book "How to Acquire Millions"**

"The innermost desire in every person's heart, is the *desire to have abundance of supply* for all necessities of life, and for luxuries and comforts; and to secure thousands and even a million dollars. There is no Lack or Limitation in the Divine Plan. The only lack or limitation is in your own mind. If you are satisfied with a small sum of money just enough to cover your daily necessities of life it is your business. If you want to acquire millions you can and will acquire them if you think righteously, and say to yourself I can and I am going to get millions, for God is on my side. I am going to follow faithfully the steps which are suggested in this book and all other steps which Divine Guidance may suggest to me to carry out my purpose. I will never stop or waver in my mind till I succeed in getting what I want. Start right now, where you are, and do not put off till tomorrow, for as we all know Procrastination is the thief of time. Do not entertain *any* doubts at the back of your mind, for if you do, you will fail in your effort. Keep up your courage and faith in God and in yourself and you surely must succeed. God knows no failure and you as His son *cannot fail,* for you have His Creative Power which knows no limit, but you must use it, and claim it as your birthright. Thoughts of doubt in this power, and doubt in your ability to manipulate it may spring up and suggest to you that all this is idle talk. If they do, then, do not entertain them for a single moment, but throw them out, for as you know, they are destructive and impede your progress. We know that thousands of persons in the United States of America have developed their money consciousness through Righteousness (right thinking) to such an extent that they have become millionaires. Picture to yourself in your mind that you are also one of these many millionaires and believe that you already possess millions. Think of all the good you can do for your fellow-men by the proper use of these millions and in this way dissipate your doubts. Fill your mind with similar constructive thoughts.

"Do not think that I am giving you a magic wand which would in an instant raise you up from the depths of poverty to the heights of prosperity. Everything has its time. In any event, do not outline beforehand the channels through which you are going to get your desire fulfilled. Leave it to God to do that. He knows how to help you, and will open up the necessary channels to you.

"Then again please remember that you cannot get something for nothing, and that you must pay in some shape or form the price for what you want to get. When you go to the market to buy your food, clothes, or other articles you require or anything else, you have to pay the price for the same in the shape of money; but when you want to acquire rich abundance, prosperity or health, you have also to pay the price for what you want to acquire. In that market you have to pay the price, not in cash, but in tokens of Patience, Perseverence, Honesty, Righteousness (right thinking), deep Concentration, Courage, Faith, Feeling and Attention, Decision and Firm Determination. For any one of these tokens the Law will give you an equivalent value.

"Every day offer thanks to God for all the blessings you enjoy in your life (and they are many), and for His loving care and protection, and especially for the blessings of perfect health and peace which you enjoy. Praise every organ and cell of your body for the intelligent and wonderful work they are doing to keep your body in perfect order. These daily practices will raise your consciousness and faith to great heights and will help you in your achievements and enterprises, and riches will flow into your coffers from the Infinite Source of Supply in such abundance that you will wonder where they come from. I daily repeat to myself, the following formula: The riches of God are flowing and rushing into my hands in abundance which no one can stop. The opulence of God is ready in my hands and for my use, which is my birthright.

"God works wonders in His mysterious ways which the human mind cannot fathom. The creative power of the mind is a wonderful gift to us from the Father, and we must realize that it can create whatever our right thoughts ask it to create. So always present to it positive and constructive righteous thoughts with courage and faith, and the results will be wonderful.

"*Cultivate Patience and Perseverence* in order to secure the attainment of the object desired. This is absolutely necessary for your success. If you fail by reason of some obstacle or some unforeseen circumstance in the outer, try and try again till the obstacle is removed or the circumstance is changed. This requires dogged perseverance. Edison failed a thousand times in his search for the electric light before he finally succeeded. There are many other instances of many failures before final success. So do not lose heart but persevere.

"*Your desire must be deeply rooted and intense in feeling.* Merely wishing for a thing or wanting to have it is not enough. You must resolve in your mind that you must have what you desire and constantly imagine that you are already in possession of it. Many people refuse to believe this statement and argue that until you have actually got the thing, it is silly to say that you possess it. But experience has proved that the creative power of the mind accepts your statement that you have got the thing and creates it for you out of the Infinite Substance in the Universe. So please do not try to argue with yourself whether such a thing is possible, but accept the statement as true for all time. When you do so, you will be Divinely guided to act and do things which will help you in your efforts.

"*Cultivate your powers of Concentration on the object of your desire.* Our mind has to be trained for this acquisition. Ordinarily people get into the habit of allowing their minds to wander from subject to subject. For instance, when you are saying your prayers on Sunday morning, you are thinking of the things you have to do on the Monday following, or of the long journey on which you are going the following week, or of the friends whom you have invited to dinner next month, etc. One has to check this habit of wool gathering before it gets deeply rooted in your affairs in life. If you are a salesman and are talking to prospective customers about the efficiency of the article you want to sell them, do not think of how you succeeded with another customer two weeks ago, or that you may be late for your next appointment, but concentrate all your attention on the customer you are talking to, and your wares. One subject at a time and fix your definite attention to it. When your desire is to acquire millions, fix your mind on that desire and concentrate upon it; ask for Divine guidance to show you what to do as your part of the work, leaving the rest to God, who knows His job and will do it for you, and you will be rolling in wealth. But, whatever you do, do not outline from what source the wealth is to come to you. God knows it better than you do."

"In concluding, I feel sure that God will guide my readers to realize the importance of the most precious gift from God, the creative power of mind, and to use it for themselves so that they may acquire Perfect Health, perfect Peace of Mind and Prosperity galore. I have every confidence that they will succeed in their efforts if they persevere and concentrate on the acquisition of whatever they desire to achieve. And when they succeed my joy will be unbounded. If there is anything I can do personally to help any one of them in their efforts, my services will always be at their disposal free of any charge."

N. H. Moos,
Los Angeles

FINIS

APPENDIX

Benefits Received

A Great Change

No book that I have ever read has so completely changed my life for the better as has Robert Collier's book. I find so many friends who need to read it that I keep it on the road all the time, and my copy is getting quite dog-eared.

So many wonderful things have happened to the people who have read my copy, and every one of them has rushed right out for a copy of her own. I wrote a book I'd planned to do for a long time because of the inspiration I received; another friend found courage to leave a job she hated and launch out on a brand new career; it kept another girl from killing herself; and the last one to read it has been using it to regain her health after several operations.

Bless you for publishing Collier's books.

Mrs. D.K.C.

$50,000 from Reading a Book

Dear Sir;

Some fourteen years ago I bought a set of your books, "The Secret of the Ages."

Believe it or not, these books were responsible for my present position, which has meant more than fifty thousand dollars to me during this time.

I am a great hand to lend books to despondent persons, usually getting them back, but the last one I loaned this set to "forgot to return them."

I would like to get another set of the books.

Yours very truly G.A.M. Waco, Texas

A Big Sale

The literature on your book recalls to mind a letter I received ten years ago. At that time I was a writer on Specialty Salesman Magazine in Chicago, writing interviews with salesmen. I had a letter from a salesman in__________________, in which he told me of his success as well as previous slumps. He said at one time he was just about down to zero when he happened onto a copy of your book. He continued that shortly after reading the copy he went out and within a half hour had sold over $1500 worth of cooking oil. His sales continued at an astounding rate. He sold cooking or salad oil to restaurants, hotels, wholesalers, etc. He told me how he sold to dealers who had previously turned him down. I still have this letter among my papers.

K. I.

"Secret of the Ages" brings $30,000

Dear Mr. Collier:

I feel that it is only fair to report to you and express my appreciation for what you have done for us through your wonderful book *The Secret of the Ages.*

In fact, both my husband and I did not believe your guarantee that $500 would be added to our income through reading your book. We received it and read it eagerly from cover to cover. We soon faced the world with a new found joy in living and anticipation of greater things to come. The very next week, without even asking for it, a $50 raise was given to my husband. Then, out of a blue sky, $30,000 came to us unexpectedly; like a gift from Heaven.

Your book is certainly amazing, and I am sure your other book will bring new surprises and blessings to us. Thank you again and again for your wonderful book and may God bless you even more than ever.

Gratefully yours M.N.

From Cebu City, Philippines

Dec. 1941

I know that you must be waiting for news; news about the good the book has done or is doing for me. Of course, at present I cannot say much, but I am sure you will have a deep feeling of satisfaction when I tell you: In a tiny spot ten thousand miles across the sea, and down into the heart of a soul lives "THE SECRET OF THE AGES"; yes, there it lives to bring cheerfulness and encouragement, love and hope, faith and life, all good—GOD! That soul was once downhearted and consequently fretful and cross—almost a wreck. But a wonderful transformation—a metamorphosis—has taken place. That miserable, despondent soul is now no more. That soul has come to the glorious recognition and unconditional acceptance of its oneness with GOD. Today that heart goes about radiant with joy, secure with a firm faith that all prayers will be heard, all yearnings satisfied, all desires fulfilled. And that heart and soul are mine.

May "THE SECRET OF THE AGES" reach the homes of millions all over the world, that it may do for theirs what it is doing for mine!

I would be doubly glad if I can express my eternal gratitude to the Colliers in person for bringing this priceless book into my life. Would you two and Mr. Collier join me in my prayers that I may have enough or rather plenty of money in order to realize this end? Would you? Well, I hope so!

THANKS A LOT. In the meantime I will be jotting down notes about my future progress in the course. AND you will always know about the bigger things.

A. A. T.

Prosperity Plus

Dear Mr. Collier:

I have derived so much good from your books that I'm most anxious to have any new books you may have put out.

About five years ago when I "hit bottom" and was seeking

something to steady my thinking, I came home one night without a dime in my pocket and without a loaf of bread in my home; a truly deplorable situation that gives one a very empty feeling.

Today I have my own business with 29 employees; my own home and car; have travelled both ways in Masonry and am a Shriner, a member of our Country Club, the Civic Association, the Kiwanis Club and have a very desirable credit rating, not only here but in Minneapolis, Chicago, St. Louis, New York, Pittsburgh, Washington, D.C., Great Bend, Kansas, Fargo, Sioux Falls, and other points where I have occasion to trade.

This may sound fantastic, and indeed, it sometimes seems so to me, except as thru continued readings of the above books I have come to believe that the above conditions are those which have been promised us under certain conditions. Surely, you can at least understand my desire for "further enlightenment" if it is available.

Yours truly W. C. L. Aberdeen, S. D.

Like Aladdin's Lamp

Dear Mr. Collier:

Aladdin and his lamp couldn't have done more for me than your book. As I wrote you previously, my husband had been unemployed for seven months and conditions were really tragic. My parents had turned us out, saying that they had asked us to stay with them temporarily but it had turned out to be quite permanent, so we would have to leave.

Every chapter in your book seemed to fit our case, so, absolutely unafraid, I put the matter up to God. Now, all in this short time, my husband has found employment and we have a little furnished apartment.

Surely you and your writings should have the blessings of the world. May God bless you, and the wonderful work you are doing.

Thankfully yours L. M. K. Port Townsend, Wash.

From the United States Senate

I told Senator ____________ the other day that if one would winnow from my own writings with reference to the relationship of the mind and body, that I would be another witness to the truths you so ably present. It has always been heartbreaking to me to see people try to get health by the taking of pills and medicine out of the bottle. We have within ourselves the forces that make for or against health.

On the fly-leaf of my Grandfather's Bible I discovered this: "The world we inhabit must have had an origin; that origin must have consisted in cause; the cause must have been intelligent; that intelligence must have been efficient; that efficiency must have been supreme, and that which always was and is supreme we know by the name of God."

Apparently my Grandfather was thinking along the same lines that we are thinking. The trouble with us is that we don't make use of our intelligence, because it is not really efficient. In any event, let's keep on trying to make the world better by thinking good thoughts. By right thinking and right living we can revolutionize the physical existence of man.

Yours truly,

Senator ______________

A Textbook from Now On

Dear Mr. Collier:

I have just finished reading "Secret of the Ages" and I don't know when I have read anything that moved me so profoundly. It is beautifully and simply written in understandable language, and I shall use it as a textbook for living from now on, I can assure you. As I mentioned above, I have just finished reading it, but it will be reread many, many, times and assimilated, I hope.

I am enclosing a check for another copy.

Yours sincerely E. D. New York, N. Y.

From the Commonwealth of the Philippines

SUPREME COURT
Manila
April 25, 1936

Sometime in 1929 I purchased from you two interesting sets of books written by you, entitled "The Secret of the Ages" and "The Secret of Gold" and "The Life Magnet." I was also one of the early subscribers to your magazine "Mind, Inc."

The magazine and the set of books have been of incalculable value to me. They have acquainted me with my hidden forces, and have instilled in me a sense of power and security that makes me a "Happy Warrior," fighting my battles for success and righteousness with a smile on my lips and a feeling of self-assurance. Since then I have forged constantly ahead, have finished my schooling, and been admitted to the practice of law. Lately, I was persuaded to accept the position of Secretary to Supreme Court Associate Justice of the Commonwealth of the Philippines. Your works have been my "talisman" all the time.

J. P. M.

From the United States Senate
Committee of the Judiciary

Please let me assure you that no time will be lost between the arrival of the short pamphlets to which your very acceptable letter of the fourteenth day of April refers and my reading of what you have said.

Indeed, I can not recall that I have ever failed to read anything from your pen that has ever become available to me. And I can now recall no page of your large literary output that, in my opinion, could be annihilated without distinct loss to humanity.

May I now again urge you to give me the pleasure of becoming better acquainted with you in the event of your being in Washington for any purpose before the adjournment of the Congress.

Since I last wrote you I have improved my every leisure moment by reading the excellent pamphlets entitled "The God in You." Indeed, night before last I was reading one of them at five minutes till two in the morning—and I do not mean by Daylight Saving Time.

I hope that I may sometime have the pleasure of telling you "face to face" of an additional case, in which the book mentioned in our previous correspondence seems to have wrought what would ordinarily be considered a miraculous result.

Sincerely wishing you long life and unlimited success and happiness to the end of your days, I am, as always,

Yours truly,

Senator _______________

Spreading the Good Word

Dear Mr. Collier:

I have heard and read of many evangelists who have preached the gospel and have undoubtedly done a great deal of good among their fellow beings in inculcating into their minds an understanding of religion. However, I doubt if any man ever lived other than our Saviour, Jesus Christ, who can be credited, like you, with bringing their fellow being to a real practical understanding of religion and the law of nature such as you have so completely accomplished through the various publications you have written.

Sincerely yours R. W. H. Chicago, Ill.

Paradise for Hell

Dear Mr. Collier,

What I want to say this morning is in regard to *The Secret of The Ages.*

A year ago I was living in a constant hell. My job had played out; my wife was divorcing me; and I was broke and near hungry. But I have never been a whiner or a quitter and I never confided my troubles to a soul.

At that time I was travelling through Amarillo, Texas and I chanced to go to the public library. As is my custom, I went to the Psychology, or "mind department" and there I chanced to run across your *Secret of the Ages.* After reading a couple of chapters, I decided to check it out and take it with me.

That night I couldn't sleep until I had read your book through. The very next day "Whoo-ee"; things started to open up for me like I had never seen before. I always knew I had some power in me but could never put my finger on it before. Things began to unfold, and I was shown the right way to go. I was able to purchase a modern *Imperial* car and within four months I had a job that is now paying me more than $25,000 per year. Best of all, I have met the most wonderful girl down in Mexico City, and we will be married April 15.

Well, so much for my success, the real reason for this letter is to obtain another book of yours. This is called *Riches Within Your Reach.* Any more books written by you will be welcomed by me, so just send them to me as they hit the press. Thanks a million for *The Secret of the Ages,* and may God be wonderful to you the rest of your life.

Yours truly, D. B.

$60,000 Received!

Dear Sir,

You may be interested to know, that I loaned most of Robert Collier's books to a very warm personal friend, in the east, and he was negotiating a business deal which required considerable capitalization. He was at a loss as to where he could obtain the funds through a private source, when one of my books reached him. He decided to try out the knowledge in this book, and Lo and Behold, a thought was inspired, which prompted him to board a train, to visit a friend who not only guaranteed financial assistance, in the amount of $60,000, but also offered my friend an opportunity to engage in a proposition which overshadowed the one for which the funds were required!!! I have documentary proof of this.

Sincerely yours F. P. Kingman, Ariz.

Absolute Necessity

Dear Seer and Soothsayer:

In seventy-six years I haven't found a volume that snuggled so comfortably into hand and mind. You put the world into a nutshell, and crack it so we can get at the kernel.

Through the years I have read a great variety of things written by savants and word-mongers in general, but none, by-and-large, that presented their subject matter in such a cogent, concise yet universally comprehensive manner as you do. You don't obscure the forest by trunks full of printed leaves. The book is one of the absolute utilities.

In His Name J. L. Los Angeles, Calif.

"It Works"

I enjoyed SECRET OF THE AGES so very much and I think it may interest you to know that the science has really worked for me. Last year I was a struggling cartoonist whose initial income from cartooning was just a poor $500; not $5000, but $500. Not much of an income, was it? Well, upon reading THE SECRET OF THE AGES just prior to the holidays, things began to change. This year, in the month of January, I've gotten $500 from cartoons, and my success as a cartoonist is rapidly building up momentum. Yes, in one month I made what I did last year. If you want, you can use this testimonial in your ads. The whole science is unusual, almost fantastic, but it works, by golly, it works.

J. G.

$500.00 Extra in Two Weeks

My dear friend:

I read and reread the book; it told me many things I should have known, appreciated and applied—but had not.

Would it surprise you to know that certain ideas and principles of your book enabled me to definitely help myself in a number of ways, and that it brought me about $500.00 extra in two weeks after I had the book.

I am,

Yours cordially J. G. H. Atlantic City, N. J.

*THE BIBLE, THINK AND GROW RICH, AND SECRET OF THE AGES BRING A FORTUNE TO A POOR NEGRO TENANT FARMER**

"We are poor—not because of God." † S. B. Fuller was one of seven children of a Negro tenant farmer in Louisiana. He started to work at the age of five. By the time he was nine, he was driving mules. There was nothing unusual in this; the children of most of the tenant farmers went to work early. These families accepted poverty as their lot and asked for no better.

Young Fuller was different from his friends in one way; he had a remarkable mother. His mother refused to accept this hand-to-mouth existence for her children, though it was all she had ever known. She knew there was something wrong with the fact that her family was barely getting along in a world of joy and plenty. She used to talk to her son about her dreams.

"We shouldn't be poor, S. B.," she used to say. "And don't ever let me hear you say that it is God's Will that we are poor. We are poor—not because of God. We are poor because father has never developed a desire to become rich. No one in our family has ever developed a desire to be anything else.

*Published by Prentice-Hall, Inc., Englewood Cliffs, New Jersey.

†From *Success Through A Positive Mental Attitude* by Napolean Hill and W. Clement Stone, the man who built $100 into a multi-million dollar organization. One of the wealthiest men in the country—worth several hundred million—he has dedicated his life to helping others.

No one had developed a *desire* to be wealthy. This idea became so deeply ingrained in Fuller's mind that it changed his whole life. He began to *want* to be rich. He kept his mind on the things he did want and off the things he didn't want. Thus he developed a burning desire to become rich. The quickest way to make money, he decided, was to sell something. He chose soap. For twelve years he sold it, door to door. Then he learned that the company which supplied him was going to be sold at auction. The firm price was $150,000. In twelve years of selling and setting aside every penny, he had saved $25,000. It was agreed that he would deposit his $25,000 and obtain the balance of $125,000 within a ten-day period. Written into the contract was the condition that if he did not raise the money, he would lose his deposit.

During his twelve years as a soap salesman, S. B. Fuller had gained the respect and admiration of many businessmen. He went to them now. He obtained money from personal friends, too, and from loan companies and investment groups. On the eve of the tenth day, he had raised $115,000. He was $10,000 short.

Search for the light. "I had exhausted every source of credit I knew", he recalls. "It was late at night. In the darkness of my room I knelt down and prayed. I asked God to lead me to a person who would let me have the $10,000 in time. I said to myself that I would drive down 61st Street until I saw the first light in a business establishment. I asked God to make the light a sign indicating His answer."

It was eleven o'clock at night when S. B. Fuller drove down Chicago's 61st Street. At last, after several blocks he saw a light in a contractor's office.

He walked in. There, seated at his desk, tired from working late at night, sat a man whom Fuller knew slightly. Fuller realized that he would have to bold.

"Do you want to make $1,000?" asked Fuller straight out.

The contractor was taken aback at the question. "Yes," he said. "Of course."

"Then make out a check for $10,000 and when I bring back the money, I'll bring back another $1,000 profit," Fuller recalls telling this man. He gave the contractor the names of the other people who had lent him money, and explained in detail exactly what the business venture was.

Let's explore his secret of success. Before he left that night, S. B. Fuller had a check for $10,000 in his pocket. Today he owns controlling interest not only in that company, but in seven others, including four cosmetic companies, a hosiery company, a label company and a newspaper. When we asked him recently to explore with us the secret of his success, he answered in terms of his mother's statement so many years before:

"We are poor—not because of God. We are poor because father has never developed a desire to become rich. No one in our family has ever developed a desire to be anything else."

"You see," he told us, "I knew what I wanted, but I didn't know how to get it. So I read *The Bible* and inspirational books for a purpose. I prayed for the knowledge to achieve my objectives. Three books played an important part in transmuting my burning desire into reality. They were: (1) *The Bible,* (2) *Think and Grow Rich,* and (3) *The Secret of the Ages.* My greatest inspiration comes from reading *The Bible.*